LIZZIE'S HEART

"Are you deliberately evading my question to keep from hurting my feelings?"

"*Nee.*" But she did experience an uncharacteristic shyness at the thought of declaring her feelings. Suddenly she felt hot and then cold. Maybe she needed some air. "I think I need to . . ." Lizzie started to scoot Sunny out of the way so she could scramble to her feet.

Stephen's fingers circling her wrist held her in place. "Please, Lizzie. Can you answer my question? I have to know."

Lizzie kept her eyes on Sunny. Stephen deserved an honest answer. She struggled to get one out. "I-I can care. I do care." She raised her gaze to Stephen's glowing face. If pure joy could be captured in a picture, it would look exactly like Stephen's face. She had only a second to look into his eyes before he crushed her to his chest.

"You had me scared. I thought you were going to say I didn't stand a chance at winning your love."

Stephen pressed a kiss to the top of her head that sent chills all down her body. "You don't have to win my love. You already have it . . ."

Books by Susan Lantz Simpson

THE PROMISE

THE MENDING

THE RECONCILIATION

ROSANNA'S GIFT

LIZZIE'S HEART

Published by Kensington Publishing Corporation

LIZZIE'S HEART

Susan Lantz Simpson

ZEBRA BOOKS
KENSINGTON PUBLISHING CORP.
www.kensingtonbooks.com

ZEBRA BOOKS are published by

Kensington Publishing Corp.
119 West 40th Street
New York, NY 10018

All Kensington titles, imprints, and distributed lines are available at special quantity discounts for bulk purchases for sales promotion, premiums, fund-raising, educational, or institutional use.

Special book excerpts or customized printings can also be created to fit specific needs. For details, write or phone the office of the Kensington Sales Manager: Attn.: Sales Department. Kensington Publishing Corp., 119 West 40th Street, New York, NY 10018. Phone: 1-800-221-2647.

Zebra and the Z logo Reg. U.S. Pat. & TM Off.
BOUQUET Reg. U.S. Pat. & TM Off.

First Printing: June 2020
ISBN-13: 978-1-4201-4982-1
ISBN-10: 1-4201-4982-2

ISBN-13: 978-1-4201-4983-8 (eBook)
ISBN-10: 1-4201-4983-0 (eBook)

10 9 8 7 6 5 4 3 2 1

Printed in the United States of America

For Dana Russell,
with gratitude for all you do!

ACKNOWLEDGMENTS

Thank you to my family and friends for your continuous love and support.

Thank you to my daughters, Rachel and Holly, for believing in me and dreaming along with me.

(Rachel, you patiently listened to my ideas and ramblings, and Holly, I couldn't have done any of the tech work without your skills!)

Thank you to my mother, who encouraged me from the time I was able to write. I know you are rejoicing in heaven.

Thank you to Dana Russell for all your information on looms, stitching, and patterns, not to mention your enthusiastic support and help. Thanks for sharing your alpacas, too!

Thank you to my Mennonite friends, Greta and Ida, for all your information.

Thank you to my wonderful agent, Julie Gwinn, for believing in me from the beginning and for all your tireless work.

Thank you to John Scognamiglio, editor-in-chief, and the entire staff at Kensington Publishing for all your efforts in turning my dream into reality.

Thank you most of all to God, giver of dreams and abilities and bestower of all blessings.

Chapter One

Lizzie Fisher practically ran down the blacktopped bike trail St. Mary's County had constructed along the old rail line. Earlier the shriek of sirens had penetrated the crisp, fall air and left a ringing sound in her ears. The acrid smell of charred wood grew stronger, and the black cloud loomed larger as she hurried along at breakneck speed. Wisps of soot and ashes rained down around her. She could almost taste the smoke, and her eyes already stung. She begged her feet to travel faster so she could see what had happened. Mamm's voice, in that admonishing tone Lizzie had heard so often in her twenty years on this earth, echoed in her ears: "You're too nosy for your own *gut*, Dochder!"

She wasn't really nosy. Lizzie preferred "curious" or "interested" or "concerned." Those sounded like more fitting terms to describe a young Amish woman. Besides, she wasn't a gossip. She didn't go around spreading tales from the information she gleaned. She merely cared about what happened in the world around her.

Right now, she cared about what was on fire that had caused what surely must be every fire truck in the county to race toward it. She offered a quick prayer for all who were involved, be they victim or rescuer, and urged her lungs to keep up with her feet. Her breath came in gasps as she tried to bring smoke-tainted oxygen in through her nose. She halted abruptly at the sight of flashing red and white lights through the trees. Lizzie would have to step off the path and part the branches and brambles to get a clear view.

For some unknown reason, she glanced around her before entering the thicket. She nearly jumped out of her black athletic shoes when a radio blasted out a message. If the volume was at that level while the rescuers rode in the truck, it was a wonder they weren't totally deaf. Lizzie reached around a prickly bush, carefully avoiding its thorns, to part the branches of several small pine trees. She squinted to peer through the little opening she'd made.

Straight in front of her sat a huge fire truck with lights flashing. Slightly to her right, she watched firefighters in full protective gear run toward the building that was barely out of her line of vision. She'd have to move just a bit . . .

"See anything interesting?"

Lizzie nearly swallowed her tongue. The prickly bush raked its teeth along her arm when she jumped at the sound of the deep voice. "Ahhh! Wh-who are you?" She patted her chest, where her heart galloped.

"You're bleeding."

Lizzie looked down at the rivulet of blood racing down her arm. She jerked her hand away from her chest to keep from staining her dress. She knew she hadn't stuck any tissues that she could use to wipe off her arm in a pocket or up her sleeve. She cast a furtive glance in each direction to see if there were any large, non-prickly leaves nearby that could serve her purposes.

"Here."

The man held out a clean-looking white handkerchief. Lizzie hadn't yet raised her eyes to look directly at the stranger's face, but from the shoes and trousers she could see with her downcast eyes, she surmised the man was Amish. "I-I can't bleed all over your white handkerchief."

"Do you want to use my shirtsleeve instead?"

Lizzie gasped. How dare he think she would want to be that close to him! She summoned up her courage, swallowed her mortification, and raised her eyes to meet the clearest, bluest eyes she'd ever seen. Even partially shaded by a straw hat, those eyes with the crinkly corners fairly sparkled.

"Here, take the handkerchief. It's better than leaves." He chuckled as he waved the handkerchief in front of her.

Was he laughing at her? Her face surely must be as red as the fire truck she'd glimpsed when she parted the bushes. If the hole in the big, old oak tree to her right had been large enough, she would have crawled inside it. When she didn't make any move to take the handkerchief, the stranger took Lizzie's arm and blotted the blood. She gasped again and jumped as if she'd been bitten by one of the copperheads she'd discovered under a pile of dried leaves last week. She attempted to squirm away, but he held fast. "Wh-what do you think you're doing? And who are you?"

A sly little smile tugged at the corners of the stranger's lips. What was that all about? Since she couldn't jerk her arm free, she used the opportunity to study his face. It was a nice face. More than nice, actually. Heat seared her cheeks. She hoped mind reading wasn't one of his talents. He certainly didn't need to know his brown hair reminded her of rich, dark chocolate and his eyes were the exact color of the clear summer sky. "Ouch!"

"Sorry. I was only trying to stop the bleeding."

Lizzie tried again to free her arm, but it was to no avail. This man was keeping her from discovering what was happening through the brambles. "You can let me go. I don't think I'll bleed to death."

"I certainly hope not. I'll accompany you to make sure you don't have any more mishaps."

"That isn't necessary. Besides, I only had a *mishap* because you scared me, uh—what did you say your name was?"

"Ah! *Gut* try. I didn't tell you my name."

Lizzie's eyes traveled up and up to meet those bluer-than-blue eyes that looked down at her. "And why might that be? Are you hiding something or hiding from someone?"

"You are a curious one, aren't you?"

Lizzie shrugged. How was she going to shake free from this fellow towering over her? "I need to leave. *Danki* for your concern and for your handkerchief." She finally slipped her arm from his grasp, leaving him holding only the soiled cloth. She studied the brambles, trying to decide where to part them to avoid another attack by thorns.

"You're welcome, Lizzie Fisher. Are you going through the briars again or taking the trail?"

Lizzie sucked in a sharp breath and turned back

to face the stranger. "H-how do you know my name? I don't believe we've ever met."

"I know lots of things."

"I don't care what else you know. I want to know how you know who I am when I don't know you from a hill of beans."

The man had the audacity to chuckle. At her! It wasn't an unpleasant sound, but it irked her nonetheless. She didn't have time for this distraction.

"Why do you look so annoyed? You are quite pretty when a frown isn't wrinkling your brow."

Lizzie fumed. How rude could he get? "Well, I'm certainly glad my looks didn't frighten you." Though maybe if they had, she wouldn't be having this ridiculous exchange right now.

"*Ach*, Lizzie. Most girls would be flattered to hear that they are considered to be pretty and to find out a man knows who they are."

"I am not most girls!"

"I can see that." A smile played with his full, pink lips.

"And you're a stranger who doesn't have the manners to tell me your name even though I've asked."

"Did you ask nicely?"

"Oooh! You are such a boor!" Lizzie knew the man wasn't from around here. She hadn't heard that anyone in her community had out-of-town visitors, either. And she would know. Everyone knew if someone else had visitors. That's just the way things were. Well, she didn't have to stay rooted to the spot struggling to endure this rude stranger any longer.

"I don't mean to be."

"Really?" Lizzie looked back at the bushes. *Jah*,

she'd risk the thorns to make her escape from this fellow.

"Maybe you should keep the handkerchief if you're going to plow through there."

"I'll be fine." Lizzie plunged through the branches and bushes, ducking and swerving to avoid injury. She heard the deep chuckle behind her.

"See you, Lizzie Fisher!"

He didn't know what had gotten into him. He really shouldn't have teased Lizzie so much. And he should have told her his name, but that would give her something else to puzzle over. He chuckled again. This was truly the most fun he'd had in a while. He'd been quite wrong, though, to think that Lizzie Fisher was pretty only when she wasn't frowning. She happened to be absolutely beautiful regardless of the expression that crossed her face. He gave a little shrug of his shoulders and carefully parted the brambles. He might as well follow and see what the ruckus was about. And keep an eye on Lizzie. He had a feeling she might need watching over.

Congratulating himself on acquiring only a few minor thorn scrapes, he exited the tangled underbrush and pushed his cockeyed straw hat aright. The scene that immediately greeted him nearly snatched the breath from his lungs. Fire shot from the windows of a sprawling, faded, once-white two-story house that looked like it had been abandoned a decade ago. He hoped it was abandoned—or that anyone who might have been holed up inside had long since escaped. Firefighters shouted at one another as they aimed hoses at the blazing house.

A different kind of movement caught his eye. Someone was running. Lizzie. What was she doing? Lizzie Fisher was running at top speed directly *toward* the inferno.

"Lizzie!" Her name burst from his lips. He sprinted, thankful for the long legs that gave him speed. What on earth was she thinking? Sparks could sail out to scorch her. The entire structure looked as if it would collapse at any second. Debris could rain down on her like a cloudburst on an April afternoon. He pushed himself to run faster. His heart hammered in his ears louder than the rumble of the nearby fire trucks. He would yell her name again, but he needed every gasping breath to drag oxygen into his lungs. Surely one of the firefighters would stop her. Didn't they see her so near the blazing building? He watched her hesitate only briefly.

He had to try to call out again. "Lizzie!" Pitiful. It sounded more like a loud whisper than a yell. With an earsplitting crash, part of the roof caved in, drawing every eye. The distraction gave her the opportunity she'd apparently been waiting for. She dashed behind the house. He spurred himself on. He must not be the fine physical specimen he had thought he was if he couldn't keep up with this little wisp of a girl who sprinted effortlessly right into danger.

Either Lizzie couldn't hear him holler above the cacophony around them or she chose to completely ignore him and instead dive headfirst into a fiery furnace. He hoped it was the former, because if it was the latter, that meant she was totally insane. He prayed that wasn't the case. She had seemed rather normal during their encounter a few minutes ago. He also prayed for a bit more strength, since it looked like he was going to have to tackle her to keep her from being burned beyond all recognition.

Was he the only one who saw this madwoman in a purple dress and white *kapp* dashing toward the burning house? Who was in charge here? Who was supposed to keep civilians away from danger? It looked like the job was his. "Stop, Lizzie!" Somehow he managed to yell the two words in between gulps of oxygen. The thick smoke threatened to cut off his supply of that precious commodity at any moment. How was Lizzie breathing? He saw her hesitate. Maybe she had heard his call after all.

To his horror, Lizzie opened her mouth as if biting off a chunk of air and then dashed onward. What was wrong with her? Did she have a death wish? That might very well be granted shortly if he couldn't force his legs to pump faster.

With a final, long-legged leap, he sailed through space and grabbed Lizzie's shoulders. She crashed to the ground with a whump. He hadn't meant to tackle her and bury her nose in the dirt, and he hadn't meant to collapse on top of her and crush her ribs. But at least he had kept her from burning to a crisp. An elbow to his own ribs sent him rolling on the ground. How had she managed to do that? Somehow he still had hold of one of her arms.

"Get off of me!" The words spewed out with a breathless grunt. She tugged her arm free. "Let go of me!" She scrambled to her feet and prepared to resume her mad dash.

He leaped up behind her, ignoring the pain in his scraped elbow. "Are you crazy? You'll die if you go much closer."

"They will die if I don't."

Chapter Two

"Who? Do you mean to tell me someone is inside that house? We've got to tell the firemen." He raised his arms to wave at the emergency responders.

"*Nee!*" Lizzie grabbed one of his arms and tugged it down.

"What?"

"Shhh! There aren't any people inside. The place has been abandoned for years. I can take care of this." She took off faster than a deer during hunting season and disappeared around a corner of the crackling house.

As he took up the chase again, he questioned his own sanity. Why was he running toward an inferno instead of away from it? And if the place had been empty for a long time, why was she willing to risk a fiery death? His feet slipped, and he momentarily staggered before getting his footing. If Lizzie Fisher planned to sacrifice herself in a fire, what was it to him? *Nee.* He really didn't feel that way. Someone had to save this beautiful but crazy girl, and it looked like he had been elected for that job. Maybe the Lord Gott had put him on that bike path today for just this purpose.

The smoke stung his eyes, making them water so

much his vision blurred. He could barely see a hazy purple shape right ahead of him. Was he going to have to tackle her again? How was she even breathing in this air as thick as his *mamm*'s navy bean soup?

"Lizzie!" He tried to call her but choked on the word. He might as well save his precious breath. She probably wouldn't acknowledge him even if he dropped out of the sky right in front of her. How did the firemen and gawkers not notice her dashing headlong into a burning house? Maybe this was all some crazy, mixed-up nightmare. If it was, though, his bedroom was on fire, and he was about to die from smoke inhalation.

He raised an arm to cover his nose and mouth with his shirtsleeve. He forced his heaving lungs and throbbing legs to press on. What a miserable rescuer he was! He couldn't even seem to catch this tiny girl with the caramel-colored hair and violet eyes. She could probably outrun his big black horse, and Blaze was the fastest horse in his community, if he did say so himself.

Why was this man chasing her? She did not need an audience or a witness. She could handle this matter all by herself. She heard him cough behind her. He must have inhaled a lungful of smoke when he hollered out to her—exactly why she kept her own mouth closed. She prayed she wasn't too late. How long could they last in the heat and smoke? Since most of the damage looked to be at the opposite end of the house, maybe they had a chance.

Her legs screamed at her, and her arm still oozed a trickle of blood. There wasn't time to worry about either right now. She had to find them and get out—unseen of course, unless she counted the fellow gasping ever closer behind her. And she didn't want to count him, that was for sure and for certain, even though he did have eyes the color of the robin's eggs she'd climbed the oak tree to peek at a few weeks ago. It was a *gut* thing Mamm hadn't seen that!

Kumm *on, legs.* Kumm *on, lungs. Just a little more.* Lizzie gave a cursory glance in each direction before yanking on the basement door that should have been open a crack. She wondered if the pressure change in the house had sucked the door closed and if the heat from the fire had caused it to stick. Otherwise, she couldn't imagine how it had gotten shut completely or how she was going to coax it open now. She grunted and pulled with all her might. The metal handle had absorbed enough heat to scorch her hand. She couldn't worry about that right now, either. She grunted and yanked so hard she slammed into a wall behind her. She gasped. What was back there?

"Let me try." The deep voice spoke directly into her ear. His breath tickled the little hairs on her neck.

Lizzie didn't want to, but she didn't have a choice. She dropped her hand from the door handle and shifted over to allow this persistent, meddling man access to the door, since she was obviously not having any success getting the thing to budge on her own.

He grabbed the handle, flinched briefly when he first touched it, and then jerked the door open with a grunt. Lizzie couldn't help but notice the muscles in his arm ripple at the effort. Okay, so he was strong. So what? She had to get past him and get inside before it was too late. "What's in here that's worth risking our lives for?"

"I didn't ask you to follow me."

"Who would pull you out of here if I didn't?"

"I plan to exit under my own steam." She elbowed him none too gently. He was using up precious time. "Let me get by."

"Please."

"What?"

"Let me get by, *please*."

"Oooh!" Lizzie pushed her way past the exasperating man, but he reached out and snagged her arm with one of his big hands. She stopped abruptly and bumped into him again.

"Tell me what's so important that you'll risk singeing your eyelashes off for and I'll get it while you wait here."

Lizzie tried to jerk her arm away. Hadn't they been in this predicament before? "Ow!"

"I'm sorry. I didn't mean to hurt you."

"Ordinarily that wouldn't have hurt." She looked down at the spot where a trickle of blood ran from her reopened wound.

"*Ach!* Your hurt arm. That really was a pretty deep scratch. You probably need some medicine on it."

"Right now I need you to let go of me." The old house crackled, and Lizzie felt sure it shuddered. "Now! I have to go right now!" She shook his hand off her arm and slithered through the slim opening of the door before he could latch onto her arm again. If he'd made her too late, she'd . . . she didn't know what she would do. She couldn't be too late. That's all there was to it.

Smoke had filtered all the way down to the basement, creating a thick, gray cloud. A crack overhead made her jump almost out of her skin. She waved a hand in front of her as if doing so would give her a breath of fresh air or clearer vision. It did neither.

Despite her attempt to hold it back, a cough erupted. Her eyes stung and watered.

"Lizzie, wait! What are you after?"

She didn't waste a breath to answer. She stumbled along with one hand out in front of her to prevent running headfirst into one of the wooden posts sprinkled sporadically throughout the basement. Lizzie assumed they were supports to hold the house up. She feared they would be hard-pressed to perform that function today—or ever again, for that matter.

The basement of the old, abandoned house, with only slits of windows to admit any daylight, was always dark. It was even darker today with all the swirling smoke. She must be almost to the far corner. If only she could move faster.

"Lizzie, we have to get out of here."

She wished he would be quiet. "Go!" she croaked. Her throat already felt raw. Where was the back wall? She waved her hand around and inched forward. Ah, there it was. The concrete was the only slightly cool thing around, she was sure. *Please Lord, let them be okay.* She strained to hear any slight sound over the roar of the fire and the splashes of water from the fire hoses. Was that it? Such a tiny sound. She dropped to her knees and crawled along the wall.

"Lizzie!"

He should save his breath. She wasn't going back when she was this close to accomplishing her mission. She had almost reached the corner. What if after all this they weren't there, or they were . . . *Nee.* She wouldn't even think that way. Gott would surely take care of them, ain't so? "Miriam, Moses, Aaron, where are you?" Her throat was as dry as dirt in an

August drought. Her heart skipped every third beat in fear—not fear for herself but fear for them.

A tiny mewling sound rewarded her effort and allayed at least a few of her worries. Relief flooded her. Now she had to determine how to get everything out of here. Quick. "Is everyone here?" She reached out a hand to pat three tiny heads. All bobbed under her touch, so she knew all three were alive, at least for the moment.

Now, not only was her throat dry, but her esophagus and windpipe felt glued together. Lizzie quickly wrapped the big fleece blanket around all three little bodies and scooped the bundle into her arms. She tried to juggle her load in one arm so she could snatch the metal case off the floor with her stinging hand, which suddenly reminded her how hot every metal object in the vicinity had become. She bent to retrieve a much smaller blanket from the floor. If she wrapped that around the handle, she should be able to lift the case. She hadn't yet figured out how she'd carry everything and still use a hand to feel her way through the thick fog. She lifted the case.

Oomph! Something banged into her, almost toppling her over. "Hey!"

"What in the world are you doing?"

The voice came out raspy. He must be experiencing the same suffocating feeling she was. "Get that case on the floor, but use this." She thrust the small blanket into his hand. She had again not said "please," but he didn't scold her this time. She could barely see him lift the case and tuck it under his arm. He grabbed her free hand and pulled her along with him. She hoped he knew the way to the door. She was too intent on balancing her bundle to blaze a trail.

Chapter Three

He thought his lungs would burst into flame any second if he didn't get some fresh air into them. Where was the door? He had a keen sense of direction—usually. It had better not fail him now, or he and this crazy girl and whatever she held in her arms would not make it out of this house before they succumbed to smoke inhalation or the whole crackling inferno collapsed on them.

Thank you, Lord Gott. His toe hit the edge of the door. With the little daylight streaming in through the crack, he could see the swirls of smoke dancing around them. Too bad he couldn't yank the old door open more than a few inches. They would have to slither out the same way they had squeezed in. He pulled Lizzie in front of him, let go of her hand, and pushed her toward the opening. "Go!"

She wobbled a little as she tried to redistribute the weight of her burden. "Aren't you *kumming*?" She tried to nudge him.

Nee, I thought I'd sacrifice myself in this blaze. He nodded but then remembered she probably couldn't see him. "*Jah.* Go first." His parched throat wouldn't let him get any other words out.

Lizzie managed to get herself and that heap she was carrying out the door faster than he would have thought possible. He sure hoped he hadn't just risked life and limb to rescue a pile of blankets that would smell like smoke forever, regardless of how many washings they got and a utility box full of tools. He elbowed his way through the narrow opening.

He blinked to get his eyes to adjust and gulped in air. Lizzie stood right there by the door. "Run! Are you waiting for the building to fall on you?" His words came out with little gasps between them.

"I was making sure you got out." Lizzie's words emerged punctuated with gasps as well.

That was sweet of her, he supposed, but he hadn't survived that fiery furnace only to perish when the whole structure rained down on top of them. He grabbed her arm and half ran, half dragged her toward the woods. Since they were now on the opposite side from where they had started, they'd have to figure out how to get back to the trail unseen by the firemen who would surely have a passel of questions after they'd recovered a bit. More than likely, Lizzie knew a shortcut to the cleared trail. She lived around here, after all.

Totally spent and needing huge gulps of oxygen, he sank to the ground, pulling Lizzie with him. The metal case clunked when he dropped it.

"Hey! Careful!" Her bundle wobbled as she dropped down beside him, and she clutched it tighter to herself.

"Please tell me . . ." He couldn't get a breath big enough to complete the entire sentence at once. "Tell me I didn't nearly get killed . . ." He paused to gasp again. "To rescue your *grossmammi*'s ancient quilts." He reached a hand out to peel back layers of her bundle.

She promptly smacked his hand away. "I didn't ask you to *kumm* with me."

How had she recovered her breath so quickly? His lungs were still screaming at him. "The least you can do is let me see what I rescued."

Lizzie shifted a little so the pile of quilts or blankets or whatever she was clutching was a little farther away from him. He almost laughed. She looked like a little girl trying to keep her toys to herself when asked to share. A dirty little girl with traces of soot on her cheeks and even on the *kapp* strings hanging over her shoulders. Well, two could play this game. He pulled the metal case closer and fumbled with the latch, which hadn't cooled off a whole lot yet.

"Wait!" Lizzie shifted her bundle and reached out to grab his hand. "That's mine!"

"Finders keepers."

"You didn't find it. I told you to grab it, remember? Now I'm telling you to leave it alone."

What a spitfire! Here this girl, who looked about fifteen, stood as high as his shoulders if she raised on tiptoe, and weighed maybe a whopping ninety pounds soaking wet, was telling him what to do. He swallowed a chuckle. "You're *telling* me?"

He heard her gulp and heave an exasperated sigh. "Asking, then."

"Ah, that's more like it." He looked into her little heart-shaped face. *Jah*, he had been right earlier. He had thought it was some kind of crazy reflection from her dress, but her eyes truly were violet. He'd never seen that before. "What's that noise?"

Lizzie hugged her bundle. "Wh-what noise?"

"You heard it. What have you got, Lizzie?" He yanked on the bundle, and a tiny ball of fur flew out. It was purely reaction that caused him to hold out his hands to catch the fluff. "A kitten? We risked our lives for a kitten?"

She wagged her head.

"Are you going to tell me this is not a kitten?"

She wagged her head again, setting the dirty *kapp* strings aflutter. To his surprise, the violet eyes watered, and he feared she would burst into tears any second. "W-we risked our lives to save three kittens."

"You're kidding me, right?"

"*N-nee.*" She held the bundle a tiny bit closer to him. Two pairs of eyes peeked out from the folds of the quilt.

He shifted the kitten he was holding to one hand and reached for the latch on the box again. "If this box is full of cat toys or cat food . . ."

"Don't! Uh, please don't open the box."

"My, my. You can dredge up manners when you want something, ain't so?"

"I actually use manners most of the time, when I'm treated with respect."

"I've been a perfect gentleman."

Lizzie cocked an eyebrow. "Really? A gentleman wouldn't try to confiscate personal property. A gentleman wouldn't have knocked me down more than once. A gentleman would have told me his name long ago."

"If I was not a gentleman, I would have refused to snatch up that red-hot metal box when you issued the command. If I wasn't a gentleman, I would have let you run alone into a blazing house to rescue kittens so you could suffer third-degree burns and smoke inhalation."

"I tried to tell you to stay out. I would have been perfectly fine on my own."

This time, he raised an eyebrow. "Who would have carried your box if I hadn't been right behind you? Tell me that."

Lizzie shrugged. "I would have figured out something." She'd like to wipe that smug smirk off his face.

"Right."

Her bundle began squirming. She gently eased it to the ground beside her. She peeled back layers of the quilt and plucked a wad of black fuzz from the folds. "Are you okay, Aaron?" She uncovered a speckled tortoiseshell ball of fur. "How about you, Miriam?"

"Let me guess. I'm holding Moses, *jah*?"

"You are."

"And why are they named after the prophet and his siblings?"

"Because Miriam ran out and found me. She led me back to the others, you know, like in the Bible story. Miriam watched over Moses in the basket. When Pharaoh's *dochder* found him, she ran to get her own *mamm* to care for the *boppli*."

"I know the story." He held up the black-and-white kitten still in his possession. "Uh-oh."

"What? What's wrong with the kitten?" Lizzie's heart skipped a beat. "He didn't get hurt in the fire, did he?" She leaned closer.

"I don't think so, but I believe you need to change *his* name to Mosette."

"Huh?"

"He's a she."

"You're kidding."

"Not a bit."

"I-I . . ." Lizzie knew her face must have turned every shade of red imaginable and settled somewhere around scarlet when this as yet unnamed man had the audacity to lift the other two kittens.

"One out of three."

"What?"

"You got one right. All three are girls."

"Are you sure?" Lizzie's cheeks would most likely burst into flame any minute now. The firemen would probably see the blaze through the trees and rush over to douse her with water. "Never mind."

"Did you *kumm* here every day to take care of the kittens?"

"Twice." Lizzie's voice came out in a whisper.

"Twice every day?"

"If I could get a few free minutes." *And could sneak away without Mamm seeing me.*

"Where's the *mudder* cat?"

"She was here at first, but then I think she got hit by a car a few weeks ago. Her *bopplin* were almost weaned. I couldn't very well let the kittens starve to death, could I? You aren't an animal hater, are you?" Lizzie felt the scowl but couldn't erase the pucker that gathered across her forehead.

"*Nee*, I'm not an animal hater. In fact, I like animals a lot. I'm not sure I'd risk my life to run in a burning building to drag out three kittens—if I'd known what I was rushing into that inferno to retrieve."

"What? How can you say that? Look at that sweet face."

He stared at Lizzie instead. "I am."

Her face surely could not grow any hotter, could it? At what point would her temperature be incompatible with life? She forced herself to look away from the mesmerizing blue eyes that were staring into her soul. Somehow she got the feeling he knew even more about her than he let on. He certainly knew more about her than she knew about him, which wasn't much at all. "Look at Moses—uh, Molly." She reached over to push his hand that held the kitten so it was right in front of his face.

He jerked his head back and sniffed. "I don't want to inhale cat hair. The smoke was bad enough."

"Well, isn't she cute?"

"I guess."

"*Hmpf!* Men! The kittens are all right, don't you think? I mean from the smoke and all."

"They seem to be. They weren't gasping like we were. They probably had their noses inside the quilt. Why didn't you just take the kittens home, anyway? It would have saved you a lot of jogs down the trail."

"I like to walk."

"Your *mamm* wouldn't let you keep the kittens at home."

Was the man so perceptive, or was she simply easy to read? He was definitely exasperating, that was for sure and for certain.

"You didn't answer."

"You didn't ask a question. You made a statement as if you already know everything. I didn't think an answer was necessary."

"Are you always so curt?"

"Not curt. Truthful. Are you always so evasive?"

"How am I evasive?"

"You've never yet told me your name, and I've asked you—politely—at least twice."

"Now that I've discovered your big cat secret, let's see what's in the box."

"Let's not." She tried to slide the box away from the infuriating man. "What's in my box is none of your business."

"Your desperate attempt to keep me from looking into the box has raised my curiosity even more."

"Curiosity killed the cat, you know."

"Hmmm. So they say." He pulled the box back toward himself.

"Give me the kitten and the box so I can go home." She wasn't sure how she'd carry everything, but she'd figure something out, just like she would have figured out how to get it all out of the burning house without his help. Some idea would materialize.

"Don't go away mad, Lizzie."

"Huh!" She wished *he* would go away.

"And don't pout. You look like a little girl."

"I am not a little girl. I'm twenty, for your information."

"That old? Well, I helped you rescue these little fur balls, so I can help you carry them home. What will your *mamm* say?"

"I can carry everything, and it isn't any of your concern what my *mamm* will say." Lizzie was concerned, though. She hoped that once Mamm saw how adorable the kittens were, she would relent and let Lizzie keep them.

"Your *mamm* doesn't want you to have the kittens." It was a statement again, not a question. Didn't she already ignore it once? How annoying. The man must be a joy to live with. Lizzie pitied his family.

"Well?"

"Well, what?"

"Your *mamm* does not want you to bring these kittens home."

Truth be told, Mamm didn't know a thing about the kittens. Lizzie shrugged. She didn't have to answer his nosy questions. She lifted the newly renamed Molly from the man's hands before he could tighten his hold on the kitten. She carefully tucked Molly into the folds of the quilt with Miriam and newly christened Annie and prepared to make her escape. When she snatched the handle of the box, it opened, spewing its contents all over the ground. That man must have loosened the latch! Lizzie gasped and stared in horror. Tears burned the backs of her eyes.

There wouldn't be any way she could hold three kittens and scoop up her belongings before he had a chance to examine them. And now he would plainly see her other secrets strewn all across the grass and dirt. Why did this man, whom she still did not have a name for, have to follow her? Why had he shown up on the trail at all today? Who was he, and where did he *kumm* from? He couldn't have merely dropped from the sky. Ugh! What did it matter? He was here. He'd seen. He'd tell. Simple as that.

Chapter Four

He knelt to pick up the papers before they could flutter away in the slight breeze that kept smoke swirling in the air. He picked up a paper in each hand, looked at them, and then looked up at Lizzie. "What . . . Who . . . ??"

She intended to snatch the papers from his hands, but she couldn't seem to control her trembling fingers. All she could do was murmur, "Please." Just when she thought things couldn't get any worse, a fat tear rolled down her cheek, jumped off her chin, and splatted right on his hand. Why couldn't the earth open up and swallow her?

"Did you draw these?"

Lizzie stared at the three little lumps bundled up in the quilt and wished she could crawl inside and hide with the kittens. "*Jah.*"

"They're *wunderbaar*!"

Was he making fun of her? She dared to lift her eyes for a quick peek at his face. She couldn't say for sure, since she'd just met the man, but he didn't appear to be teasing. Her voice had taken a hike and had apparently carried her brain along with it. She couldn't form a thought or squeak out a syllable.

"I'm serious, Lizzie. These cat drawings are superb." He picked up other papers off the ground. "This is the house that burned. You've captured its charm—or the charm I imagine it used to have. You have real talent."

"A talent an Amish girl is not supposed to have."

"We don't have control over the talents the Lord Gott gives us. We can only control how we use them."

Lizzie hadn't thought of that. She stood with mouth agape and with what she was sure must be the most dumbfounded expression ever on her face. She only knew her parents probably wouldn't be at all pleased if they had any idea how much she liked drawing pictures. Creativity must have been a component of her genetic makeup, though, since she'd enjoyed creating things ever since she could remember. She was happiest when she was drawing or weaving or knitting . . . or caring for animals.

The church, however, frowned on pictures or anything prideful. Even though she never drew people—only animals or buildings or objects in nature—and had never displayed her work to a living soul, not a human soul, leastways, she would still most likely be reprimanded and told to give up her drawing. Now her secret was out, and this stranger would probably trip all over himself as he raced to tattle on her.

"Please put everything back in the box." She should have left the whole thing in the house to be destroyed by the fire or water or falling debris. Could he listen to her? Of course not. He turned over other pictures that had landed facedown. All her most recent artwork had been stored in the box, along with her small sketch pad and charcoal pencils. She had sketched kittens, horses, buggies, trees, flowers, squirrels, and even a doe with her fawn.

He gave a long, low whistle. "These are amazing!"

"Please put them in the box." She now spoke through gritted teeth and had only barely managed to choke out the word "please."

"Are you ashamed of them?"

"Of course not."

"Then why do you hide them?"

"Look, I don't know where you're from or even what your name is, since *you* seem to be ashamed to tell me, but my sketches would most likely not be looked upon favorably by my ministers or my bishop or even my parents."

"How do you know? Have you ever asked?"

"I don't need to." Again he ignored her reference to his name. What was he hiding or hiding from? He didn't seem dangerous. She wasn't afraid—just annoyed.

"Don't you all send greeting cards or write on note cards or use calendars?"

"Sure we do . . . sometimes."

"Well, it looks to me like your pictures would be perfect for cards. Or maybe you can put them all together and publish a book."

A chortle escaped before she could catch it. "That would go over well. I only draw because I like it. It's calming, a way to wind down after a busy day."

"But you have to hide to do it. How relaxing is that?"

"I have to get home. Give me my box . . . please."

He quickly looked at each picture one more time before neatly stacking them inside the box. "Do you want me to carry the kittens or the box?"

Lizzie juggled her load and stabilized it in the crook

of one arm. "There. Now if you'll be so kind as to hand me the case, I'll be all set."

"How far do you have to walk?"

"A ways."

"Meaning quite a ways. You'll never make it before your aching arms wear out."

"I'm used to hard work."

"I'm sure you are. I'm used to being a gentleman. I'll help."

"A gentleman? Really?" The words had just slipped out. Flushing, she continued, "You must have some other business besides rescuing kittens and, as you say, nearly getting killed in a fire. I won't keep you any longer."

"You aren't keeping me. Besides, the walk will help clear any residual smoke from my lungs."

"A simple cough will do the same thing, and then you can be on your way."

"Why, Lizzie Fisher, I do believe you're trying to get rid of me. That pains me greatly." He slapped a hand across his chest.

"You're *narrisch*!"

"I've been called crazy a time or two."

"Well, as the saying goes, if the shoe fits—"

"*Ach!* Don't say it." He put a finger to her lips. "Be kind to strangers."

She jerked away from his intruding touch. "You aren't a total stranger anymore, even though I don't know your name or where you're from."

"I suppose you're right. If two people share a near-death experience, they can hardly be complete strangers. Perhaps we bonded over the kittens."

"Don't get your hopes up. And your name is . . . ?"

"Do you even have food for these cats?"

"Why won't you tell me your name? Are you a fugitive? If I go to the post office, will I find your picture on a poster?"

"Funny."

"Well then, what's the problem? You do have a name, don't you? Or a number or something that people call you? Because 'Hey, you' must get pretty confusing." Lizzie hazarded a glance up toward his face in time to catch his lips twitching. My, but he was tall. Or maybe she was short. Maybe both. She'd likely get a crick in her neck if she kept her head tilted up to look at him.

"I don't answer to 'Hey, you.' Generally I answer to Stephen."

"Whew! You do have a name. Was that so hard to spit out?"

"Not really."

"I suppose it would be way too much to ask for a last name."

"Don't you think we should get these kittens settled somewhere? It is probably getting late."

"*Ach!* Mamm will wonder what happened to me."

"And she'll be ever so delighted to see you've brought three kittens home, ain't so?"

"I'm not sure 'delighted' is the right word." She would be even less thrilled to learn about Lizzie's sketches. But the absolute icing on the cake would be learning that her *dochder* had been in the woods with a strange man, innocent though it was.

"Okay. Less than thrilled."

"That's more like it."

"Do we have to go back the way we came and parade through the crowd of firemen and gawkers?"

Stephen looked around as if trying to identify an escape route.

"We do if we want to get back to the trail as quickly as possible."

"And if we don't take the quickest route, is there another way to go, or can we not get there from here?"

"Of course we can get there from here. I'm here, aren't I?"

"Actually, you were walking, or more like jogging, on the trail."

"Walking fast."

"Whatever."

"I don't always use the bike trail, though."

"Which implies there is another trail."

"There is indeed. It just isn't nice and paved and free of underbrush and thorns."

"And you've already lost one battle with those today."

Lizzie glanced at the dried blood on her arm. That was going to sting something fierce when she cleaned it up. "I sort of called a truce with the briars."

"It was more like you used my handkerchief to wave as a flag of surrender."

Lizzie chuckled. "Maybe."

"Do you have cat food?"

"I did. It's a little well-done now."

"It was at the house, I presume."

"*Jah.* So were the litter and the litter box."

"Now your *mudder* will be even more overjoyed. You've brought her three cats without any food and without a way to, um, take care of business."

"Would you like to go back to the house and crawl through the cloud of smoke to find those items for me? I'm sure the fire is out by now. You'd just have soot, ashes, smoke, and a collapsing building to worry about."

"I'll pass."

"But I do have to take care of those needs." Lizzie's brain whirred. Where could she at least find some kind of makeshift provisions for her kittens until she could get to the store? *Her kittens.* They probably wouldn't be that for long if Mamm had her way. But she couldn't let them starve. And she couldn't, in desperation, feed them table scraps like she could a dog. Cats were a lot more finicky.

"So how do we get to your house? Lead on."

"I've warned you that it's not a nice, smooth path like the bike trail. Are you sure you want to risk it?" She really didn't want him traipsing home with her. He didn't need to know where she lived, and she didn't need to fend off questions from Mamm or any of the other people who would likely be outside somewhere.

"Lizzie, I just fought my way through a smoke-filled, burning building about to crash down on my head. I don't think I'll be intimidated by a few briars."

"I suppose you're right. *Ach!*" She grappled to keep hold of her bundle when the kittens changed positions.

"Do you want to change loads?"

"*Nee*, I'm fine. They just shifted a bit. Besides you don't like kittens." Lizzie started off through the woods, following a barely visible path.

"I never said I didn't like kittens."

"You certainly didn't seem too pleased with them after we rescued the poor little things."

"Actually, it was the fact that my entire life flashed

before my eyes several times that I wasn't too pleased
with. That was hardly the kittens' fault."

"That was my fault." Lizzie scooted under a low-
hanging branch. "Sorry," she mumbled.

"Sorry? Did I just hear you apologize?"

She threw a scowl over her shoulder.

"Duck!"

Lizzie didn't heed the warning quickly enough. She
turned around just in time for another low branch
wrapped with a thorny vine to scrape across her cheek.
She cried out and fell backward. Strong arms grabbed
her, and she felt herself wrapped in a tight embrace.
Her stinging face took precedence over her position
at the moment. She raised a hand to swipe at the wet-
ness on her cheek. Tears? She held red fingers out in
front of her. Blood. Finally realizing where she was, she
pulled against the arms that still held her. "Y-you can
let me go now."

Immediately his hands dropped, but he slithered
around her to look down into her face. "*Ach*, Lizzie!
You have another battle wound. I'd offer you my handkerchief, but . . ."

"But I already used it."

"That, and it's probably gray from the soot."

"I-I think I dropped it in the house anyway. I'll buy
you another one."

Stephen laughed. He had a nice laugh. In fact, he
was quite pleasing to look at, with his hair the color of
a starless night sky and robin's egg blue eyes. Even
after clawing his way through a burning building, he
looked relatively neat. She, on the other hand, must
look a fright. She felt wisps of hair clinging to her
neck. Her *kapp* must be dingy, if the ties dangling over
her shoulders were any indication. She supposed she

should be grateful it still sat atop her head. Her face had to be as dirty as her dress.

"I'm not worried about a handkerchief." His voice dragged her back from the place her mind had no business wandering to. "I'm more concerned about wiping the blood from your face."

"It's just a scratch. I'm fine. Are you ready to move on?"

"After you." He bent in an exaggerated bow.

This time, she scrunched down low to avoid the evil branch. It would not attack her again. After scooting under it, she waited for Stephen to push through. She swiped the back of one hand across her injured cheek and frowned when she saw more blood. The scratch must be a little deeper than she had thought. Great! Now, how was she ever going to explain that, as well as the gash on her arm?

"You're still bleeding, Lizzie. Maybe I can tear off the hem of my shirt so we can wipe your face—though I'm not sure how clean my shirt is." He reached to untuck his shirt.

Lizzie threw out a hand in the universal "stop" sign and nearly dropped the kittens. "Don't you dare!"

"I'm only trying to help."

Lizzie softened her tone as much as her exasperation allowed. "I appreciate that. I don't think a scratch will kill me. It will clot and stop bleeding. Eventually."

"How about if I carry the squirmy kittens for a while?"

The offer was tempting only because she wanted her sketches back in her possession. "I'm okay. We need to hurry." She plodded on. "The going might get a little rough," she called over her shoulder.

"I can handle it."

Lizzie tried to pay closer attention to limbs that

could conk her on the head, briars that could reach out to snag her, or stumps that could trip her. She didn't need to look any clumsier than she already did. Now she was sure that, on top of thinking she was a little girl, Stephen thought she was a silly girl who drew pictures and carried stray animals home.

But she didn't have time to think about Stephen's opinion of her at the moment. Right now, she had to *kumm* up with some kind of plan to get Mamm to accept the kittens. And she had to find them something to eat.

"Will our journey take us near any place that might sell cat food?"

Apparently the man really did read minds. How did he always seem to know her thoughts? That was a bit unnerving. "I haven't seen any door-to-door cat food peddlers in the area." Oops! She shouldn't have been so sarcastic. She should apologize. To her surprise, Stephen burst out laughing.

"I'm glad you still have your sense of humor after the injuries and perils you've faced today."

"I'm glad you aren't put off by my smart mouth. Mamm always tells me to hold my tongue because other people might not appreciate my sense of humor."

"Well, I think it's rather refreshing. By all means, feel free to speak your mind around me."

"I believe I have—probably too much."

"Not at all. What I meant before was if there is some kind of store on the other side of the woods where we could purchase a small bag of cat food."

"Even if there was a store around the next bend, we wouldn't be buying cat food, because I don't have any money with me."

"I would be happy to contribute to the cause."

"You? You don't like animals."

"You keep saying that, but I don't go around kicking puppies or stepping on cats' tails. I actually like animals. I like them better than some people, to tell the truth, but I'm sure I shouldn't have said that."

Lizzie giggled. "I really didn't think you abused animals, and I'll ignore that last part, because I'm probably one of those people on your list who ranks lower than animals."

"*Nee*, you definitely are not in that category. Really, though, we have several cats who call our place home, and I am nothing but kind to them."

"I see."

"Now, we can't show up at your house and expect your *mudder* to accept three starving kittens without any way to feed them."

"*We*" *can't show up there at all.* How was she going to get him to go away once they reached the edge of the Fisher property? There wasn't any way she could enter the house with stray kittens *and* a stray man.

Chapter Five

"You do know your way home, ain't so? We aren't wandering aimlessly in the woods only to be found when someone notices the buzzards circling?"

Lizzie stopped tramping across brittle leaves, broken branches, and protruding roots to glare over her shoulder. "Of course I know my way home."

"I was just making sure. This doesn't look like a very well-worn path, or even a path at all, for that matter."

"Most people use the paved bike trail. It's easier, but since we wanted to avoid the trail, this is pretty much our only option."

"Tell me again—why are we avoiding the trail?"

"I believe that was your idea, but I agreed. Since we both look like we crawled out from under a campfire, we decided it would be best not to draw the attention of the firemen or police or whatever authorities were back there."

"We did?"

"We did. You must have a memory problem."

"Not really. I'm testing yours."

"There's not a thing wrong with my memory or my sense of direction."

"If you say so."

To prove her point, Lizzie turned around and stomped off.

"Do we really look that bad?"

Lizzie laughed. "I'm sure I must. And we probably smell like a belching chimney."

"You do have a way with words. Maybe you should write stories to go with your pictures."

"I think the pictures will get me in enough trouble all by themselves."

"If anybody knew about them."

"You know about them."

"I'm not planning to tattle."

Lizzie stopped so suddenly that Stephen smacked into her. "Oomph!" She juggled her meowing load. "Really? You won't say anything to anyone?"

"It's not any of my business, so I'm keeping my mouth shut. I think you have real talent, though, and should ask your bishop or someone about making notecards or something."

"I just draw for me."

"It's a shame to hide your light under a bushel."

"I've got more than a light hidden under my bushel."

Stephen threw back his head and laughed. "You've got three kittens under there, too. You can't have room for much more."

"You're probably right. I'd better speed up this walk, or I'll be reprimanded for being late on top of the scolding I'm bound to get for dragging the kittens home." Lizzie set off, with Stephen at her heels. She paused but didn't stop, for fear he'd crash into her again. "Hey, you wouldn't want to take the kittens, would you? I'm sure you could give them a *gut* home. Maybe your *mamm* would be more understanding."

Lizzie didn't think he was married, since he didn't have a beard or even the beginning of one, but for *gut* measure she added, "Or your *fraa*."

"I don't have one of those. My *mudder* likes animals, but I doubt she wants me to return home with three kittens."

"But they're so cute."

"I'm certain she would say we already have too many critters."

Lizzie sighed. "I just thought I'd try." She picked up her pace again.

"Do you think a neighbor would let you borrow some cat food?"

"I wouldn't want to ask anyone, but the poor little things can't eat dirt or people food." The brambles grew sparser and the walk a bit easier as they neared the edge of the woods.

"I passed a little hardware store earlier. Are we anywhere near that, and do they sell pet food?"

"I think they sell a small amount of pet food, but we aren't very near there. And I have to get home. Where did you *kumm* from?" Lizzie meant not only where he had ventured from before finding her on the trail but also where he lived.

"My driver needed to take his car to the auto repair shop on the main highway."

"And you simply rode along to pass the time away?"

"*Nee.* I, uh, had business to attend to."

"Where did you say you lived?"

"I didn't say."

"Why the secret? How did you happen to be on the trail? And don't say the wind blew you there, because it's not breezy enough to stir up leaves, much less blow you from one place to another."

Stephen chuckled. "I saw you racing along and followed."

"*Ach!* You're a stalker? That's kind of creepy."

He laughed again. "I'm not a stalker."

"It sure sounds like it."

"You were in a big hurry with a look of determination—or was it desperation?—on your face. You stoked my curiosity."

"Maybe I should throw a bucket of water on you and douse that real quick."

"But you don't have a bucket of water."

"I can get one as soon as I get home." Except she had to get him to leave before they came within sight of the house.

"When will that be?"

"What?"

"Home. Where is your home?"

"I can take that box and point you in the right direction to meet your driver. You don't have to traipse the rest of the way with me." He really didn't need to know where her home was.

"I'm not complaining. And I think my driver will be a long time getting his car repairs done, so I'm not in a big hurry."

"Oh."

They emerged from the woods at a blacktopped road. Ordinarily Lizzie would have hopped across the ditch to reach the pavement. She thought better of that today, with her arms full of squirming kittens. Stephen, however, stepped across the ditch in one long-legged stride. He turned back and reached for Lizzie's arm to help her across. She could have made it fine on her own, but she found his consideration touching, even if she wasn't entirely certain if he was being considerate of her or of the kittens.

Lizzie adjusted her load when Stephen let go of her arm. She still hadn't concocted a story for her *mudder*. She didn't plan to lie; that wasn't the case at all. She simply needed to find the approach that would best appeal to Mamm's tender side. She sighed. There wasn't any use putting off the inevitable. She marched down the road, giving only a cursory glance at the farm across the road from them to assure herself she had no witnesses. How fast would news travel along the Amish grapevine that Lizzie Fisher had strolled down the road with a strange man? That she had been in the woods with him, no less? She shuddered at that thought.

She stopped at the end of the long dirt driveway leading to the two-story white farmhouse. "You can leave the box here, and I'll walk down to fetch it later." She couldn't very well hide the kittens, but she could put off revealing her sketching secret for a little while longer. There was only so much tongue-lashing a person could take in one day.

"You don't want me to walk to the house with you?"

Lizzie's eyes shifted from side to side in case one of her siblings was wandering around. "Uh, that won't be necessary."

"Are you ashamed to be seen with me?"

He was a very nice-looking man, so that wasn't her concern at all. Her cheeks burned at that thought. "Well, how will it look if I tell my *mamm* that a strange man who won't tell me anything about himself other than his first name—and I had to pry that tidbit out, by the way—followed me through the woods? Do you think she would be overjoyed at that revelation?"

"I don't want to leave your box here. Something could happen to it."

"Trust me, it's too close to supper time for my siblings to venture down here. My *schweschders* should be helping Mamm. My *bruders* should be helping Daed. And the little ones should be playing. I'll make sure there isn't any mail in the box, just in case someone says they want to check."

"What about the cat food?"

"I haven't figured out that part yet. Right now, I'm only hoping the kittens can stay."

"I hope so, since you like them so much. They are cute. I'll admit that. And you were right to rescue them. I'd walk barefoot across hot coals to save my dogs."

"Well, that's *gut* to know."

"What do you think your *mamm* will say about the kittens?"

I'm more worried what she'll say about you. "I guess I'll find out in a few minutes." Lizzie brushed at her dress as if she could obliterate the grime. Out of the corner of her eye she could detect Stephen wagging his head. "It didn't help a bit, did it?" She stopped brushing.

"Not really, but honest, Lizzie, you don't look that bad."

"I'm not sure that's a compliment."

"I meant it as one. You merely look like you've been outside and maybe dragged kittens out from under a bush."

"This is getting better."

"Do you think I should quit while I'm ahead, if I'm ahead?"

Lizzie smiled and nodded. "That would probably be the best idea. If you'll set my box in the middle of that clump of bushes, I would appreciate it. I'll retrieve it later. *Danki* for your help and for risking your life when you didn't even know why."

"This has certainly been an interesting day."

"If you won't say any more about yourself, I won't bother to ask again. I'll be sure to check the post office walls the next time I'm in there. But at least tell me how you knew who I was. You called me by name when you first saw me on the trail."

"I, uh, someone pointed you out as you raced by."

"Does that someone have a name, or is he or she nameless like you?"

"He's anonymous."

"Interesting name." Lizzie turned away from the captivating blue eyes and tried to shut out the man that owned them. She'd most likely never see him again, so she really didn't need to know anything else about him. Her curiosity would have to be satisfied with a first name and an image of a tall, dark-haired man with a wry sense of humor to match her own.

"Say, Lizzie?"

"*Jah?*" She turned her head to bring him into view.

"Is your *mudder's* name Lizzie, too?"

"*Nee.* Her name is Anna. Why?"

"Is there another Lizzie Fisher around here?"

"Not that I'm aware of. Why do you ask?"

Stephen shrugged. "Just asking."

"Well, that's a strange question." Lizzie waited a moment, hoping he would offer more of an explanation. When he didn't make any further comments, she turned back to face the house. She still had a plea to construct.

"Hey, Lizzie?"

She stopped but didn't turn around this time.

"Could I have one of your sketches?"

She gasped, turned her whole body around, and marched back to the man with the suddenly humble expression and sparkling blue eyes. The hint of a smile tugged at his lips. "Why in the world do you want one of my sketches? Do you want to get into trouble, or is your goal only to get *me* into trouble?"

"I don't want either of us to get into trouble. I don't plan to share the picture with the world. I'd just like to have one to keep, if that's not a problem for you. I can always say I know an artist."

"I'm hardly an artist."

"Sure you are."

Lizzie gazed at the ground. Her face must be as red as an overripe tomato. Did he truly want one of her sketches because he liked them, or did he have some ulterior motive?

"Don't get shy on me now."

"I'm not shy. Which picture do you want?" She'd probably regret this hasty decision sooner rather than later.

"You choose. I wouldn't want to take your favorite one."

"I have several of the kittens and several of that farmhouse. You could take one of those."

"Great! I'll take one of the kittens."

She raised an eyebrow but kept any further comments to herself, lest they emerge laced with a healthy dose of sarcasm.

"What? I like the kittens."

She held the bundle out toward him. If he'd take the kittens instead of the drawing, it would save her a heap of trouble.

Stephen gently pushed the quilt back toward Lizzie. "I said I liked them, not that I wanted to own them.

My dogs might not be too happy if I brought kittens home with me."

"You can take whichever picture you want and then put the box under the bushes."

"*Danki.*"

Lizzie nodded and trudged on toward the house. Now she was extra late *and* bore an unwanted gift. She stole a glance over her shoulder in time to see Stephen push her art box under the bush. A piece of paper fluttered in his hand. Now, why did he really want a picture? And why had he asked her if there was another Lizzie Fisher?

Chapter Six

Stephen smiled at the sketch of the three kittens. Lizzie had done a fine job of capturing their likeness. He didn't know what had possessed him to ask for a picture, but once the words had leaped from his mouth, he couldn't have taken back the request without hurting her feelings. Anyone who had such a tender heart toward animals and would risk life and limb to rescue stray cats had to be a sensitive person. Maybe he wanted the sketch as a memento of the day, but he didn't see how he'd ever forget rushing into a crumbling, blazing building to rescue kittens.

He carefully rolled the paper to avoid creasing it and tucked it into a pocket. He'd told Lizzie he wouldn't divulge her secret, so he'd have to hide the sketch from observing eyes. He'd have to remember to remove the paper as soon as he got home so he didn't throw it into the laundry basket with his pants. He didn't know how he'd explain that.

Stephen needed to hurry. He increased his pace to nearly a jog so he'd have time to dash into the hardware store before meeting his ride. He wanted to grab a bag of cat food and leave it under the bush with

Lizzie's art box. He'd pay Lester extra to drive him by the Fisher house if need be.

His *mudder* must have gotten the name wrong, or else there was a Lizzie Fisher in the vicinity that this Lizzie didn't know about. That seemed highly unlikely, though. Even if she lived in a different Amish district, his Lizzie would surely know of another person with the same name as hers. *His* Lizzie? Why on earth would he think of her that way? His brain must be starved for oxygen. He'd better slow down so some of the oxygen he took in could shift from the muscles in his legs to his obviously deprived brain.

What Stephen had meant to think—can a person intend to think something?—was that *this* Lizzie would have heard of someone with her name. Mamm had to be wrong. That's all there was to it. She would be disappointed when he didn't bring home the information she needed, but how could this Lizzie possibly be the person she sought?

The Lizzie Fisher he had met today was part girl and part woman. He chuckled aloud when he remembered how offended she'd been when he thought she was young. She'd puffed up and informed him she was twenty years old. Stephen glanced around in every direction to make sure there wasn't anyone around to see him laughing to himself. His appearance attested to the fact that he was Plain, so he wouldn't likely be talking on a cell phone. *Nee*, anyone around would believe he was plain crazy. He almost laughed again at his unintentional pun. Plain crazy. That was him.

His thoughts weren't usually this discombobulated. The smoke inhalation must have done something to his brain. *Or the girl did*, a little voice whispered. Now he knew his brain must have suffered some kind of oxygen deprivation. He was hearing voices. He shook his head to jiggle that little voice out. He'd better try to focus on the tasks at hand. He'd purchase the cat food, meet Lester, drop off the food, and prepare to tell Mamm to check her sources for the correct name of the person she needed. If he saw that fellow who pointed Lizzie out to him again, he would ask the man if *he* had heard of another Lizzie Fisher.

Stephen barely made it back to the automotive shop before Lester finished his business there. He must have put a hundred miles on his feet today, and they were beginning to protest. In response to Lester's questioning glance at the bag of cat food tucked under his arm, Stephen explained he'd picked it up for an acquaintance who couldn't get to the store. Lester said he didn't mind altering their route home so Stephen could drop off his purchase.

Did it ever feel great to collapse onto the seat of Lester's car! Even the cracks in the vinyl didn't bother him so long as they didn't grab at his pants and tear a hole in them. He directed Lester to the Fishers' house and had him stop at the end of the driveway. Stephen jumped out and left the bag beside the bushes. He peeked between the leaves. *Gut.* The art box was still there, so Lizzie was bound to see the bag of food sitting in open view. He hurried back to Lester's idling, rusty tin can on wheels. He wondered how things were going with Lizzie and the kittens. He'd probably never know, so he might as well put it out of his mind.

"Don't you want to take that to the house?" Lester fixed him with a curious stare when Stephen repositioned his backside over the gaps in the seat.

"*Nee.* The person knows to *kumm* to the end of the

driveway." She knew to fetch her box, but she didn't know about the food. He hoped it would ease her burdens at least a little.

There. He'd done his *gut* deed for the day. He could relax. Actually, he normally tried to do more than one such deed each day. And "relaxing"! What exactly was that? Simply remaining calm with Lester behind the wheel was a challenge. Relaxing would be totally out of the question.

Lester had a heart of gold, but he was a terrible driver. Stephen never knew if he should shut his eyes so he wouldn't see any danger or keep them open so he could warn Lester of an oncoming car or a mailbox that was about to become a hood ornament. Sometimes, though, it was best to close his eyes, keep his mouth shut, and pray the whole way.

Stephen checked the surroundings and didn't discover any imminent danger. Traffic was light, and mailboxes were few and far between. Maybe he could let his mind wander and try to shut out the twangy country music blasting from the radio and Lester's annoying tapping on the steering wheel in time with the beat.

Suddenly it occurred to him that he should have asked Lizzie if there was an Elizabeth or a Liz Fisher. The woman Mamm sought could go by a different name or nickname. Mamm might have thought her informants had said "Lizzie" when they'd actually said a variation of the name. Either way, though, Mamm would be disappointed. It would probably be better for her to do her own search anyway. He could tell her to skip this Lizzie Fisher, though. It was highly unlikely this one possessed the knowledge and skills Mamm required.

* * *

"But, Mamm, look at them. Aren't they the most adorable little things?" Lizzie held the quilt closer and opened the folds enough to let three fuzzy little heads pop out.

"*Nee* critter is adorable in my house!"

"They're just babies. They're sweet."

"They are animals, and animals do not belong in the house."

"They'll die if I don't take care of them."

"Lizzie!"

She knew she'd better think of something to calm Mamm down fast before she threw Lizzie and the kittens out the back door. "Can I make them a place in the shed? They won't bother anyone there."

"They will make a mess."

"They'll go outside to do their business if I leave the door cracked. Cats are *gut* about that. They just need a safe, warm place to stay."

"They are kittens. They'll run around and get into everything in the shed."

"I'll make sure things are put away. There can't be much more than gardening tools and flowerpots and such in there. I'll use a cinder block to prop the door open only wide enough for the kittens to go in and out but not so wide that the wind blows things around." Lizzie put on her best pitiful, pleading face. If she had thought tears would be persuasive, she'd have squeezed some out.

Anna laughed. "Lizzie, you're incorrigible."

"I think you've told me that before, maybe once or twice."

"Maybe a lot more than that. What happened to

your cheek? Did one of those cats claw you? And your arm, too?"

"It wasn't the cats." Lizzie had forgotten about her telltale injuries. "I, uh, had a run-in with a briar."

"It looks like it was more than one."

"I'm fine, Mamm. Can the kittens stay? Please?"

"You've got such a tender heart. If you could bring home every stray animal in the world, I'm convinced you would do so."

"They're so helpless. You have to admit they're cute, ain't so? And when they get a little bigger, they will be *gut* mousers."

"You'll probably spoil them too much for them to become decent hunters, but *jah*, they are cute."

Lizzie's hopes soared. Could Mamm be relenting? "Does this mean I can keep them?" That would be highly unusual, but there was a first time for everything.

"For now. We'll see how it goes, though. Your *daed* might have other thoughts entirely."

Daed was an animal lover like her. Lizzie knew he wouldn't make her turn the kittens loose to fend for themselves. He'd probably be in the shed playing with them as much as she was. "*Danki*, Mamm. I'll make them a quick bed and then help with supper."

"Supper is taken care of. If I waited for you, we'd all starve."

"I'm sorry I'm so late."

"And you're filthy."

"I'll clean up after I take the kittens out." Lizzie wanted to hurry and get them out of sight before Mamm changed her mind. She had almost made it to the door when Mamm spoke again.

"Why do you smell like you just crawled out of the chimney and look like you've wrestled with pigs?"

Lizzie shrugged. If she told the truth, Mamm would lock her in the house until she married her off. If she told anything otherwise, it would be a lie. And lying was a sin. At a loss for words, she shrugged again and changed the subject. "I'll get the kittens settled." She headed for the door again until Mamm's words stopped her once more. At this rate, she'd never escape.

"Have you thought what you are going to feed them?"

"I'm working on that. I'll buy the cat food myself, but, uh, I don't have any yet."

"I suppose Ruff's food won't kill them tonight."

"Dog food?"

"Have you got another plan? They certainly aren't sitting at the table with us."

"I guess Ruff will have to share. I hope he doesn't make one of the kittens his midnight snack in retaliation. I'll have to make sure he can't get into the shed."

"He'll get used to them—if they stay around long enough."

Now, what did she mean by that? Lizzie hurried outside to check on the shed. If she was quick enough, she might have time to retrieve her art box before dinner. Darkness would soon be upon them. The days had been growing shorter as fall approached.

When she reached the potting shed, Lizzie stooped down to let the kittens out of their cocoon. They would probably be eager to stretch their legs. She hoped they didn't run off while she readied the shed for them. They meowed and wound themselves around her feet until they got up the nerve to explore their surroundings. Lizzie would have to work quickly in the shed and search for food for them. Ruff might not take too kindly to sharing his food, so she would try to sneak some kibble from the bag when he wasn't around.

She secured tools and terra-cotta flowerpots so they wouldn't get knocked over and broken. She made sure all potting soil containers were closed and there was nothing around that could get destroyed by little claws or teeth. She hoped she hadn't missed anything. The last thing she needed was for Mamm to enter the shed and find a huge mess. She even found a bowl for water and ran to the outside pump to fill it. The kittens trotted back and forth behind her like ducklings following a *mudder* duck. Lizzie smiled as they tumbled over one another in their bid for her attention.

While the kittens lapped at the water, Lizzie stole away to sneak a little food from Ruff. His huge bag of dog food was stored in a big metal can with a tight-fitting lid. If he heard the clang of the metal or the rustle of the bag, he would be right there with his tongue hanging out and his tail thumping. She'd have to be ever so quiet.

Lizzie glanced in all directions. Since none of her siblings were in sight, this might be the best time to dash to the end of the driveway. It could be the only chance she had to slip away unnoticed. She felt like a naughty scholar as she sped down the driveway. She hadn't planned what she would do if someone came out and spied the box in her hand. She'd have to cross that bridge when she came to it. Would it be wrong to pray she wouldn't *kumm* to it?

Honestly, how much trouble would she be in if her secret was discovered? Lots, probably. Why was it okay to design quilts and to construct furniture and trinket boxes but not okay to sketch the Lord Gott's creation? Lizzie supposed the buildings she drew weren't exactly the Lord's creations, but He created the people who constructed them. If the Lord Gott gave her any talent for drawing, as Stephen had said, was it wrong for her to use it? *Ach!* Who was she to question?

Her breath came in gasps by the time she reached the bushes. What was that propped against a bush? Had someone gotten here before her? She squatted down to investigate. Cat food? A bag of cat food leaned against the very bush that concealed her box. Stephen must have bought food and brought it back here. Lizzie smiled. For all his secretive behavior and seeming nonchalance, he had again saved the kittens. That was a point in his favor. But he hadn't taken her box, had he? He had some strange interest in her drawings.

Lizzie pushed aside the medium-sized bag of cat food—kitten food, actually. He'd even thought to purchase the appropriate food. Another point for Stephen, but all points would be obliterated if her artwork was gone. Her fingers trembled as she felt around beneath the bush. Her box had to be there!

Chapter Seven

Lizzie forced down the rising panic that threatened to swallow her whole when her fingers didn't immediately grasp the metal box with her treasured drawings, paper, and pencils. She'd spent *gut* money on her supplies at a rare visit to the craft store months ago. And she'd put her heart and soul into her drawings.

She knew one of her siblings hadn't retrieved the box, because they would have blabbed to Mamm or Daed by now. Surely Stephen whatever-his-last-name-was wouldn't have exchanged the kitten food for her box. He didn't give her the impression of being the artsy type, but he did seem to like her drawings.

Lizzie wiggled closer to the bush to stretch her uninjured arm farther back. Maybe he had moved the box to play a trick on her and was watching in amusement as she searched. She could picture the smirk on his face and the crinkles around his sparkling blue eyes. *Nee.* He didn't seem to be the prankster type, either—or a thief, for that matter.

She nearly cried in relief when her fingers touched the cool metal box. Her pictures better still be inside. She would only truly be relieved once she'd checked the contents. Lizzie tugged the box forward, freeing it from the clutches of the bush. *Hurry! Hurry! Before someone discovers you!* She wanted to heed the warning of the wee voice in her head, but she had to peek into the box before she headed back to the shed to herd the kittens inside. She had left them outside to do their business, but that might not have been the best idea. She needed to move faster.

Lizzie sucked in a breath and held it as she fumbled with the latch. Did Stephen take anything besides a single picture, like he had asked? Which one did he take? More important, what did he plan to do with it? At last her fingers cooperated, and she popped open the lid of the box. Lizzie dug through the pencils and tablets to reach the sketches hidden underneath. Aha! Stephen had taken one of her kitten pictures, but everything else was exactly as she'd left it. *Forgive me, Lord Gott, for suspecting him of any wrongdoing.*

She returned everything to the box and grunted as she pushed herself to her feet. She threw another glance in all directions to make sure she didn't have any observers. Hoisting the bag of cat food in one arm and her beloved box in the other, Lizzie tried to determine how to return to the shed unnoticed. Great! Now she had two things to hide—the box because she was not now and probably never would be ready to reveal her secret passion, and the bag because Mamm would ask where it came from if she left it in plain sight. She certainly couldn't tell Mamm the bag had appeared under the bush as if by magic. Tomorrow she could leave the bag in view, because then everyone would assume she had purchased it while out and about.

Please let everyone still be busy with whatever they've been doing. Please don't let me be discovered. I'll be really fast.

Were her actions truly so wrong? Wouldn't the Lord Gott want her to take care of His creatures? Would He be upset that she drew pictures of kittens, rabbits, deer, trees, and houses?

Lizzie sighed. She didn't have any answers to her questions. She would, however, have to *kumm* up with answers to Mamm's questions if she got caught with the box and bag in her hands. She sauntered up the driveway as normally as possible, even though she wanted to run to hide the incriminating evidence she carried.

With the sun sinking lower in the sky, the once-warm afternoon morphed into a chilly early evening. Lizzie loved the fall, when they would have a break from all the canning, weeding, and mowing. She would have leaves to rake, but that was okay. It was a hard job, but she didn't mind too much. Soon they would need to drag out scarves and gloves and keep the woodstove burning constantly. Lizzie loved the scent of the wood smoke that curled from the chimney. Somehow, that smoke smelled a whole lot better than the awful smell that now clung to her hair and clothes.

Gut! She'd reached the halfway point on the long dirt driveway and hadn't yet encountered another human. She might make it back to the shed undetected. Oops! Maybe not. She stepped up her pace when the sound of laughter reached her. Apparently her younger *schweschders* had run outside. Either Mamm had let them off the hook from helping with supper preparations or she had gotten tired of hearing their banter and ordered them out of the house. Whatever the reason, if they saw her with the kittens, they would stick to her like gum on the bottom of her shoe.

Lizzie exhaled the breath she'd held almost to the

exploding point as soon as she safely entered the dimly lit shed. She'd have to hide her things in here for the time being and hope to retrieve them later. The problem was where in this shed would she hide them? She had only a few seconds to ponder her choices. The kittens couldn't hurt the metal box, but would they claw into the bag of food? The voices and giggles grew louder. Quick! Where would she hide her treasures?

Not the best choice, for sure and for certain, but Lizzie shoved the box and bag into a far dark corner. She set bags of potting soil and fertilizer in front of them and draped a couple of rags over the top. That would simply have to do for now. If she could slip out alone to check on the kittens before bedtime, she'd at least try to move the box to her room.

"Kittens!"

Six-year-old Sadie's squeal pulled Lizzie away from the back of the shed. Eight-year-old Nancy would, without a doubt, be right on Sadie's heels.

"*Ach!* Three of them!" a second voice squealed.

Jah. Just as Lizzie had predicted. She'd better rescue the poor little critters from her two well-meaning but overly exuberant younger siblings. She made it to the doorway right as Sadie bent to nab a kitten. "Wait, Sadie!"

The little girl jumped back with a shriek. She jerked her hand away as if she'd discovered she was about to pet a skunk. "Y-you scared me, Lizzie. Whose kitties are they? Why can't I pick one up? What—?"

"Whoa!" Lizzie held up a hand. In typical Sadie fashion, the questions flew one after another without a pause to insert an answer. Lizzie crouched down to gently stroke the frightened black kitten at her feet.

The other two had zoomed into the shed. The poor babies weren't used to eager little hands grabbing at them or to loud voices. "They're my kittens, at least for now. They aren't very used to people, so you need to be gentle and use a quiet voice. They'll adjust soon." *If they stay.*

"Can I touch the kitty?"

"Sure, but pet her easy. This one is Annie."

"Are there only three of them?" Nancy dropped to her knees and reached out to stroke the kitten.

"*Jah*, there are three kittens. The other two ran into the shed."

"What are their names? Can we see them?" Sadie attempted to keep her voice calm, but it increased in volume in proportion to her level of excitement.

Lizzie scooped Annie into her arms and stood. The frightened animal buried her face in the crook of Lizzie's arm. "You can meet them. Then we need to let them settle in and go help with supper."

"Frannie already helped with supper, and Sadie and I set the table." Nancy, the informer, stood and crossed her arms over her chest in a "So there!" stance.

Lizzie's lips twitched. She got a kick out of her little *schweschders*. Nancy was a take-charge kind of girl, while Sadie was mellower, except where animals were concerned. Both had dark hair and big, brown eyes like their oldest sister, Frannie. Even their *bruders*, Melvin and Caleb, had the same hair and eyes. Lizzie was the only odd one, with hair that was neither brown nor blonde and eyes of a delicate violet hue.

She remembered when she went through a period where she felt as if she didn't belong in the family. Even Mamm and Daed had dark hair and eyes. It didn't help matters that Melvin teased her and told her Mamm found her growing under the big leaves of the zucchini plants. When Mamm's *grossmammi* invited her to Pennsylvania to stay for a while, Lizzie understood her unusual appearance. The woman had been small, wrinkly, and gray-haired for as long as Lizzie had been on the planet, but Lizzie learned a whole lot that summer when she cared for the lady after her surgery.

She and Mammi Lena, as Lizzie called her, had the same violet eyes! Lizzie hadn't lived nearby growing up and hadn't noticed her eye color during childhood visits. All she had ever seen was the silver, wire-rimmed glasses. But that summer, Mammi Lena told Lizzie stories of her own youth and how she always had the same unusual shade of hair as Lizzie. How uncanny that the genes, or whatever was responsible for eye and hair color, had skipped two generations and landed on Lizzie!

The more Lizzie learned about Mammi Lena, the more she admired her. She had weathered many storms in life but never lost her hope, her faith, or her sense of humor. And Mammi Lena liked to create, too! Another link. She showed Lizzie many sketches of quilt designs she'd created herself. The older woman had unique patterns stored in her head as well, and she could weave about anything imaginable on her *wunderbaar* loom—the very same loom Lizzie now owned.

Mammi Lena taught Lizzie all about that loom and was tickled pink someone else showed an interest in it and had a natural ability for weaving. And Lizzie learned very quickly. She took to the loom like a fly to honey. Mammi Lena said it was Lizzie's calling to create beautiful but useful items. She even caught Lizzie sketching a picture of the big old orange and white cat that slept in Mammi Lena's rocking chair whenever Mammi vacated the spot. And of all things, the old woman didn't reprimand her. Instead she praised Lizzie's talent.

Lizzie couldn't believe how spry the woman was for her advanced age. She bounced back from her surgery lickety-split and devoted the weeks of her recovery to teaching Lizzie. And how the young girl adored her time spent with the wise old woman. She fell in love with weaving and revered the loom as much as Mammi Lena did. Mammi called Lizzie her little sponge because she soaked up every tidbit of information offered yet always craved more.

When it was time for Lizzie to return to Maryland, she hated leaving the woman and the loom behind. She begged Mammi Lena to move in with her family, but Mammi wanted to spend whatever remaining days the Lord Gott gave her in her own little house.

Lizzie had visited Mammi Lena several more times before she passed away. She missed her great-*grossmammi* fiercely, but now had the loom to keep her memories alive. Lizzie experienced something akin to pride that Mammi left the loom to her. An Amish girl should not be proud, but her emotions rivaled that. Daed had given her space in one section of the smaller barn. Lizzie spruced the place up and dragged in a kerosene heater. Now she spent as much time as possible weaving and creating designs.

That's it! She'd stash her hidden items in the workroom. They'd be far less likely to be found in there than in the bedroom she shared with Frannie. "Let's go put Annie in her bed, and you can meet Miriam and Molly."

"You've named them already?" Sadie skipped along

beside Lizzie. Without waiting for an answer, she added, "That's okay. I like their names."

"I'm glad. Are you ready to meet the kittens, too, Nancy?"

"Sure. I was wondering where you got them."

"I found them near the bike trail."

"Don't they belong to someone?" Nancy's brow wrinkled as if in deep thought.

Lizzie walked faster. If she could get the girls in and out of the shed, maybe she could avoid a ton of questions she couldn't answer. "They're strays."

"Where is their *mudder*? They seem young to be all alone, ain't so?"

Ugh. Leave it to Nancy to want details. "There was a *mudder*, but I think she must have gotten hit by a car."

"The poor thing. And poor babies, to be left alone." Sadie sniffed.

Lizzie reached to tweak her youngest sibling's nose. The little girl was so sensitive, so compassionate. Lizzie hoped she would keep those qualities as she grew up. "That's why I'm taking care of them."

"Did Mamm say you could keep them?" Nancy stopped walking and planted her hands on her hips.

If Nancy was *Englisch*, she would make a great detective. "She said I could keep them for now. I have to make sure they stay out of trouble." *And out of Mamm's way.*

"We'll help you, won't we, Nancy?" Sadie tugged at the bigger girl's arm.

"Sure."

Lizzie opened the shed door a little wider to let in the waning daylight. The other kittens were huddled beneath a workbench. Sadie got down on all fours, ready to crawl under the bench. "Let's leave them for now. They're a little scared. The black-and-white one is Molly, and the tortoiseshell one is Miriam."

"I want to hold one." Sadie backed out and jumped to her feet.

"Maybe tomorrow they will be ready for that. Why don't you two run back to the house and wash up for supper? I'll fix the kittens a little bed and be right in."

"Don't they need food and water?" Practical Nancy would naturally consider that.

"They sure do. I'll leave them something. Tell Mamm I'll be inside in a few minutes."

Nancy nudged Sadie. "I'll race you." The girls scrambled out the door and shot toward the house.

Lizzie laughed. Unless Nancy fell in a hole, her longer legs would surely get her to the house way ahead of Sadie. At least they were gone. She arranged the smoky quilt in a corner to make a bed for the kittens. Tomorrow she'd find something else. That quilt would likely make the whole shed reek of smoke. She hoped the kittens wouldn't venture out of the shed during the night. More importantly, she hoped nothing crept in to get them.

She filled one small pie tin with food and another with water before snatching her art box and the bag of food from the hiding place. She'd slip over to her work area and bury the items among her weaving supplies before heading to the house. Lizzie left the door open only far enough for the kittens to get out to take care of their business. If she'd had a litter box, she would have closed the door all the way to keep them safe. She would pray for them. The Lord Gott cared about all of His creatures, didn't He?

Lizzie's work area was as neat and orderly as she had left it. She was ever so glad Daed had partitioned off an area to be her workshop and store. He had even run in a propane light so she could see on cloudy days or if she worked until dusk. Thankfully, this was a storage barn where Daed kept implements, tools, extra bales of hay, and grain, so she didn't have animal smells to contend with. That would not be *gut* for business, at least as far as *Englisch* customers were concerned. Most of them weren't as used to farm smells as her Amish patrons.

She didn't know why Frannie always called her a scatterbrain. There was nothing haphazard about Lizzie's little corner of the barn. Her little world. Weaving soothed her mind and calmed her spirit even if everything else around her was in a jumble. Mammi Lena must have sensed Lizzie would feel this way. She had even confessed that she found the same peace in weaving and designing that Lizzie did. Kindred spirits, Mammi Lena had called the two of them.

Mammi Lena held a special place in Lizzie's heart, for sure and for certain. Lizzie wished she could have had more time with the dear lady, but she cherished every single memory she had. Lizzie paused a moment to shift her load so she could finger the alpaca fleece in a big woven basket. Designs already swirled in her mind. At least she could give free reign to her creativity for her *Englisch* customers' projects, even if she did have to stick to plainer items for the Amish folk.

Lizzie lovingly ran her hand along the loom. Her fingers twitched, anxious to weave more of the blanket in progress. But that would have to wait. If she didn't hurry and get in the house, Mamm would send Nancy and Sadie back out to fetch her. They'd pester her with more questions. Even worse, Mamm might send Frannie out to bring her in. Lizzie loved her older *schweschder,* but they were as different as pigs and cows. Although Frannie was a mere two years older, Mammi Lena would have called the girl an old soul.

Frannie would be perfectly content to spend her whole life indoors cooking, cleaning, or mending. She generally only went outdoors when Mamm sent her to weed the garden, pick vegetables, or hang clothes on the line. Personally, Lizzie thought the girl needed to get outside more to get some color in those cheeks. Frannie's dark hair and big, brown eyes were lovely, but her complexion was much too pale. Even Melvin told Frannie she looked like she lived under one of those huge mushrooms that grew where the yard met the woods. Perhaps she could entice Frannie outside to play with the kittens tomorrow.

Lizzie squatted beside a big plastic tote where she stored weaving supplies. She laid her bundle down to pop off the lid. Surely if she rearranged things she could hide her secret items in here. She rummaged and reorganized as quickly as possible. Even with all her poking and prodding, she only barely managed to conceal the box and bag in the full tote. She should be able to remove the bag of cat food tomorrow, and that would make it possible to close the tote without sitting on it.

If times were different and she was at Mammi Lena's house, she wouldn't have to worry about keeping her treasures a secret. Mammi had loved animals as much as Lizzie. She even kept her big, lazy cat inside her house. Few Amish people allowed house pets, but Mammi marched to the beat of her own drum. Her cat wasn't even a stray. She had adopted him from the animal shelter. She actually paid *gut* money for him and justified that by saying it was for a noble cause. Mammi Lena had been a character, all right.

The girls' voices brought Lizzie back to the present in a hurry. She slid the storage box out of the way and set a basket of yarn on top of it. She'd slip outside and chase the little girls so they'd forget all about asking her what she had been doing.

Her idea worked. They all arrived at the house breathless and laughing. Nancy didn't ask a single nosy question, and Sadie didn't beg to see the kittens "just one more time." Lizzie cleaned herself up the best she could. There wasn't any time for her to change her filthy dress or dingy *kapp*, since Daed and her *bruders* had already stomped inside eager for supper. She still smelled like the remnants of a campfire, but at least her hands had been scrubbed clean.

Lizzie hustled to the kitchen and carried bowls and platters to the table. She ignored Frannie's wrinkled nose but stuck her tongue out at her *schweschder*'s back. Easy to keep all prim and proper if you stayed inside all day like Frannie! *Bad, bad, Lizzie. Don't add "mean" to your list of transgressions.*

Once everyone had been seated, Frannie leaned so far away from Lizzie that she expected Frannie to drop off her chair at any second. Now, why would Frannie be in such a snit? Lizzie had scrubbed her hands and face. She'd shower and wash her hair later. She didn't reek that bad, did she? Lizzie knew she'd hear all about Frannie's problem—whatever it was—once they were in their room. Hopefully, it didn't involve her, but she wouldn't count on that.

The supper conversation went along just fine, with six boisterous *kinner* of varying ages vying for a turn to speak. Fine, that is, until Daed paused with a forkful of mashed potatoes halfway to his mouth to look Lizzie in the eye. She struggled not to cringe but would have liked to slide right under the big oak table. He could nail a person to the wall with his piercing brown eyes.

"What's this I hear about more mouths to feed, Dochder?" Emanuel Fisher slipped the bite of potatoes into his mouth but kept his eyes on Lizzie.

"Kittens, Daed." Lizzie gulped down a sip of water to moisten her throat, which had suddenly become as dry as a clod of dirt in an August drought. She cleared her throat. "I'll take care of them. They're awfully cute, ain't so, Sadie?" If she involved the *boppli* of the family, Daed might soften a bit more, but she prayed his concern for animals would kick in.

"They're ever so sweet. And they're all different." Sadie became so animated she nearly toppled her glass of milk.

"Easy there, little one." Daed laid his fork on his plate and turned to Lizzie again. "How do you plan to take care of them?"

Before Lizzie could answer, Nancy rushed in. "Lizzie made a bed for them in the shed. She's going to give them a little of Ruff's food until she buys cat food. She left the door open a crack so they can get out to, well, you know." She paused for breath.

Nancy the Informer, at it again. Did every family have such a member? While Nancy inhaled, Lizzie plunged in. "I'll buy the kitten food with my money. You won't have to buy anything, Daed."

From the corner of her eye, she caught Frannie's eye roll. The girl could be infuriating. Even though she never showed any interest in learning to use the loom, or even in hand knitting, which she could do in the safety of the house, she always seemed to begrudge

Lizzie her love of weaving and needlework. And now she was begrudging her the kittens, too? Lizzie couldn't quite determine the reason for the older girl's persnicketiness, if that was a word, or her shyness or whatever caused her attitude, but she could be downright aggravating. She'd likely never find a husband holed up in the kitchen nursing a nasty disposition. The girl simply had to get out more. That's all there was to it.

Chapter Eight

"You didn't find hide nor hair of Lizzie Fisher?" Mary Zimmerman pushed an escaped strand of dark brown hair beneath her white *kapp*. She turned from the kitchen counter where she'd been assembling a salad, eyebrows raised, to stare into her second-oldest son's blue eyes.

"*Nee.* Well, not the person you wanted. I don't know, Mamm. Either you got the name wrong or there is some other Lizzie Fisher, because the girl I saw today was just that—a girl. She came up to about here on me." Stephen indicated a spot right below his shoulder. "And she was young, very young." Twenty, he distinctly remembered. And scatterbrained, or maybe "animal-brained." She was a *gut* artist, though. He raised a hand to subtly pat the pocket that held her drawing.

"Just because a person is short or young doesn't mean she can't have skills and talents and can't help people."

"I know. I'm just saying this wisp of a girl can't be the one you're looking for." He reached to pluck a cherry tomato from the salad bowl, but jerked his hand back before his *mamm* could swat it.

"*Nee* dirty hands in my salad. Whew! Why do you smell like last week's stove ashes?"

"That's a long story."

"I'm listening."

Great! Now what was he going to say? That he had chased after a girl named Lizzie Fisher and ran into a blazing building behind her to rescue kittens? That he risked life and limb and inhaled enough smoke to fill both lungs because he had thought he needed to save the aforementioned girl from becoming charred beyond all recognition? He'd have to do better than that to avoid an inquisition. "I, uh, helped someone rescue their belongings from a smoky room." Not entirely true, but not entirely untrue, either. He had rescued Lizzie's art box, and he assumed the kittens belonged to her, if her *mudder* allowed them to stay. And they had been in a room. It's just that said room happened to be located in a crumbling, burning house.

"Hmmm. Smells like you crawled into a stove to rescue those belongings."

It had rather felt like it at the time, too. Instead of replying, he shrugged and, quick as a flash, pilfered a tomato.

"*Ach!* I saw that. You're filthy!"

"I only touched the one tomato."

"And probably contaminated the rest by reaching over the bowl." Mary bent close to the salad and sniffed.

"The smell didn't jump off of me and into the bowl, Mamm."

"I was just checking. So tell me about your Lizzie Fisher."

"She's not *my* Lizzie Fisher." The tomato almost squirted out of his mouth.

"You know what I mean." Mary set the salad aside, grabbed a quilted hot pad, and pulled open the door on the wood cookstove.

Stephen often wondered why Mamm didn't use the propane stove, but she apparently liked the woodstove best. He peeked around her to determine the source of the delectable smell that had set his stomach rumbling. Ah! He thought so. Meat loaf. Mamm did something special to meat loaf that made it much more than an ordinary meal.

"Well?"

Stephen swallowed the tomato with a gulp. "Well what?"

"Tell me about the girl you met and why you believe she isn't the right person."

"She's young."

"So? You already mentioned that."

"She's barely out of girlhood. How could she possibly know all the ins and outs of your mysterious loom?"

"Don't you think young people have skills?"

"Sure I do." The Lizzie he had met was a talented artist. She might sit still long enough to draw magnificent pictures, but he doubted she could spend hours glued to a loom. Besides, how would she know about the thing if his *mudder* didn't? He suddenly realized Mamm had said something else that he missed with his internal rambling. "Huh?"

"I said *you* have talents, ain't so? You design and construct some very nice pieces of furniture in that shop back there, don't you?" Mary nodded at the kitchen window, beyond which lay the building where he built desks, dressers, rocking chairs, and most any kind of wooden furniture a person could want.

"I do all right."

"You do far better than that, and you're only twenty-three. Don't you think you could teach some of the older men a thing or two about woodworking?"

Stephen shrugged again. "I don't know. I never thought about it."

"Well, I'm sure you could. And don't you have a way with those dogs that none of us has?"

"Maybe." Stephen grew a little uncomfortable with Mamm's litany of his accomplishments.

"Now, about this girl . . ."

"Mamm, do you think you could have gotten the name mixed up or the wrong community or something?"

"I'm sure there could very well be more than one Lizzie Fisher. Did you ask that?"

"I asked *her* if she knew of another Lizzie Fisher or if her *mamm* had the same name."

"And?"

"She didn't know of a single other woman with that name. But that doesn't mean there isn't another one."

"Did you ask if she was the weaver who owned the same kind of loom Aenti Martha left me?"

"Uh, *nee*, I didn't ask that."

She made a clucking sound with her tongue. Her disappointment in him was practically palpable, and he regretted letting her down. "I'm sorry. From talking to her, I simply didn't think she was the person you sought, so I didn't ask more questions."

Mary shoved the meat loaf back into the oven. "What's that expression? 'Don't judge a book by its cover'? Something like that?"

"I didn't mean to judge her. I truly didn't get any indication she was *your* Lizzie Fisher." He should have asked if she owned a loom, but he had gotten the impression she wouldn't know one end of a loom from the other. He sighed. Risking his life for kittens, racing to meet his driver, dropping off cat food, and enduring a wild ride home at Lester's mercy had made for an interesting but exhausting day.

His *mamm* tapped her fingers on the countertop. "I have to find out about this loom. I can't let Aenti's art die."

"I can search again." Stephen made the offer but secretly hoped Mamm wouldn't take him up on it. He supposed there was nothing really wrong with Lizzie, per se, but she belonged to the gender he was leery of after his last disaster. Couldn't Mamm send one of his *bruders* next time? Maybe his older *bruder*, Seth, would have a more successful mission. "I'm going to check on the dogs before supper." Stephen backpedaled from the kitchen before Mamm had a chance to make another request, but he could hear her mumbling to herself before he reached the door.

"Maybe I did get the name wrong." Although quiet, her voice floated out to him.

Stephen hoped she checked her sources for the correct name. Even more, he hoped Mamm searched for the mysterious lady herself. He picked up his pace as he neared the kennel area. From the yipping and barking, he knew the pups sensed his approach. He broke into a smile when he saw the eight golden retriever puppies tumbling over one another while their *mudder* looked on. This was going to be an especially hard litter to part with. Each little ball of fuzz had its own personality, but all were loving and just plain funny.

He couldn't help but laugh out loud at the pups.

Once he entered the kennel, they bounced over to him, each one begging for his attention. "You've got a good group of pups there, Goldie." The big, beautiful female nodded as if she understood. Stephen was convinced she smiled at him as if to say, "Of course they are *wunderbaar*, you silly human."

Stephen counted himself fortunate indeed. He enjoyed crafting furniture, he enjoyed raising golden retrievers, and he loved his family, even if his *bruders* could sometimes be annoying. The only negatives in his otherwise positive life were that he had to let the puppies go when the time came and that he had not yet found a girl he wanted to spend his life with. Mamm told him he was too picky, but that was Seth's problem, not his. Seth, older by only one year, was obviously waiting for the perfect girl to happen along. He'd probably be waiting for a long time.

Nee, Stephen wasn't looking for someone perfect. He certainly had his faults, so he didn't expect anyone else to be the model of perfection. All he wanted was someone kind. Someone who could be serious but fun-loving. Someone who liked animals as much as he did. A pleasing appearance would be nice, but inner beauty was far more important. Would he find such a girl? He hadn't so far. He'd thought he had once, but that hadn't turned out as he planned. He would keep attending the young folks' gatherings, even though he still smarted from that disastrous relationship, and he'd keep dragging Seth with him.

Stephen made sure he lavished the same amount of attention on each of the puppies and on Goldie. It wouldn't do to have jealous dogs. He stroked their soft fur. Some of them were blond, while others had an almost caramel color. Hmmm. He'd thought of caramel earlier in the day. He kept an eye on the puppies' antics while he cleaned and refilled water bowls and added kibble to the food bowls. The pups still nursed but had begun to eat solid foods. He sure would be sad when they were weaned; since that would mean they would soon be ready to leave.

"Mamm wants to know if you're going to play with the puppies all night and eat dog food or *kumm* to supper with the rest of us." Thirteen-year-old Daniel had probably reworded Mamm's comment. He had a habit of doing that.

"Tell her I'll be right there."

Chapter Nine

Lizzie snagged the comb through her wet, waist-length hair. She grabbed a hunk of hair and held it under her nose. *Gut.* After three latherings with strawberry-scented shampoo, it no longer smelled like smoke. Her skin still tingled from the scrubbing she had given it so her body would be free of that burnt wood scent. She had even scrubbed the bathtub after she finished bathing so prissy Frannie wouldn't whine about the condition of the bathroom.

She laid the comb on the dresser and hopped onto the throw rug. Her bare feet had grown cold standing on the wood floor. Lizzie gave in to the shiver that worked its way up her body. The evening had grown quite chilly, a sure harbinger of fall and winter. She skipped across the room to close the window. She'd leave it open a crack to let in the fresh air—unless that fresh air made her shivers intensify.

Lizzie gasped at the sight of a light outside. Then she patted her thumping heart and smiled. Daed's big flashlight wove along the path. As she had suspected, he was heading out to see the kittens. She almost laughed aloud when he looked around before slipping inside the shed. He'd fall in love with the kittens, too, for sure and for certain.

"What are you looking at?"

Lizzie jumped at the voice and the click of the door. So much for pleasant, serene thoughts. "*Ach*, Frannie! You scared me."

"I don't know why. This is my room, too."

"I'm aware of that." Was she ever! "I just didn't hear you enter, that's all."

"Well, I don't stomp down the hall like some people."

Lizzie counted to ten forward and backward. She did not stomp down the hall, but she wouldn't bother trying to defend herself. That never worked. Frannie believed whatever Frannie wanted to believe or whatever she made up. *Oops! That was not nice. Shame on you, Lizzie.* She could only hope that if she kept quiet Frannie would leave her alone. At least if she didn't reply, her tongue couldn't get her into trouble.

"Are you going to answer me or not?"

Had Frannie asked something else? "What?"

Frannie huffed. "What's so interesting outside?"

Her big *schweschder* would make an excellent schoolteacher. The scholars would definitely toe the line. One of her mean scowls would have them cowering at their desks with their heads down all day. Lizzie almost smiled at the image but thought better of it. "I saw Daed sneak into the shed where the kittens are sleeping. You should have seen him." Lizzie chuckled and turned to face Frannie. Her laughter died a sudden death at the girl's scowl.

"You and animals. You'd turn the place into a zoo if you could."

"What's wrong with animals?" *They are a lot nicer than some people.* "How can you not like adorable little kittens?"

"I didn't say I didn't like them."

"*Kumm* look at them tomorrow. Maybe you'll adopt one for your own."

"I'll pass." Frannie grunted as she dragged her comb through a tangle.

"What's wrong with you, Frannie? You seem so out of sorts." Now that she'd opened the can of worms, she'd have to endure whatever venom her *schweschder* spit out.

"*Hmpf!* I'm not." Frannie's nimble fingers quickly braided her long, dark hair.

"Well, you're awfully grumpy." *Bad, bad tongue! You were supposed to keep still.*

"If you were around and hadn't run off to who knows where, you might understand."

"I didn't run off. I asked Mamm before I left. I needed a few things from the hardware store. Mamm didn't need me for anything." *I didn't know I had to clear my plans with you.* Thank goodness her brain kept her tongue from making that comment! A battle surely would have ensued, and she was too tired for that.

Frannie wrapped a band around the end of her braid and flung it over her shoulder like she was hurling a spear. She dropped the comb onto the dresser with a clatter. Lizzie sought a way to soothe the beast but wasn't sure she should even try. Anything she said could be misconstrued. She'd make an attempt anyway. "Did something happen today?"

"If you'd been here, you'd know. Why didn't you take the buggy so you wouldn't have been gone so long?"

"As I said before, Mamm didn't need me. Canning

is done until the rest of the apples are ready. Cleaning and chores had been completed. It was a beautiful day for a walk. You could have accompanied me, you know. The fresh air would do you *gut.*"

"What does that crack mean?"

"I didn't mean anything bad. I find a walk in the fresh air puts me in a peaceful frame of mind." *Except when I'm chased down the bike path by some stranger who doesn't want to give his name or I have to rescue helpless animals from a burning building or both.*

Frannie shrugged again.

"Tell me what's bothering you. Maybe I can help."

"Nothing is bothering me." Frannie whirled around so Lizzie couldn't see her face. "You can't help anyway."

The last four words had been mumbled, but Lizzie heard them. "I'm a great listener."

"Ha!"

Lizzie dared to approach her *schweschder* and laid a hand on her arm. "Talk to me, Frannie. You've been in a sour mood ever since we heard Aaron Kurtz wasn't returning from Pennsylvania. Is that it?"

"Who cares about Aaron Kurtz?" A sniff punctuated Frannie's words.

"I think you do—or you did."

"Aaron and I had nothing going on."

"But you wished you had, ain't so? You used to go to singings before he left. You haven't been to one since we heard the news." Lizzie's heart ached for her *schweschder.* She'd seen Frannie's eyes dart to Aaron many times during singings. Apparently she'd been hoping he would ask to drive her home. Lizzie knew for a fact that had never happened, because she and Frannie always rode home together. "I'm sorry, Frannie."

"There's nothing you can do." Frannie jerked her arm away. "But you could have been here today."

"What happened today?"

"Mamm got a letter from Ohio."

"From whom?"

"Her *aenti* Grace." Frannie sniffed again and wiped a hand across her face.

"Has something happened to the woman? She must be close to eighty by now."

"I don't know how old she is, but she needs someone to stay with her for a while after she has hip surgery."

"There are relatives there, though. Her husband grew up there and must have tons of family in the area."

"Mamm volunteered me for the job!"

"What?" Lizzie crossed the room to snatch a couple of tissues from the box on the dresser. She expected Frannie to break down into full-fledged sobs at any second. Maybe she should take the whole box. She tiptoed across the cold floor and pressed the tissues into the quaking girl's hand. "Tell me."

"Apparently Mamm knew about the upcoming surgery and mentioned sending her *dochder* out to help. Aenti Grace must have jumped on that idea."

"Mamm has four *dochders*. How do you know which one she planned to send? I mean, I know Sadie and Nancy are too young, but she could have meant me."

"I begged Mamm to send you." Frannie gasped at her outburst and then clapped a hand across her mouth. Obviously, she hadn't meant to reveal that tidbit.

"Gee, I appreciate that."

"Don't worry. Mamm said you have your *business* to take care of."

"You don't have to say the word like it's a bad grape

you need to spit out of your mouth. I do have orders to fill. People do want my products."

"Whatever."

Lizzie knew Frannie never took any interest in the weaving, but she hadn't known the girl resented her work or was jealous of it. Before she could think of a suitable reply, Frannie continued.

"Mamm said you already went to help someone."

"That's true. I went to Mammi Lena's several times."

"But you liked that."

"I did. Mammi was such a *wunderbaar* lady, and so interesting. And fun—even at her age."

"Well, I don't know Aenti Grace or anyone else there, and I don't want to go to Ohio." She crossed her arms over her chest. A defiant gesture if ever Lizzie had seen one.

"Did you tell Mamm you don't want to go?"

"How could I do that? It would make me look like a selfish, uncaring person."

Lizzie gnawed her tongue nearly in half to keep from uttering, "Well?"

"It's not that I don't care. Really. I just don't want to go to Ohio and stay with strangers. I'd rather help someone right here."

"Why don't you tell Mamm you aren't comfortable living away from home, even if it is only for a few weeks?"

"Ugh!" Frannie slumped onto her bed. "Why can't Aenti Grace's local relatives step up to help her? And why did Mamm have to volunteer me without even asking me first?"

"Maybe she thinks a change will be *gut* for you."

"How could it possibly be *gut* for me if it's making me so miserable?"

Lizzie tried to choose her words carefully. Since Frannie had finally opened up a bit, she didn't want to slam the door shut by making her angry all over again. "Maybe Mamm thinks you're stuck in a rut and need to meet new people. You stopped going to singings and pretty much stay in the house all the time."

"Do you think if I tell Mamm I'll go to every singing and I'll bake and clean for any of our sick folks or I'll help out the widows and young *mudders*, she'll let me stay here?"

When Frannie paused to gulp in a breath, Lizzie jumped in. "I don't believe Mamm expects you to single-handedly tackle every problem in the community."

The older girl sighed loud and long. "I don't want to be sent away."

"You act like Mamm is punishing you."

"That's exactly how it feels to me."

"I think you should tell Mamm what your concerns are and see what she says."

"I don't know."

"There's a quilting frolic for a couple of the brides-to-be soon. You could say you were planning to attend."

"*Hmpf!* I'll probably never get to be one of them."

Not with your surly attitude. "Of course you will. You're pretty and nice." Pretty for sure. Nice when she chose to be.

"Everyone knows I'm lousy at sewing. That's your talent, not mine. Actually, I'm not sure I even have any talents." Frannie flopped back on the bed.

"You're a first-class baker. You could bake and serve at the frolic. You know, you could probably do quite well selling baked items."

"Do you think so?" Frannie rolled onto her side and stared at Lizzie.

"I do." Lizzie reached for the lamp. Her *schwesch-der*'s relentless gaze made her jittery. What thoughts were roaming through the girl's head? Whatever they were, Lizzie was pretty certain she'd rather have the discussion in the dark so Frannie's eyes didn't bore into her heart and soul. Lizzie never knew when she might have to stretch the truth a teensy bit, and she didn't want Frannie to be able to read that from her expression or body language. It wasn't a sin to fudge the truth if it kept her from hurting someone else, was it? "Is it okay to turn out the lamp?"

"Sure."

Moonlight streaming in through the bare window gave Lizzie enough light to hop to her bed from rug to rug without stubbing her toe on something. Maybe Frannie would simply crawl beneath her covers and go to sleep. That's certainly what she wanted to do. It had been a long, exhausting day. The throbbing in her injured arm would probably make sleep difficult enough as it was, but she had a nagging suspicion the day wasn't over yet. Lizzie plumped her pillow and slid beneath the sheet and blanket.

"Lizzie?"

The voice was faint, but not so weak that Lizzie could pretend she didn't hear it.

"I know you didn't go to sleep that fast."

If only she had. "I'm awake."

"Don't you ever think about getting married?"

Could a person possibly swallow her own tongue? Lizzie coughed. Now where did that question emerge from, completely out of the blue? "Sure, one day."

"'One day' sounds like a long time off. You're twenty years old."

"Not exactly ready to be put out to pasture."

"*Nee,* but you aren't getting any younger."

"I don't believe any of us are moving backward. You're older than I am. Do you think about getting married?"

"*Jah.* A lot."

Thinking about it isn't going to make it happen. You've got to get out of the house. Lizzie bit back those words. "What exactly are you thinking?" Lizzie rose up on an elbow and peered through the moonlit room toward her *schweschder's* bed. Shadows prevented her from seeing Frannie's face clearly. "Does that mean you'd like to get married soon?"

"I'm ready to settle down."

"You need to attend the singings, then."

"I did that."

"But you stopped when Aaron left. There are plenty of other *buwe.*"

"Maybe if I was courting someone, Mamm wouldn't make me go to Ohio."

Lizzie bolted upright. "Frannie! You can't court someone just to get out of doing something you don't want to do. Marriage is forever, you know."

"Of course I know that. And I wouldn't court someone I didn't like."

"I think it needs to be more than 'like.' What about 'love'?"

"Maybe that's all a fantasy, like the *Englischers'* happily-ever-after stories. Maybe real people don't actually experience that."

"Don't you think Mamm and Daed love each other?"

"I suppose they do."

"You know they do. It's obvious by the way they still look at each other after all these years."

"But they might not have felt like that at the beginning. They might have learned to love each other over time."

"I don't believe that for a minute. Frannie, don't you dare settle for someone you don't love and count on happiness finding you later. Besides, don't you think the man would want you to love him?"

"Who knows what fellows think? A widower who needed a *mudder* for his little ones wouldn't care so much about love."

Now Lizzie was wide awake without a shred of hope that sleep would claim her in the foreseeable future. "You're young. You have plenty of time. You don't have to be so desperate to get married that you settle for someone who only wants a housekeeper and a caregiver. Give yourself a chance. You know, maybe there would be someone in Ohio who was just right for you."

"I don't want to find that out. I don't want to go. I'm not at all *gut* in strange, new situations."

"Don't you think marriage would be such a situation, especially if you joined with a man you didn't love?"

"I don't know. Do you have your eye on someone? You've been going to singings."

For a split second, the face of a dark-haired stranger with robin's egg blue eyes flashed into her mind. She eased back down onto her pillow and sent that image scurrying to some distant, shadowy corner inside her head. Maybe in a day or two it would vanish permanently.

"Do you, Lizzie?"

Lizzie heard Frannie's bed creak and knew it was her *schweschder*'s turn to raise up and stare through the darkness. Thank goodness she'd doused the light and her squirming couldn't be detected. "Of course not."

"Hmmm. I'm not so sure about that. You hesitated."

"You know very well I'm either helping out around the house or working on a weaving project." *Or rescuing animals with handsome strangers.*

"I don't know. There are plenty of times you traipse off on some errand all by yourself. That would give you plenty of opportunities to meet up with someone."

"You can put that silly notion out of your mind. I'm usually going to the hardware store to pick up some gizmo for the shop or to one of the neighboring farms to buy fleece for a project."

"Or gathering up stray animals."

"That, too." Lizzie sighed. "I have to help animals who can't fend for themselves or who need a bit of care."

"You have a soft heart."

Lizzie's jaw dropped. Was that a compliment from her *schweschder*? "I guess I do. I can't help it."

"Are you sure you haven't met any prospects at the singings?"

Apparently Frannie was not going to abandon this hashed-out topic. "Honest, I've only been singing, talking to the girls and grabbing a snack afterward, and then heading home."

"None of the fellows who sneak peeks at you during church services talk to you? I find that hard to believe. You're outgoing and fun."

"They aren't looking at me. They're looking at you. You're the pretty one."

"You must not have glanced in a mirror in a long while. You've turned into a beautiful young woman, with your light hair and unique eyes. Even the freckles on your nose are cute."

"Weird, you mean. I'm the only one in the family with different hair and eyes." Who did Frannie think had been glancing at her? Since they hadn't approached her after a singing, they must not have been looking at her.

"Different can be very appealing."

"I don't think so. Why don't you attend the next singing with me? Then we'll see who the fellows are really interested in."

"I might not be here."

"When is Aenti Grace's surgery?"

"Not for three weeks, but knowing Mamm, she'll have me go early to adjust."

"That's awfully soon."

"I know." Frannie's voice ended as a wail. "You've got to help me, Lizzie. The very thought of going petrifies me. Why don't you offer to go instead?"

"Mamm volunteered you."

"But I need to help Mamm with things. She can't count on you—oops!"

"She can, too, count on me. I do my share of chores. I just don't sit around the house all day."

"I don't sit around all day. I stay plenty busy."

"Okay. Don't get huffy. We're both tired and need to sleep." *Before we say hurtful words we'll regret.*

"Okay. But you'll help me stay here?"

"I won't volunteer to go, because I have three orders to finish, but I'll try to think of something.

Just don't up and marry some prickly old man you'll have to spend the rest of your life with. Ohio can't be *that* bad."

Frannie giggled. "*Danki*, Schweschder."

Lizzie sincerely hoped Frannie could rest easier, because now *she* would have to stay awake to devise some scheme to keep her *schweschder* in Maryland. She rolled over, punched her pillow extra hard, and yanked the covers over her head.

Chapter Ten

Lizzie slithered out of bed feeling every bit as weary as she had when she had crawled into it the night before. If she could move very quietly, she might be able to dress and slip from the room before Frannie awoke and demanded to know the brilliant plan she'd devised overnight. Unfortunately she did not have a brilliant plan, or even a lousy one.

She sucked in a sharp breath when her bare feet hit the wood floor. Cold weather definitely lurked right around the corner. Soon even the midday sun wouldn't give out much heat. Lizzie shivered. Would it be wrong to pray for a mild winter?

After years of doing the same thing the same way day after day, Lizzie could pin her dress, twist her hair into a bun, and secure the white *kapp* on top of her head in the dark. She could probably perform the tasks in her sleep, or in a deep coma. She snatched up her shoes from their resting place and crept from the room in stocking feet. The soft snores she heard assured her Frannie was still asleep.

Lizzie tiptoed down the steps, taking care to avoid the creaky one near the top. She sank onto the bottom step to thrust her feet into her black athletic shoes.

She resisted the urge to sigh. This day promised to be a long one, but at least her weaving would perk her up, like it always did.

She must have beat Mamm out of bed this morning. Not so much as a hint of light glowed from the kitchen. She would get the *kaffi* brewing before heading out to check on the kittens. She hoped they fared well through the night.

Lizzie stole into the kitchen and lit only one oil lamp instead of turning on a brighter propane light. She filled the pot with water and measured out the *kaffi*. Tempted though she was to dump in an extra scoop or two, she didn't. The rest of the family probably did not want the additional caffeine jolt she needed this morning. Lizzie yanked a shawl off the hook and eased open the back door. Maybe the crisp air would clear the cobwebs from her mind. And maybe, just maybe, the cool breeze that smacked her in the face would blow a plausible idea into her tired brain.

Tiny, squeaky meows met Lizzie as soon as she pulled the shed door open far enough to ease inside. "How are my *bopplin* this morning? Did you do all right through the night?" The three kittens tumbled over one another to be petted first. She sniffed twice but couldn't detect any nasty odors, so they must have found their way outside to take care of their business. *Gut.* One less thing for Mamm to complain about.

Lizzie picked up and nuzzled each kitten before pouring a small amount of Ruff's dog food in the bowl. "I'll give you kitty food later. I promise." She couldn't give them the appropriate food right now in case someone walked into the shed and saw it. How would she explain the sudden appearance of kitten chow? She couldn't very well say it had dropped out of the sky.

A scuffling noise near the door drew her attention. Melvin or Caleb must have gotten curious about the kittens. But how had they finished their chores so quickly? Daed would have their hides if he caught them shirking.

"Any problem here, Dochder?"

Lizzie almost tossed the bowl of food into the air. "*Ach*, Daed! You scared me." She set the bowl near the kittens' bed. "*Nee* problems that I can tell. The kittens seem fine."

Emanuel pushed his way into the shed. His body blocked the breeze and gave Lizzie a respite from the chill. He peered over her shoulder at the kittens. "They need cat food."

"I know. I'll have some for them today." As soon as she could safely sneak it out of its hiding place.

"*Hmpf!* More critters!"

"You know you like them, Daed. Didn't I see you out here checking on them last night?"

"Me?"

"It sure looked like you."

He grunted and turned toward the door but not before smiling at Lizzie. "I need to check on your *bruders*."

And Lizzie needed to get back inside to help with breakfast. So far not a single idea had presented itself to her. She would have to wing it with whatever thoughts popped into her head at the time. *I sure hope they're great ones!*

* * *

Mamm was standing at the kitchen counter cracking eggs into the big blue ceramic bowl by the time Lizzie had washed her hands and entered the room. "*Gut mariye*, Mamm." She infused as much cheerfulness as she could into those three words. Then maybe she wouldn't be chastised for being outside instead of in the kitchen. Mamm was forever telling her to get her head out of the clouds or to mind her own business or some other well-worn phrase whenever Lizzie fell short of Mamm's expectations. And that seemed to occur more often than Lizzie liked. She didn't intentionally do things to raise Mamm's ire, but her head always seemed to be filled with weaving patterns and projects or some animal in need of care.

"Where were you?"

For some reason, it didn't matter that Frannie hadn't yet put in an appearance. It was always *her* whereabouts that were questioned. Perhaps that was because Mamm didn't have to look much farther than her own arm to find Frannie. The girl acted like she was on a short leash and couldn't make it past the clothesline.

"I, uh, I . . ." What would go over better? She paused to consider. "I spoke to Daed for a minute while I was checking on the kittens."

"*Hmpf!*"

"They're really cute. Where is Frannie?"

"I sent her back upstairs to drag Sadie and Nancy out of bed."

The wind evaporated from Lizzie's sails. So Frannie had already made her way to the kitchen. Lizzie couldn't spot any evidence that her *schweschder* had actually performed any breakfast duties, though. "Would you like me to put water on for oatmeal?"

"Frannie already did that."

Of course. Now Lizzie spied the pot on the back of the wood-burning cookstove Mamm preferred over the gas stove. "Would you like me to make pancakes?"

"How about French toast? I've got to use up that loaf of bread."

"Sure. Are lunches already made?" Only Nancy and Sadie attended school. Since the Amish school stopped at age fourteen, Lizzie, Frannie, Melvin, and Caleb had already finished.

"I threw those together before I started on the eggs."

"Oh." Lizzie stood on tiptoe to slide another mixing bowl toward the edge of the shelf. She wasn't as tall as Frannie or Mamm, and she wished they wouldn't push dishes so far back in the cabinet. When she put them away, she kept them near the front so she could reach them easier. This particular mixing bowl must have a mind of its own today. Every time Lizzie thought she could grasp it, it slid away. Now she was going to have to drag a chair over and climb up after the thing.

"Here."

Hands reached over her head and easily lowered the bowl to the counter. "*Danki.*" Now Frannie would be expecting to hear the plan Lizzie had devised. The nonexistent plan. Lizzie couldn't meet her *schweschder*'s eyes. She deliberately kept her back to Frannie as she mixed the egg and milk coating for the French toast. She dipped bread slices into the bowl and dropped them into the cast-iron skillet heating on the stove. Each slice hissed as it hit the pan. She'd have to pay attention so they didn't turn out as black as coal. If that happened, everyone would be disappointed in her. As of right now, Mamm was the only one disappointed in her. But that would definitely change if Lizzie didn't devise a plan soon. Frannie's disappointment would lead to anger and to a serious tongue-lashing.

Think! Think! Think! Lizzie flipped over the three sizzling bread slices. Golden brown. *Gut.* She slid an empty plate closer to the stove so she could transfer the pieces of toast when they were done. She could feel Frannie's eyes shooting darts into her back. She almost winced.

Everything would be so simple if Lizzie could simply say, *Mamm, Frannie doesn't want to go to Ohio. She will be miserable, and I can pretty much guarantee the rest of us will be miserable, too, until her departure. Especially me. I have to share a room with her so will surely receive the brunt of her surliness. Please, Mamm, spare me. Spare us all.*

But of course she could never utter those words. There had to be some need here for Frannie to fulfill. Lizzie couldn't believe Mamm had instigated this mission of mercy. Frannie was her right arm. If Frannie left, Lizzie would have to take up the slack and perform extra duties. Long stretches of weaving time would fly right out the window. Oooh, that was a pretty selfish thought. She needed to do better.

Lizzie gasped when a pointed elbow dug into her ribs. She jumped and turned slightly to find Frannie standing practically on top of her. She'd been so lost in thought she hadn't noticed Frannie's approach.

"Well?" Frannie mouthed the single word.

Lizzie nodded, indicating she understood the silent request. She eased the spatula under the edge of another bread slice and raised it enough to peek underneath.

"Here." Frannie held the plate out.

"Let me make sure it's ready." Lizzie flipped the bread over and repeated her peek-and-flip process with the remaining slices of bread.

"Say something before the others get here." If a whisper could be a growl, then that one surely was.

Lizzie nodded again. What could she say? What made Frannie think Mamm would listen to her, anyway? She transferred all three slices of French toast to the plate and dipped more bread into the egg mixture. Frannie stirred oats into the simmering pot of water. She'd invaded Lizzie's space and stayed there, making Lizzie nervous.

"I need to scramble these eggs, girls, so you'll have to make some room for me."

"I can do it, Mamm." Lizzie reached for the bowl of eggs.

"You're doing the French toast."

"I can do two things."

Mamm's raised eyebrows told Lizzie her *mudder* had qualms about that. Honestly, Lizzie wasn't that terrible a cook. None of her family had ever gotten sick from eating anything she had prepared. She simply never got much chance to hone her skills, since Frannie had attached herself to Mamm's apron. Of course, weaving claimed a lot of her time, too.

"I'll do it." Frannie grabbed the bowl of eggs before Lizzie could move a muscle.

Lizzie didn't miss Mamm's relieved expression. She really could have cooked two things at once if she'd been given the chance, she was sure of it—but now she didn't have the opportunity to prove that.

Frannie plunked a second skillet onto the stove. She scooped a dollop of bacon grease from the little canister Mamm kept on the shelf over the stove and banged the spoon on the edge of the skillet to pry the glob loose. Lizzie struggled not to gag. For some reason, the sight of that congealed grease and the sound of it plunking onto the pan made her stomach a bit queasy. Frannie nudged her a little harder this time.

Lizzie grunted and resisted both the urge to rub her arm and the stronger urge to elbow Frannie in return. "Uh, Mamm?"

"What?"

"I was thinking. Uh, you know with the quilt auction *kumming* up, uh, maybe Frannie could bake things to auction off or sell. She's such a *gut* baker." Lizzie hazarded a glance at her big *schweschder*. Frannie's brow puckered, and her lips formed the silent word "What?"

"That's a possibility, I suppose, but November is weeks off yet." Mamm never stopped pulling plates and mugs out of the cabinet to even glance at the girls at the stove.

Lizzie took some small measure of comfort from the fact that Mamm hadn't seen Frannie's scowl or her own burning face. Frannie's glare more than made up for Mamm's inattention. *If looks could maim, I'd be limping right about now.* Since she had started the ball rolling, she had to continue. "I was also thinking maybe Frannie could bake things to sell at Yoder's Store. They never seem to have enough fresh-baked items. You know, lots of *Englischers* stop there, too, and they always like our homemade treats."

This time Mamm paused in her busyness and stared straight at Lizzie. "Why the sudden interest in finding things for your *schweschder* to do?"

"Well, uh, she seems to have a real talent for baking, and it seems a shame not to share that with others. She wouldn't want to hide it under a bushel." Hadn't she heard that expression somewhere recently? She was on too much of a roll to consider that now. "She could also make treats for some of our older folks who don't bake much anymore. The Lord Gott wants us to use our gifts to help others, ain't so?"

Frannie shot her a murderous look. Lizzie could almost read the girl's thoughts, and it didn't make for pleasant reading. Without a doubt, Frannie would lay into her as soon as they were alone. What would she say? Probably something like, *How could you suggest sending me out among strangers when that's the very thing I'm trying to avoid?* And the words would be flung at her at a high volume.

Lizzie sighed and slid the skillet off the heat. She carried the plate piled high with French toast slices to the table to get out of elbow range. Two bruises already this morning were two too many.

Frannie mumbled something incoherent under her breath and scrambled the eggs with such force that Lizzie feared there would be nothing at all left to chew. They would be sipping eggs through a straw or using them for syrup. Lizzie hadn't intended to upset her *schweschder*, but she hadn't had much time to devise a better plan. This was the best she could *kumm* up with on such short notice. If Frannie didn't like it, she should have thought of her own excuses.

Mamm plucked a handful of paper napkins from the plastic package and handed them to Lizzie. "You've made some *gut* points. Frannie's baking is right tasty. I know that Sophie Hostetler isn't seeing so well or getting around so well these days. She'd surely like some treats. But that will have to wait awhile. Frannie is supposed to stay with Aenti Grace in Ohio for a few weeks."

"Really?" Lizzie acted surprised but took care not to overexaggerate her reaction. "That's a shame, Mamm, since there is a need here. Aren't there some relatives out there who could help out?"

"I don't know. When Grace mentioned her upcoming surgery in one of her letters, I asked if she'd like Frannie to help her."

Lizzie stole a glance in her *schweschder*'s direction. The girl stood as stiff as if she had been lashed to a board. Her hands had curled into fists at her sides. Lizzie couldn't tell if Frannie's expression showed fear, disgust, or anger, but the grimace was far from pleasant. "Oh." She couldn't think of anything else to say. Frannie jerked her head toward Mamm and mouthed, "Go on!" Go on with what? If she kept badgering, she would be bound to raise Mamm's ire.

Ach! That was it! What a *dummchen* she was! If Lizzie kept pestering, Mamm would get mad at her but not at Frannie. What a clever girl her *schweschder* was! Maybe "devious" would be a better word. When Frannie gave her the evil eye again, Lizzie ignored it. Since she had started this whole business, let Frannie figure out how to finish it. Lizzie marched to the refrigerator to find the butter and a bottle of maple syrup. She heard Frannie's sigh but ignored that, too.

"Do you think you could write Aenti Grace?" Frannie's voice sounded hesitant, like it took all her courage to ask Mamm a simple question.

Lizzie peeked over the refrigerator door. She had to see how this scenario played out. She certainly didn't miss the scowl Frannie threw her way before turning an innocent, wide-eyed look on Mamm.

"Well, I don't know if there would be enough time, and I hate to go back on my word. Besides, the change might do you *gut*."

Lizzie's sentiments exactly.

"I don't need a change." Frannie mumbled the words, but if Lizzie heard them, Mamm probably did, too.

"You've never been to Ohio. You might enjoy seeing another area of the country." Mamm fiddled with the napkin package until little slivers of paper floated to the floor.

"I-I don't have a desire to see another area. I-I'm happy here."

Guilt tugged at Lizzie. She felt sorry for Frannie. While she had enjoyed her visits with Mammi Lena and looked forward to them, she probably wouldn't be too keen on going to a strange place and staying with people she'd never met. She had to try again to get Frannie out of this dilemma. "Winter will be upon us soon. They get lots more snow in Ohio than we get. I'd hate for Frannie to get stranded there for the holidays." There. That was the last idea she had to throw out. Frannie's gasp meant she apparently hadn't considered that possibility.

Mamm dropped the napkin package on the counter and tapped her chin with an index finger. "Hmmm! I hadn't thought of that. I'll write Grace tonight."

The *schweschders* exchanged a secret smile.

Chapter Eleven

"You're in a happy mood." Stephen swiped his still-damp hands down his pants legs after morning chores the following week.

"Wasn't there a towel in the bathroom?" Mary stopped singing and turned from stirring oatmeal to look up at her tall second-born son. She held the spoon aloft, but the oatmeal was too thick to drip off. "And for your information, I am always—or nearly always—happy."

"I know, Mamm. I'm teasing." He crossed the kitchen in three long strides and gave his *mudder* a brief hug. Some families, he knew, rarely showed affection. His family was different. They talked and laughed at mealtimes, after their silent prayer. They hugged or showed their love in other ways. They teased but never poked fun at one another. "And *jah*, there was a towel in the bathroom. My hands were still a little damp, that's all."

"Uh-huh." Mary turned back to the pan on the stove.

"I thought I smelled bacon."

"You did. I set it in the oven to keep warm. I haven't scrambled the eggs yet. You're earlier than usual. Where are Daed and your *bruders*?"

"They'll be along shortly. I finished up outside early.

Those pups are growing like weeds. They're such silly little things." Stephen smiled at the thought of the roly-poly puppies tumbling over one another. "I've got a furniture order to get out today. I need to get it out of the way so I can work on the holiday orders."

"The holidays will be here before we know it."

"That's for sure."

"Are you going to have a hard time letting this litter go?"

"It's always hard, but I am sure they will be well loved by their new families when the time *kumms*."

"You're such an animal lover. You've done a fine job with the pups. Do you need to go ahead and eat so you can get your order out?"

"I guess I can wait. I can gather up things I need to take out to the shop. You can finish singing your song."

Mary banged the spoon on the side of the pan and laid it in the ceramic spoon rest. She covered the pan and slid it away from the heat. "I might just do that. And you are right. I'm extra happy today."

"Any special reason why?"

"I'm going to start learning how to use my loom today."

"That's great. Did you find someone to help you?"

"I most certainly did. Lizzie Fisher."

Stephen paused in midstep. "You found her?"

"I did indeed."

"Was she in a different district?"

"*Nee*. The same one you visited."

"Okay. I guess there were two of them after all."

"I don't know about that, but the Lizzie who does weaving is visiting this afternoon."

"How did you find the right person?"

"I thought about what you said that maybe I got the name wrong, so I went back to the quilt shop and asked Norma again. She's the one who gave me the name to begin with. I thought I'd clarify it with her."

"And you had the name right but I found the wrong Lizzie, right?"

"I don't know about the person you found, but Norma had a customer who knew exactly where to find the person I wanted."

"Did you go there by yourself?" Stephen didn't recall a hired driver picking his *mudder* up any day the past week, but he could have been too busy to notice.

"I didn't have to. Norma's customer was going over to the Amish community in Maryville and offered to deliver a note. I asked Lizzie to call me out at the phone shack. She did, and we made arrangements for today."

"I'm glad you'll finally get started on your loom." Stephen shook his head as he left in search of more rags to use in his furniture shop. He wouldn't have been surprised if his *mamm* had danced a little jig right there in the kitchen. He didn't quite understand her fascination with that big loom, but she deserved a little time for herself to do what she wanted to do. She'd lived in a house full of rowdy fellows all these years. If she could put up with him and his *bruders*, she deserved a medal, as far as he was concerned. He might have to invent an excuse to peek into Mamm's sewing room this afternoon, though, so he could catch a glimpse of this Lizzie Fisher she had rounded up.

"Why do I have to go with you to Yoder's Store? You've been there a million times at least." Lizzie crossed her arms across her chest and stared into Frannie's brown eyes. It had taken her a whole week to convince her *schweschder* to take on this venture, and now she was going to have to accompany Frannie to the store and be her mouthpiece, to boot? Ugh!

"It was your idea to have me sell baked items at the store, so you can *kumm* with me to ask Martha Yoder about it." Frannie's lower lip protruded in a pretty little pout.

"That pout might work with Mamm and Daed, but it won't work with me. I've got lots of weaving to do, and I'm already going to lose the afternoon."

"It won't take long to go to Yoder's."

"It certainly will. You know how Martha loves to talk. Ordinarily I wouldn't mind chatting with her, but—"

"You thrive on getting all the latest news, and Martha is bound to have it."

"Not today."

"I'm going to ask Mamm to *tell* you to accompany me."

"And she'll probably say for you to act like a big girl and do your own bidding. By the way, I am not a gossip. I simply like to keep informed."

"Right. Please *kumm* with me, Lizzie."

"Oooh! Hurry up, then!" Lizzie flounced from their shared room and galloped down the steps, muttering under her breath the whole way. Why did she always give in to Frannie? Evidently the pout did work on her, too.

Just as Lizzie had suspected, Martha Yoder talked a blue streak. That was all fine and *gut* for the first fifteen or twenty minutes, but when Martha started retelling things for the third time and still Frannie didn't break in to say exactly why they were there, Lizzie had to take matters into her own hands.

She suggested the store needed more freshly baked items on the shelves and explained how Frannie wanted to help. She listed some of her *schweschder*'s specialties and described their delectable flavors. She closed the deal and set up all the arrangements. Lizzie almost asked Frannie why she had bothered to tag along at all. The girl had only smiled or nodded or mumbled by way of communication. Honestly, maybe Lizzie shouldn't have intervened on Frannie's behalf. It might very well have been to Frannie's advantage to go to Ohio. Maybe she would have learned to speak up for herself.

By the time the girls arrived home, their *mudder* was deep into noon meal preparations. Frannie and Lizzie hustled to wash up and help.

"How did it go?" Anna looked at Frannie with raised eyebrows.

You really should ask me, since Frannie stood like a statue the whole time. Would Frannie find her tongue and answer Mamm, or would Lizzie have to do that, too?

"It went fine." Frannie began slicing fresh-baked whole wheat bread. "Martha said she could use cookies, brownies, and the like. She'll pay me for them."

Wonder of wonders! The girl could speak! And apparently she had listened to the transaction at the store, even if her comments had been few and far between.

"That's great, dear. When does Martha want you to start taking things to the store?"

"Uh . . ." Frannie looked to Lizzie.

Okay. So maybe Frannie hadn't zoned in on the entire conversation with Martha Yoder. "Tomorrow, if possible." Lizzie supplied the missing information.

"*Ach!* You'd better get busy baking as soon as we eat. Lizzie can clean up the kitchen while you get started."

"Mamm, did you forget a driver is due to pick me up in about thirty minutes? We were later getting back than I planned on." She scowled at her *schweschder.*

"I can clean up from the meal before I start baking, Mamm. Lizzie was kind enough to go with me. I don't want her to be late for her appointment."

Lizzie's jaw dropped. Frannie offering to do her chores? Surely the world was going to turn upside down. "I appreciate that, Frannie."

"We'd best hurry and get food on the table, then." Anna bustled about spooning vegetables into bowls and slicing ham left over from yesterday. "Daed and the *buwe* will be in any moment. They worked on the hay this morning. It will probably be the final cutting, since frost will likely coat the ground soon."

Lizzie hoped she could eat fast so she had time to check on the kittens before she left. She would be gone for several hours and wanted her charges to be safe. She would leave them a little extra food—real kitten food—just in case she was later getting back than planned. Thank goodness she'd been able to run an errand for Mamm the day after the kittens had arrived so she could pretend she had purchased kitten food. They took to it much better than they had to Ruff's food.

A big blue van rumbled up the gravel driveway while Lizzie gave the kittens a final pat. She slipped out of the shed after promising to play with them later. She snatched up her bag of samples and supplies from her workshop and scurried to the van.

"Hey, Lizzie. How are you doing?"

"Hi, Patti." The Fishers' *Englisch* neighbor Patti

Stanley often drove the Amish to destinations that would take too long to reach by horse and buggy.

"I'm cold today, so I've got the heater blasting. Let me know if it's too warm for you."

"I'm fine." Even if Lizzie was sweating buckets, she probably wouldn't tell Patti. She knew the woman had experienced some health issue and was still quite thin. The poor lady was probably cold most of the time, but she was always cheerful and pleasant. Lizzie didn't think she'd ever seen Patti with her curly blonde hair hanging down. She always wore it gathered into a big brown clip at the back of her neck, and today was no different. Lizzie guessed the woman was in her early forties and always thought Patti was very pretty despite her thinness.

The twelve-mile trip from Lizzie's house in Maryville to Parsonville passed quickly. Patti kept a lively conversation going. Lizzie was happy to listen and offer a brief comment whenever necessary. A person could learn so much simply by listening to other people, and Lizzie always loved learning new things. She hoped she'd be able to pass on some of her weaving knowledge as easily as she had learned it herself. She was still a little surprised Mamm hadn't kicked up a fuss about her going to the Mennonite community. At least the woman who had sought her out, this Mary Zimmerman, was Old Order Mennonite if she was indeed a member of the same community as Norma, the message bearer. Their beliefs weren't drastically different from those of the Amish.

"This is the address you gave me. The sign says Zimmerman's furniture. Would this be the right place?"

"Mary said her son builds furniture."

"Then this must be right. I have errands to run. Do you think a couple of hours will be enough time for you?"

"It should be fine."

"If you need longer, I can wait. I don't have to buy any perishable foods or anything, though I think it's too cool out for any food to spoil anyway."

Lizzie wasn't sure it was that cold outside, but she smiled and nodded. "Okay, Patti. Take your time. When I get started doing anything with the loom, I kind of get lost in it and ignore the time altogether."

Patti laughed. "I can do the same thing with a good book."

Lizzie slid open the van door and hopped to the ground, pulling her bag out behind her. For some unfathomable reason, butterflies took flight in her stomach. She dragged in a few deep breaths to calm her nerves. Mary Zimmerman was probably a perfectly pleasant woman. Lizzie didn't have any reason to be jittery. She definitely did not need to become all backward like her older *schweschder*. She shored up her confidence and marched up the cement walkway leading to the front porch of the large pale green two-story farmhouse. She pasted a smile on her face. There. That was more like it. It would be fun sharing her knowledge of the loom with someone so eager to learn. Everything would be just fine.

Chapter Twelve

Something blue caught Stephen's eye as he looked up from the oak hope chest he'd been sanding. He cocked his head to better see out the front window of his workshop. He was right. Something blue had passed by. A long blue van pulled up to the house. He assumed his *mudder*'s guest had arrived. If he could see the woman get out of the van, he might be able to determine if it was indeed a different Lizzie Fisher without having to actually enter the house. He had not yet dreamed up an excuse for barging into Mamm's sewing room anyway.

Stephen didn't know why, since he was completely alone in the building, but he tiptoed closer to the window. "*Ach!*" He slapped his forehead. How stupid could he be? The woman wore a black cape with a royal blue dress peeking out at the bottom. The black bonnet not only covered her hair but shielded her face from view as well. Black stockings and black athletic shoes completed her ensemble. Exactly like every other Amish woman! What was he thinking? There wasn't any way he could discern the woman's identity from his lookout spot at the window.

If the weather had been warmer and outerwear

hadn't been necessary, Stephen might have been able to see if the woman's hair—what wasn't covered by her *kapp*—was the color of the caramel they dipped apples in every fall. He might have been able to see the heart-shaped face with the smattering of freckles the same color as her hair. He might connect with those unusual but lovely violet eyes.

He smacked his head again, only harder this time. He'd only see those features if he got closer to the woman or if he looked through binoculars. He shook his head to get images of the Lizzie Fisher he'd met out of his brain. He hoped that, once he figured out an excuse to enter the house, he would find a wrinkled, gray-haired woman wearing big, ugly glasses working with his *mamm*. But the spritely, almost perky, gait of the woman bouncing up the front steps didn't seem to fit that description.

Get back to work! Stephen clomped back to his project and sanded the chest with renewed vigor. He needed to work off the tension that had mounted in his shoulders and neck. He'd finish the task at hand and stride right into the house. He'd get a glass of water or something. He lived there. It was his home. He could enter whenever he pleased. Why did he need an excuse?

Because Mamm will know you came in to check out her guest, a little voice deep inside his mind dared to point out. Stephen rarely went back inside the house until after the evening chores were done and smells of supper wafted out to beckon him in. Maybe some plausible excuse, uh, reason would *kumm* to him by the time he finished the sanding.

Besides, Mamm probably had enough questions to keep the woman here for a week. She'd be so grateful to have another woman around the house that she'd want to stretch this visit out as long as possible. There wouldn't be any need to hurry his foray into women's territory. He hummed a song from the Ausbund as he worked in a vain attempt to drown out those nagging images and voices.

"*Ach!* I'm afraid I'm all thumbs." Mary lifted her hands and wiggled her fingers. She stared at them as if checking to make sure she had a variety of digits.

Lizzie laughed. "Not at all, Mary. You're doing quite well."

"You're young. Young people learn things faster."

Lizzie laughed again. "I hardly think you're ancient. I had intense instruction. I stayed with my *mammi* Lena several times—for several weeks each time. I watched Mammi and asked her about a million questions. She patiently answered every one about three times each. I probably badgered the poor, dear woman to death."

"I doubt that."

"Mammi Lena never got flustered or weary of my pestering. My *mudder* taught me to knit and crochet when I was very young, but the loom was special. I was in awe of it. I wanted to learn so badly that I soaked up every morsel of information Mammi could offer me. I was so honored that she left it to me when she passed."

"You must have been an exceptional scholar. I've been in awe of the loom, too. I always wanted to learn. When my *aenti* sent this one to me because her arthritis got too bad to perform the work, I became determined to learn." Mary flexed her fingers. "Should we try again, or have I completely plucked your last nerve?"

"You've done nothing of the kind. Remember, this is your first real try at working the loom. You're catching on quickly."

"Hmmm. If you say so. I guess I don't have a lot of patience with myself."

"Just take a deep breath and let it out slowly."

Mary obeyed.

"Do it again."

Mary repeated the action.

"There. Did that help you calm down a teensy bit? Mammi Lena had me do that whenever I got so frustrated I wanted to yank out all the stitches."

"That did help, dear. I can't imagine you getting frustrated. You've been a most patient teacher. I daresay needlework must be an innate skill for you. Were you born with knitting needles in your tiny hands?"

Lizzie laughed so hard that tears gathered in her eyes. She swiped the moisture away and poked a loose strand of hair back where it belonged. "Hardly, but Mamm had me knitting by the time I was six. I think I hung over her shoulder so much she figured she might as well teach me to knit on my own so I'd quit breathing down her neck. My *schweschder* wasn't anxious to learn, so I guess we all have our own special likes."

"And talents. I didn't have any *dochders* to share these moments with. I've enjoyed having you here today, Lizzie."

"It has been fun. Are you ready to start again?"

"Sure."

Lizzie glanced up toward the window at the sound of barking. There must be several dogs out there, and they sounded young.

"Don't worry. The dogs are penned up. Most are

puppies. I don't think they'd hurt a soul. They might lick you to death, though."

"I'm not afraid of dogs. I love animals. In fact, I just rescued three kittens that Mamm has agreed to let me keep—for now, at least."

"I take it your *mudder* isn't fond of animals."

"I think she can take them or leave them. What she isn't too fond of is me bringing home strays."

Mary laughed. "Do you do that often?"

"Whenever I find them. I just can't leave a helpless animal to fend for itself. It might get hurt or worse. But Mamm usually makes me find a home for them. She always tells me I'd have a whole zoo if she would go along with it."

Mary laughed again. She reached over to squeeze Lizzie's arm. "You have a soft heart. You're just like my son."

"Does your little *bu* like all kinds of animals, too?"

"I'm afraid I don't have any more little *buwe*. My youngest is thirteen. It's my second oldest who is the animal lover. He used to sneak home strays, too."

"Did you let him keep them?"

"Usually. I guess I have a soft spot for animals, too."

"Did he outgrow the habit?" Lizzie didn't think she'd ever outgrow her need to protect and shelter the helpless animals she came across. Mamm probably wished she would. She probably wished Lizzie was more like Frannie, a homebody content to stay in the house and do chores all day. But Lizzie was totally different. She did her share of chores, but she simply had to get outside—and, of course, she had to work on her loom. She pulled her mind from its meandering to focus on Mary.

"I don't think he outgrew the practice. I think he

got too busy with working and chores. But the puppies you hear are his. He raises them for a service dog organization."

"*Ach*, how *wunderbaar*! He gets to enjoy the animals and know they will be helping someone else later. He must be a very special person." Lizzie leaned over to correct a small mistake on the loom.

"I think he is. Oops! I guess I need to concentrate more."

"*Nee*. You're doing fine."

"I wonder if I'll remember everything later on."

"You probably will, but I can write some things down for you if you have paper and pencil."

Mary looked up from the loom and glanced around the room. "I don't seem to have either in this room. If you don't mind, you can go in the kitchen and look in the little drawer of the end cabinet. There should be a pad of paper and pencils in there, unless Daniel, my youngest, carted them off somewhere."

"I'll go check."

The woman had been in with Mamm for a couple of hours, for sure. If he planned to get a glimpse of her, he'd better slip into the house now. It's too bad a plausible excuse for going inside hadn't presented itself to him. He'd sanded furiously and gotten the chest ready for staining. He could always say he needed a drink of water. Stephen glanced at the half-full thermos of water he'd set on the windowsill. He'd have to dump that out to make his story true.

He pushed himself up from his stooped position and twisted to ease the strain in his lower back. Why hadn't he hoisted the chest to a worktable before he had started? He probably could have lifted it by himself. His brain didn't seem to be functioning properly lately. A little break might be a *gut* thing.

Stephen snatched the thermos from its perch and marched out the door. He should be able to walk into his own home whenever he wanted. He cast a quick glance in each direction before emptying the thermos onto the ground near his shed. Fresh water. That's what he needed. He would sneak into the kitchen to get it. The woman's voice might be all he needed to make an identification. Then he wouldn't have to face her at all.

Chapter Thirteen

Lizzie easily found the correct drawer in Mary's orderly kitchen. The pad of paper and pencils were exactly where Mary said they would be. Lizzie smiled. In her house, a pencil or pen was sometimes hard to locate, with her two little *schweschders* moving things hither and yon. She didn't hear footsteps, but she felt a presence. Mary must have decided to make sure she found what she needed.

"I found them, Mary." Lizzie turned around. A gasp chased the smile from her lips. Her heart thundered. She grabbed the edge of the counter to help her maintain her balance.

"What are you doing here?"

Lizzie wasn't sure if she spoke the words or heard them spoken. Were her eyes playing tricks on her, or was this tall, dark-haired man with the shocked expression the same man who had helped her rescue the kittens from the blazing farmhouse? Lizzie blinked to clear her vision. The robin's egg blue eyes she remembered so well stared at her now.

"Lizzie?"

"Stephen?"

"You're the Lizzie Fisher who has the loom like my *mudder*'s?"

"You're the son of the woman who asked for my help?" Lizzie wondered if her own face showed the same bewilderment that she saw displayed on Stephen's.

"You never said you were the weaver."

"You never asked. Why would I mention that, considering the events of the day?"

The man before her shrugged his broad shoulders.

"You never told me your last name was Zimmerman. You were so secretive."

"I didn't think my name was important in the grand scheme of things. As you said, we were rather preoccupied."

"I did *kumm* right out and ask your name several times, if I remember correctly."

Stephen remained silent. His blue eyes continued to stare at her. She fought not to squirm under the intense scrutiny. She would not let this man know he unnerved her. "What are you staring at?" The question flew from Lizzie's mouth practically before she'd finished thinking it. Had she suddenly sprouted a second head? Was her *kapp* askew? He made her feel as if she needed to search for a paper bag to pull over her head. Then, of all things, he had the audacity to chuckle at her discomfiture.

"Sorry. You look different without the smudges of soot on your cheeks and with a white *kapp* instead of a gray one."

Lizzie lifted her chin. "You look a little different yourself." Even better, if that was possible. She was certainly glad that thought hadn't found its way to her tongue.

"Don't go getting offended. I didn't mean anything bad. I thought you looked cute with the dirt. But you look even prettier now."

Lizzie barely heard the last whispered comment, but she assumed she had correctly deciphered his words since his face changed from pink to spiced crabapple red in a matter of seconds.

"*Ach*, I see you two have met." Mary appeared in the kitchen doorway. A smile played across her lips. How much of the conversation had she heard? Now Lizzie's cheeks probably matched Stephen's. Mary grasped her son's upper arm. "Is this your Lizzie?"

"M-my Lizzie?"

Lizzie hadn't thought it would be possible for Stephen's face to glow any redder, but somehow it did. Her own face threatened to burst into flame.

Mary squeezed the arm she still held. "You know, is this the girl you met before and discounted as being the person I sought?"

"Uh, *jah*. I, uh, met Lizzie before."

"See? She isn't too young to be an expert weaver. If you had asked her about the loom before, you would have saved me the trouble of hunting her down, but never mind. She's here now, and she's been ever so much help."

The sheepish expression crossing Stephen's face made it clear he wished the floor would split open and swallow him. Lizzie pitied him. Even though his opinion of her wasn't entirely favorable and he obviously considered her an inept, bumbling little girl, she felt compelled to ease his awkwardness. "I probably didn't give him much of an opportunity to ask, Mary." Lizzie forced a little laugh. "That was the day I rescued the kittens, so a lot was going on."

Mary looked from Lizzie to Stephen. "That was the day you returned home smelling like a campfire."

"*Jah.*"

"Again, I take the blame. Rescuing the kittens was entirely my idea."

"I'm sure you didn't have to twist Stephen's arm. He loves animals. He's the son I told you about who raises the puppies."

"Really? Maybe I could see the puppies before I leave?" Now, why did she ask that? Why would she want to spend any more time in the presence of a man who didn't even consider her capable of operating a loom? A man who couldn't even tell her his full name, like he had some big secret. It was the puppies. Her love of animals—and her curiosity—would win over logic every time. Lizzie wanted to see the puppies, not spend more time with Stephen Zimmerman. At last she had a last name for the man. End of puzzle. End of thoughts of the man with the gorgeous blue eyes. Right!

"I-I only came in to refill my thermos." Stephen held it up and jiggled it to prove his point.

A sly smile tugged at the corners of Mary's mouth. "Did the outside spigot stop working?"

"I wanted some ice." Stephen freed himself from his *mudder*'s hold and slunk off to the gas-powered refrigerator.

"I found the paper and pencils." Lizzie held the items up like trophies. "I can write down some points you need to remember." She had to force her attention back on the loom.

"Excellent. I'm sure I'll need something to jog my memory."

"How did you do while I was gone?" Lizzie deliberately kept her eyes on Mary and refused to let them stray the slightest bit in Stephen's direction.

"Okay, I think. I'll let you be the judge of that."

"I'm sure you did fine. You are an apt scholar."

"That would only be because I have such a *gut* teacher."

Lizzie got the distinct impression Mary's comment had been uttered mainly for Stephen's benefit. She clutched the paper and pencil and trailed out of the kitchen on Mary's heels. When Mary stopped abruptly, Lizzie almost mowed her down.

Mary turned to call over her shoulder. "I'm sending our guest out to you when we're finished so you can show her the puppies and tell her all about the organization."

Lizzie wanted to fade into the woodwork. She zoomed back to Mary's sewing room before she could hear any grunts or groans from Stephen.

Now who seemed a total bumbling, fumbling scatterbrain? Stephen bent to chase down the ice that had skittered across the floor. He couldn't even coax ice into the thermos without making a mess. Never mind that he couldn't string a succession of coherent words together to complete a sentence. And here he'd thought Lizzie Fisher was a naive scatterbrain. After a brief fluster, she'd recovered nicely and come across as quite mature and in control. Stephen ground his teeth together and filled his thermos with water. The sooner he reached the safety of his workshop, the better.

Why had he bothered to leave his comfort zone? He could have drunk the lukewarm water in the thermos and begun staining the chest. But *nee*. He had to let curiosity get the best of him. He was as bad as Lizzie! Maybe worse. And what was behind Mamm's smirk? Why did she make a point of telling him she would send Lizzie out to see him? The less he had to do with Lizzie Fisher, the less chance he would grow to like her more, and the happier he would be.

Stephen stomped from the house and marched straight to his shop. He resisted the urge to slam the door. There wasn't any use breaking something he would have to take the time to fix. He could always hope Mamm kept Lizzie busy until her ride returned so there wouldn't be an opportunity for him to expound the virtues of his special pups and the role they would later perform.

He pulled the door back open a crack so he could hear when the bothersome girl left. He twisted his mouth to blow out a sideways breath that ruffled the hair hanging across his forehead. His aggravation must have provided extra strength, since he was able to lift the chest to the workbench with minimal groaning and straining. Work. That would calm him. He reached for the cherry stain and soon became totally absorbed in his project.

"H-hello?"

The soft voice at the door startled Stephen enough to make him drop his cloth. He barely managed to capture the can of stain before it toppled from the shelf. So much for being able to hear when she left the premises.

"I'm sorry." Lizzie pushed the door open a speck more.

Now he could see her entire heart-shaped face and the smattering of freckles across her nose. Big violet eyes stared at him. "It's okay." Stephen tried not to growl, but he did not need the distraction of a girl—even an uncommonly pretty one. He'd traveled that road before and didn't plan to do so again at this point.

"Your *mamm* sent me out here. If you don't have time to show me the puppies, that's okay. I'm only following instructions."

If he knew what was *gut* for him, he'd better follow them, too. Mamm had probably stationed herself at the window to make sure he did her bidding. "It's okay." Didn't he just say that? This girl got him all turned around. "Let me finish this last little spot, and then I'll show you."

Lizzie nodded. "It looks very nice. The chest, I mean." Stephen nodded in return but kept silent.

What was he brooding about? Had he been that perturbed that she had discovered who he was, like his identity was some big hush-hush mystery? Was he upset that he had been wrong about her, that she wasn't the unintelligent person he had imagined her to be? He had been a bit sarcastic when they first met, but in a humorous way. Now she felt like she should tiptoe back out and leave Stephen Zimmerman alone.

As she turned to do that very thing, a scrap of paper fluttering on a sudden whoosh of air caught her attention. Something about it seemed familiar. She side-stepped to get a closer look. Stephen must have been following her gaze, because he reached for the paper to intercept Lizzie's scrutiny. She got a good enough look to recognize her cat sketch, though. "You kept it!"

Stephen shrugged. "I told you I thought it was *gut*." He avoided looking at Lizzie and slid the picture beneath some other papers on the counter, as if he was embarrassed to be caught with it in his possession.

Lizzie suppressed a smile and tamped down the little thrill she felt that Stephen had held on to her drawing. He had even moved it carefully so as to avoid bending the edges. Funny that this virtual stranger was the only person who knew about her drawings. Funnier still, he actually liked her pictures.

"Let's go."

"Huh?" Lizzie mentally shook herself out of her reverie.

"Don't you want to see the puppies?"

"Sure, but I thought you needed to finish your work."

"I can do it later."

"Okay." Apparently he wanted to appease his *mudder* and then get Lizzie out of his hair. She would be pleasant even if she had to swallow her tongue to hold back a retort. She trotted along behind Stephen, needing to take two steps for each of his long-legged strides. "How long have you been raising puppies?" At first Lizzie thought he hadn't heard her or had chosen to ignore her, but then he spoke. Maybe he'd had to ponder her question.

"Three years now."

"What kind of dogs are they?"

"Golden retrievers. They're easy to train. They're loyal, and they make excellent service dogs."

The yipping drew Lizzie's attention away from the tall, broad-shouldered man she was following. "Oh my! They're adorable!" Lizzie laughed at the golden balls of fluff wrestling and tumbling over one another. "Look at them!" She could hardly keep from racing into the fenced area where the dogs were playing, but she figured she'd better take her cue from Stephen.

She sneaked a peek at his face and was pleasantly surprised to find a wide smile in place of a scowl. His entire face glowed, and crinkly laugh lines appeared around his brilliant blue eyes as if by magic. Lizzie's joy increased. The puppies made her happy, but for some strange reason, the amusement on Stephen's face practically rendered her giddy. "May I go in there to pet them?"

"They're still excited pups yet. They'll jump all over you. I've been working with them, but they're young."

"I don't mind."

Stephen looked down at her and smiled. A real smile. Meant for her and not for the puppies. She could tell. Her heart did a ridiculous little dance. She almost missed his question.

"You really do like animals, don't you?"

"Of course I do. Otherwise I would not have—"

"Risked your life and that of your companion by barreling into a crumbling, flaming building to rescue three kittens."

"Well, that, too. But I was going to say I would not have risked Mamm's wrath by bringing the kittens home. Hey, you didn't have to go into that house with me. I didn't *ask* you to."

"That's true, but there had to be someone to drag you out if you got into trouble or overcome by smoke. Who knows what could have been lying around in that old house? The place could have exploded like fireworks over the river on the Fourth of July."

"It didn't, though. And we're safe."

"And the kittens have a home."

"They do. At least for now."

"Don't you believe your *mudder* will let them stay? Does she really dislike animals that much?"

"I don't believe she truly dislikes them, but they might mess up her ordered life. I don't mean anything bad by that. She likes things done a certain way and frowns on anything that messes up or alters her plan."

"She sounds pretty set in her ways."

"I guess she is about some things, like when chores are to be done and how long it should take to do them. I think it throws her off balance when something gets out of order. So if the kittens take up too much time or get in the way or get under her feet when she's outside or, worst of all, try to sneak into the house, her day will be ruined."

"And then the kittens will be sent on their way."

"Something like that. Your *mamm* doesn't seem to be that way at all."

Stephen laughed. "Hardly. She's raised four *buwe*, so she's had to be flexible."

"I'm sure you were all perfect angels."

Stephen laughed again. "I wouldn't exactly say that. And don't ask her. She could give you an earful of our antics." He unlocked the gate. "I'll slip in the pen first. Maybe they'll take out their hyperactivity on me and you'll be spared."

"They're puppies. They're going to be rambunctious. I don't mind at all."

"Okay, if you say so. But don't say I didn't warn you."

As soon as Stephen got both feet inside the fenced-in area, the puppies dashed over to him, yipping and wagging their tails. Lizzie skittered through the gate right on Stephen's heels. Immediately the puppies shifted their attention to the newcomer.

Lizzie crouched down and tried to pet each squirming

body. She lifted the smallest one and held it close to her. She bent down to rub her chin on its soft fur and was rewarded with a giant doggy kiss. The puppy's exuberance caused her to lose her balance, and she landed on her behind in a most unladylike fashion. She laughed until tears ran down her cheeks. The other puppies hurried to investigate, instantly adding to the melee. Lizzie squealed as each one slurped her cheek with a fat, pink tongue.

Stephen whistled, calling the puppies away to give her time to collect herself and to assume a more dignified position. "Sorry about that."

"It's okay. I expected their excitement. They are adorable. I'd love to draw them. I hope I can remember details when I get home . . . Only now I don't know where I can draw." The puppies waddled back to where Lizzie now sat in a more demure manner. She studied their soft fur.

"Were you using that old house as your studio?"

"Sort of. I'll have to either think of something else or give up my drawing."

"Don't do that."

Why should he care?

"I mean, unless you want to, but I think you have talent. I'd like to see any pictures you draw of the puppies."

"Really?" Hope blossomed in Lizzie's heart. Someone thought her drawings were worthwhile. Stephen actually said he wanted to see them. That meant he'd have to see her. Did he realize that? *Stop it, Lizzie. He's Mennonite. You're Amish. End of story.*

But he's Old Order Mennonite! That nagging little voice had to be silenced before it instigated a whole heap of trouble.

* * *

Why had he said he wanted to see her drawings? That would mean she'd have to return here. He couldn't very well knock on her door and tell her *mudder* he'd *kumm* to see Lizzie's pictures, could he? And who knew? Mamm might have already arranged for Lizzie to help with the loom some more. Mamm seemed bound and determined to master the thing, and like it or not, Lizzie was the proclaimed expert.

She looked at him now with those big violet eyes shimmering with excitement. She seemed truly thrilled that he had complimented her artwork. He hadn't been merely saying pretty words. Her drawings were *gut*. He wasn't any art expert, but he knew what he liked. His heart did a strange little flip-flop like a fish thrashing about on the deck of the little rowboat he liked to take out on the river. Knowing he'd made Lizzie happy caused warmth to flood through him.

Ach! He had to get out of this situation. He had to forget how cute Lizzie looked on the ground with the pups climbing all over her and licking her. Any other girl would have shrieked at him to call the dogs off. But not Lizzie. She enjoyed the puppies and didn't mind dirt and slobber.

"Stephen! Help Lizzie up off the ground and get those dogs off of her. She said she wanted to *see* the puppies, not be attacked by them." His *mamm*'s voice came from the back door. He whistled again for the puppies.

"It's all right, Mary. I don't mind them climbing on me at all."

Stephen figured he'd better do as his *mudder* asked

or he'd hear about it later. He reached out a hand to Lizzie. "Here, let me help you up."

When she placed her small hand in his and looked up at him with an unbelievably cute, shy smile, something like a lightning bolt shot through him. At least he thought that's what it felt like. Having never been struck by lightning, he couldn't be sure. What he could be sure of was the tingling that traveled up his arm and wrapped around his heart. This nonsense had to stop! He dropped her hand as soon as she'd gotten steady on her feet.

"*Danki.*"

"I-I'd better feed them now."

"Can I help?"

"I've got it. Your ride should be here soon." He knew he sounded rude, but he couldn't seem to help it. He turned away from her disappointed face.

"You didn't tell me about the rescue group."

"I, uh . . ."

"Maybe next time." Lizzie gave the puppies a final pat and wiggled through the gate.

Next time? Would Stephen be able to be more cordial then?

Chapter Fourteen

"I hope I didn't keep you waiting." Lizzie hopped into the back seat of the van parked near the Zimmermans' house after retrieving her supplies from where she'd dropped them by the puppy pen. She waved to Mary, who still stood in the doorway, before tugging the heavy van door closed.

"Not at all. I just got here, actually. My errands took a bit longer than I'd planned. That always seems to happen." Patti's blonde curly ponytail bobbed as she laughed.

"Well, it worked out perfectly for me." Lizzie situated herself and her bag and clicked her seat belt shut.

Patti turned the big van around and started back down the driveway. She braked and pulled over onto the grass, giving Lizzie a jolt. "Sorry about that. A buggy is coming."

Lizzie strained to peer inside the black buggy. She'd never questioned why the Old Order Mennonites in St. Mary's County used black buggies while the Amish used gray ones. Maybe she should ask Daed. He'd probably know the reason. A lone man glanced at the van and then back out the front of his buggy. That must be Seth. Mary had said her oldest son, Seth, worked at the nearby feed mill. Was it late enough to be quitting time? If so, Mamm would be preparing supper—without Lizzie's help again. Mamm had Frannie, though.

Lizzie turned to look at the retreating buggy. She couldn't see the man or even his silhouette any longer. She wondered if he had Stephen's blue eyes. *Ach!* She had to stop thinking of those. She let her head drop against the headrest as Patti eased the van onto the driveway and continued toward home.

She closed her eyes briefly but popped them open when her brain conjured up blue robin's eggs in the blackness. Would she forever be plagued by visions of those eyes? She needed to think of something different.

Mary. She'd think of Mary. The woman had been such an eager learner. She had gotten the hang of the loom quicker than most people would have. Lizzie had given the older woman a simple project and gotten her started on it. She had promised to return next week to check on Mary's progress. Would Stephen be there?

Stephen Zimmerman was a puzzle. One minute he seemed gruff and out of sorts. Then two minutes later, he'd smile and make some kind of wisecrack. He obviously loved the dogs. Lizzie could see that in the way he cared for them and his gentle treatment of them. He apparently loved and respected his *mudder*, too. His tone of voice and whole demeanor softened when he spoke of her. And why not? In the few short hours Lizzie had spent in the Zimmerman home, she'd grown rather fond of Mary herself. The woman had an easygoing way, though Lizzie knew she had to be a strong person to have kept four *buwe* in line.

Mary, Lizzie could figure out and relate to. Stephen? Not so much. It might be fun to try, though. *Ach! Stop it, Lizzie!*

Lizzie Fisher was a puzzle. Stephen reached beneath his straw hat to scratch his head. For a moment he didn't even hear the puppies yipping as they hopped around his feet nipping at one another. He shook his head but couldn't dislodge thoughts of the caramel-haired girl. One minute Lizzie presented herself as a confident, competent young woman who had apparently earned the title of "local loom expert." The next minute, she sat in the dirt with puppies climbing all over her and licking her until she giggled like a little girl. He chuckled at the memory of that scene. Lizzie could spar with him, matching him barb for barb, but then she could be demure and hesitant to accept a compliment. She was passionate about animals and art.

Stephen absentmindedly stooped to pet the puppies. He had been planning to do something before thoughts of Lizzie had invaded his brain. What was it? He simply had to stop seeing violet eyes every time he closed his own eyes. She was Amish, for Pete's sake, and he was Mennonite. A baptized Mennonite. An already-joined-the-church Mennonite. A sure-to-be-shunned Mennonite, if he left the faith.

Left the faith? He didn't have any intention of doing that. He'd never had any desire to try out any other lifestyle, even during his *rumspringa*. He had joined the church as soon as he was able, unlike Seth, who hadn't yet joined, despite being the oldest son. Stephen was what he was and planned to stay that way.

Like his *bruder*, Lizzie must not have joined her church yet, or else she would have put the artwork away once and for all. Hmmm.

A loud bark brought Stephen's attention to the task at hand. Right. He'd been getting ready to feed the puppies. How could that have possibly slipped his mind with all these little fur balls cavorting around him? "Okay. Okay." Stephen struggled to free himself and get to his feet. "Your supper is *kumming*. You're still nursing, so don't act like you're starving." The puppies nursed, for sure, but they had begun demanding more and more kibble.

Lizzie sure seemed to like the runt of the litter. She definitely was a feisty one—like Lizzie. *Ach!* There he went again. Would that girl get out of his mind and stay out? He needed to feed and water the dogs and get back to work. He didn't have time for nonsense. He was not in the market for a girlfriend, not after Joanna Brubacher had played with his heart before smashing it. And he definitely wasn't in the market for an *Amish* girlfriend.

Lizzie burst into the kitchen gasping for breath. "I'm here to help, Mamm. I'm sorry it took a little longer than I thought."

"Ew! You smell like a dog." Frannie wrinkled her nose when she passed by Lizzie with plates and silverware. She made a big show of putting as much space as possible between them, like some terrible stench would hop off of Lizzie and affix itself to her.

"*Danki*, Schweschder. It's so nice of you to notice." Lizzie would smell like a rose, too, if she stayed in the house all day. She chewed her tongue. Thank goodness she had kept that comment from slipping out. It surely would have been the beginning of a battle Lizzie would never win, especially since Mamm would side with Frannie. Sometimes Lizzie feared that if she grew old and senile like Mattie Glick, all the retorts she usually suppressed would gush out like water over a dam. That was a scary thought indeed!

"One day you reek like ashes from a week-old fire and the next you smell like a pack of dogs. What is it with you?" Frannie flounced off to the big oak table and methodically arranged silverware at each place.

"Maybe you have an overly sensitive nose." And here Lizzie had helped Frannie get out of going to Ohio, only to be treated so shabbily.

"Then I must have a sensitive nose, too."

Lizzie's shoulders slumped. She felt like a balloon with a pinprick. Frannie just had to keep harping on the subject and get Mamm involved.

"I thought you went to help someone with a loom." Mamm glanced up from the ham she was slicing.

"I did."

"Did the Zimmermans have dogs in the house?"

"Not inside the house."

"Did you roll around in the yard with their dogs?" Frannie burst into a fit of giggles. "I can picture that."

Lizzie made a face at her *schweschder*. "Very funny." She turned her back on Frannie and directed her comment to her *mudder*. "Do you want me to change clothes if I'm so offensive?"

"You don't have time. Here, put the ham on the table." Mamm held the platter out to Lizzie.

"Just don't let any of the food touch you." Frannie wrinkled her nose again.

Lizzie held the platter piled high with ham slices as far away from her body as possible. "Happy?"

"I guess that will do. You didn't tell us about the dogs. Did you fall into a dog pen?"

Lizzie scowled. Why was Frannie so persistent? Why was she so prissy? Her *schweschder* was another enigma. Last night Lizzie had had the silly thought that the girls might be on the same wavelength. She had risked Mamm's anger to plead Frannie's case, and her *schweschder* had seemed so grateful. Now that she had gotten her way, Frannie must not have a reason to be nice anymore. *I should have let her go to Aenti Grace's house.*

"Well?"

"'Well' what, Frannie?" When her *schweschder* looked directly at her, Lizzie mouthed, "What's wrong with you?"

Frannie ignored the unspoken question. "Where were the dogs?"

"I don't really think it's important, but if you must know, the Zimmermans had adorable puppies that I petted before leaving."

"Petted? Smells like you napped with them."

"Let it go, will you?" Lizzie spoke loud enough for only Frannie to hear. "Why are you so mean?"

Frannie whirled around and waltzed away. "I'll finish dishing up the vegetables, Mamm."

"*Danki*, dear."

Lizzie rolled her eyes. She always came out lacking, while Frannie always shone like the brightest star in the sky. Always. Lizzie should be used to that by now. "Do you want me to get the clothes off the line, Mamm?"

"Frannie got them earlier. Didn't you notice?"

Of course Frannie brought them in. Silly me! "Okay. I'll go check on the kittens since everything is done here."

Lizzie strode toward the door, anxious to be with animals, who didn't criticize.

"Great! Then she'll smell like cats, too."

Lizzie slipped outside and sighed with relief. At least she would have a little peace outside. Sometimes it was so much easier to be with animals. Maybe she would work on the loom until Frannie went to bed so she wouldn't have to fend off any more attacks.

Uh-oh. The shed door stood open a *gut* four or five inches more than Lizzie had left it. Either the kittens had decided to explore or they'd had visitors. She hoped the cats hadn't wandered off. That meant a hawk could easily scoop them up for a snack. *Wait! What was that sound?* Now Lizzie knew why the door was open wider.

"*Nee*, Sadie, this one is Miriam."

"Is not. It's Annie."

"*Nee*."

"*Jah*."

Lizzie cleared her throat. Two guilty faces turned toward her. The black kitten squirmed in Sadie's hands before letting out a pitiful mew. Lizzie gently lifted it into her own arms. "You're right, Sadie. The black kitten is Annie." She nuzzled the fuzzy head with her chin. "The tortoiseshell kitten is Miriam."

"And the black-and-white one is Molly." Sadie looked so pleased with herself that she'd gotten all the names correct.

"Now, tell me why you two are out here."

"We can visit the kittens, can't we?" Nancy crossed her arms over her chest as if getting ready for a battle.

"It's okay to visit them, but I don't want them to wander off. That's why we need to leave the door nearly closed. This place is new to them. We don't want them to get hurt or lost or snatched up by the hawk."

Sadie giggled. "A bird can't take a cat."

"Hawks are big birds with sharp claws." Lizzie chose her words carefully so she wouldn't frighten the little girl.

Nancy was not so considerate. "You've seen it, Sadie. It's a big, mean, scary bird with beady eyes. If you were a little smaller it would grab you."

"Ahhh!" Sadie shuffled closer to Lizzie.

"It won't get you." Lizzie frowned at Nancy over Sadie's head. "But it could hurt helpless little kittens."

"I don't want that to happen."

"I know you don't. Didn't Mamm need you two to help with anything?"

"*Nee.* We did our homework and got ready to set the table, but Frannie shrieked at us."

Lizzie could always count on Nancy to divulge any morsel of information she knew. "Why would Frannie shriek at you?"

"Because she's mean."

"That's not very nice, Nancy." Out of the corner of her eye, Lizzie caught Sadie's nod of agreement with Nancy's assessment.

Nancy plopped her fists on her hips. "It might not be nice, but it's true."

"She's been even meaner today," Sadie whispered. The poor little girl probably feared her oldest *schweschder* lurked around the corner.

Lizzie stroked the kitten. To tell the truth, she thought the girls were right. Frannie had certainly been meaner to her, and she'd only been home a short time. "Maybe she had a bad day."

"Maybe it's because of the news." Now Nancy was whispering, too.

"What news would that be?"

"I heard Frannie and Mamm talking." Nancy pulled herself up as tall as possible, obviously thrilled to know something that Lizzie wasn't aware of.

"And you just happened to overhear, right?"

"I did, but I wasn't eavesdropping."

"Of course not." Lizzie hugged the little girl so she would know Lizzie was teasing.

"All right. Sometimes I do, but I wasn't today. Honest. I headed for the kitchen to get an after-school snack. I do that every day."

"And?" Lizzie probably shouldn't encourage any gossip, but if Nancy knew something that would help her understand Frannie's mood better, she needed to hear it—fast. Since Lizzie had to share a room with Frannie, the more knowledge she had, the better.

Nancy stepped closer to Lizzie. Sadie inched her way closer as well. Nancy glanced toward the door before speaking.

Lizzie tried her best to keep a straight face, but the girls presented such a comical sight that a giggle sneaked out. She covered it with a cough to keep from hurting Nancy's feelings. "I think it's safe to tell me."

"Shhh! You never know. Mamm might send Frannie out to fetch us for supper." Nancy's whispered words were probably loud enough to be heard by anyone passing by, despite her attempt to be secretive.

"You'd better spill the beans fast, then." Lizzie dropped her voice to match Nancy's whisper.

"Okay. Like I said, I was going to the kitchen to get a snack. You know how much I love those peanut butter chocolate chip cookies. I wanted to see if there were any left. I could eat a whole—"

Lizzie cleared her throat and tapped a foot. "I got that part, Nancy."

"Oh, well, Frannie was stirring a pot of kale. I hate kale. I have to hold my breath to eat that slimy green stuff."

Lizzie rolled her eyes. With Nancy, nothing was ever straightforward. Lizzie tapped her foot again.

"Anyway, I heard Frannie sniffing over the top of the noise she made banging the spoon against the pot. Mamm said, 'Aaron Kurtz must not have been the right fellow for you.' Frannie put the spoon down—slammed it down, actually. When she looked at Mamm, her nose was all red and tears were running down her cheeks."

Lizzie's sensitivity kicked in. Poor Frannie. What on earth had happened? Had Aaron returned? "What happened to Aaron?" Lizzie hated grilling an eight-year-old, but she needed Nancy to finish her story.

"He got married."

"What?"

"He got married," Nancy whispered louder.

"Did not!"

"He did. I'm telling you the truth."

Lizzie frowned. "Aaron went to stay in Pennsylvania for a while. I thought he planned to return to Maryland."

"If he does, he'll bring his *fraa* with him."

Sadie reached around Nancy to tug on Lizzie's sleeve. "Was Frannie going to marry him?"

"Not that I know of." As far as Lizzie knew, and from what she'd observed at singings, Aaron had never even hinted at asking to take Frannie home. He had never tossed pebbles at or shone a light into their bedroom window. Lizzie was a light sleeper. She would know. Apparently the attraction had all been one-sided— Frannie's side. Had he ever given Frannie any reason to hope he would return to court her? If he had, that would have been so mean. Frannie didn't always treat her siblings well, but she didn't deserve to have her heart broken. But somehow Lizzie didn't think the miscommunication was Aaron's fault.

"Did you hear me?"

"What did you say, Nancy?"

"I asked if you're going to get married?"

"Not any time soon. Why do you ask?"

"Well, you are getting old."

"I know at my advanced age of twenty, time is running out. I'll be an old *maedel* before you know it." Lizzie made a silly face at her little *schweschders*. "Getting old, my foot!"

"You know what I mean. I don't think you're all that old yet."

"You might want to quit while you're ahead, Nancy. If you dig yourself any deeper a hole, I might not be able to pull you out." Lizzie tickled each of the girls. "I'm afraid you're stuck with me for a while longer."

"*Gut!*" they cried in unison.

"Lizzie Fisher, where are you? You go outside and lose all track of time." The shrill voice rode the gust of wind to the shed.

"Uh-oh! We're in trouble." Lizzie tucked the kittens back into their basket.

"Do you see what I mean about Frannie?" Nancy nudged Lizzie and nodded toward the doorway. "She's shrewish."

"That is not very nice. Where did you ever hear that word?"

"Melvin."

"That figures. It's best you don't go around repeating everything you hear our dear *bruder* say."

"What does 'shrewish' mean?" Sadie looked from Lizzie to Nancy.

Lizzie searched for words, but Nancy answered quickly. "It means shrieking in that voice that hurts my ears and being nasty to people like Frannie does."

"Shame on you, Nancy Fisher."

"Lizzie! Nancy! Sadie! If you don't *kumm* right now, I'll tell Mamm you won't listen."

Nancy rolled her eyes. "See? Now she's going to tattle on us."

"Will Mamm get a switch?" Fear clouded Sadie's eyes.

"Not if we get moving right now." Lizzie threw a final glance at the kittens before steering her little *schweschders* out of the shed. "We're on our way, Frannie!" Lizzie turned to prop the shed door just so. "You two run ahead."

"*Jah*, before she yells again." Nancy grabbed Sadie's hand. They took off in a trot toward the house.

"It's about time. Do you two smell like cats and dogs and who knows what else, too?" Frannie's voice probably carried to the next farm.

Maybe Nancy was right, after all.

Chapter Fifteen

Lizzie tried her best to be pleasant all throughout supper. She didn't let Frannie get a rise out of her. She ate her meal and ignored her older *schweschder* except for whenever she had to pass a bowl Frannie's way. Melvin and Caleb talked about a neighbor's new horse practically nonstop. Lizzie noticed Frannie didn't accuse them of smelling like a horse, which they did. Her barbs seemed directed only at Lizzie. For the life of her, Lizzie couldn't determine a single thing she'd done to rile the girl. She planned to slip out to her loom if she survived cleaning the kitchen with Frannie.

Mamm helped clear the table and get the kitchen cleanup started. Thank goodness! She could always hope Frannie would harness her sharp tongue in Mamm's presence.

Frannie marched to the sink and turned on the water so forcefully a stream shot across the floor.

Lizzie sighed. "Maybe not," she muttered.

"What?"

"I didn't say anything to you, Frannie. In case you didn't notice, you just splashed water all over the floor."

"Well, clean it up!"

"I didn't make the mess." Mamm handed Lizzie a

roll of paper towels. *But I guess I'll be cleaning it up.* If Frannie was behaving so hatefully with Mamm in the room with them, Lizzie dreaded being alone with her in their bedroom.

Despite the fact that she was tired enough to fall asleep on her feet, Lizzie made a beeline for the door as soon as she'd hung the dish towel on a hook.

"Where do you think you're going?"

You are only two years older. You are not my mudder. *What gives you the right to question me or order me about?* Lizzie continued on the course she'd begun without answering, lest she say something she regretted. She tried to be patient with Frannie. Really she did. But her patience had been stretched to the limits.

"Did you forget about Bible reading and prayers?"

Lizzie clamped her teeth together. She had forgotten. How she could let a daily occurrence slip her mind was beyond her comprehension. Her brain hurt. Her head hurt. She needed the soothing, rhythmic motion of weaving. Lizzie spun around to change directions. She'd try to focus on Daed's Bible passage and hope that would provide the peace she needed. *Please let Daed's words calm that beast living inside of Frannie.*

To her dismay, Lizzie's mind wandered terribly. How could Frannie be so upset over Aaron's marriage when she and Aaron had never even ridden home from a singing together? She sincerely doubted Frannie had sneaked out at night to meet Aaron, so they probably didn't have any kind of understanding. Lizzie's brain hurt even more trying to rationalize her *schweschder*'s behavior.

What must the atmosphere be like in the Zimmerman household? Mary appeared to be a kind, caring person. She hadn't met Seth, Aaron, or Daniel or

Mary's husband, Matthew, so she had only observed the family dynamics between Mary and Stephen. Those two obviously got along well. At least serenity and peace reigned in that household. Tension reigned more often than not in the Fisher home, much to Lizzie's chagrin. She'd rather run from conflict than participate in it, but she often got dragged into the tiff of the day.

Daed closed the big Bible and bowed his head. Uh-oh. Lizzie had missed the entire reading. Her silent prayer better be one seeking forgiveness for her inattention to the Lord Gott's word. She bowed her head and closed her eyes. When Daed cleared his throat, Lizzie's eyes popped open. She prepared to bolt.

"It's too late and too cold to go out there now."

How could *mudders* always read their *kinners'* minds? Lizzie looked over her shoulder and caught Mamm's stern expression. There would not be any weaving tonight. Lizzie swallowed her disappointment and the sigh she wanted to heave. "Okay, Mamm. *Gut nacht.*"

She forced herself to ascend the stairs in a dignified manner. She would not stomp her feet or mumble under her breath. She would get ready for bed and brace herself for whatever Frannie dished out.

At least Lizzie made it in and out of the bathroom in record time. Frannie didn't even have a chance to bang on the door and yell for her to hurry up. Lizzie practically tiptoed into their shared bedroom. Blessed peace ruled momentarily. *The calm before the storm.*

Since Frannie hadn't made her way to the bedroom yet, Lizzie sped up her bedtime preparations. If she could jump into bed and pull the covers up to her head, she could feign sleep. She quickly hung up her clothes and pulled on her nightgown. She removed her *kapp* and yanked the pins from her hair. *Hurry! Hurry!* She brushed and braided her hair in a loose braid. She might make it!

Lizzie hopped across the cold wood floor, her bare toes tingling, and flung back the quilt and blanket. She would say her prayers in bed tonight. She had lifted one knee to hoist herself onto the high mattress when the door jerked open. *I almost made it!* She paused with her leg still hovering over the bed.

"What on earth are you doing?"

"Getting into bed."

"You look like you're trying to do some weird dance or acrobatic stunt."

Lizzie dropped her knee onto the mattress. "I'm not. I'm only trying to get up on the bed. I'm so short I practically need a ladder to get in." She gave a nervous little giggle. She shouldn't be nervous. Frannie was her *schweschder*, and this was her room.

"Technically, I suppose you *could* dance, since you haven't yet joined the church."

Lizzie let the comment slide. She situated herself on her back, untwisted her nightgown, and drew the covers up to her chin. She had opened her mouth to say *gut nacht* when Frannie spoke again.

"When are you going to join the church, Lizzie? You are planning to join, ain't so?"

"Of course I am."

"What are you waiting for?"

First the dogs and now joining the church. Was there anything else Frannie could find fault with? Frannie would *kumm* up with something, for sure and for certain. "I'm only twenty. I have time."

"I was twenty when I joined."

Hooray for you! "I guess we're all different." Lizzie

rolled onto her side—the side facing away from her *schweschder*. Would Frannie take the hint and leave her alone?

"Where else did you go today?"

"You already know I spent the afternoon with Mary Zimmerman working on her loom. Mary recently got it from a family member but didn't know how to use it."

"And you're the expert, of course."

Lizzie didn't like the tone or the sarcasm. She turned back over and raised up on her elbows. "I'm not the expert, and I never said I was. But I have learned enough about the loom to help Mary out. Why are you so mean this evening?" She barely resisted qualifying that with *meaner than usual*.

"I'm not mean. I . . ."

To Lizzie's surprise, Frannie burst into tears. She covered her face with her hands and rocked back and forth like she was attempting to soothe herself. Lizzie threw off the warm covers and hopped to the floor. She skipped from throw rug to throw rug until she stood right in front of Frannie. She hesitated a second, unsure how her gesture would be received. Throwing caution to the wind, she wrapped her arms around her *schweschder*. "What is it? What's wrong?"

"*Ach*, Lizzie." Frannie sniffed. She stiffened and tried to pull away. "Y-you wouldn't understand."

Lizzie didn't loosen her grip. Even though Frannie was several inches taller, she held tight. "Try me. I'm a *gut* listener."

"How could I have been so wrong?"

Lizzie rocked Frannie and patted her heaving back. "Wrong about what?"

"About Aaron."

"How were you wrong about him?"

"Didn't you hear? He got m-married to someone he met in Pennsylvania." Frannie drew back to look into Lizzie's face. "To someone he just met. He hardly knew the girl! And here he's known me all these years, and . . ." She paused to sniff so loud that Lizzie almost moved her hands to clap them over her ears. "And he never paid attention to me." Her last word ended in a wail.

"Maybe he knew the girl from previous visits."

"What about me? He's known me forever."

"Maybe that's it. Sometimes when you've known someone for a long time they become too familiar, like family."

"He should never have talked to me after singings and gotten my hopes up."

Aaron had talked to her at singings? "Did he seek you out?" Lizzie spoke as gently as she could to keep from upsetting Frannie any more than she already was.

"Well, uh, I guess I approached him first."

"Every time?"

Frannie looked pensive for a moment. "I suppose so. But he could have walked away. He didn't have to stay and talk to me."

"I've never known Aaron to be rude, have you?"

"*Nee.* He could have been truthful, though."

"Did he tell you he was interested in you, Frannie? Did he ask to take you home from a singing? Because I never saw you leave with him."

"H-he never asked. But I thought he would." Her voice dropped to a whisper. "I hoped he would." After a pause, her voice grew louder, angrier. "It's me. It was only my wishful thinking. Aaron never did anything, because he didn't have any interest in me. I'm a terrible person."

"*Nee,* you aren't. I'm sorry things didn't work out like you wanted."

"Nothing works out like I want."

"Like what? You've always seemed happy with your life. You seem content to cook and clean."

"'Seem.' That's the key word." Frannie frowned, but then her angry facade melted into the saddest expression Lizzie had ever seen. "I cook and clean because I can't do anything else. I don't have any talents like you do."

Lizzie swallowed a gasp. Surely Frannie wasn't referring to her artwork. Her *schweschder* hadn't discovered that secret, had she? "What talents?"

"Your weaving. You can make beautiful blankets and things. You're at ease talking to Plain or *Englisch* customers. You like to do things outside. You l-like people."

Whew! Her drawing secret was safe for the moment. "I do like being outside and caring for animals. I enjoy weaving very much. I'm not always comfortable talking to people, but I get along with most folks." Lizzie paused. The image of a certain tall, dark-haired, blue-eyed man appeared in her mind. She wasn't sure how well she got along with Stephen Zimmerman.

"See. You have lots of skills." Frannie freed herself from Lizzie's grasp and turned her back.

"You have talents, Frannie. Not everyone can bake the delicious pastries you bake. It takes skill to keep a house running smoothly. I believe you could do that without any trouble at all. And I could teach you to use the loom, if you'd like." Lizzie couldn't imagine where she'd find the patience to deal with Frannie's whining, but she'd try.

"*Nee*. Needlework is definitely not my talent. I'm twenty-two years old. I want to get married and have my own home."

"You will. Twenty-two isn't over-the-hill, you know." Lizzie moved to squeeze Frannie's hand. "The right fellow will *kumm* along. You'll see." Lizzie couldn't be too sure of that, though.

He played with the puppies until it got too dark and cold, and then he returned to his shop to apply a second coat of cherry stain to the chest. Still those violet eyes haunted his thoughts. Mamm's excited chatter about weaving all during supper didn't help much. It was "Lizzie this" and "Lizzie that." And then she had to go and remind them that the girl would return to help her again. Stephen planned to find out exactly when that would be and make himself scarce.

The puppies and work proved to be only temporary distractions. Those eyes stared at him again as he lay in bed. Why? He'd never been so affected by a person's eyes or maybe it was the person herself. *Nee*. That couldn't be it. He had too many responsibilities to be distracted by a little girl.

You're only three years older, that nagging little voice in his brain pointed out.

But I have a job and raise dogs and work on the farm.

That important, are you? Lizzie is three years younger. She works and probably does a lot of household and childcare chores as well.

I've joined the church. I'm settled. I know what I want.

Really? What's that?

Great! Now he was having entire conversations with himself. What exactly did he want? Didn't he want what every Plain man wanted—a *fraa*, a home, a family? Hmmm. Didn't he? Stephen rolled onto his side and covered his head with the pillow. If only he could snuff out that little voice with the pillow.

Once upon a time he had thought he had those desires in his heart. But he'd hesitated, and the girl who had captured his attention and his heart had happily traipsed off with another fellow. He didn't have any intention of traveling down that road again, especially not with an Amish girl, even if his *mudder* did seem to adore her. Maybe Seth would be interested, though. Despite being a year older, Seth had not yet joined the Mennonite Church.

Stephen flopped onto his other side. He had to get some sleep. Tomorrow promised to be busy. He didn't particularly want to saw off a finger while working on his next project. The caramel-haired girl with purple eyes had to leave him alone. Now!

Chapter Sixteen

Apparently Frannie had sniffled herself to sleep after unloading her burdens on Lizzie. Lizzie, on the other hand, thrashed about most of the night alternately wondering if she'd said the right words to her *schweschder* and tamping down visions of bluer-than-blue eyes. She'd dozed off about the time the rooster crowed and groaned as she opened one eye and squinted toward the next bed. As best she could tell in the darkness, it stood neatly made. Frannie must have slipped from the room in those few brief moments Lizzie had slept. *Well, she certainly must feel better to be up and out. I feel like I've been kicked by a mule.*

Ten minutes later Lizzie stumbled into the kitchen. Mamm stood at the wood cookstove frying bacon with her back toward the door. Frannie leaned over the counter, furiously stirring a bowl of pancake batter. She appeared well rested and perfectly normal. How did she manage that? Lizzie needed toothpicks to prop her eyes open and a gallon of strong *kaffi* to clear the sludge from her brain. She shook her head. It didn't seem right. Whatever time Lizzie stepped into the kitchen, regardless of how early, she always felt like she was a day late and a dollar short. Today was not any different, only she now felt groggy and unkempt as well.

"There you are." Frannie glanced up. The wooden spoon in her hand dripped batter down the side of the big glass mixing bowl and onto the counter.

"I'm glad to see you're better." Lizzie poked a misbehaving strand of hair under her *kapp*.

"Better? I'm fine. Why wouldn't I be?" Frannie stared with wide, innocent eyes. Mamm turned only halfway toward them. Maybe she was only half paying attention.

Okay. So this was the way Frannie wanted to play it. Apparently she wanted to pretend her outburst last night had never occurred. Lizzie hadn't imagined it or dreamed it, had she? Now she was thoroughly confused. "You were upset last night." Frannie's frown and slight head shake stopped Lizzie in midsentence.

Mamm slid the frying pan to the back of the stove and turned all the way around. She fixed Frannie with a concerned expression. Lizzie couldn't recall if Mamm had ever gazed at her quite that way. "Did you have too much on your mind or weren't you feeling well?"

Frannie turned on a bright smile. "I'm fine. You know how mixed-up Lizzie gets."

Mixed-up? Her? Lizzie knew reality from pretense. Perhaps she could understand why Frannie wanted Mamm to believe she was all right, but she couldn't understand why Frannie would deliberately try to paint her in a bad light. Lizzie sighed. That was Frannie. Well, she would not take the bait this morning. She was too tired to argue. "What would you like me to do, Mamm?"

"You can make sure Nancy and Sadie are up and

ready. Those two need to get moving before they're late."

"Okay." Lizzie wasn't sure if she'd rather pull her little *schweschders* out of bed and listen to their grumbling or deal with more abuse from Frannie. But she decided coaxing Nancy and Sadie out of their warm beds would most likely be less stressful than holding her tongue around Frannie. Actually, wrestling a grizzly bear might be less stressful—and painful.

What happened between last night and this morning? Frannie needed me then, and she was even nice. Lizzie resisted the urge to stomp up the stairs and to mumble aloud. She paused at the top step and dragged in a deep breath before proceeding to the little girls' room. Then she inched the door open, poked in her head, and sang out, "Rise and shine!" She ran across the room, pounced on the bed, and tickled both girls until they crawled from beneath the covers giggling and gasping. Lizzie helped them dress and braided their hair. "Now you two monkeys need to get downstairs before Daed gets inside."

Sadie threw her arms around Lizzie's waist. "I love you, Lizzie!"

Nancy squeezed Lizzie from the other direction. "Me, too. I'm glad you're such a fun big *schweschder*."

Lizzie hugged both girls in return and sent them on their way. She wiped a tear from her eye as she straightened their room. At least her younger *schweschders* were sweet.

"How are the puppies getting along?" Mary handed a mug of *kaffi* to the broad-shouldered son towering over her.

Stephen swallowed the chunk of chocolate chip cookie he'd pilfered from the bear-shaped cookie jar and reached for the mug. "*Gut*. They're doing fine, except for the runt. I'm not sure if she's got what it takes to be a service dog."

"Give her time." Mary stretched to wipe a crumb from Stephen's cheek. "Honestly, cookies for breakfast?"

"Only a little fragment. Besides, I ate breakfast. The bite of cookie was an extra little treat before I head out to the shop."

Seth, Aaron, and their *daed* had already left for their respective workplaces, and Daniel had tromped off to school. Stephen planned to get started on a cabinet for an *Englisch* customer and had decided a little bite of sugar would give him extra fortification.

"She sure enjoyed the puppies, didn't she?"

"She who?" He had a pretty *gut* idea who his *mudder* was referring to but didn't want to voice it.

"Lizzie Fisher, of course. She didn't mind the pups' yipping, nudging, and licking one bit."

Stephen gave a noncommittal shrug.

"She's such a sweet girl, ain't so?"

"I wouldn't know. She spent time with you, not me." Stephen frowned. Did they have to discuss Lizzie Fisher? He'd been trying to forget she existed.

"Why the surly mood this morning?"

"I'm not surly."

"*Hmpf!* Well, you certainly must have noticed how lovely she is."

Stephen didn't miss his *mamm*'s sly smile. "If you say so." He turned away and gulped his *kaffi*. His eyes watered as the steaming liquid burned all the way down his throat and esophagus. He didn't plan to take her bait.

"You can't fool me one bit, Stephen Zimmerman. I'm your *mudder*, and I can read you like a book."

She always could do that. He had never been able to hide anything or dodge the truth with Mary Zimmerman. When he could speak past the fire in his throat, he mumbled, "She's fine to look at, I suppose."

Mary laughed as if she'd just heard the best joke ever. "She's beautiful, and you know it. I know you know it, because even your neck and earlobes are blood red."

Stephen set his mug on the counter a little harder than he had intended. *Kaffi* sloshed over the side to burn a whole in his finger to match the ones in his entire digestive tract. "It really doesn't matter if she's pretty as a peach or ugly as a goat—she's Amish."

"So?"

"So if you're trying to play matchmaker, I'm Mennonite, in case you've forgotten. I'm a baptized member of the church. Period. You can play matchmaker with Seth. He hasn't joined yet."

"Lizzie hasn't joined the Amish church yet."

"How would you know that?"

"We talked as we worked at the loom."

"It sounds like you got pretty chummy awfully fast."

"Lizzie is very open and honest. She's easy to get to know and to like."

The girl had easily wormed her way into his thoughts. Stephen knew that for sure. What he didn't know was how to get her out. "I'd better get to work." He headed for the door and deliberately whistled an upbeat tune from the Ausbund to throw his *mamm* off track.

"She'll be back next week."

Stephen could practically hear the smile in her voice. A little hiccup interrupted his tune momentarily, but he forced himself to keep whistling. He could grumble all he wanted once he reached his shop.

"They're so nice to you. You're the fun *schweschder*."

Lizzie wasn't sure whether Frannie's muttered words were meant to be heard or not, but she certainly caught them. She had just closed the door behind Nancy and Sadie. Both little girls had hugged her before departing for school. Both had broad smiles on their faces after another brief tickling session. Lizzie always tried to send them off in a pleasant mood. She'd always found that a smile at the start of the day made things go better whether she was scrubbing the kitchen, fighting with the gas-powered wringer washing machine, or working at her loom. Now she had to try to hold on to her own smile while dealing with her grumpy older sibling. "You could be the fun *schweschder*, too." She tried to keep her tone light and not accusatory.

"Ha! All those two care about is Lizzie. I heard them before they came downstairs."

Frannie must mean she heard the girls say they loved her and were glad she was their big *schweschder*. So that's why Frannie was even more prickly at breakfast than she had been earlier. She was jealous along with whatever other emotions were rolling around inside of her. Lizzie coaxed a smile onto her face before looking at Frannie. "They love you, too."

"I don't get hugs and giggles."

"Do you hug them or play with them?"

"I don't have time to play."

"Sure you do. It only takes a few minutes here and there. And the girls are so much more cooperative if I try to make things fun instead of nag at them."

"So I'm a nag, too, in addition to all my other faults?"

"I never said that." The smile tried to run away. Lizzie silently begged it to stay put. "I've never criticized or tried to find fault with you, Frannie." Not out loud, anyway. "If I've said something that hurt your feelings, I'm sorry."

Frannie shrugged. "It's them." She jerked her head toward the door. "They don't care about me. Nobody does, except maybe Mamm."

"That's not at all true! We all care about you. We all love you and want you to be happy."

"*Hmpf!*"

"Why don't you try reading to Nancy and Sadie when they get home, or playing a game with them?"

"They have homework and chores to do. And I have to help with supper."

"Supper is usually well underway by the time they get home from school."

"Well, they have things to do, and I . . ."

"You aren't their *mudder*. Be their *schweschder*, not their watchdog."

"I've gone from being a nag to being a dog. *Danki*, Lizzie."

"*Ach*, Frannie! You turn my words all around. The kitchen is clean. The downstairs has been swept and dusted. The laundry is flapping in the wind. I'll be out in my shop. I hope you're feeling better later." *And in a better mood.* When Frannie was down in the dumps, she tried to pull everyone else down there with her. Well, Lizzie wasn't going there. She was going to check on the kittens and weave.

Animals always brought a smile to Lizzie's face. The kittens had become a bit more adventurous and definitely liked to play. So far, they had stayed out of Mamm's way. If they kept behaving, they might get to stay here. Lizzie spent a *gut* fifteen minutes playing with the three little balls of fluff. She fed and watered them before continuing on to the weaving project that awaited her.

She was tempted to extract her drawing materials from their hiding place so she could sketch the puppies while they were still fresh in her memory, but she didn't dare. With Frannie on the warpath, she wouldn't hesitate to tattle if she caught Lizzie drawing. Her art project would have to wait until she finished weaving. If only she could keep her supplies in her room, she could draw at night. But sharing a room with Frannie made that totally out of the question.

The rhythm of weaving always brought Lizzie peace. Even if her mind was troubled, working at the loom could soothe her. Balm for the heart, mind, and soul. It's too bad Frannie didn't have such a hobby to provide her peace. As the blanket took shape beneath her fingers, Lizzie resolved to find a way to help her *schweschder.* Devising a plan for Frannie might be a great way to keep her brain too occupied to call forth memories of laughing, blue eyes.

"Ahhh!" Lizzie yelped at a touch on her arm. Her

hand flew to pat her chest, where her heart pounded like a jackhammer.

"Sorry."

"You nearly frightened me to death."

"Sorry."

"It's okay. I was lost in thought. I didn't expect anyone to sneak up on me." *It's a* gut *thing I didn't drag out the art supplies.*

"I wasn't sneaking."

Here we go again. Wrong choice of words. "You know what I mean, Frannie. *Was ist letz?*"

"Nothing's wrong. *Nee,* that's not true. Everything is wrong." Frannie heaved a sigh that made it sound as if she bore the burdens of the world.

Lizzie chewed her lower lip. What should she say? Most of the time Frannie misconstrued her words so much she'd have been better off to save her breath. "Do you want to tell me about it?" There. That shouldn't be offensive. Now it would be up to Frannie to take the conversation further.

"How do you do it?"

"Do what? The weaving? I can teach—"

"Not the weaving. How do you stay so upbeat? It's as if nothing ever bothers you."

"Things bother me sometimes. I try not to dwell on them. I pray and then try to distract myself. Weaving and knitting help me. Is there some activity you enjoy that could be soothing when you're upset?"

"It certainly wouldn't be anything involving needles and yarn. I get too frustrated sewing and knitting. I'd end up ripping out all my mistakes over and over again. Then I'd be more miserable." Frannie sighed again. She continued to watch Lizzie. "That's pretty."

Lizzie started to ask Frannie to repeat her last

words. Surely she hadn't just offered a compliment. Lizzie opened her mouth but closed it quickly. It would be best not to call attention to Frannie's uncharacteristically kind words. Instead she mumbled, "*Danki.*"

Silence fell as thick as a blanket over the workroom. Lizzie's unease increased. Usually she tolerated lapses in conversation with Frannie quite well. In fact, she often welcomed them. Today was altogether different. Lizzie's gaze followed Frannie as she paced like an animal in a cage.

That was it! Frannie must feel trapped. She did the same thing the same way day after day and had fallen into a rut. She was a young woman living an old woman's life. What could Lizzie say without offending her *schweschder*? How could she help Frannie see her way out of the pit she'd hurled herself into? "What do you enjoy doing, Frannie? What feels fun to you?"

Frannie stopped pacing and stared at Lizzie like she'd sprouted a horn in the middle of her forehead. "Fun? What's that?"

"*Kumm* on, Frannie. You're young. You're supposed to have fun mixed in with the work and chores. What brings you joy or satisfaction?"

Frannie shrugged. Lizzie wondered if the girl could even imagine a fun activity. Surely she could. When they were *kinner*, they used to play outside or play board games. "We used to play croquet and checkers, and . . ."

"*Kinner* play games."

"Adults do, too. Why, the young folks often play volleyball or horseshoes. You could join in the next time they play."

Frannie shrugged yet again.

"What about your baking? You enjoy that, ain't so?

Because if you don't, you should stop baking for Yoder's Store. That will make you feel more miserable." When Frannie turned around, Lizzie thought she saw a spark of interest.

"I do like baking. I want to continue baking for the store. Maybe that is one thing I'm adequate at doing."

"I'm sure there are many things, but your baking is definitely a talent. Why don't you attend the next singing? That could be fun."

"Uh, I don't think so."

"Why not?"

"Everyone will whisper. They'll say, 'Poor Frannie Fisher chased Aaron Kurtz off so he up and married the first girl he met in Pennsylvania.' I'll be laughed at—or worse, pitied."

"That won't happen. I doubt other folks even know you were interested in Aaron."

"You don't think they saw me corner him after every singing?"

"To tell the truth, Frannie, they were probably all too interested in their own pursuits to even notice your conversations."

"Huh!"

"Really. Please attend next time. You can have fun with the rest of us girls. I'm not planning to ride home with anyone. I simply like singing and talking to my *freinden*."

"You don't think people will whisper and point?"

"Absolutely not." Lizzie sure hoped not, anyway. "It will do you a world of *gut* to have fun with us. And who knows? Maybe there will be some visitors there."

"I-I don't know."

"It will be fun. You'll see." Lizzie couldn't believe

she was begging Frannie to attend the singing. "Besides, your *freinden* will wonder where you are."

"They all have fellows they're either already courting or hoping to court."

"Not everyone."

Suddenly Frannie stomped her foot, nearly causing Lizzie to slide off her high stool. "All I want is to have a home of my own, a husband who loves me, and *kinner*. Is that too much to ask?"

Once Lizzie caught her breath and her heart started beating in a regular rhythm again, she tried to formulate a gentle response. "You will, Frannie. You're a-a special person. And you're pretty, too." Lizzie didn't dare throw in the adjectives "grumpy" or "moody." Perhaps if Frannie had a steady fellow, she'd mellow out some.

"Do you really think so?"

"For sure and for certain." Now Lizzie just had to find a *bu* who would agree with that assessment and court her *schweschder*.

Chapter Seventeen

"What on earth are you doing in there?"

The loud, ferocious bellow caused Lizzie to lose her balance. She plopped on her backside in the dirt but somehow managed to cling to the littlest puppy in her arms.

"I . . . what . . . why are you yelling at me? You nearly caused me to have a heart attack!"

"Why are you in there with my dogs?"

The frown and grim set of his lips would have warned Lizzie of Stephen's displeasure if the shout hadn't gotten his point across. But it had. She should have been contrite, but at the moment all she felt was anger at being yelled at as if she was a misbehaving little girl. And here she'd thought they might be making some headway at becoming *freinden* of sorts, for Mary's sake if nothing else. "You can lower your voice and speak to me in a civil tone." She spoke through clenched teeth but kept her stroking of the puppy's head as gentle as possible.

"It's a little difficult to be civil when someone is trespassing and interfering with my animals."

"Well, I never!" Lizzie couldn't stop sputtering long

enough to utter a coherent statement. Her petting increased in speed but not in intensity.

"You're right. You should never have—"

"Wait just a minute. Your *mudder* said I could visit with the puppies while I wait for her to finish mopping the floors. She gave me permission to be here."

"They aren't her dogs."

Even though he had mumbled, Lizzie heard every syllable. "I guess you'll have to take that up with her. But for your information, I am not trespassing. Hard as it may be for you to believe, Mary invited me here today. I am a guest, not a trespasser."

"*Hmpf! Her* guest."

This time Lizzie barely caught his words. Why was he so grumpy? Was he that protective of his dogs? Did he get up on the wrong side of the bed this morning? Did he dislike her that much? Her breath caught and her heart wrenched at that last thought. But why should they? The man was being perfectly unreasonable and overbearing. That's all there was to it.

Lizzie couldn't help but giggle when the puppy hopped up and slurped her tongue across Lizzie's cheek. At least the puppy liked her. She looked back at the big man who still stood glaring at her. "I wasn't hurting your puppies. You should at least know me well enough to understand how much I care about animals."

"These puppies are raised to be working dogs."

"But they're practically newborns."

"That might be, but I start their training right away, learning to obey commands and such, before I hand them over to the professionals."

"Oh. I don't think I interfered with that. I'm only

showing them some affection. I hope that's okay."
She hung her head. Her penitence was genuine. She
certainly hadn't set out to thwart Stephen's work with
the dogs. Now she felt awful. If she had set the puppies
back in their training she would be so angry with herself.

"*Ach*, Lizzie! There you are on the ground again.
Those animals are too rambunctious. Stephen, help
her up."

"I'm okay, Mary. The puppies didn't knock me
down." Lizzie gnawed on her tongue to keep herself
from telling Mary her surly son had caused her to
assume the unladylike position this time.

Stephen hesitantly reached out a hand that Lizzie
promptly ignored. She set the puppy on the ground
and gave her one last pat. She pushed herself to her
feet under her own steam. Stephen snatched back
his hand. Lizzie almost smiled. "Ready, Mary?" She
brushed off her dress, mumbled another apology to
Stephen, and marched to the house with all the dignity
she could muster.

Why had he snarled at her like some big mangy
mutt? She hadn't been harming the puppies in the
least. She had actually looked kind of cute sitting there
surrounded by eager puppies. That runt had sure taken
to her. Stephen's lips stretched into an unbidden smile
that he quickly wiped from his face. He didn't want
Lizzie sitting in *his* dog pen looking cute with *his*
dogs. He didn't want her here, period. He sure hoped
Mamm quickly learned all she needed to learn about

that loom so Lizzie Fisher could stay in her Amish community where she belonged.

He leaned down to absently stroke the *mudder* retriever, who had approached for a little attention of her own. Lizzie had appeared to be contrite and maybe a little deflated when she trotted off. It could be possible that he had *kumm* down a little too hard, a bit too gruff. Nothing he could do about that now.

"Don't mind Stephen." Mary squeezed Lizzie's hand. "He's a little persnickety when it pertains to his dogs." She laughed.

A little? How about a lot? Lizzie merely nodded.

"I probably should have checked with him before telling you to go into the pen, but you're such an animal lover that I knew you would be fine with the pups."

Lizzie smiled. She didn't want to take on Stephen's grumpy mood. "I'm sure Stephen wants the puppies to be cared for just right so they can complete their training without problems. They really are adorable." Too bad she couldn't say the same for their caregiver.

"They are indeed. The runt seems as taken with you as you are with her."

"Her? I wasn't sure if that one was a girl, but I thought it might be."

"*Jah.* That one's a girl. Stephen didn't tell you?"

"I didn't ask. Does she have a name?"

"I haven't heard Stephen say. Sometimes I think he hesitates to name them because that might make it harder to part with them."

"That makes sense."

"Maybe he'll let you name that one."

Lizzie's eyebrows shot upward. "I doubt it," she

mumbled. He probably wouldn't even allow her back into the pen to play with the puppies again. Was he so surly with everyone, or had she done something to irritate him? "Probably me."

"What, dear?"

"Uh, let me see how you've done with your weaving." Lizzie needed to get her mind off of cantankerous Stephen Zimmerman.

Mary had progressed so quickly that Lizzie only needed to offer a few pointers; the woman seemed well on her way to mastering this new skill. But Mary's confidence still lagged, so Lizzie agreed to visit again. Right now, though, she needed to get home to help with supper preparations. She didn't want to be late and further irritate Frannie or Mamm. Apparently she possessed a real talent for irritating people. Lizzie planned to steer clear of Stephen as she waited for her ride to return, but she sure would like to see the puppies again.

Ignoring her brain's admonitions, Lizzie's feet carried her closer to the dog pen. She simply couldn't ignore the eager eyes watching her every move, the happy dance performed for her benefit, or the excited tail thumping the ground. "Hey, Sunny." Lizzie didn't dare enter the pen, but she might be able to wiggle her hand through the fence to pet the puppy once more before she left.

"What did you call my dog?"

Chapter Eighteen

Lizzie jumped back like she'd laid her hand on a hot stove. She banged into a wall of muscle behind her. A large hand grasped each of her upper arms to keep her steady on her feet. She hazarded a sideways glance into the blue eyes of the tall man who kept her upright. "You have a habit of sneaking up on people."

"I don't sneak."

"It sure seems that way to me." She tugged against his hold. "You can turn me loose now."

Stephen dropped his hands and took two steps backward. "What did you call the pup?"

As if on cue, the puppy yipped and jumped.

"I-I called her Sunny." Lizzie kept her eyes averted and rushed to explain. "I'm not naming her, of course. I certainly wouldn't be that presumptuous, but look at her. All the puppies are adorable, but this one has such a sunny disposition. She's always excited and happy. I even think she smiles." Lizzie snagged her lower lip between her teeth. She'd been babbling like an idiot. Stephen would surely believe she had lost her mind. Hesitantly, she raised her eyes to his face, expecting to find a mocking expression.

"I think you're right."

Was he actually grinning? More surprising, was he actually agreeing with her? "I am?"

"This little runt is always glad for any scrap of attention. I'm not sure she will make a *gut* service dog, though."

"Why not? She will probably be very gentle and loyal."

"Most golden retrievers are."

"Then why couldn't she be used?" Lizzie's heart ached for the little dog. This must be how parents feel when the schoolteacher tells them their little one can't learn.

"She's so small. I'm not sure how strong she will be. The vet said she's healthy, but I'll have to see how much stamina she has. Ultimately, it will be up to the professionals to decide."

Sadness dropped over Lizzie like a shroud. A mountainous lump clogged her throat. "What will happen to her if they can't use her? They don't get rid of the dogs they can't use, do they?" Surely they wouldn't do that. She'd heard of puppy mills, but didn't know much about them. Surely they would not be so inhumane. She couldn't believe Stephen could possibly be connected to any group that mistreated animals. He acted as if he truly cared about them. He had risked his life for kittens, hadn't he? But then, he didn't really know about the kittens when he followed her to the burning house. Lizzie jumped again when a big hand patted her shoulder.

"They try to find homes for the dogs who don't make it as service dogs. I wouldn't work with a group that didn't treat animals right."

"Whew! That's a relief." Lizzie's shoulder tingled even though the big hand was no longer patting it.

She should put a little more distance between them, but the puppy captured her attention before she could move. All the other puppies had dropped in exhaustion to doze in the sunshine near their *mudder*. Not the little runt, though. She chased her tail and then chased a dried brown leaf blowing around the pen. Lizzie laughed aloud. She almost startled yet again at the sudden deep chuckle behind her.

"I suppose if I kept her, Sunny would be a right fitting name for her."

Lizzie gazed up into the clear blue eyes. A smile continued to tug at Stephen's lips. My, he was handsome! The softened expression made his face even more appealing. She lost her train of thought and had to glance away for a moment to recall it. "Don't you ever want to keep the puppies?"

"Sure. There are usually at least one or two in every litter I have an especially hard time letting go. But I'm raising them for a reason. They usually only stay with me a few weeks after they are weaned so they can start their specific training as young as possible. Occasionally a litter stays a bit longer while waiting for the trainers to be free."

That was probably the longest speech Lizzie had ever heard Stephen make. He certainly grew animated when talking about the dogs. Being an animal lover was definitely a point in his favor—if Lizzie had been keeping tabs, that is. "I hope this litter stays around awhile." She wasn't sure why she whispered the words. It certainly wasn't like she would be invited over to play with the puppies, but she would be returning soon to help Mary.

"*Jah*, this has been an especially fine litter."

"If Sunny doesn't get accepted for training, will you keep her?"

"I haven't kept any dogs yet. The organization usually finds some other way to use the dogs or else finds homes for them."

"Oh." Lizzie truly would like to keep tabs on the puppy. If Sunny stayed here, Lizzie could always use the excuse of helping Mary to visit the dog. "She's special." Lizzie whispered the words so was surprised and embarrassed that Stephen heard them.

"That she is." He removed his straw hat and ran a hand through his thick, dark hair. He plopped the hat back on his head. "So have you sketched any puppy pictures yet?"

Lizzie gasped. "Shhh! That's my secret." Unfortunately, Stephen now knew it. She prayed he hadn't shared that little tidbit with anyone.

"It's okay. Only animals are close by. Don't worry. I haven't announced your secret talent to anyone. I'd really like to see any pictures you draw of the pups, though."

This nice Stephen took Lizzie by surprise. Had he let down his guard and allowed an amenable man to emerge? What a refreshing change! She searched for her voice but only managed a tiny croak. "Why?"

"You are a *gut* artist. You know that I still have your kitten drawing."

If she couldn't get her brain and mouth to communicate soon, she was going to look like the most unintelligent person on earth. Stephen already considered her a silly little girl. He didn't need to add "hopelessly stupid" to his list of descriptions of her. Not that she should care.

"And it is still in my workshop."

"Not on display for the whole world to see, I hope."
Out of fear, the words poured out.

"You aren't ashamed of the picture, are you?"

"Not of the picture." She dropped her gaze to her
foot, which circled in the dirt. "I should be ashamed
of myself, though, for drawing in the first place."

"But you aren't."

"How can something as harmless as drawing be
wrong? How can something that brings me peace and
joy be so awful? It's okay for me to design items to
weave and quilt, but I can't draw pictures of the Lord
Gott's creations. What is so horribly, awfully sinful
about that?" Lizzie gasped and slapped both hands
over her mouth. She hadn't intended to say any of
that. The words had sort of taken on a life of their own
and wrestled one another to jump out of her mouth.
Her cheeks burned. Tears clouded her vision. She
couldn't be more mortified if she fell into a hog pen
and got covered with stinky muck.

Lizzie bit her lip hard to stop its trembling. If she
didn't gain control soon, she'd start blubbering like a
boppli. A surprisingly gentle tug on her chin forced her
to look up. Stephen's expression showed concern. A
tiny smile tugged at the corners of his lips. Lizzie was
spellbound. "I-I'm sorry."

"Don't be. That's the feisty Lizzie I know who runs
through brambles that tear into her arms and dashes
into a smoke- and flame-filled building without regard
for her own safety."

"I figured you considered that a foolish venture that
could have gotten me, uh, us killed."

"As you pointed out to me several times that day, I
was not forced to tag along with you. I entered that
house on your heels by my own choice."

"Sorry." Standing so close to Stephen Zimmerman with his hand still holding her chin made even breathing difficult.

"Stop apologizing. There isn't any need. You and I and the kittens are safe and sound, and the day is only a memory now. As for your outburst a moment ago . . ."

Lizzie tried to look down, but he tilted her chin higher. She had to look at him or roll her eyes to the sky. That might actually be the best option.

"You don't need to apologize for that, either."

"I-I was wrong to question."

"I don't think so. And I honestly don't see the harm in drawing your pictures."

"A-are you allowed to do that? I mean in the Mennonite church?"

"I'm not sure. I never asked. I only draw designs of the furniture I'm planning to build. I am certainly allowed to do that."

"But that's for your work."

"We read books. Little ones have picture books. Hey! There's a logical explanation. If picture books are all right, why aren't drawings?"

"The authors and illustrators of those books are probably not Amish or Mennonite." Lizzie tried to be practical even though a little spark of hope ignited in her soul. Would the bishop and ministers be okay with her artwork if she likened the idea to books? They were allowed to read, usually books pertaining to nature or gardening, or even inspirational fiction. Maybe comparing her art to illustrations in books was an idea she could chew on later.

"I don't know, Lizzie. Some of the books I've seen around are fairy tales. They certainly aren't written by

Plain people. I can see what my *mudder* might know about all of this."

"You can't!"

"I won't tell her about your drawings. But I can tell you for sure and for certain she would not hold that against you in any way. Mamm is fair and open to new ideas—within reason, of course. And she's loyal. If you are her *freind* now, you will always be her *freind*."

Lizzie had sensed all those things about Mary even though she hadn't known the woman long. She had also picked up on a creative flair. Mary experimented with colors and patterns in her quilts and probably would do the same with her weaving. Even the Mennonite ladies' dresses were a little fancier than those of the Amish. Oh, they all wore the same style, which was similar to but not exactly the same as what the Amish wore, but Mennonites were allowed to have small prints on their fabric. They didn't have to stick to only solid colors.

A buggy traveling a little faster than expected rumbled up the driveway, interrupting all conversation. Lizzie squinted to identify the driver—not that she would actually know the person. She could tell from the black buggy that he would be Mennonite. From the scowl on the young man's face, she deduced he was not a happy person.

"*Nee.* Generally he isn't."

Lizzie gasped. Had she spoken that thought aloud? She'd better pay more attention. "I didn't mean anything bad. In fact, I didn't mean to voice the thought at all."

"It's okay, and you are exactly right."

"Do you know him?"

"He's my older *bruder*, Seth."

"Why does he look so, uh, so . . ."

"Mean?"

"I was going to say 'miserable.' Or maybe he's deep in thought or had a bad day."

"Then every day must be a bad day."

From the quick glimpse she got, Lizzie thought the man's face would be quite pleasant if the snarl was erased. In fact, it seemed he looked a lot like Stephen. Did he have the same blue eyes? "Are things not well with him? Oops! I'm sorry. That is none of my business. It's a shame to be so young and so unhappy."

"Seth is twenty-five, two years older than me, and he hasn't found what he wants to do with his life. So generally, he frowns and stomps around and tries to make everyone else miserable."

"That sounds like Frannie."

"Who?"

"My older *schweschder*. She's been down in the dumps lately and tries to drag everyone else down there with her."

"Maybe we should introduce them to each other."

Stephen chuckled, but Lizzie entertained the idea. Frannie needed to meet someone new and get her mind off of Aaron Kurtz. Seth appeared to be in need of a *freind*. Could two gloomy people be *gut* for each other? *Ach!* What was she thinking? "Your *mamm* would be heartbroken if your *bruder* had to be shunned for leaving the community. I know my *mudder* would be beside herself if Frannie left. Frannie got baptized and joined the church a year ago."

"Seth hasn't joined yet."

"What?"

"I joined already, but Seth hasn't made the commitment yet."

"So he wouldn't be shunned."

"I don't suppose so. A few people have left and stayed in the area. Since they hadn't joined the church, they can associate with the rest of us."

"How interesting. You've joined but Seth hasn't. We're the opposite. Frannie has joined but I haven't."

"Because of your art?"

Lizzie shrugged. She'd unintentionally voiced her thoughts again. How could she bridle her tongue? It always wanted to spout out any thought that entered her mind. She'd have to add that to her prayer list. Oops! Stephen was staring at her, waiting for an answer. "I guess because of my art. I'm not ready to give that up yet, and I don't want to be deceitful. If I sneak around to draw or paint, I'll be going against the Ordnung. Right now, I might be reprimanded, but I haven't yet vowed to uphold all the tenets of our faith."

"So you didn't feel deceitful hiding your art supplies in an abandoned house with feral cats?"

Heat spread from Lizzie's toes all the way up to her cheeks. "I, uh . . ."

Stephen patted her arm and smiled a broad smile that lit his face and made his blue eyes dance. "I'm teasing, Lizzie. I don't see anything wrong with your art, so I don't believe you are deceitful at all. Besides, if you haven't spoken any vows, you aren't breaking any promises."

Lizzie blew out the breath she'd been holding. A little giggle escaped behind it. "I like your way of thinking. You know, you can be quite pleasant when you want to be." Now her cheeks burned like fire. She should cut out her tongue and fling it into the woods.

Stephen burst out laughing. "See, Lizzie, you don't

have a deceitful bone in your body. You don't hide your thoughts at all."

"Maybe I should. I didn't mean anything bad. Sometimes you are a bit grumpy, but we all are." Lizzie kept digging the hole deeper. She wished she could drop into a hole right now and pull it in behind her.

Stephen laughed again. "I'm sure you're right. Before you apologize again, let me tell you that you don't need to hide your thoughts around me—or your artwork or your kittens or whatever other stray animals you've encountered."

Lizzie should be relieved that Stephen let her off the proverbial hook, but she was still a little peeved with herself. He could have taken offense at her words. Any of them. All of them. But he didn't, thank goodness. He laughed. Amazing!

"So how can we devise a way to get Snarly Seth to meet Ferocious Frannie?"

Chapter Nineteen

Was Stephen serious? Lizzie had never played matchmaker in all her life. Nor had she ever wanted to do so. Frannie would be mortified, wouldn't she? Lizzie pondered the idea for a moment. Maybe Frannie would be grateful to have someone intervene on her behalf. Before she could reply, Stephen shouted out to his *bruder*.

"Hey, Seth!"

The other young man glanced their way. Lizzie could see the frown still in place, only it had deepened into more of a scowl. Perhaps this fellow wouldn't be at all right for Frannie. But then again, Frannie wore a grumpy expression most of the time, too.

By the time Seth reached them, his brow had smoothed significantly. *Gut* manners must have won out over his mood. He wasn't quite as handsome as Stephen, but without the scowl, his appearance was quite nice. His eyes were dark brown instead of blue.

"Seth, this is Lizzie Fisher."

"You're the one helping Mamm with the loom. She's talked about you nonstop."

Not sure how to respond, Lizzie merely offered, "Mary is doing fine with her weaving."

"Nice to meet you." Seth turned toward the house.

Was that the extent of the pleasantries he could exchange? "Nice to meet you, too."

"Wait, Seth. Why don't you stay and talk to us?" Stephen called.

Lizzie raised an eyebrow but didn't voice her question. What was Stephen up to? Seth obviously wanted to get away.

Seth hesitated and then turned back. "Do you want to talk about anything in particular?"

Stephen looked at Lizzie as if he expected her to fill in the silence. What was she supposed to say? "Uh, so, what do you do?" Lame question. She might as well have asked about the weather.

"I work at the feed mill."

"Do you like it there?" Why wasn't Stephen jumping in to rescue her?

Seth shrugged. "It's a job."

"It sounds like you'd rather do something else." There went that runaway tongue again.

"Maybe. Stephen, did you need me for something?"

Stephen cleared his throat. Twice. "I thought you might like to get to know Lizzie. Were you aware that she weaves all sorts of things to sell?"

"Mamm mentioned that at least several times."

"Right. She has an older *schweschder* named Frannie, too."

So this was where Stephen was going. He was trying to turn the conversation to Frannie? Why? Was he merely trying to gauge Seth's reaction?

"That's nice. Does she weave, too?"

"*Nee.* She doesn't have any interest in weaving, but she's an excellent baker. She's providing baked items for Yoder's Store."

Stephen jumped back into the conversation. "We'll have to try that out next time we're in that area, huh, Seth?"

"Sure."

"Maybe I'll bring you some treats next time I help Mary with the loom." Lizzie forced a smile. What an awkward situation! She would only feel relief if the earth opened and swallowed her.

"Anything else, Stephen?" Seth's eyes darted from his *bruder* to Lizzie.

"*Nee.* You can go ahead inside."

"*Danki* for your permission." Seth shook his head as he loped off toward the house.

"Well, how did that go over?"

Lizzie wrinkled her nose. "Like ants at a Fourth of July picnic."

"That well, huh?"

"It looks like my ride is here. Have fun explaining to your *bruder* what that was all about."

Stephen's gaze followed Lizzie to the big blue van that pulled to a stop near the back door of the house. *Jah*, Seth was bound to have questions. The first one would most likely deal with Stephen's sanity or lack thereof. Stephen sighed. Thoughts of Seth got pre-empted by the violet-eyed girl who smiled out the window at him. He'd better purge that image immediately.

After the fiasco with Joanna Brubacher, Stephen had vowed not to look at or think about another girl for a long time. He did not plan to have his heart trounced and handed back to him as flat as a pancake ever again. It had taken him ages to plump it back up and encase it in a hard shell.

Despite his best efforts to remain aloof, Stephen chuckled at the memory of Lizzie's expression when he asked how that ridiculous conversation with Seth had gone. Her scrunched-up face had made her freckles dance across her slightly upturned nose. And why couldn't she have ordinary mud brown eyes? Those unusual violet ones threatened to bore through his carefully erected shell. He could not let that happen.

Lizzie had said she would be back. Knowing Mamm, she'd keep the girl returning if only for the female companionship. But he had a hunch Lizzie and Mamm had forged a bond that went beyond their love of weaving. He was glad Lizzie would return—for his *mudder*'s sake, of course.

What about for your own sake? a little voice whispered in his brain.

Absolutely not!

Lizzie came to help Mamm. If he and Lizzie hurried to hatch a plot to link Frannie and Seth, he would be able to avoid her altogether. If Lizzie's *schweschder* could make his *bruder* happy, he'd risk a few more meetings with her.

Stephen turned back toward his shop. A forlorn little fur ball pressed her nose against the fence. Could a puppy feel lonely? Little Sunny, as Lizzie had dubbed her, didn't seem so cheerful at the moment. Could she miss Lizzie? Impossible! She had her puppy siblings to play with. Stephen's eyes followed the puppy's gaze. Sunny sat stone still, watching the big blue van disappear from sight.

He detoured to the dog pen and reached through the fence to pet the fuzzy little head. "You miss her, huh, girl? Don't worry. She'll be back." But had he spoken the words to comfort the dog or himself?

Lizzie blew out a sigh and then wished she hadn't. She glanced up at the rearview mirror and experienced great relief that the driver hadn't heard her. Patti seemed absorbed in the music leaking from the radio speakers. Whatever had possessed Lizzie to go along with Stephen's harebrained scheme to connect Seth and Frannie? Her *schweschder* would undoubtedly throw a huge fit if she ever found out. Besides, was it even possible for two negative people to end up with a positive relationship?

She leaned her head against the cool, vibrating window. She supposed there wouldn't actually be any harm in Frannie meeting Seth. Whatever happened after that would be up to them. Probably nothing, since Frannie would never forsake her commitment to the church, and it would be highly unlikely for Seth to want to become Amish. *Lizzie, you keep getting yourself into one mess after another.*

Lizzie bolted upright when the radio announcer gave the time.

"Are you okay?" Patti's concerned face peered at her in the mirror.

"Did he give the correct time?"

Lizzie saw Patti's eyes drop to the dashboard and then back to the mirror. "Yes, he did. Why?"

"Nothing." She didn't want Patti to feel bad about Lizzie's own tardiness, but she was so late. Again!

Chapter Twenty

"*Nee*, Mamm, you can't! Lizzie will be so upset!"

Lizzie heard Nancy's wail as soon as she jerked open the back door of the house. What had distressed Nancy, and why would *she* be upset? Was that Sadie sniffing?

"Lizzie will get over it, and you will be fetching a switch if you sass me again."

"I don't mean to sass, Mamm. Honest. Just please don't get rid of the kittens."

Lizzie's heart leaped to her throat and lodged there, threatening to cut off her oxygen supply. Why was Mamm planning to get rid of the kittens? She rushed into the kitchen. Her eyes did a quick sweep of the room to take in the entire picture. Nancy and Sadie stood facing Mamm with their hands clasped tightly together. Normally, a scowl such as Mamm wore right now would send the little girls scurrying for cover. The situation must be grave indeed.

When she shifted her eyes slightly, Lizzie spotted Frannie standing in front of the wood cookstove twisting a quilted pot holder all out of shape. Although Frannie's attitude was one of disinterest, Lizzie could tell by the set of her mouth that her *schweschder* was taking in every detail of the unfolding drama.

"What happened?" Lizzie's heart pounded.

"*Ach*, Lizzie! Mamm wants to send the kittens away!" Nancy towed Sadie behind her as she ran to Lizzie. She buried her head in her big *schweschder*'s cloak.

Lizzie patted Nancy's back. She looked from the little girls to Frannie to Mamm. She forced herself to speak calmly, though she really wanted to shriek. "Will someone please tell me what's going on?"

Nancy heaved a shuddering sigh, sniffed, and spoke into Lizzie's cloak. "Frannie said she got scratched by one of the kittens, but I'm sure it was an accident. She probably stepped on its tail or something. Anyway the scratch is a little, bitty thing and couldn't possibly hurt that much." The little girl finally stopped speaking to drag in a gulp of air. How could she say so much in one breath?

"Hush, Nancy!" Mamm's scowl deepened. "If animals are going to scratch or bite, they don't belong here."

"Let me see." Lizzie broke free from Nancy's grasp. She crossed the room to Frannie in three quick strides. She grabbed the pot holder from Frannie's hands and flung it onto the counter. "Where?" She turned Frannie's hands over and over searching for a wound. Frannie tried to pull her hand away, but Lizzie held fast. "I don't see anything."

"Here." Frannie turned her hand over.

"Where?"

"Right there on my wrist."

"This tiny mark?" Lizzie pointed to a surface scratch about half an inch long and scarcely red at all. "This? This teensy weensy mark? Really? Frannie, you've had worse paper cuts than this."

"Well, it hurt."

"Honestly?"

Frannie hung her head. "*Jah.*"

"What difference does it make if it hurts or not? She got scratched, and we can't have that," Mamm snapped. "What if it was one of the little ones who got hurt?"

"Ruff has scratched me before, Mamm, and it didn't really hurt," Sadie ventured.

"And she didn't even cry. Ruff didn't get sent away," Nancy added.

Lizzie feared Nancy had gone too far this time. She rushed in before Nancy could incriminate herself further or be sent out to select a switch. "Mamm, kittens play. They don't aim to hurt anyone. And if they are provoked, they try to defend themselves."

"So you think your *schweschder* provoked the kitten? Is that what you're saying?"

"Of course not. I'm not saying Frannie deliberately did anything to the kitten." *Though she probably did.* "But you know kittens. They can get spooked at the strangest things." Lizzie ignored the daggers Frannie hurled at her with her eyes. For a split second, Lizzie regretted helping her older *schweschder* get out of going to stay with Aenti Grace. Perhaps a little time away would have been *gut* for her. And *gut* for Lizzie and the kittens, too.

"Huh!" Mamm crossed her arms over her chest. "Those kittens weave in and out around our feet whenever we go outside. They are going to make someone fall. And with cold weather upon us, they'll try to run into the house every time the door opens."

Mamm had built quite a case against the darling kittens. Frannie's minute scratch must be the icing on the cake, so to speak. Didn't Mamm have any pets growing up? Lizzie tried to figure out a way to ask without sounding insolent.

"Kittens only want attention. Didn't you have any pets when you were a little girl?" Leave it to Nancy. Her tongue misbehaved more than Lizzie's. When Mamm didn't answer right away, Nancy continued. "Didn't you have a cat or a dog or a rabbit or any critter you cared about?" Nancy's foot tapped on the oak floor. She kept her eyes fixed on their *mudder*.

Lizzie swallowed her gasp. Surely Nancy would be in boiling water now. How could Lizzie defuse this situation before Mamm exploded? Obviously, Frannie had no intention of stepping in. "Nancy, why don't you and Sadie help me make sure the kittens have food and water before we set the table?" She jerked her head toward the door.

"But, Lizzie, I—"

"Nancy, *kumm*," Lizzie cut her off. The girl apparently hadn't caught on that Lizzie was trying to save her hide—her backside, at least. She grabbed Nancy's hand and tugged her toward the door. Sadie still clung to Nancy's other hand, so she stumbled along as the caboose of the train of girls. Lizzie glanced over her shoulder. "Which kitten did the dastardly deed, Frannie?"

"That motley one."

"Tortoiseshell. She's a tortie." Lizzie shook her head and clicked her tongue. She'd better tow this train outside before her own mouth got them into trouble. But she couldn't resist one little barb. "Is that meat loaf I smell burning?"

"*Ach*, Frannie!" Mamm's attention was instantly diverted. "Grab that pan from the oven before our supper is ruined."

Lizzie had another forgiveness request to add to tonight's prayers. She hustled the little girls out the door.

"Miriam didn't mean to hurt Frannie, ain't so?" Sadie's eyes brimmed with tears poised to run down her cheeks.

"I'm sure she didn't, dear one. Kittens like to play."

"*Hmpf!* Frannie didn't look too hurt to me." Nancy stomped a foot for emphasis. Lizzie agreed but didn't say so.

"Will Mamm make you get rid of the kittens? I don't want them to go away." At least one tear escaped and trickled down Sadie's cheek.

"I don't want them to go away, either." Lizzie had risked her life to save the kittens. She certainly didn't want to abandon them now.

"Let's talk to Daed. He likes animals. Why, I even saw him playing with the kittens a time or two." Nancy squeezed Lizzie's fingers. "Would you talk to him?"

"I'll try. Let's let everyone calm down a bit. Don't mention the kittens at supper, and ignore Frannie if she does. Talk about school or anything else. I'll try to talk to Daed before he goes to bed."

"Is Miriam okay?" Nancy squatted down to pet the tortoiseshell kitten rubbing against their legs. Since Sadie still clutched Nancy's hand, she squatted, too.

"Why wouldn't she be?" Lizzie bent to get a closer look at the purring kitten. Immediately Molly and Annie trotted over to be included in the petting.

"Mean ol' Frannie might have hurt her," Nancy mumbled.

"I don't think Frannie would intentionally hurt a kitten." All the same, Lizzie leaned a little closer for further inspection. Once she deemed the kitten fine, she turned her attention to the other two mewing kittens. She scooped up Annie and placed her in Sadie's arms, then cradled Molly in her own.

Nancy held Miriam close and kissed the fuzzy little head. "Did mean ol' Frannie hurt you?"

Lizzie couldn't let the little girls continue to malign their oldest *schweschder*, even though she sometimes had misgivings about Frannie herself. "Nancy, I really don't believe Frannie is a mean person. I don't think she would harm an animal or a person. Some people simply aren't very fond of animals."

"That's *narrisch*!"

"Not crazy, just different. Not everyone likes the same things. Sadie adores strawberry ice cream. Do you?"

Nancy wrinkled her nose. "Ick! I like chocolate."

"See? You and Sadie don't like the same flavor of ice cream, but that doesn't mean one of you is a bad person, ain't so?"

"I guess." Nancy kissed the kitten again. "But who wouldn't like sweet little kittens?"

"Mamm." Lizzie thought Sadie hadn't been paying attention to them, but her single whispered word proved otherwise. "Why doesn't Mamm like animals?" She rocked the kitten in her arms.

"I don't know, Sadie. Maybe she didn't have pets growing up. Or maybe she got hurt or frightened by an animal." Lizzie shrugged. She'd probably never know the answer. If Mamm didn't want to tell them something, wild horses wouldn't be able to drag it out of her. Lizzie sighed. "We'd better get these kitties settled for the night and go set the table."

Lizzie paused in brushing her hair when Frannie entered their shared bedroom. Frannie watched her feet and never lifted her gaze to meet Lizzie's stare. *She ought to be ashamed to look me in the eye. She didn't have any reason to do what she did.* Lizzie mentally counted backward from twenty to give herself a bit more time before speaking.

Frannie shuffled to her bed and pulled back the covers. She snatched the *kapp* off her head and yanked out the hairpins securing her bun. She shook her head so that dark hair tumbled down, forming a tent to hide behind.

You ought to hide. Lizzie started at twenty again. Why didn't Frannie at least apologize or mumble some sort of explanation? Did she dislike the kittens so much that she'd do anything to make sure Mamm sent them away? Was she angry with Lizzie for some reason?

Lizzie flipped through the pages of her memory. She couldn't locate a single instance—lately, anyway— where she might possibly have offended Frannie. She'd had such hopes that the two of them could be closer after Frannie's meltdown. Apparently not. Frannie was still behaving as if that brief moment of bonding had never occurred.

Frannie continued to avert her gaze and remained silent. Like Lizzie was in the wrong! She got to twelve in her third countdown, but her tongue could not stay bridled any longer. She marched over to stand right in front of Frannie. She balled her hands into fists and planted them on her hips. She fixed her *schweschder* with a glare. "Do you want to tell me what that was all about?"

Chapter Twenty-One

"Do you want to tell me what that was all about?"

Stephen had just pulled off his shoes. He'd had a busy day and hoped to avoid any confrontation with Seth. How did he tell his *bruder* he'd been attempting to play matchmaker? That would not go over well at all. He decided to play dumb instead. "Tell you what what was about?"

"'*Kumm* meet Lizzie,'" Seth's voice singsonged. "Or how about 'She has an older *schweschder* who bakes delectable treats'?" He paused to run a hand through his hair. "Or—this is my favorite one—'We'll have to stop in and try some.'"

Stephen shrugged. His brain hadn't yet concocted any plausible explanations.

"How often are we in the Amish community to try anything?"

"It isn't like it's on the moon. And we do occasionally have business out that way, you know."

"Maybe you do. What were you trying to do?"

"I was only trying to be sociable. Lizzie was waiting for her ride. I thought it would be polite to keep her company while she waited."

"You can do better than that."

"Huh?"

"You can invent a better excuse. Do you want to try again?"

Not really. "I don't have anything else to say." Because if he spoke the truth, Seth would be as mad as that cranky old hen they once had that had squawked and pecked every time Stephen tried to gather eggs.

"If you're trying to fix me up with Lizzie, forget it."

Lizzie? Stephen started. He sure hadn't meant to give that impression, but he couldn't very well say, *Frannie, not Lizzie,* even if the words were on the tip of his tongue. "I wasn't trying to fix you up with Lizzie." He hoped he didn't emphasize the last word, but from Seth's reaction, he must have.

"If not Lizzie, then who?" After a pause, Seth continued. "I don't want to meet her *schweschder*, either, even if she can bake a peach pie fit for a king. I can find my own girl, if I want one."

Stephen half expected Seth to stomp his foot and storm off like he used to do when he was young. "'If'? Don't you want to get married and have a family?"

Seth shrugged. "Someday, I suppose, but I'll find my own girl when I'm ready."

"I haven't seen any evidence of that happening." Stephen mumbled his thoughts before he could censor them.

"I don't see you tearing out of here to court anyone."

"Maybe not, but you're older."

"By one whole year. I also haven't joined the church yet, but you have, so I'd say you were closer to marriage than I am."

"When are you going to join?"

"When I'm *gut* and ready!"

If Stephen had learned one thing about dealing with his older *bruder*, it was not to push. If Seth felt pressured, he dug in his heels and resisted anything mentioned to him. "I suppose that's a fair answer."

Seth nodded and strode from the room.

Whew! Close one! Stephen had barely managed to preserve his own civility. He truly did believe Seth needed help finding a girl if he was ever going to get married. Could Lizzie's *schweschder* be the one who could tame him?

"Do you want to tell me why you're glaring at me like you could lop my head off and feed it to the buzzards?"

Lizzie blinked and tried to soften her expression. "You honestly don't have any idea why I'm upset?"

Frannie pushed the dark hair out of her face and finally gazed at Lizzie with wide, innocent eyes. Her mouth formed an O, but not a single sound came out, not even a gasp. She pulled her hair across one shoulder and began to braid it. "Did someone say something at supper to raise your dander?"

You raise my dander! Twenty was not a high enough number. Lizzie took a deep breath, held it, and let it out ever so slowly. She spoke as softly as she could. "Frannie, you know very well I am upset about the molehill you turned into a mountain."

"The what?"

"Don't pretend you don't understand! Why did you have to make a big deal over that tiny scratch? Why did you have to say anything about it to Mamm at all? You knew how she would react. You knew she would say the kittens would have to go. Haven't you seen how much

Nancy and Sadie love the kittens? How much I love them?" Lizzie's voice broke. She did not want to cry now. Maybe after Frannie fell asleep. She sniffed hard. "H-how could you be so cruel?" Lizzie turned away. She didn't even want to look at Frannie, and she certainly didn't want to shed tears in front of her.

"I-I'm sorry, Lizzie."

Confused, Lizzie kept silent. Was Frannie sorry Lizzie was upset? Was she sorry the kittens would have to go? Was she sorry she'd made such a big deal over a miniscule scratch that hadn't even broken the skin? Or was she sorry she'd been in such a lousy mood lately and made everyone else suffer along with her?

"Did you hear me, Lizzie?"

Lizzie felt a hand on her shoulder. She wanted to shrug it off but didn't. "I heard you. What exactly are you apologizing for?"

"*Ach*, for everything! I shouldn't have mentioned that silly scratch to Mamm. That was worse than a scholar on the playground tattling to the teacher because he didn't get a turn at a game."

"Why did you do it? Did you want to hurt me or Nancy and Sadie that much?"

Frannie's hand dropped from Lizzie's shoulder. "I didn't want to hurt anyone. I was in a bad mood and complaining about everything. When I went outside, I accidentally stepped on the kitten. I bent down to pet her, and she scratched me."

"It didn't even break the skin! There wasn't a single drop of blood. You didn't even cover it with a bandage."

"*Nee.*"

"Why did you tell Mamm? You knew she didn't like animals to begin with. I had to work hard to convince her to let the kittens stay. You knew one little slipup and Mamm would make me relocate them."

"I shouldn't have said anything. I'm sorry."

"Go tell that to Nancy and Sadie. They're probably sobbing into their pillows." Lizzie hadn't intended to heap guilt on Frannie's head, but she needed to be aware of the repercussions of her actions. The girl had always been a little spoiled—at least to Lizzie's way of thinking—and a little selfish as a result. She needed to consider someone else's feelings for a change. Lizzie tried to calm down. Getting more upset wouldn't improve the situation. The damage had been done.

"I'll tell Mamm it was all my fault, that the kitten didn't deliberately attack me."

"You can try, but I don't think that will make a speck of difference now. Mamm had been looking for an excuse to get rid of the kittens. I only hope she'll give me time to find *gut* homes for them."

"I truly am sorry."

"Why were you in such a nasty mood that the kittens had to be your scapegoats?"

Frannie shrugged.

"Aaron again?"

Frannie nodded. "I heard through the grapevine that he might be returning to Maryland. I can't bear the thought of seeing him with someone else."

"But you two didn't have any kind of understanding, ain't so?"

Frannie shook her head. "It still hurts all the same."

"You can't believe everything you hear, you know. He might not be on his way back, and he might not have gotten married." Lizzie still didn't think Frannie had the right to be hateful to everyone else because she was upset, but she would not hold a grudge. That wouldn't be right, either.

"I'll try to talk to Mamm tomorrow. I need to bake for the store, so I'll have plenty of time to try to get her to change her mind."

"Okay, but I won't hold my breath."

Chapter Twenty-Two

"You're always delightful, dear, but today you seem a tiny bit glum. Is everything all right?"

Was Mary always so perceptive? Maybe it was a trait of all *mudders*, except for perhaps her own. Mamm seemed oblivious to Lizzie's moods or needs. "I'm sorry, Mary. I guess I have a lot on my mind."

"Do you have a lot of projects to complete for Christmas? I'm sorry if I'm keeping you from your work."

"You aren't interfering with my work at all. I do have quite a few orders, but I'm making fine progress with them. I enjoy spending time with you."

"So your troubles aren't work-related, then." Mary reached over to pat Lizzie's hand where it lay next to the loom. "I don't mean to pry, but I am a *gut* listener if you ever want to unburden yourself."

Lizzie hadn't intended to let her tongue have its way, but it seemed to have its own agenda. Mary's kindness and concern so touched Lizzie that she dropped all pretense of bravery. The words tumbled over one another as she told Mary about Frannie's trumped-up injury, Mamm's declaration that the kittens had to go, and her own inability to find homes for them. To her horror, tears sprang to Lizzie's eyes. She swiped at them and sniffed. "I-if I don't find homes by the end of the week, Mamm will have someone take them to the animal shelter."

Mary squeezed Lizzie's hand. "We can't let that happen."

"I don't know what else to do. I've asked everyone I know. The kittens really are sweet. My little *schweschders* love them almost as much as I do."

"We'll think of something."

"I've been thinking until my brain hurts."

"Well, as the saying goes, two heads are better than one. Let's let our brains wander a bit, and then we'll attack the problem again later."

"Okay." Lizzie heard the skepticism in her voice, but she'd trust Mary's judgment.

"Look at these samples." Mary produced several swatches she'd woven. "What do you think of the color scheme?" They pored over Mary's work.

Surprised she'd been distracted for so long, Lizzie looked up when Mary's stomach rumbled. "Oh my! I didn't know it had gotten so late. You probably need to prepare supper, and it sounds like you missed your noon meal."

Mary laughed. "Weaving has a way of capturing your attention, doesn't it?"

"It always does for me. I'm sorry to have stayed so long and interrupted your routine."

"You didn't do any such thing. Believe it or not, I did eat at noontime, and I have soup simmering for supper, so everything is just fine."

"I forgot all about the treats I brought." Lizzie hopped off the stool she'd been glued to for the past few hours and reached for her bag.

"You brought treats?"

"I did. I know you are a *wunderbaar* baker, Mary, but I brought some of Frannie's specialty brownies. She does something different to give them a unique flavor. She won't share her secret. She's quite an accomplished baker and is baking items to sell in our local store."

"You're amazing!"

"Me? I didn't do anything. Frannie baked these." Lizzie pulled the tin from her bag, pried off the lid, and held the container over for Mary to get a whiff of the brownies.

"You are amazing because you can still sing your *schweschder*'s praises after she did something to hurt you. You have a forgiving heart."

"That's what we're supposed to do, ain't so? We're supposed to forgive and not hold grudges."

"Indeed, but that can be difficult, especially when the wound is still open."

"I'll admit I don't always understand Frannie, and I get peeved with her almost daily, but I still love her. I don't think she's a bad person. I don't think she wants to be mean."

Mary reached into the tin to break off a chunk of a brownie. "Why do you suppose she does the things she does?"

"I've pondered that on more than one occasion. I think Frannie might be a little . . . I shouldn't talk bad about her."

"Spoiled? Selfish?"

"Maybe." Lizzie hung her head.

Mary tapped her arm. "You aren't an evil person for thinking that. Those are simply character traits, like honest or kind or forgiving."

"I guess, but they aren't very nice ones."

"Some people have those traits, though. It doesn't mean they are bad people. And it doesn't mean they can't change. I'm sure Frannie is a lovely girl if she shares any of your genetic makeup at all. When she's more mature, she'll probably lose those more childish traits."

"She's older than I am."

"Some people mature earlier than others. When I think of my sons, I know Stephen is much more mature and settled than Seth. There. I've said something about my sons that some people might not think was right, but I simply spoke the truth. I love my sons equally, but they are very different fellows. And I'm sure Aaron and Daniel will be totally different from either of the other two." Mary popped the bite of brownie into her mouth and chewed.

Lizzie's eyes never strayed from Mary's face. Did Stephen know how special his *mudder* was? How amazing it would be for a person to tell her *mamm* all her deepest thoughts and desires and know she would listen without judging. Lizzie loved her own *mudder* but couldn't imagine having a conversation with her such as she'd just had with Mary. Maybe Mamm and Frannie had that sort of relationship, but Lizzie always felt held at arm's length.

Mary's expression changed from serene to excited as she chewed the brownie. "These are delicious!"

"I told you Frannie was a skillful baker."

"I'm sure she will sell many treats if they are all as tasty as this."

"They are."

"You are a remarkable young woman, Lizzie Fisher. I hope your family realizes how special you are."

Lizzie's cheeks burned. She didn't feel special at all.

She was just Lizzie. But how *wunderbaar* to have Mary's approval!

As Mary had requested, Lizzie trotted outside bearing a brownie for Stephen. It certainly hadn't been her intention to seek him out with a gift of food. She didn't need him to get any wrong ideas. She'd make sure he understood his *mudder* had sent her out to his shop.

Lizzie paused in the doorway. Should she knock or simply poke her head inside to announce her presence? She shifted her weight from one foot to the other. She sure hoped she couldn't be observed from any windows. She surely must look pretty silly—a grown woman hopping about in indecision. She'd rather sneak around to the dog pen and play with Sunny. Knock? Don't knock?

Stephen bolted through the door, practically crashing into Lizzie and thereby removing the decision from her hands entirely. What on earth possessed him? Lizzie wobbled and clutched the brownie tighter.

"*Ach*, Lizzie!" Stephen reached out to grab her. "I didn't see you."

"Obviously."

"What were you doing lurking outside the door?"

"I wasn't lurking. You can let go of my arm now."

"Huh?"

Lizzie looked down at his big, strong hand wrapped firmly around her arm.

"Sorry." He instantly released her.

Lizzie teetered a smidgen but quickly regained her balance. A chill replaced the burning sensation in her arm. How could a simple touch create such confusing emotions and chaotic thoughts? *Focus, Lizzie. He just asked you something. What was it?* "Your *mamm* sent me out here with this." She thrust the napkin-wrapped brownie under his nose.

"Whatever it is, it sure smells *gut.*" He took the napkin from her hand.

Those silly fingers tingled when Stephen's fingers brushed them. She needed to scramble back to the house and away from this man who caused such perplexing sensations.

"Were you and Mamm baking instead of weaving?"

"I brought these from home. This is one of Frannie's specialty brownies. Mary wanted you to try one."

"Hmmm. She could have waited until I went inside, but she does occasionally bring me treats while I'm working. So this is a sample of some of the infamous Frannie's wares, is it?" He unwrapped the brownie and pinched off a bite.

Now Lizzie's quandary involved whether she should hang around to be polite or hightail it to the house. Most of her wanted to go with plan B, but a teeny part of her opted for plan A. Again, Stephen relieved her of the decision.

"This is terrific. I'll have to make sure Mamm squirrels one away for Seth before Daniel spies them. Is Frannie baking these to sell?"

"Among other things. She's planning to take her treats to Yoder's Store on Wednesdays and Saturdays."

"Wednesdays and Saturdays, huh? I might have to persuade Seth to take a little trip with me. Will she drop her treats off early in the morning?"

"Probably. The store opens at eight. I'll probably help her." Now, why did she add that bit of trivia?

Stephen wouldn't care if she was there or not. Besides, this was about Seth and Frannie.

"Hey, Lizzie, do you want to see Sunny?"

Lizzie frowned. Had she missed some thread of conversation, or had Stephen so abruptly changed the topic? She searched his face for a clue. She couldn't figure the man out. One day he snapped at her for visiting with the puppies, and now he offered to let her visit them. He even called the runt by the name she'd given her. "Sure."

Before Stephen polished off the brownie, he held out the last bite to her. "Would you like this? I'm sorry. I was such a pig. I should have offered to share with you."

"That's all right. I've had the brownies zillions of times. Please go ahead and finish." She waved toward the last chunk, which Stephen held between his thumb and forefinger.

"Tell your *schweschder* these are great." He stuffed the last bite into his mouth.

Lizzie turned aside as if suddenly absorbed in the colorful leaves clinging to the tree limbs. She didn't want him to see her smile for fear he'd think she was laughing at him. She could tell he was chewing that last morsel slowly to savor the flavor. She did the same thing.

A tug on her arm brought Lizzie's attention back to the man standing so close to her. That tingling warmth crawled up her arms again. *Step back. Turn around. Run.*

"Let's check the pups." Stephen led the way to the dog pen.

"They're getting bigger already. How is the training going?"

"Fine, except Sunny doesn't seem to keep up as well as the others."

"She's smaller. Maybe it will take her a little longer."

"That's possible."

Fear struck Lizzie's heart. She didn't want to think about what might happen if Sunny didn't catch on and couldn't be trained with the other dogs. She scanned the throng of puppies but couldn't detect Sunny. "Where is she?"

Stephen whistled. The smallest ball of fur trotted out of the doghouse.

Lizzie laughed. "Here she *kumms*." Could dogs smile?

"I think she's glad to see you. Look how happy she is. It's almost as if she is smiling at you."

Lizzie's heart skipped a beat. How could they think the same thing at practically the same time? She hazarded a glance in Stephen's direction, but he was focused on the pup. His expression clearly told how much he cared about the dogs. There couldn't be a better person for this job.

"Do you want to pet her?"

"Absolutely." Lizzie wouldn't turn down a chance to play with an animal, and this puppy had definitely captured her heart. She would be sad when the puppy left for training. Stephen must have a very hard time letting his puppies go. Sunny leaped up, nearly knocking her to the ground.

"Get down!" Stephen used a stern but not loud voice.

Instantly the puppy sat, looking at Lizzie with big, sad eyes as if she knew she had broken some rule. Lizzie wanted to kneel down, wrap her arms around the animal, and tell her it was all right, but she didn't want to undo any of Stephen's training. She searched his face for some sign. His stern expression disappeared when he smiled at Lizzie. She must have the same pitiful countenance as the dog.

"You can pet her."

Lizzie stooped down and rubbed the fuzzy little head. "What a greeting, Sunny! I missed you, too."

"She has to learn not to do that. A service dog can't be jumping on people."

"She's only a puppy. She's learning." Lizzie defended the dog as if she was Sunny's *mudder*. She would most likely be at least that protective of her own *kinner* one day.

The other puppies approached more cautiously, waiting for a signal from Stephen. Sunny must be a challenge for Stephen. But she was the sweetest, most affectionate of all the dogs.

Stephen squatted down near Lizzie. "They have been a *gut* litter. I think the service organization will be pleased with them."

"Even Sunny?"

"I'm not so sure about that. We'll have to wait and see."

I want her! Lizzie almost shouted the words, but she needed to push such thoughts far away. If Mamm wouldn't allow the kittens, who would one day be *gut* mousers, to stay, she'd never agree to a puppy. Lizzie would have to lavish as much affection as possible on Sunny whenever she visited the Zimmermans' home. Thank goodness Mary continued to request her help with the loom.

"There you are. I should have known." Mary laughed as she made her way across the yard to the dog pen.

"Stephen offered to let me visit the puppies, and I couldn't pass up the opportunity." Sunny used the momentary distraction to slurp her tongue across

Lizzie's cheek. Lizzie giggled and swiped a hand across the wet spot. She dropped her hand to Sunny's head. "You got me, didn't you?"

"See what I mean?" Stephen muttered.

"Stephen, can't you make that one mind? She's always knocking Lizzie down or getting her all gooky."

"'Gooky'?" Stephen chuckled. "I'm trying, Mamm, but this one seems to have her own agenda—especially when Lizzie is around."

"So it's my fault, is it?" Lizzie giggled again as the puppy nudged her. She successfully warded off the long pink tongue this time. "I really don't mind, Mary. I love animals. This little one might not be as quick to obey as the others, but I have a feeling she is very smart. And she's very affectionate."

"'Very determined' is more like it." Stephen jumped to his feet and held out a hand to help Lizzie up.

She hesitated for a fraction of a second, dreading but anticipating the shot of electricity bound to shoot up her arm at his touch. She would have to pretend she felt nothing. Lizzie gave Stephen her hand and let him tug her to her feet. Sure enough, the bolt struck and fingers of fire raced up her arm. Thankfully, Mary didn't seem to notice any change in Lizzie's expression.

"I suddenly realized we had not resolved your dilemma, Lizzie. We were supposed to get back to our discussion but got sidetracked."

"Dilemma?" Stephen looked from one woman to the other.

Lizzie's brain, temporarily numbed by Stephen's touch, whirred back to the business of thinking. "The kittens!"

"What's wrong with the kittens?" Stephen asked.

"Lizzie's *mudder* wants her to find other homes for them."

"Why?"

"Mamm is not really an animal lover, I guess you could say. I should be grateful she let me keep them as long as she did. I'm sure going to miss them, and so will my two little *schweschders*. Even though Daed enjoyed playing with them, too, he couldn't sway Mamm."

Lizzie had enlisted his aid, as Nancy and Sadie had urged her to do, and he had tried to reason with Mamm. In the end, though, he had given in to keep the peace. Even Frannie had appealed to Mamm, as she had promised, but once Mamm's mind was set, nothing would change it.

"Do you have an answer for Lizzie, Mamm?" Stephen snapped his fingers at Sunny, and this time the puppy sat.

"I believe I do. I'll take the kittens."

"You?" Lizzie and Stephen asked at the same time.

Mary burst out laughing. "You'd think I said I planned to flap my arms and fly to the moon. The kittens will be fine here. I've always liked cats. We certainly have plenty of room for them to play or roam about. And they will keep the barns free of mice. But best of all, Lizzie will get to see them whenever she visits."

Evidently Mary did not want their weaving sessions to end. That was fine with Lizzie. She so enjoyed Mary's company. "Will your husband mind?"

"Matthew won't mind one bit."

"Daed caters to your whims, you mean," Stephen teased.

"That, too." Mary laughed. "They shouldn't interfere with your puppies or their training, right?"

"I wouldn't think so."

"Then it's settled. Bring the kittens over whenever you're ready, Lizzie."

Lizzie scrambled out of the dog pen and threw her arms around the older woman. "*Danki* so much. I appreciate this more than you know."

"And I appreciate all your help." Mary hugged her back. "Besides, this will be another reason for you to keep visiting."

Lizzie laughed. She didn't dare turn her head to gauge Stephen's reaction. Did he smile or frown?

Chapter Twenty-Three

"I don't understand why you insisted I accompany you on this mission. It's clearly something you could accomplish on your own." Seth spoke in Pennsylvania Dutch but still kept his voice low.

Stephen always thought it was rather rude to speak in their language in front of someone who couldn't understand—not that Lester, their *Englisch* driver, would really care. With the music blasting from the radio's speakers, he probably didn't even hear them. "Relax and enjoy the ride, Bruder."

"Mamm should have made this trip with you. She's the one who wants the kittens. Besides, I thought Lizzie was supposed to bring them to our house."

Stephen couldn't reveal that he had volunteered them for this task. "It would have been a bit difficult for one girl to bring three kittens and their paraphernalia all by herself, don't you think?" If anyone could manage such a feat, though, it would be Lizzie Fisher. "If I need help with it, don't you think she would?"

Seth shrugged, obviously still perturbed by the change in his usual routine. "I should be at work, but instead I'm chasing down kittens."

How would you ever meet Frannie if you didn't accompany

me today? "Don't worry. You'll be at work before midday. A change of schedule can be *gut* for the body and mind, ain't so?"

"I like sticking to a schedule." Seth grunted and folded his arms across his chest.

"Enjoy the scenery." However much he could, with it whizzing by so quickly due to Lester's lead foot.

"I can see plenty of trees and fields at home."

Stephen elbowed his older *bruder*. "Don't be a grumpy old man."

"I'm not old."

Stephen laughed. "But you'll concede to the 'grumpy' part, huh?"

"You're not funny."

How was he ever going to get Seth out of the doldrums? Frannie would run in the opposite direction after five minutes in Seth's presence, unless she was wallowing in that same pit herself. Stephen and Lizzie would have their work cut out for them trying to get their siblings to be civil. He leaned forward as much as his seat belt would allow so Lester could hear him over the twangy music. "Say, Lester, could you stop at the country store for a minute, if you have time?"

"Sure thing. I've got all the time in the world. Since I retired from driving the school bus, my time is my own."

"*Danki*, uh, thanks." Stephen pitied the poor scholars who must have clung to their seats for dear life with Lester behind the wheel.

"Why are you prolonging this agony?" This time Seth spoke in *Englisch*. He must have figured Lester wouldn't even be able to hear a bulldozer driving alongside them.

"I thought we'd pick up a little snack."

Seth rolled his eyes but refrained from further comment. Stephen hoped they didn't arrive before Frannie and Lizzie had gotten to the store. He'd tried to time the trip exactly right, but Lester's erratic driving might have thrown them off schedule. He wanted to catch them here in case Frannie stayed hidden in the house, as Lizzie said the girl was wont to do. Seth would never be able to talk to her if that scenario played out.

When the van screeched to a halt in front of the Amish store, Stephen spotted two buggies off to the side of the parking area. Since he'd never seen the Fishers' horses or buggy, he had no clue if one of these belonged to them. He nudged Seth. "Let's go."

"I don't need anything."

"Get out and look around anyway. There's bound to be a treat that will appeal to you."

"I ate breakfast. I'm not hungry."

"Stretch your legs, then, and browse a little. You might be surprised." Stephen hoped his *bruder* would be pleasantly surprised by Frannie Fisher. But first he had to convince him to get out of the van. Why did he make everything so difficult?

"It isn't like we've been riding for hours. We've been in the van for, what—twenty minutes? Go ahead and get what you want, and make it fast. You're wasting time."

"*Kumm* on, Seth. Maybe you'll find something that amuses you and gets you out of your grumpy mood." Stephen could only hope so.

Seth heaved the biggest exasperated sigh Stephen had ever heard, but, miracle of miracles, he pushed open the door and slid out. "Let's get this over with," he snarled.

Stephen ignored the muttering as they strode toward the door but shot Seth a warning look before twisting the doorknob. Would Lizzie be here? More importantly, would Frannie be here?

His eyes flew around the huge room, but he couldn't see up and down all the aisles. Wouldn't fresh-baked items be in the front? He didn't see any. Maybe they had a special place to enjoy treats at the rear of the store. Female voices drew his attention. That melodic laugh could only belong to Lizzie. They simply needed to follow that merry sound.

Stephen nudged Seth and nodded toward the far side of the store. Lizzie must be in that back corner. He would soon find out if Frannie had come with her. Seth grunted but trudged along behind him.

Lizzie's back was toward them, and she blocked the view of whoever she was sharing a laugh with. When Stephen edged slightly to the right, he could glimpse the other woman. He almost groaned in disappointment. That woman looked much older than Lizzie and couldn't possibly be her *schweschder*.

"Martha, I didn't find . . ." The young woman racing up the aisle with an aluminum foil–covered plate stopped in her tracks. "You have customers already."

This girl had to be Frannie. She looked to be about Lizzie's age. She had brown hair and eyes, like Lizzie had once mentioned. She stood at least four or five inches taller than Lizzie and had a large build but would not be considered plump at all. She was panting as if she had run a mile.

At the precise moment Stephen glanced her way, Lizzie turned around. Her violet eyes grew as big and round as dinner plates. "*Ach!* Stephen and Seth. It's nice to see you."

Her comment included both of them, but those magnificent eyes focused on Stephen, causing him to feel like he was the only person in the room. She acted surprised and flustered, but she should have been expecting them, unless she hadn't received the note his *mudder* sent. Lizzie quickly regained her composure and tugged her *schweschder*'s arm so she would turn around. "This is Frannie, and this is the store owner, Martha Yoder."

Both women murmured greetings, which Stephen and Seth returned. Stephen sought for a way to begin a conversation, but Lizzie relieved him of that duty.

"We came to drop off some baked items for Martha to sell. Frannie made some of her scrumptious brownies and some cookies."

"What was it you couldn't find?" Martha rescued the shaking plate from Frannie's trembling hands.

"I thought I brought a box of little plastic baggies in case you wanted to package the brownies individually."

"Not to worry, dear. I have plenty of those. Let me arrange these delectable treats."

After Frannie handed over the plate, she didn't seem to know what to do with her hands. She clasped them together in front of her.

Stephen sought to relieve some of the tension that had spread like wildfire throughout the room. "If those are the same kind of brownies Lizzie brought over to our house, they will be big sellers for sure. They were great, weren't they, Seth?" He elbowed his mute *bruder*. Was the fellow still breathing?

"Huh? Oh, the brownies were very *gut*."

"*Danki*." Frannie's gaze fell to the floor.

This meeting was not getting off to a great start. Seth had to be prompted to speak, and Frannie barely mumbled. Stephen raised his eyebrows at Lizzie. *Help!* he wanted to plead.

"Frannie has loved baking forever and even makes up her own recipes, ain't so?" Lizzie tapped her *schweschder*'s arm.

"Sometimes."

Another one-word answer. Would either Seth or Frannie even holler "Fire!" if the place went up in smoke around them? "Well, we plan to buy some of your brownies, and maybe some cookies, too, as soon as Martha has them packaged."

"What brings you over this way today?" Lizzie offered a sweet smile. The little freckles fairly danced across her nose. Was she trying to put him on the spot? She knew very well why he had dragged Seth into the shop, but maybe she didn't know the rest of the plan. "Did you get my *mudder*'s note?"

"*Nee*, I didn't receive any notes."

"She sent us to fetch the kittens."

"Sent *you*, you mean," Seth mumbled.

Stephen ignored the remark but only barely resisted stomping on Seth's foot. "You haven't found other homes for them, have you?"

"Not yet, and Mamm is ready to explode."

"My *mamm* sent you a note saying we'd pick them up today."

"I never received it, but that's fine. We'll be finished here in a few minutes. I'll need to gather their food and everything once we get to the house, if you don't mind waiting."

"Sure. That's fine."

"Work," Seth ground out between clenched teeth.

Stephen coughed and cleared his throat in an effort to cover Seth's rude remark.

"I have the treats packaged whenever you're ready, *buwe*, but take your time."

Stephen smiled at Martha. He didn't need anything, either, but he'd make a few small additional purchases to support a local business. But what should he buy?

Whew! Was Stephen half as flustered as she was? If Lizzie had received that note, she would have had a little time to devise some sort of plan. Winging it did not seem to be working out very well.

"Are you looking for anything in particular?" That was Martha—always eager to help and to make a sale.

Stephen cast a helpless look at his *bruder*.

Lizzie could have told him that would be a waste of time. Seth appeared perfectly content to watch Stephen squirm. She had to try to help him somehow. "You know, Stephen, Mary said she was running low on some thread the last time I helped her with the loom. I think I know the colors she needs. And she wanted to get a new pack of needles, too. Do you know if she bought those already?"

"I don't believe so."

Stephen's relief was palpable. He trailed after Lizzie to the aisle of sewing notions. They left Frannie and Seth staring at each other.

"Do you think they will start talking?"

Stephen had leaned so close his breath tickled her ear and sent shivers down her spine. "It doesn't look too promising."

"That's what I was afraid of."

Lizzie scooted over to the shelf and put a little space between them. She selected spools of basic white, black, dark blue, and dark green thread and a package of sewing needles. She raised her voice loud enough for the others to hear. "I think these will be fine." She thrust the items into Stephen's hands. "Frannie and I will head home while you pay. You can meet us there. It's—"

"I know where it is."

"Right. We'll see you soon, then."

They were halfway home before Frannie broke the strained silence. "What was that all about?"

Lizzie had feared Frannie would ask that very question. She had anticipated it and even prepared for it. With the words now actually hanging out there in the air between them, all her ideas fled. "Apparently Mary sent a letter telling me her sons would pick up the kittens today. Somehow, I didn't receive it." Lizzie sucked in a breath and held it. Would that explanation fly?

"And they just happened to show up at Yoder's Store while we were there?"

Rats! "Apparently." Lizzie jiggled the reins. The sooner they got home, the sooner she could escape Frannie's scrutiny.

"Did you really arrange for their *mudder* to take the kittens?"

"I didn't have a choice. Mamm's been almost fit to be tied. I was afraid she'd have someone take them to the shelter. When Mary said she'd take all three of them, I jumped at the chance to keep the poor little things together."

"I'm sorry, Lizzie." Frannie picked at imaginary lint on her black cloak. "I did try to talk to Mamm."

"I know." Lizzie sighed. "Mamm is that proverbial stubborn mule. Nothing in the world can make her budge. Daed couldn't even make any headway. I don't know why she's so against animals. They're the Lord Gott's creatures, too."

"It's hard to tell, but I really am sorry the kittens have to go."

Lizzie had struggled not to bear a grudge. She didn't trust herself to speak at the moment so settled for a nod. She tugged on the reins to coax the horse to turn onto the dirt driveway. Not an automobile in sight. "They must have dawdled to give us time to get here first."

"Not for long."

"Huh?"

"They're getting ready to turn onto the driveway."

"Oh. This won't be easy. I'm glad Sadie and Nancy are at school." She tossed the reins to Frannie and hopped from the buggy as soon as it stopped rolling. Stephen crawled out of the back of the van at the same time. Lizzie turned back and raised her voice so Frannie could hear her over the hum of the van's motor. "If you see to the horse, I'll round up the kittens."

Stephen called back to the van as soon as Lizzie's words died on her lips. "Seth, why don't you help Frannie with the horse, and I'll help Lizzie with the kittens."

Seth must have uttered some retort, but Lizzie couldn't hear it. She only heard Stephen's reply. "We'll get finished sooner that way so you can get to work."

With obvious reluctance, Seth exited the van and lumbered off toward the buggy. Stephen hurried to catch up with Lizzie. "You don't think that was too obvious, do you?"

"Do you mean Seth's disdain for helping or your scheme to get him with Frannie?"

"It's not that Seth doesn't like to help people. He's

normally at work at this time of day and is worried about getting there soon. I had to cajole him to accompany me."

"More like drag him kicking and screaming."

"Almost. Wait a minute. I have a carrier for the kittens in the back of the van."

"I hope you didn't buy one for the occasion."

"I have several for when I need to haul puppies to the vet or something."

"That makes sense." Lizzie waited while Stephen fetched the carrier. Together they approached the shed. She stole a peek over her shoulder. "Hey, it looks like they're talking."

"Really?" Stephen took a quick glance. "I know it's hard for you to part with the kittens, but maybe something *gut* will *kumm* from this after all."

"Very hard." Lizzie bit her lip. She would not cry or otherwise act like a *boppli*. She would be mature. She would round up the kittens, their food, and their toys. She could do this, couldn't she?

Chapter Twenty-Four

She had waited all day to talk to Frannie, and now that they were alone in their bedroom, Lizzie didn't know how to broach the subject. Granted, conversation hadn't been a priority after Stephen and Seth had taken the kittens. *Her* kittens. And then she'd had to comfort Sadie and Nancy after they arrived home from school when she really felt like wailing along with them. It had taken a lot of coaxing to get them to play a game with her.

After the supper cleanup, she could finally slip out to her workshop, where she cried and worked until the cold made her fingers too stiff and the tears had threatened to freeze on her face. Physical and emotional exhaustion were now staking their claim, but she still wanted to talk to Frannie. Had the first step in the plan she and Stephen had hatched been successful?

"Stop fidgeting!"

"What?"

"If you bang that hairbrush on the dresser one more time, I'm going to throw it out the window."

"Sorry. I didn't realize I was tapping it and bothering you." Figuring out what would set Frannie off had become a real chore. What did she have to be so grumpy about, anyway? It wasn't her kittens who were sent away. It was her fault, though. *Don't think that way, Lizzie. Mamm would have found some other reason to get rid of them.* She fumbled with her hairpins.

"And why is your face so blotchy?"

Lizzie pressed both hands to her cheeks. She had been unable to conceal the evidence of tears. Honestly, couldn't Frannie hazard even a teensy guess as to why she had been crying? "Cold. I was working in the cold."

"Why didn't you turn on a kerosene heater like a normal person?"

Lizzie shrugged. So now she wasn't normal. She needed to turn this conversation around. She'd never been adept at beating around the bush, so she might as well be her usual straightforward self. "What did you and Seth talk about?"

"Seth? How did he get into the conversation?"

I just brought him in, that's how. Lizzie began her mental counting. "I suddenly remembered you two were talking while unhitching the horse." If Frannie had been this snippy when they chatted, the poor fellow would never want to see her again. Lizzie was used to being the recipient of Frannie's barbs, so she was immune. Almost. But poor Seth would probably want to run for his life.

"I thought you were too busy talking to Stephen to notice if the sun fell from the sky."

Lizzie swallowed a gasp. Her heart stopped in midbeat and then pounded back into action. "Me and Stephen?" She cringed at the squeak her voice made and cleared her throat. "All we did was pack up the kittens for the trip to their new home."

"Well, if you two discussed kittens, Seth and I discussed horses."

"Horses?"

"*Jah*, you know, as in the beast we unhitched and others like him."

"Oh."

"And he talked a tiny bit about the job he was late getting to because Stephen had him chasing down kittens."

"Was he nice?"

"As far as I could tell. He was polite and helpful, as most strangers would be when pressed to perform a task."

"He doesn't have to be a stranger." Lizzie hadn't meant to say that aloud.

Frannie plunked one fist on her hip, scowled, and wagged her other index finger at Lizzie. "Don't you go playing matchmaker." As she advanced, Lizzie imagined she could see steam escaping from her *schweschder*'s ears. Frannie stopped within inches of Lizzie, towering over her with an angry glare. She jabbed the index finger into Lizzie's upper chest. "I mean it, Lizzie!"

"I-I . . ."

"He's not even Amish."

"He hasn't joined the Mennonite church yet."

"And how do you know this sliver of information?"

"Mary or Stephen mentioned it."

"Sort of like you haven't joined the Amish church yet?"

This conversation was heading in a direction Lizzie hadn't anticipated. "I plan to."

"When? You might not want to wait until you're eighty years old."

"I'm only twenty. I've got time."

"Aren't you considering marrying and having *kinner*?"

"One day. I'm not ready yet." Could that be because she wasn't ready to put away childish things, like drawing pencils and paints? "Are you ready for that?"

Frannie turned away, but not before whispering, "*Jah.*"

Lizzie dared to touch Frannie's arm. "You'll find someone. Don't worry."

"You make it sound like I'm some sort of troll who needs pity because I'll never be worthy of love."

Wow! Frannie had gotten that from Lizzie's five little words? So much for attempting to offer reassurance. "I meant nothing of the kind. How you came to that conclusion is beyond me. I only meant you have plenty of time to find the person who is just right for you."

"I'm not sure such a person exists."

"Just because your first crush didn't work out, don't let it sour you."

"Aren't you full of wisdom."

"I'm not. I'm only trying to help. You could consider Seth."

"Don't go there, Lizzie. We both know that would never work out."

"Never say 'never.'"

"Ha! I'm sure about this. I might have been wrong about Aaron, but I am not wrong about Seth, so stop trying to make something out of nothing." Frannie whirled away to finish getting ready for bed.

Lizzie would have to tell Stephen their plan had backfired. Unless he had a foolproof plan B, they'd have to abandon the idea of helping their older siblings find matches.

Frannie merely mumbled an incoherent response

to Lizzie's "*Gut nacht*," so Lizzie assumed her *schweschder* was still miffed. Over nothing! Lizzie had been trying to offer kindness and reassurance. How could that have been misconstrued? Frannie was the only person she knew who could find fault with a totally innocent comment. Perhaps she shouldn't bother to speak to the girl at all. Did Stephen feel that way about Seth?

Lizzie knelt beside her bed to say her prayers. She tried to remember all the little slipups she wanted to ask forgiveness for. She might have to start writing them down in a notebook if they kept piling up like this. "Notebook" made her think of "sketchbook," which made her think of drawing. She wanted to sketch the puppies, especially Sunny. She had hoped to draw more pictures of the kittens, but that opportunity had been stolen, unless she hauled her art materials to Mary's house the next time she visited.

That would never work. Her secret would surely be discovered if someone noticed her carrying a lot of extra gear. She would have to rely on memory to create future drawings of the kittens. Oh dear. She was supposed to be praying, not thinking about drawing. Another item to jot down in her notebook of sins.

At last she climbed into bed and pulled the covers up to her chin. What a hard day! Her body was so weary. Why wouldn't her brain shut down? She missed the kittens already. She would try her very best not to hold a grudge against Mamm or Frannie. What was done was done. Wishing wouldn't change a thing.

Stephen had been more than kind when he helped her collect the kittens and their things. He'd expressed his regret and repeated Mary's invitation to visit them whenever she wanted. He regaled her with humorous stories from his childhood and even succeeded in making her laugh. He didn't poke fun at her tears when she placed the last meowing kitten in the carrier. Instead, he had squeezed her arm and assured her they would be loved and cared for.

Lizzie flipped her pillow over so the cool side pressed against her warm cheek. How did thoughts of Stephen send warmth through her body? She needed to bridle that reaction immediately. They had a common mission to help their siblings find love and happiness. Nothing more. Right? *Absolutely right! Now go to sleep!*

Chapter Twenty-Five

When threads started blurring and blending together, Lizzie decided a break was in order. She'd tried all the usual tricks for tired eyes, like blinking and staring at some faraway object, but nothing brought more than a few seconds of relief. If she hadn't tossed and turned all night, her brain might function normally, but she might as well have left it under the pillow for all the use it had been today. She kept making careless mistakes and backtracking to fix them. She didn't want to ruin her *Englisch* customer's blanket, so she'd better take a little break. It might save her some time in the long run. She had plenty of time to finish the project before Christmas.

Lizzie hopped off her stool with a groan. Her lower back made sure she knew it did not appreciate the position she'd assumed for so long. She bent forward at the waist and then twisted from side to side to loosen the stiff muscles. She listened for footsteps and peeked out the single window. Satisfied she would not be interrupted anytime soon, she fished her art box from its hiding place.

Thoughts of kittens brought too much sadness. She needed another subject for her sketch. She would draw the first thing that came to mind. Lizzie set up her sketch pad and opened her box of pencils. She squeezed her eyes shut and took several deep breaths. She'd read such actions were calming. *Not so.*

She opened her eyes and chose a pencil. The first image to flash across her mind was a little ball of golden fur with a puppy grin. Sunny made her smile. Sunny provided the stress relief she needed. Lizzie's fingers drew what her brain pictured. She lost track of time and blocked out every other sight or sound until she had added the last detail to her sketch.

She sat back and massaged her neck. The picture was a pretty *gut* likeness, if she said so herself. Lizzie would tuck it away to show Stephen—maybe. A scratchy noise instantly grabbed her attention. She leaped up and tiptoed to the door. She edged it open only a crack so she could peek out unnoticed. Ruff. He must have bumped against the door. Close call. Lizzie scrambled to tuck her art materials away. She should be able to concentrate on her weaving now.

"You are doing fine, Mary. You don't really need my help at all."

"Oops! Now look what I did!"

Lizzie playfully swatted Mary's arm. "You messed that up on purpose."

Mary laughed. "Guilty. Can I help it if I enjoy your company? I'm afraid you won't visit at all if you don't help me with my weaving." She squeezed Lizzie's hand. "And I would surely miss you."

Lizzie squeezed back. "I would miss you, too."

"I suppose I should correct my mistake, ain't so?"

"That might be nice. You know, I think you're ready for something a bit more advanced."

"What? I've barely gotten this down pat."

"You lack only confidence. Your skills are great. When you're ready for a break, I brought some patterns for you to look at."

"Something harder?" Mary's eyes widened and a hand flew up to pat her chest.

"Think of it as something more challenging. You like challenges. I can tell."

"That all depends. If it's something I think I'd be able to do, then I would like a challenge. Otherwise, probably not."

"There's your lack of confidence again. I'm sure you can handle any of the patterns I brought."

"I don't know, but you're the teacher."

"I've been concentrating so hard that my eyes are crossed. Let's have a snack." Mary pushed back from the loom an hour later and rubbed her eyes. "I've got a caramel cocoa mix. Would you like to try some?"

"Mmmm! It sounds great."

"I have some chocolate brownies, too, if that won't be too much chocolate for you."

"As my little *schweschder* Nancy says, you can never have too much chocolate."

Mary laughed. "I'd have to agree. The brownies aren't nearly as *gut* as Frannie's, but they'll do."

"I'm sure they are fine. I'll bring my bag, and we can study patterns for your next project."

"You are awfully optimistic that I will finish the current one."

"You're nearly finished now. I have confidence in

you." Lizzie snatched her bag and followed Mary to the kitchen.

Mary pulled two flowered mugs from the cupboard and dropped a scoop of cocoa mix into each. "If you would, could you grab a couple of napkins and that pan of brownies on the counter?"

Lizzie lifted the lid on the brownies and inhaled. "I don't know which smells better—the cocoa or the brownies." She carried the pan and napkins to the big, well-used oak table.

"Here you go." Mary set a steaming mug in front of Lizzie. "Help yourself to a brownie."

Lizzie spread a paper napkin open on the table and selected a medium-sized brownie. She ventured a tiny sip of cocoa. "This is delicious. I know my *schweschders* and *bruders* would love it." She nibbled a corner off her brownie. "And the brownies are every bit as *gut* as Frannie's."

"Hardly, but you're a dear to say so."

They ate in companionable silence. Lizzie pressed her finger to the napkin and raised it to her lips to consume the last few crumbs of her treat. Since the cocoa had cooled to merely hot instead of scalding, she took a bigger gulp. "Are you ready to examine the patterns?" Seeing Mary's skeptical expression, she hastened to add, "I promise they aren't that hard. Only a little more advanced. I wouldn't have brought them if I didn't believe you could do them. But they are only ideas. You don't have to do any if you don't want to."

"I suppose it won't hurt to look at them—if you say they aren't too hard."

"They aren't. Trust me. You're ready to move on."

"I'm not nearly as sure as you are."

"Take a look. That can't hurt, right?" Lizzie stood to

rummage through her bag and extracted a handful of papers. One page flew from her hands as if it had wings to soar on its own power. It fluttered and dropped to the table smack in front of Mary. Lizzie gasped. She dropped the other papers and gripped the edge of the table.

"What's this?"

Lizzie couldn't find her voice. She could scarcely breathe. She watched in horror as Mary turned the paper over.

"Why, it's the puppy, the one you call Sunny!"

Stephen sanded the bookcase with a little more vigor than usual. His thoughts had wandered aimlessly, and his hands performed their task by rote. When he came to his senses, he realized he'd better lighten up a bit. In fact, the edges already felt as smooth as a newborn's skin. He'd heard that expression. Having practically zero experience with newborns, he wasn't sure how accurate the comparison really was.

He stood back a little to eyeball his latest project. Every curlicue looked even and in its proper place. His *Englisch* customer had requested a slightly fancier bookcase than he usually built, but the construction had turned out well. He wished the meeting between Seth and Frannie had turned out as well. That had been more like a disaster.

Stephen brushed bits of sawdust off the bookcase to prepare it for the cherry stain. His mind hiked backward to that more than awkward meeting. He should have planned it better, but that would have been difficult to do since he couldn't even be sure Frannie would even *kumm* out of the house so that she and

Seth would actually meet that day if they hadn't met at the store. Would a second meeting go better now that the ice was broken? All he knew for sure was that his *bruder* needed help finding someone to make him smile and warm his heart. After meeting Frannie, though, Stephen wasn't totally convinced she would be the right person for the job. But who knows?

He opened the can of cherry stain. After applying one coat, he would work on the walnut coffee table for another *Englisch* customer while it dried. He whistled as he brushed on the deep reddish-brown stain. Would one more meeting between Frannie and Seth be worth the effort? Mamm might get upset with him for trying to fix Seth up with a girl who was not Mennonite, but Amish was pretty close. At least he wasn't encouraging a relationship with an *Englischer*.

Stephen chuckled when he thought of Frannie and his *bruder*. They were two peas in a pod. From what Lizzie had told him, Frannie might be even moodier than Seth. The *schweschders* seemed as different as night and day. He'd never detected any moodiness in Lizzie. Spunk, for sure. He smiled. He liked spunk and a quick wit. She definitely had that, too. But Frannie and Seth apparently lacked wit, or suppressed it. He could imagine the two of them in a snit and neither one would budge an inch. It could be comical—to the observer, anyway.

He set the can of stain on the workbench and examined his effort. He believed his customer would be pleased with the finished product. On to the next project and concocting a plan B for Seth and Frannie. Had Lizzie had more success in that area?

Chapter Twenty-Six

Lizzie stood rooted to the spot. All she could do was stare at the picture in Mary's hands. She couldn't even raise her eyes to Mary's face. Would she see accusation or disgust or repulsion?

"Lizzie? Did you draw this picture?"

Lizzie sank to the chair. Her wobbly legs would not support her weight, slight though it was, any longer. Her voice would only emerge in a whisper. "I did."

"It's *wunderbaar*! Such an amazing likeness! Did you do this from memory?"

"Huh?" No chastisement? No outrage?

"Did you draw the puppy here one day or from memory?"

Lizzie cleared her throat to get her voice to project as something louder than a faint croak. "I drew it at home. From memory." Before she could consider her next words or actions, she burst into tears and covered her face with shaking hands. "I'm so sorry, Mary. I didn't mean . . ." She sensed Mary at her side but couldn't move her hands to look at the sweet woman who would probably not want her as a *freind* any longer. She might even ban Lizzie from the premises.

Mary tugged Lizzie's hands away from her face. "Look at me, Lizzie."

Lizzie sniffed and raised her eyes to peer through the cloud of tears.

"Why are you crying, dear?"

"I-I know I'm not supposed t-to engage in artwork, b-but I enjoy it so much."

"That's why you haven't joined your church yet, ain't so?"

Lizzie nodded. "Partly. I-I feel so ashamed. I-I brought the picture to show Stephen."

"He knew about your art?"

"*Jah.*" More tears threatened. "I didn't mean to involve him or get him into any trouble." At least now she knew Stephen could be trusted. He had never revealed her secret to his *mudder.*

"He didn't tell me."

"I asked him not to tell anyone. I-I'm so sorry. You see, I'm n-not a *gut* person. I'll get my things and leave." Lizzie reached for her bag, but the tears blinded her.

"*Nee.*"

Lizzie stood still. She blinked to try to focus on Mary's face.

"You are not a bad person, and I do not want you to leave."

"But I kept my drawing a secret and involved your son." Lizzie hung her head.

"How did Stephen happen to discover your talent?"

"It was an accident. Really. He helped me rescue the kittens. My art supplies were in that abandoned house. He saw my pictures that day."

"Do you have lots of pictures?"

"A fair amount." Lizzie couldn't lower her head any

farther. If she could have dropped completely to the floor and slithered out the door like a worm, she surely would. A tug at her chin forced her gaze upward.

"Look at me, Lizzie. You have nothing to be ashamed of."

Lizzie sniffed but kept silent.

"Do you hear me?" Mary gave her a little shake.

Lizzie nodded. "I hear you, but I don't understand."

"If your other pictures are as fine as this one, you have real talent. I'm not surprised, actually, since you are so creative with your weaving." Mary smiled.

"You aren't angry with me?"

"Why would I be angry?"

"Isn't art wrong for Mennonites?"

"We have pictures on our calendars, don't we? We give Christmas cards. We just don't have pictures of people, though there have been many times I wished I had pictures of my sons when they were little or of loved ones who are gone."

"You have?"

"For sure. I don't see anything wrong with your drawings. You don't worship them or set pictures up and pray to them."

Lizzie gasped. "Never. I'd never do that. There is only one Lord Gott. I worship Him alone."

"That's all I need to know. Of course, I already believed that. So Lizzie, dear, stop beating yourself up and feeling guilty. Personally, I don't consider your artwork a sin."

"You don't?"

"I consider it a talent. A gift. You have a marvelous gift of creativity. I don't believe the Lord wants us to hide our gifts. We aren't supposed to set them up as gods in our life. They aren't supposed to rule us. But if your gift can bring joy to others, then I think it would be wrong *not* to draw or create beautiful woven items."

"I told her the same thing."

Lizzie nearly jumped to the ceiling at the sound of the deep voice at the doorway.

"We didn't hear you *kumm* in, Stephen."

"Apparently. I didn't mean to interrupt, but I couldn't help overhearing your conversation."

If their heat was any sort of gauge, Lizzie's cheeks must be the color of an overripe strawberry. With puffy eyes and a tear-streaked face, her appearance must be frightful.

"Look, Stephen. Isn't this picture absolutely delightful?" Mary held out the sketch of Sunny.

Lizzie couldn't meet his gaze when he took the picture from Mary's hands. She didn't know why she cared what he thought of it, but she did.

"It's a great likeness. You've somehow captured her personality in this picture."

Lizzie exhaled, crazily relieved Stephen liked the drawing. She froze at Mary's next words.

"You didn't tell me Lizzie was an artist."

Was Mary angry that her son had kept the information from her? She hadn't seemed angry earlier, but maybe she felt differently with Stephen standing right in front of her. Why, oh why did she bring that sketch with her today? She couldn't help that Stephen had discovered her secret, but she should never have brought the picture here. Would she ever learn to do the right thing? What would Stephen say? Should she jump in to offer a defense? Too late. Stephen glanced at her with a little smile before addressing his *mudder*.

"It wasn't my place to tell. Besides, I discovered

Lizzie's talent quite by accident. She asked me not to tell anyone, so I kept my word."

"*Gut.*"

"*Gut?*" Lizzie could squeak out only the single word. She stared at Mary. The woman was full of surprises.

"*Jah.* Stephen is a grown man and doesn't have to tell me everything. I'm glad he is a man of his word. If he told you he wouldn't reveal your secret to anyone, then he did exactly the right thing. I would have been very disappointed in him if he had given his word and then broken his promise. Of course, if your secret had been something horrible that would endanger someone, then I would expect him to tell the proper people. But your secret was harmless. It's delightful, truth be told."

Lizzie sighed. "It wouldn't be so harmless if my *mudder* found out."

"Don't you think she would enjoy your pictures?"

"I'm sure she wouldn't even look at them. And she'd have me confessing my sinful ways before the whole church."

Stephen chuckled. "You aren't practicing voodoo. You're drawing pictures of things the Lord Gott put on this earth."

"That's what I always thought, but then I figured I was only looking for a way to justify my sin."

"Don't your people send cards?" Mary's tone was gentle, not accusatory.

"I suppose. On occasion."

"And don't *kinner* color pictures?"

"Sure, but they're little and they're learning motor skills and whatnot."

"Has your *mamm* ever received a card from someone?" Mary patted Lizzie's arm. "I'm sorry, dear. I shouldn't probe. It's not my place. And I'm certainly not criticizing your *mudder*."

"It's okay. I'm not offended. To answer your question, I'm sure Mamm has received cards, and she's even kept them for a while." Lizzie paused while her own words sank in. "So my pictures shouldn't be regarded any differently. Right? But they probably would be."

"Well, your secret is safe with us, dear. I, for one, would love to see more of your pictures."

"I have one."

Mary gaped at her son. "What?"

"I have a picture Lizzie drew of the kittens."

"How long have you had it?"

"Since the first day I met Lizzie. I helped her cart her stuff home from that burning house and badgered her into giving me a picture."

"And you've kept it hidden all this time?"

"I didn't want to let the cat out of the bag." Stephen chuckled at his own joke.

Mary playfully swatted her son. "You've known about our Lizzie's talent all this time and even had one of her drawings. My, you are *gut* at keeping secrets. It makes me wonder how many other things you've hidden from me over the years."

"Not a thing, Mamm."

Lizzie saw Stephen cross his fingers behind his back and laughed. *"Our Lizzie"?* Mary had said that as if she belonged with them. The very idea gave Lizzie a strange little jolt. She heard Mary's and Stephen's banter but couldn't focus on it. The fact that Mary considered her like family filled every nook and cranny of Lizzie's mind with peace. Her heart swelled with joy. Her body instantly warmed, as though big, loving arms had wrapped themselves around her. What must it be like to truly belong to the Zimmerman family? *Ach!* What was she thinking?

"Is that okay with you, Lizzie?"

Lizzie tried to clear her mind. She hadn't any idea what Stephen had asked her. "I-I'm sorry?"

"I said, is it okay to show Mamm your kitten picture?"

"Of course. She knows my deep, dark secret and hasn't condemned me, so why not?"

Mary threw an arm around Lizzie and hugged her tight. "You silly girl! Of course I don't condemn you." Mary laughed and gave her another gentle squeeze.

The hug felt every bit as loving as the one in Lizzie's imagination had. The same warmth spread throughout her body. When had her own *mamm* hugged her? She couldn't remember.

She believed Mamm loved her, loved all of them, but she did not openly express it.

"I'll get it." Stephen started for the door.

"Where is it?" Mary asked.

"In my shop. I knew it would be safe there."

"And you could pull it out to look at whenever you wanted to think of the kittens or Lizzie?"

Stephen's face flushed pink, then red, then bright red. "I knew it would be safe from prying eyes, and as you said, I keep my word." Stephen again started for the door.

Lizzie suspected he wanted to hide his glowing face. Mary's words sent a tingle up her spine. Did Stephen ever pull out the picture and think of her? *Right, Lizzie. He probably thinks what a nuisance you've been.* Did she want him to think about her?

"Wait, Stephen!" Mary called. "We'll *kumm* visit the kittens and see the picture, if that's okay with you two."

"Suit yourself." Stephen tried to sound gruff, but Lizzie detected a faint smile on his face.

"And maybe see Sunny, too?" Lizzie's fondness for the puppy continued to grow.

"Why not?"

Chapter Twenty-Seven

Stephen led the way outside with the two women following him. He wished they had given him a moment alone to compose himself. Why had he blushed like some silly scholar? His cheeks still burned. Maybe the cool breeze would douse the fire.

He didn't dare hazard a glance behind him. Mamm had always been able to read his thoughts simply by looking at his face. And if she could look into his eyes, it would be like peeking into his soul. He couldn't let her know she'd hit the nail on the head. Stephen *did* slide the picture of the kittens out of its hiding place from time to time, and not because he had been thinking about the tiny fur balls. It was the artist he thought about. Somehow, gazing at the drawing made him feel like Lizzie was there sparring with him. Memories of their rows made him smile again.

Knock it off, Stephen. Lizzie is not interested in you in the least. She has only wanted to find a safe home for the kittens and a husband for her schweschder. *Gut luck with that!* If Frannie was always as touchy as she had been when they met, any self-respecting fellow would run the other way with a quickness. But if anyone could possibly understand the girl's moodiness, it would have to be Seth. However, while he didn't run away, he did emphatically declare he was not interested in Frannie Fisher.

"*Ach!* There's Miriam. Where are Molly and Annie?"

Lizzie's exclamation behind him called Stephen's mind back from its meanderings. "They're probably in the shed." He answered without turning around in case his face still glowed.

"We made a nice place for them in my potting shed,'" Mary explained. "But, of course, they're free to roam about. So far, I believe they've stayed pretty close by."

"I hope they're adjusting well. Here, kitty!"

Stephen could tell Lizzie had stopped walking. He halfway turned around and dropped his gaze to the ground. There sat Lizzie on her haunches, petting the tortoiseshell kitten.

"You look like you've grown in the short time it's been since I've seen you. You are such a pretty kitty. Where are your *schweschders*?"

Stephen couldn't have prevented his lips from curving into a smile if he had tried. Lizzie cooing to the kitten made the most adorable sight. He wished he could have a picture of that! A sense of being watched stole over him, and he dared to glance in his *mudder*'s direction. Caught! Mamm had caught him smiling at Lizzie and the kitten. He'd probably never hear the end of that. Wouldn't smiling at such a sight be normal? It didn't signify anything else, because he certainly didn't need any complications in his life. He erased the smile and cast his eyes skyward at a V of geese flying overhead.

"Here *kumm* the others." Mary pointed toward the potting shed. "They must have heard your voice, Lizzie."

A yip from the dog pen alerted them to the fact that another critter sought attention.

"I'll be there in a minute, Sunny," Lizzie called. She played with the kittens a moment longer and then sprang to her feet with the agility of an athlete. The kittens wound their way around Mary's feet. "It looks like they have already grown attached to you, Mary. I'm glad."

When she turned those big violet eyes to meet Stephen's gaze, his heart lurched. Did she know how very lovely she was? *Ach!* Those thoughts had to stop. Immediately.

"Can I see Sunny now, Stephen?"

"Sure." His response came out more gruff than he intended. He didn't miss Mamm's frown or Lizzie's shocked expression. "She's waiting for you," he added to soften his previous response.

Lizzie puzzled over Stephen's demeanor. Had she annoyed him by asking to see the puppy? Well, he didn't have to accompany her if it was such a hardship for him. She was perfectly capable of playing with a dog all by herself. Humph! Men! She tried not to stomp off like a spoiled little girl. She forced herself to walk normally and not act miffed.

"Oh my! I need to check on my stew," Mary called from behind her. "You take your time with the puppy, Lizzie. We can finish up at the loom whenever you're ready."

"Okay." Lizzie wasn't sure she was pleased about being left alone with Stephen, especially if he continued to be in a surly mood.

Mary headed toward the house, stopped abruptly, and faced her son. "Would you show me Lizzie's picture of the kittens?"

"I'll bring it inside in a bit."

"Or you can tell me where it is in your shop. I'll peek at it on my way to the house."

"I'll have to dig it out. I'll bring it inside in a bit."

Mary shrugged. "Don't forget."

Lizzie almost let herself into the pen but didn't want to risk raising Stephen's dander, so she stood at the fence and talked to the puppies.

"Lizzie?"

Her arm tingled at his touch. She couldn't control the warmth that traveled all the way up that arm and flooded her face. "*Jah?*" She kept her eyes focused on the puppies.

"I'm sorry."

"What?" She must have heard wrong.

Stephen cleared his throat and spoke a tiny bit louder. "I'm sorry I spoke sharply earlier. I didn't mean to be rude."

"It's okay. I know I'm bothering you. You have work to do, and I'm preventing you from getting it done. You need to tell me to go away and leave . . ." Lizzie broke off with a gasp when Stephen tugged her around to face him. Now she couldn't help but look into his eyes.

"*Nee.* You did nothing wrong. It was me, and I'm sorry. I'm not so busy that I can't take a few minutes to let you see the puppies. They will be gone in a couple of weeks, so you should enjoy them while you can. You are a true animal lover." Under his breath, he added,

"Like me." He dropped his hand from her arm but didn't step away.

"What do you mean they will be gone soon?" Her heart skidded to a halt. She couldn't be sure if its irregularity was due to Stephen's nearness or his words or both.

"You know I raise them for the service organization."

Lizzie nodded. Of course she remembered that. She knew the puppies would be moving on, but so soon?

"It's about time for them to go on for their specific training."

"All the puppies?"

"*Jah.*"

"Even Sunny?"

"*Jah.*" The word came out whisper soft.

"I thought you said they might not take Sunny. I thought . . ." She couldn't continue without bursting into tears, and she would not do that in front of Stephen. She blinked hard. She felt his hand on her arm again, lightly, like a caress.

"I know you really like Sunny. Often I hate to let the pups go myself. That's the hardest part about the job. I get attached to some of the dogs, too, but I tell myself they are going to be a big help to someone who needs it."

Lizzie's tight throat made swallowing and even breathing difficult. Her voice emerged as a croak. "I thought Sunny wouldn't work out as a service dog."

"They plan to give her a trial. They'll put her through the paces with the other pups and see if she'll work out."

"And if they can't use her, we've—I mean, you've—

already lost her." Lizzie sniffed. "I'm sorry. She's not my dog, so I don't have any right to ask or to be sad." Her voice caught, and she sniffed harder. Stephen squeezed her arm, sending a little shock wave along every nerve pathway.

"You don't have to apologize for caring. That's what makes you *you*. I don't know how Sunny will work out. She's a sweet, gentle dog. She obeys, but she kind of cowers at any raised voice or harshness. I don't know if her personality will mesh with the rigorous training. I'm sure she will have the stamina, and she's smart, but it's almost like she gets her feelings hurt easily—if that's possible."

"I think it's possible. I think animals have feelings the same as we do. Sunny would make a terrific pet."

"I agree."

"Will they let you know how she does?"

"I can ask them."

"That's *gut*. I mean, it's up to you, but it would be great to know whether she keeps up with the other dogs."

"Are you ready to visit with her? I think she's eager to play with you, and she's been waiting awfully patiently."

"I'm ready."

As soon as Stephen opened the gate, Sunny darted out and made a beeline for Lizzie, nearly knocking her off her feet.

"Sunny, down!" Stephen snapped his fingers and pointed. Immediately the puppy sat.

Lizzie squatted. "*Gut* girl." She giggled at the doggy kisses and hugged the puppy to her. She probably looked like a little girl, but she didn't care at the moment. She could be embarrassed later. "Don't scold," she said when Stephen took a breath to speak. "I encouraged her. I know I'm probably messing up her training, but I might not see her again."

Stephen sighed. "I'm outnumbered. Have fun."

"I'll only play a few minutes, and then I can put her back in the pen, if you need to get back to work."

"Okay. Holler if you need me."

If she needs you? Stephen shook his head. Surely Lizzie had understood what he meant. He needed to occupy his mind and hands with his waiting project and stop thinking about Lizzie and the puppy.

Before he began working on the walnut coffee table, Stephen fished through his file of orders until his fingers touched a thicker sheet of paper. Ever so carefully, he slipped it out, holding it gingerly to avoid crimping the edges. He'd used such caution every time he had extracted the paper from its hiding place. And he'd done that more often than he cared to admit.

Stephen couldn't resist a smile at the drawing. Such lively little animals. The picture was so realistic, he could practically see the kittens rolling and tumbling over one another on the page. Lizzie really had a special way of bringing her drawings alive. All the pictures he'd glimpsed on the day of the fire had captured the essence of life. The puppy picture did as well. Her talent was way too special to hide away. Would she really have to sacrifice it to join her church? Why was it okay to weave beautiful cloth but not draw these *wunderbaar* pictures?

He left the picture on his little desk so he'd remember

to take it into the house. Now that Mamm knew about Lizzie's art, maybe he'd buy a frame so the picture wouldn't get ruined. That way he could look at it whenever he wanted. Ugh! Stephen pushed that thought away. He needed to get to work.

He rubbed sandpaper over the edges of the table until every inch felt smooth. He ran a cloth over the sanded areas to make sure there weren't any rough spots. If the cloth snagged on something, he'd know he needed to sand more. The walnut was as beautiful as the cherry.

Suddenly Stephen straightened up and snapped his fingers. That's it! He would construct a frame for the puppy picture and give it to Lizzie for Christmas. Sunny would probably be gone by then, so the drawing could be a memento for her. He wondered which wood she would prefer. Would she be allowed to accept such a gift? Pictures must not be permitted by her church, or maybe by her *mudder*. Well, if she couldn't take it home, she could keep the framed picture here and look at it whenever she visited.

Would Mamm continue needing Lizzie's help? He'd heard Lizzie say Mamm was catching on to the weaving very quickly. Stephen frowned. It should not make him feel empty or lonely when he considered the idea that Lizzie wouldn't visit again. As much as he didn't want her presence in his heart and mind, she continued to show up there.

It also should not make him happy to hope Mamm would keep finding reasons for Lizzie to visit. The two seemed to have become *freinden*, and *freinden* visited each other, didn't they?

Too bad Frannie wasn't half as nice as Lizzie. Maybe then Seth would take an interest.

Stephen didn't discover any nicks or rough spots on the table, so he set it upright to make sure it did not wobble. He didn't want to have to repair anything after the table was stained. He backed up to study it from a different perspective. "*Ach!*" Were those toes he'd just mashed under his heavy work shoes?

Chapter Twenty-Eight

"Ooooh!" She put out her hand to try to regain her balance. When he had moved off of her foot, she had jerked backward and began to teeter. She should have announced her presence by calling out or clearing her throat or something. Now she had squashed toes to show for her poor judgment.

In a single motion, Stephen spun around and grabbed Lizzie to keep her from falling. "Oh, Lizzie, I'm so sorry. I didn't know you were there."

"It's my fault. I should have said something." Her breath came out in little gasps.

"Are you all right?"

"I-I think so."

"Clumsy me! All my weight and this heavy shoe on your itty-bitty foot! I probably broke all your toes."

"I-I don't think so." The throbbing eased slightly. Her breath began to return to normal.

"Sit. Take off your shoe and let me check."

She must have turned ten shades of red at the very thought of doing such a thing. "That's all right. I'm sure I'll be fine." She'd probably be even better if he let go of her and didn't stand so close. She felt funny.

Her heart fluttered. Her stomach rolled over itself. Rational thought fled. Did the injury cause these reactions?

"At least sit for a minute. Can you walk to the stool?"

"I'm sure I can." With the first bit of weight on her injured foot, she wasn't so sure about that. But she'd manage somehow. Stephen felt bad enough for stepping on her. She didn't want him to think he'd done permanent damage. She'd put most of her weight on her uninjured foot and do a little hop, if she could manage that with Stephen still clinging to her arm.

"Let me help. Lean on me."

Lizzie had little choice but to do so, since she couldn't hop with him attached to her. Now she found herself even closer to him, considering that he had shifted to wrap an arm around her waist. With little effort at all, she could snuggle against him with her head leaning on his chest. But she wouldn't allow that. She kept her back ramrod straight and limped awkwardly to the stool.

"Maybe I should fetch Mamm or get you some ice." After he had helped her onto the stool, Stephen jammed his hands into his pockets and looked completely flabbergasted.

"Don't bother your *mamm*. I'll be fine in a minute."

"Do you think your foot is swollen? A little ice would help that."

"I don't think I'm hurt that badly. I'll rest a minute and then go to the house. Please don't let me keep you from your work." Her eyes darted around his workshop. She inhaled, savoring the scents of wood and stain. Pleasant smells. "That bookcase is beautiful."

"It's for an *Englisch* customer. It's a little fancier than I usually do, but it's what the customer wanted."

"I'm sure they will be very pleased. It would look

lovely in the living room or wherever they plan to keep it. I would think they would want it in a room where people could see it." Why was she babbling? His closeness and his concern affected her thought processes—and her tongue, which had apparently jimmied loose at both ends and flapped at will. She needed to tame it before it spouted out more foolish words. "Are you finished with it?" She should have stuck with such a simple question to begin with.

"It's waiting for a second coat of stain."

"The table isn't cherry, is it?" She nodded at the table he had been eyeballing when he had backed over her.

"It's walnut. I'm about ready to stain it."

"Go right ahead. I don't mind if you work. I rather like the smells of wood and stain and varnish."

"You do?"

"Sure. They remind me of my *grossdaddi*. He used to do woodworking."

"I thought I was the only one who liked these scents. It's nice to know someone else does, too."

Lizzie circled her ankle round and round and flexed her toes. Everything seemed to be functioning normally.

"Is your foot okay?"

"It's a lot better."

"I don't see how, after an elephant smashed it."

Lizzie broke out in a fit of giggles. "You are not an elephant. I happened to be in the wrong place at the wrong time." She looked up and caught Stephen's smile that caused little crinkles at the corners of his brilliant blue eyes. My, but he was nice looking! And when he smiled, he nearly stole her breath away. She should jump from this stool and escape to the house this very second!

"I take full responsibility for your injury and am deeply sorry." Stephen bent from the waist in an exaggerated bow, sending Lizzie into another gale of laughter.

She wiped the moisture from her eyes. "What I actually came out to tell you was that I secured the puppies in the pen, and I refilled their water bowl. They must drink a lot even in this colder weather."

"I suppose they get thirsty cavorting about."

"That makes sense." Lizzie scooted to the edge of the stool so her feet reached the floor. She tested her foot by putting a little weight on it.

"Everything okay?"

"Fine."

"Say, Lizzie, have you given any thought to our plan?"

"You mean as in our plan that backfired?"

Stephen chuckled. "That would be the one."

"I'm not sure anything will work between those two. Frannie is barely speaking to me."

"Because of our attempt to introduce her to Seth?"

"Well, we did succeed in that part. We introduced them. I'm not sure how it went after that. That's probably why Frannie is giving me the cold shoulder, though I'm not really sure. I never really know what I do to set her off."

"That doesn't sound like a fun way to live. What does your *mudder* say?"

"Mamm and Frannie are two peas in a pod. I don't mean Mamm is as moody as Frannie, but she seems to understand my *schweschder*'s moods. I think they both thrive on negative thoughts."

"How do you cope with that? You don't seem negative at all."

Lizzie laughed. "Generally, I try to stay out of their way as much as possible, but since Frannie and I share a room, that isn't always easy to do. I prefer to think positive thoughts. I'd rather be happy than grumpy. I do escape to my workshop as often as I can." Her voice dropped to a whisper. "I used to go out and play with the kittens, too. Before the fire, I used to take long walks to visit them and to draw."

"I'm sorry you can't do that anymore."

"Me, too, but I should be grateful Mamm let me keep them at all. At least I got to enjoy them for a little while. How's that for positive thinking?"

"You're a better person than I am. I'm afraid I'd be pretty bitter and plenty angry at my *schweschder* for causing a problem."

"I was at first, but I figure Frannie's dramatics provided a convenient excuse for Mamm. Frannie's teeny tiny scratch gave Mamm a reason to exile the kittens. If Frannie hadn't whined about a scratch, Mamm would have found another excuse." Lizzie shrugged her shoulders. "I had to let the anger and the hurt go. I'm thankful the kittens get to stay together and that Mary took them."

"Mamm dotes on them, that's for sure."

"I'd better get inside and see if she needs help with anything before I leave."

"Can you walk okay?"

"Sure. My foot is almost as *gut* as new." Lizzie concentrated on walking without hobbling even though every step generated some degree of pain. She glanced at Stephen's desk and stopped in her tracks. "My picture. You have my cat picture out."

"Mamm wanted to see it. Remember?"

Lizzie nodded. "I remember." Why had his face

turned into a giant tomato if he had only pulled it out to show Mary? Certainly that wasn't something to be embarrassed about. "I can take it inside." As she reached the door, Stephen called out after her.

"What about Frannie and Seth?"

"We might have to let that go and let them find their own way."

Stephen sighed. "You're probably right. I just hate seeing my *bruder* so miserable."

"You see, Stephen, you are a *gut* person. You're concerned for someone else's happiness."

"Or lack thereof."

"Right."

Lizzie turned thoughtful for a moment. "So how do *you* stay positive with a, uh, kind of grumpy *bruder*?"

Stephen threw back his head and laughed. "You don't have to mince words or tiptoe around the truth. Seth is grumpy a lot of the time. I try to ignore him or, like you, escape to my shop. Sometimes I simply hang around Mamm. It's hard to be grumpy around her. Seth should try that."

"It must have been fun growing up with Mary for a *mudder*."

"She did have a way of making mundane chores fun."

Lizzie banished her wistfulness. She loved her own *mudder*, even if she was totally different from Mary Zimmerman. The world needed all kinds of folks, ain't so? Even grumpy ones. She turned the doorknob and braced herself for the breeze that had kicked up while she was playing with the puppies. "Let me know if you devise any brilliant schemes for Seth and Frannie. I guess we could give it one more try." She beat down the nagging little voice that said another try would provide another chance to see Stephen. That should not be important. It could not be important.

"I'll think on it."

"Lizzie, you're limping! Are you hurt?"

She had tried so hard to walk normally. She couldn't hide anything from Mary, though. "I'm fine."

"What happened?"

"Stephen accidentally stepped on my foot." Before Mary could interject a comment, Lizzie rushed on. "It was completely my fault. I was in the way. He didn't hear me enter the shop, and he backed right into me."

"Sit down and let me get you some ice."

"It's all right now."

"I certainly hope he apologized."

"He did, but it truly was an accident."

"I hope he apologized for his snippy attitude earlier, too."

"He did."

"I think every now and then he forgets every girl isn't Joanna."

"Joanna?" Did Stephen have feelings for some girl? That shouldn't make a person grumpy. She'd never been in love or even had a fellow call on her, so she didn't know for sure, but she thought love should make a person happy. Frannie had certainly been nicer when she thought she had a chance with Aaron Kurtz.

"Oops! That should not have slipped out." Mary smacked her mouth.

"Is Joanna someone special to Stephen?" She shouldn't probe or act nosy, but Lizzie did want to understand. When Mary had made her comment about Stephen sneaking peeks at the kitten drawing, Lizzie had thought his embarrassment might be because he cared. She should shelve that idea right now.

"I shouldn't say anything, but it's over now, so I guess it doesn't much matter."

"What's over?"

"I'm sorry, dear. I'm not making much sense. Joanna Brubacher was a girl Stephen became interested in for a while."

"For a while?"

"I don't know if he ever took her home after a singing. *Mamms* aren't supposed to know those things, but I do know they sometimes talked after church. Anyway, she thanked him for making Enoch, her real beau, jealous, since it pushed him into formally courting her. Enoch and Joanna married shortly after that."

"How awful for Stephen."

"True. At least the happy couple moved to Pennsylvania, which helped Stephen get over it."

"Well, I can see how that would make a person snippy."

"But he shouldn't be with you. You are the sweetest girl ever. Why, if . . . Never mind."

What had Mary been about to say? Should she ask? Before she could decide, the woman spoke again.

"Stephen is really a very kind, caring person, so please forgive any slipups he might have."

"We all have grumpy moments."

"Some of us more than others." Mary stared out the window at the buggy that rolled past. "That young man, for one." She shook her head and clucked her tongue.

"You're worried about Seth, ain't so?"

Mary heaved a sigh that carried the weight of the world. "I try not to worry. He's in the Lord Gott's hands, but I surely wish he would settle down and join the church."

Lizzie squeezed Mary's hand. "I don't mean to pry, but does Seth have someone special?"

"I don't know, but it could only improve his mood! If he doesn't change, he won't ever attract a girl, though. Did that make any sense?"

"Perfect sense. That's exactly what I often think about Frannie."

"But she joined your church, didn't she?"

"She did. I'm the one who hasn't joined yet, so my *mudder* probably frets about me."

"But you are a levelheaded, kind person. I've never seen you in an unpleasant mood, even when you are troubled. Is there a reason you haven't joined?"

"I'm not ready to give up my drawing yet—or I guess you could say my freedom. I don't mean that I want to jump the fence, but right now I can still draw, take long hikes, and rescue animals. I have my weaving business to tend to. If I join the church, that will tell people I'm ready to settle down and get married."

"That would indicate marriageability to the young men, you mean?"

"I suppose. And what man would put up with a *fraa* who loves animals and rescues cats from burning buildings and sneaks around to draw pictures?"

Mary hugged Lizzie and laughed. "You are a very special young woman. Any man should consider himself fortunate to win your heart. There are animal-loving and art-loving men out there, I'm sure."

"Maybe. Why do you suppose Seth hasn't joined your church? You don't think he's planning to move, do you?"

"I certainly hope not. I know sometimes grown

kinner leave the area for work or other reasons even after they join the church, but as long as they don't leave the faith, they aren't lost to their loved ones."

"So if Seth was thinking of leaving the faith, it would be better if he hasn't joined the church, the same as for us?"

"Right, but I would be heartbroken if Seth decided not to join. I'll keep praying for my firstborn."

"*Jah.*" Lizzie's heart ached for Mary. She needed to tell Stephen they should not institute a plan B. Unless Seth joined the Amish church, Frannie would be under the *bann* if she got involved with him, and Mary would be crushed if Seth left the Mennonite faith. Lizzie and Stephen were going to have to forego their matchmaking efforts and leave their siblings to their own devices.

A fleeting thought made Lizzie's breath catch in her throat. Had Mamm been praying for her to join their church? Would she be heartbroken if Lizzie didn't join? Somehow Lizzie didn't think so. Mamm loved her, but they didn't have that warm, close relationship that Mary had with her sons.

"What do you have in your hand?"

Lizzie mentally shook herself to return to the present. "Stephen dug out the kitten drawing."

"I have a feeling he didn't have to dig too deeply to find it." Mary's broad smile brightened her face and dispelled the solemn mood that had crept over the room.

"Pardon me?"

Mary laughed. "I have a feeling my son keeps this picture pretty close at hand."

"Why would he do that? I know he likes animals, but this picture isn't anything special."

"The artist is special."

Fire singed Lizzie's cheeks. Maybe Mary meant *she* thought the artist was special, not Stephen. That had to be it. "I think you're special, too, Mary."

"Of course you are dear to me, but I'm quite sure Stephen considers you special, too."

A crazy little hope sprang to life in Lizzie's heart. "I don't know about that."

Mary smiled and patted Lizzie's arm. "I didn't mean to embarrass you, child, but I would be completely delighted if something developed between you and Stephen."

"*Ach*, Mary! I'm Amish."

"But not baptized yet."

"*Nee.*" Lizzie's reply sounded like a mewing kitten even to her own ears. How uncanny! Mary assumed the same thing about her that she did about Seth.

"Let's have a look at your masterpiece." Mary tugged the drawing from Lizzie's hand.

Chapter Twenty-Nine

This time Lizzie knocked and cleared her throat to give fair warning of her approach.

"It's safe to enter. I promise not to step on you."

"I'm not worried about that. I didn't want to startle you and make you mess up your work." Lizzie pushed the door all the way open and stepped into the shop. The kerosene heater provided just enough warmth to knock off the chill in the air. Still, Lizzie's hand that clutched the drawing trembled. "I'm returning your picture." She willed herself not to blush at the memory of Mary's words about Stephen and the drawing.

"*Danki*." He straightened from his crouched position and set the can of stain on the workbench, then glanced at his less than clean hands. "Maybe you'd better lay the picture on the table so I don't spill something on it or leave my dirty fingerprints all over it. You know how clumsy I am." His lips twitched.

Lizzie smiled. "You are not clumsy. I should have knocked earlier."

"How is your foot?"

"Fine." Almost. But she wouldn't dwell on that. "Stephen, I think we need to forget about any plan B."

He swiped a hand across his forehead, leaving a

brown smudge behind. Lizzie had the ridiculous urge to pick up the cloth lying on the workbench and wipe his face. She nearly laughed aloud at the idea.

"What's so funny?"

"You left a big brown blob on your forehead."

Stephen reached up and rubbed his face.

Now Lizzie did laugh. "You smeared it from one side to the other. Here." She snatched up the cloth and dabbed at the smudge. Her heart flipped and flopped when Stephen grasped her hand as she lowered it from its cleaning mission. What had gotten into her? And why wouldn't her feet move to carry her away from those mesmerizing eyes?

"*Danki.*"

His voice broke the spell. Lizzie dropped the cloth and jumped back. Stephen had to let go of her hand or be pulled off balance by Lizzie's sudden jerk. Her fingers tingled. Her usually uncontrollable tongue refused to form a single word.

"Lizzie?"

"Huh?"

"I asked what you meant about forgetting plan B."

He did? When did he do that? "Well, if anything *should* work out between Frannie and Seth, one of them would have to leave their faith."

"We knew that at the start."

"Frannie would be under the *bann* if she left."

"True, but Seth wouldn't be, since he hasn't joined the church yet."

"It would break your *mudder*'s heart if Seth left."

"It isn't like he would be leaving the planet. He would be close by and could visit."

"Right, but I'm sure Mary wants all her *kinner* to stay in the faith."

"How would you know that?"

Lizzie didn't want to reveal the details of her earlier conversation with Mary, but she wanted to answer truthfully. "I've gotten to know her quite well during the time we've spent together at the loom. She has talked about her family, and, well, I know it's important to her that her family stays intact."

Stephen blew out a sigh that ruffled the dark hair hanging on his forehead. "I'm always going to have a grumpy *bruder*, huh?"

Lizzie smiled. "He'll find someone. I hope Frannie does, too. I'll be keeping my grumpy *schweschder*, too."

Stephen smoothed his hair back into place. "To tell the truth, I didn't see any hint of a spark between them. Did you?"

"Not even a glimmer. Who knows? Maybe since we've introduced them, they will gravitate toward each other on their own."

"If they get desperate enough."

Lizzie laughed. "You make them both sound hopeless. I'm sure they have redeemable qualities. If they're meant to be together, they will be."

"Gott's will?"

"Gott's will."

Gott's will. The words swirled through Lizzie's brain her whole way home on the county commuter bus, which was actually an oversized van. While the bus wasn't quite as reliable as a hired driver, it was less expensive. She couldn't shake those words as she trudged up the long driveway toward her house. What was Gott's will for her? He had given her weaving skills. She believed that, since she had learned so easily. Didn't He also give her the drawing abilities? Did He want her to give up one but not the other? Was it really okay to design blankets and garments but totally wrong to draw pictures? She couldn't make sense of it any which way her poor, tired brain tried to decipher it.

She glanced at the potting shed and frowned. She missed the kittens' little meows and their furry bodies rubbing against her. There had been nothing she could do to prevent their departure, and there was nothing she could do now to bring them back. At least they were safe and well cared for.

"Where's Lizzie? She should be helping."

How could she hear Frannie's voice with the door closed tight against the cold? Apparently it was Gott's will for her to have a nasty *schweschder*.

Forgive me, Gott, for my unkind thoughts. Please give me strength and an understanding heart. She sucked in a deep breath and started counting backward—from fifty this time—before turning the doorknob.

Lizzie heard the familiar tongue cluck Mamm made when she was displeased with something or someone. Unfortunately, in her twenty years on the planet, Lizzie had heard that distinctive sound more often than she cared to admit. She seemed to be forever in hot water for one reason or another, usually some trumped-up infraction reported by Frannie. *Think pleasant thoughts.* She persuaded the muscles in her forehead to release their pucker and tried to smile.

"Hello, Mamm and Frannie. What can I do to help?" Lizzie even managed to infuse cheerfulness into her voice. There was plenty of time until supper, so she couldn't imagine why the two women staring at her would be in a tizzy.

"You smell like a dog." Frannie wrinkled her nose.

"It could be worse. I could smell like a pig. Don't let your face freeze that way, *Schweschder*." Sarcasm wouldn't win her any points. Her dratted tongue had run away with itself again. She directed her attention to Mamm. "Would you like me to get the laundry off the line, or do you have something in here you need me to do?" From her brief glance around the kitchen, Lizzie surmised that supper preparations were well underway.

"Were you visiting the dogs again?"

One hundred ninety-nine, one hundred ninety-eight. "I was helping Mary Zimmerman with her weaving." Why couldn't Frannie let a topic die a natural death?

"Are you turning Mennonite?"

"Why would you ask me such a thing, Frannie? I go to the grocery store and you don't ask if I'm turning *Englisch*."

"It seems you spend a lot of time there."

"At the grocery store?"

"You know very well what I mean!" Frannie's dark eyes snapped, the same as her voice.

Of course she knew what Frannie meant. Her resolution to be nice had flown right out the window. *One hundred ninety-seven.* "You know how much I enjoy weaving, and if I can help someone else learn the art and experience the same joy, then I'm happy to do so."

"Art?"

"Weaving is an art, just like knitting or baking. At least I think so." Lizzie turned her back on Frannie and looked to her *mudder* for any instructions she might have.

"I would have thought you had plenty of your own work to do with the holidays so near."

Drop it, Frannie. Lizzie looked over her shoulder at

her *schweschder* and forced a tiny smile. "I do have
orders to finish. I plan to work on them after supper."
That way I won't have to be closed up in a room with you!

Finally Mamm assigned her a task. "If you can scrub
your hands clean, you can get the laundry in."

"If you can scrub off that smell, it will be even
better. Try not to transfer the stench to the clothes. I
don't want any of my things to smell like a dog." Frannie wrinkled her nose again.

Lizzie almost bit her tongue in half to keep from
telling Frannie she could have gotten the clothes in instead of standing around criticizing her. "I'll wash my
hands and bring in the laundry, Mamm." The sooner
she got away from Frannie, the better. On her way to
the bathroom, she paused to call out, "I can leave your
things on the line for you to get, Frannie. That way I
won't contaminate any of them."

"I'll trust you to wash your hands, so you can go
ahead and get my laundry, too."

That's what Lizzie had thought Frannie would say.
Why should the girl step a foot outside when she could
stay in the warm kitchen doing nothing? Lizzie willed
herself to walk normally to the bathroom and not
stomp her feet like she wanted to do. She lathered her
hands to scrub away nonexistent dirt. Honestly! Lizzie
had washed her hands after playing with the puppies,
so even if they weren't sterile, they were clean enough
to bring in clothes.

Don't mumble. Don't grumble. Lizzie repeated the
words silently over and over. She snatched up the laundry basket and headed outside to wrestle the flapping
clothes. She would think about her day and put
thoughts of Frannie aside for at least a few minutes.

She had had a great time helping Mary at the loom.

She had enjoyed playing with the puppies, especially Sunny. She had happily petted the kittens. And if she was totally honest with herself, she would have to admit she had even liked spending time with Stephen—all except for the foot-crushing part. Lizzie wiggled her toes. They were a little sore, but she'd live.

Lizzie understood Stephen's moods a bit more after Mary's revelation. Stephen must have been very hurt when he discovered that Joanna had only been using him and hadn't had any affection for him at all. What was wrong with that girl? Didn't she almost drown in Stephen's eyes? Lizzie sighed. After being hurt like that it probably would be hard to trust again. In time, he would find someone else to care for. Why did that thought prick her heart?

She reached for a pair of pants dancing around her head and jerked it from the clothespins. The wind had grown stronger and colder. She should have located a pair of gloves before coming out. Now she would have chapped hands. Well, chapped hands were a small price to pay to escape from Frannie. What was wrong with that girl?

Lizzie hated tiptoeing around her *schweschder*. She was going to have to simply ask Frannie what real or imaginary sin she had committed against her. Truly, Lizzie didn't try to aggravate the girl. She would much rather live in peace and harmony than have to worry about when the next explosion would occur.

If only Frannie got out more maybe her moods would improve. Lizzie had hoped baking for Yoder's Store would help. She resolved to try to persuade Frannie to attend the next singing with her. Lizzie stretched to yank down the next pair of pants before it could attack her. This job would go a lot quicker if

Frannie came out to help. *Don't mumble. Don't grumble.*
Lizzie laughed at her silly mantra. Laughing was ever so
much better than sulking.

Lizzie was still smiling as she clumped inside with
the full basket. "Brrr! It sure has turned colder!"

"Were you talking to the laundry and laughing?"

Did Frannie have to try to spoil every *gut* mood?
Well, Lizzie wouldn't let her. "I was talking to myself
and laughing at myself."

"Weird."

Not half as weird as trying to pick fights all the time.
Lizzie wondered if all her unsaid words would build up
so much that she would explode one day, releasing
them to the world. The image almost made her giggle
again, but she didn't dare let out a sound. She would
find her little *schweschders* and help them do something. Anything.

Chapter Thirty

Stephen rummaged through his scrap wood searching for exactly the right pieces. He wasn't sure what those were but figured he'd know when he found them. Violet eyes haunted him. They peeked into his mind and into his dreams. If he tried to think of something else, the eyes penetrated those thoughts. And now here he was scouting out wood to make something for the fascinating owner of those incredible eyes.

Cherry or walnut or oak? Which should he choose? He pulled out scraps of each and studied them. She had said both his projects were pretty, the cherry bookcase and the walnut table, but he thought she favored the cherry a teensy bit more.

Ach! What was he doing thinking about Lizzie Fisher and making something to please her? He must be totally daft. She was a woman. Women were not to be trusted—except for Mamm, of course. And Lizzie wasn't even Mennonite. *She hasn't joined the church yet.*

Stephen's head jerked up. He looked around to see who had crept into his shop and uttered those words. The door remained closed. Everything was just as he had left it. Not a single form, human or animal, lurked in the shadows. He was alone. Great! Now he was hearing voices, too.

He freed enough pieces of cherry wood from the pile and planned his project. He didn't have to make the frame for Lizzie. He could make it for Mamm instead. That's what he'd do. Lizzie might not be allowed to have such a thing anyway. *Ach!* There she was, invading his thoughts. Would he ever know peace again?

He heard the door. This time someone had entered the shop. He felt the cold air rush in to bite his fingers and nose. He couldn't have imagined that unless he truly had lost his mind. He glanced up, halfway afraid there wouldn't be anyone there, forcing him to question his sanity. "Seth! What brings you out here?" Stephen hoped his *bruder* couldn't hear the relief in his voice. He didn't have any idea how he'd explain his crazy thoughts.

"Can't I see what my little *bruder* is up to?"

Stephen chuckled. He might be a year younger than Seth, but he certainly was not smaller. In fact, he stood at least an inch taller and had slightly broader shoulders. "Of course you can. You just don't usually do that."

Seth shrugged. Never one to beat around the bush, he got right down to business. "Are you done playing matchmaker?"

Stephen coughed. *Gut* thing he hadn't stuck nails in his mouth like he sometimes did. He would have surely choked on them or spit them across the room pinning Seth to the wall. "Matchmaker?"

"*Jah.* With Frannie Fisher. It won't work, you know."

Stephen searched for words. "We, uh, I just thought you two could be *freinden*."

Seth burst out laughing. "Since when would a Mennonite man and an Amish woman want to become *freinden?*"

Stephen shrugged. "A person can never have too many *freinden*, ain't so?"

"Who is 'we'?"

"What?"

"You started to say 'we.' You mean you and Lizzie, don't you?"

"*Jah.*"

"Why is she trying to marry off her *schweschder?* What's wrong with the girl?"

"Nothing. You saw her. She was nice, and pleasing to look at, too."

"She looked fine. We didn't say much to each other besides basic pleasantries. Why can't she find her own fellow, and why do you think you have to find me a girl?"

Even though Seth kept his voice even, Stephen could sense his *bruder's* rising ire. He wanted to choose the right words, if only he knew what they were. "Lizzie felt like her *schweschder* needed to get out and meet people. She said Frannie tends to be too much of a homebody. Lizzie wanted to help. You've seemed a little lonely, and I, uh, we . . ."

"Did it ever occur to either of you amateur match-makers that I'm Mennonite and Frannie is Amish?"

"Of course it did, but you haven't been baptized yet."

"So you thought I'd jump at the chance to court Frannie and leave my faith and family?"

"We figured you wouldn't be shunned since you haven't joined the church, but Frannie would be since she's already joined hers."

Seth sighed loud enough to shake the rafters. He rubbed a hand across his eyes. Stephen braced himself for a barrage of angry words, but his *bruder* surprised him. "Just because I haven't joined the church yet doesn't mean I don't plan to. I don't have any intention of leaving my faith." He sighed again. "I suppose I should appreciate your concern, but I'm really not so desperate that I need you and Lizzie to parade girls around for me to choose from."

"Girl."

"Huh?"

"Girl. Only one girl. We had hoped to help you and Frannie. We thought you two would hit it off, but I guess we were wrong. I'm sorry, Seth. We shouldn't have meddled. You are certainly capable of finding your own girl."

"*Danki*. So there won't be any more matchmaking attempts? You and Lizzie haven't designed any future meetings?"

"None whatsoever."

"That's a relief." Seth turned to leave the shop. "Nice bookcase."

"*Danki*."

Seth paused and looked over his shoulder. "You know, you and Lizzie would make a *gut* match. If she hasn't joined her church yet, she could join ours. You two seem well suited. Maybe you should work on that match." He chuckled and slipped out into the darkness.

Stephen stared at the door. He hadn't even been able to manage a reply, either serious or flippant. Seth was the one who'd lost his mind to think Stephen and Lizzie were well suited. Just because they both liked animals, cared about their families, tried to look on

the bright side, liked to joke and laugh, and possessed
creative abilities didn't mean they were well suited.
Did it? Were they a *gut* match? Stephen shook his head.
Ridiculous!

Lizzie blew on her fingers to warm them. She wiggled them to get the blood circulating before returning to her weaving. The kerosene heater didn't seem
to be doing a stellar job this evening, but she wanted
to make a bit more headway on the blanket she'd been
weaving for an *Englisch* customer.

A whoosh of cold air assailed her, making her
shiver. Had she forgotten to tightly close the door?
The bang made her jump, causing the stool to teeter.

"Oops! I didn't mean to slam the door. The wind
yanked it out of my hand."

So much for her calm, peaceful evening. Frannie
rarely set foot in her workshop. Why had she picked
tonight to grace Lizzie with her presence? Surely she
didn't want to continue the nitpicking she'd begun
the instant Lizzie had arrived home. Thank goodness
Lizzie hadn't been sketching. Unable to gauge Frannie's current mood, Lizzie waited for her *schweschder*
to speak.

Frannie rubbed her hands up and down her arms.
"It has gotten much colder. Aren't you freezing out
here?"

"It's rather chilly, but as long as I keep busy, I don't
notice the cold so much."

Frannie shuffled across the small room. She reached
down to touch Lizzie's hands. "Your fingers are like ice.
Can't you work with gloves on?"

"Gloves make my fingers clumsier. I need to feel what I'm doing." Had Frannie braved the elements merely to talk about the weather? Lizzie braced herself for whatever accusation or criticism was forthcoming.

"Why don't you *kumm* inside for some cocoa to warm up? You can work out here when the sun streams in the window to warm the place up a little."

Why was Frannie suddenly concerned about her well-being? Sometimes Lizzie wondered if two people lived inside Frannie's body. "I'll probably head inside soon. I want to get a little more work done."

"It's pretty. It must be for an *Englischer*, with those bright colors."

"It is."

"It's still pretty."

"*Danki*." Compliments from Frannie were rarities. How should she react? She wanted to ask Frannie why she had come into the shop but didn't want to chase the "nice" Frannie away. She'd wait to see if her *schweschder* chose to enlighten her.

Frannie coughed and glanced around the workshop. Was she looking for something in particular? She seemed to be searching for words and expecting them to be written on the walls somewhere.

"I know what you were trying to do."

What was she talking about? Lizzie had been trying to stay out of her *schweschder*'s way. "Trying to do when?"

"At Yoder's Store."

"I accompanied you to help you take your baked foods there."

"And you didn't have any idea the Zimmerman *bruders* would waltz in."

Hmmm. How should she respond? She hadn't been

certain they would show up while Lizzie and Frannie were at the store, but she and Stephen had hoped that would happen. Lizzie stared at the blanket on the loom. She brushed away an imaginary speck of lint. What should she say? She was actually surprised Frannie hadn't jumped all over her with both feet. "I wasn't sure we would meet right then, but Stephen knew we were going to the store that day." She wished she could crawl under the loom.

"Why?"

One calm little word? No whining or screaming? Frannie must be ill. Lizzie stole a peek at Frannie's face. She didn't see anger, hatred, or any other belligerent expression. "Why?" Lizzie twirled one white *kapp* string around an index finger.

"*Jah.* Why?"

"I had met Seth before while at Mary's house. Stephen mentioned he thought his *bruder* was lonely. I suppose I talked about my family and happened to mention that you were unattached and—"

Frannie tugged Lizzie's finger away from the *kapp*. "You told them I'd been jilted?" Only a hint of the usual screech crept into her voice.

"Of course not! I said you spent a lot of time baking your delicious treats and didn't go out a lot."

"And the two of you decided to do a little match-making? Was Seth in on that, too?"

"*Nee.* He was as unsuspecting as you were. Stephen and I didn't mean any harm. We both wanted to see our siblings happy."

"How happy could two totally different people be together? He's Mennonite. I'm Amish."

"We aren't so very different in our beliefs, you know. Besides, Seth hasn't yet joined the church."

"I have."

"True, but—"

"You thought Seth would fall madly in love with me at first sight, forsake his family and faith, become Amish, and marry me so we could all live happily ever after?"

"Something like that." It did sound pretty far-fetched when Frannie put it like that. "I'm sorry, Frannie. We shouldn't have meddled. I guess you and Seth didn't hit it off, and Stephen and I should have minded our own business."

"You definitely should have. It was downright embarrassing to be forced on someone like that."

"I hadn't thought of it that way. I only hoped you could meet and talk and see if there was any kind of spark between you."

"Well, we met and we talked. He seemed nice enough, but I can assure you there weren't any sparks. I did notice some fireworks between you and Stephen, though."

Lizzie clapped her hands to her cheeks. "*Ach*, Frannie, ain't so! There's nothing going on between Stephen and me."

A sly smile played at Frannie's lips. "You, my dear *schweschder*, must be blind. Maybe blinded by love?"

"You are completely wrong."

"I don't think so."

Lizzie needed to turn this conversation around fast. "Have you been mad at me since the meeting at the store? Is that why you've been in a snit?" Lizzie almost added *this time*, but caught herself. Frannie had been quite subdued during this conversation, not at all like the usual ranting, raving girl, so Lizzie didn't want to upset the applecart.

Frannie fidgeted. She plucked at a loose strand of dark hair. It was so unlike her to think before spewing out venomous words. Dare Lizzie hope her *schweschder* had turned over a new leaf?

"That and other things." Frannie's voice died off at the end of her sentence. Such a sad look crossed her face.

"I'm a *gut* listener if you want to talk. I mean, I won't blab to anyone." Lizzie would have hugged Frannie but didn't know how that action would be received. "But maybe you've already talked to Mamm."

"I haven't said anything to Mamm."

Lizzie didn't see how the two of them could work alongside each other all day without Mamm prying the reason for Frannie's glumness out of her. Lizzie threw caution to the wind and reached out to touch her *schweschder*'s arm. The worst that could happen would be that Frannie would smack her hand away, and that would cause only emotional pain. Lizzie was pretty used to that. To her amazement, Frannie grabbed her hand and clung to it like a drowning man clung to a rope.

"*Ach*, Lizzie!"

"What's troubling you? I know my meddling was wrong even though my intentions were *gut*, and I am truly sorry."

Frannie squeezed Lizzie's hand harder and shook her head. She dragged in a ragged breath and cleared her throat. "Aaron is supposed to be home soon. He might already be home."

"I know it will be hard to see him again, but you

won't have to spend any time with him. Just hold your head high, say 'Hello,' and move on."

"That will be hard to do, but I'll try. How do I *wilkom* her, though? His *fraa*? Seeing Aaron by himself will be bad enough, but seeing him beside her . . ." Frannie shook her head and sniffed.

"I'll help you. I'll stay right beside you. In fact, I'll do the talking. You can just smile sweetly."

"I'll have to see her at church, at gatherings, at frolics. I'll run into her in Yoder's Store or the quilt shop or somewhere. Oooh, why do things have to be so hard?"

Lizzie fished around in a pocket with her free hand trying to locate a tissue for Frannie. She hadn't known Frannie's feelings for Aaron ran so deep. She had assumed Frannie was merely interested in the *bu*. Was she actually in love with him? It sure sounded like it. She extracted a crumpled tissue and held it out to Frannie. "It's unused. I promise." Lizzie almost giggled at Frannie's disgusted expression. "Truly, I haven't used it. Take it, unless you prefer to use your sleeve."

"Eww!" Frannie grabbed the tissue and dabbed it at her eyes and nose.

"I'm sorry you're hurting, Frannie. I'll try to help . . . Who in the world is visiting at this late hour?"

Frannie wiped her eyes again. She grasped the unruly strand of hair blowing around her face and poked it beneath her *kapp*. "Were you expecting someone?"

"Me? *Nee*. Who would be visiting me? My customers all *kumm* during the day."

"A suitor, perhaps?"

Lizzie swatted at Frannie's arm. "You know better than that."

Frannie scooted over to the door, opened it a crack, and peeked out. One second later she pushed it closed and leaned against it. She patted her chest.

"Frannie! Whatever is the matter?" Could a twenty-two-year-old, healthy woman suffer a sudden heart attack? Lizzie rushed to her side.

"I-it's him." Frannie could barely gasp out the two words. She continued patting her chest.

"Him who?"

"A-Aaron K-Kurtz."

Chapter Thirty-One

"Here? Why would Aaron be here?" Lizzie's own heart began beating in double time. Surely Aaron hadn't made it a point to drive his new *fraa* over here to meet Frannie. He wouldn't be that cruel, would he? Surely he had some inkling that Frannie had feelings for him, didn't he? If Lizzie, a distant observer at singings, had picked up on Frannie's cues, the man those special looks were aimed at would have. Or were men that dense?

"I-I don't know why he's here."

"Maybe you were mistaken. You only took a quick peek."

"Do you think I wouldn't recognize him? I'd know him if he was wrapped in a grain sack with a stocking cap pulled over his head."

Lizzie nodded. Frannie would undoubtedly know Aaron anywhere. She'd probably dreamed about him time and time again. She wouldn't need more than a quick glance.

"I've got to hide. I don't want to face him. I'm not ready yet." Frannie's eyes darted around the shop and stopped on the loom.

"You are not crawling under the loom."

"How did you know I was considering that?"

"I can read your mind. Sometimes." Other times she was completely clueless.

"Quick, put out the lamp."

"Then we'll fall over something and break our necks."

"That's preferable to facing Aaron right now."

"I think I'll slip outside and give him a piece of my mind. How dare he appear here in the black of night to cause you pain!" Lizzie stomped to the door.

"*Nee!*" Frannie caught her arm. "You'll make things worse."

"I'll behave. I'll be perfectly polite. Let me see what he wants before he wakes up the whole household. I guess everyone else went to bed, didn't they?"

"Melvin and Caleb were finishing a game of checkers. The little ones were in bed. Mamm and Daed were about to turn in when I came out."

"Okay. Let me see if I can find out what Aaron wants without an audience of six additional curious people."

"If we're quiet, he might go away."

"I doubt it. I'm sure he's already seen the light out here. Let me make sure someone isn't sick or hurt or something."

Frannie stepped aside. Lizzie expected she'd find her *schweschder* stuck under the loom when she returned. She willed herself to stay calm. She couldn't rush out and start accusing Aaron of something without having all the facts.

Lizzie stepped livelier so she could head Aaron off before he stomped up the porch steps. "Psst, Aaron!" She didn't want to yell. Even though the windows were closed against the cold, some light sleeper might be able to hear a loud voice. Aaron jumped and turned.

"Lizzie?"

"*Jah.*"

"You startled me." Aaron headed in her direction. "Is anything wrong at your house?"

"*Jah. Nee.* I mean, not at my house. My family is fine."

How about your fraa? Lizzie didn't ask that question, but her tongue quivered with the weight of it. She'd try very hard to wait for Aaron to explain the meaning of this nocturnal visit. When the silence became unbearable, she broke her resolve. "Can I help you with something?"

"Uh, *nee*, uh, *jah.*"

"Which is it?" Lizzie feared she would freeze before he made up his mind.

"Is Frannie here?"

"If you don't mind my asking, why do you need to see Frannie? Shouldn't you be home with your new *fraa*?"

"That's what I need to talk to Frannie about."

"Your *fraa*? Do you really think Frannie needs to hear all about her right now? That's pretty mean, Aaron Kurtz."

"You don't understand."

"I'll say. I don't understand why a man would possibly think a woman who cared for him would want to hear about his bride." Lizzie felt her blood pressure rise along with her voice.

"Frannie cares about me?"

"Forget I said that." Lizzie turned her back on the tall man in the shadows. "We'll meet your *fraa* next church day. Don't trouble Frannie now. She's—"

"Frannie?" Aaron called a little louder.

Lizzie looked at the shaft of light streaming from her workshop. Frannie stood silhouetted in the doorway.

Now, why did she open the door? Lizzie had almost gotten rid of Aaron for her.

Aaron strode toward the workshop. Lizzie trotted to keep up. She did not want to miss any of this conversation, and she wanted to help Frannie gather up the pieces of her heart afterward. She reached the doorway right as Aaron opened his mouth to speak. "You don't have to talk to him and whoever he has in the buggy, Frannie."

"There isn't anyone in the buggy. I came here alone."

"What made you think Frannie would want to talk to you? What would you have done if we were all in bed?"

Aaron held up his hand like he was stopping traffic at an intersection. "Please?"

From what Lizzie could see in the dim light, he did seem contrite or worried or something. She glanced at Frannie. Would her *schweschder* hear him out or run to the house?

"Please give me a chance to explain, Frannie. Please listen to me."

Lizzie held her breath, waiting for Frannie's decision. "All right, Aaron. I'll listen to you."

"Could you talk inside? I'm freezing." Lizzie scooted past Aaron and Frannie, who stood staring at each other in the doorway. She darted over to the kerosene heater and held her hands in front of it. "You two can talk. Don't mind me."

"Lizzie . . ." Frannie began.

"I'm not going to wait outside, Frannie, so don't even ask. You two can stay out there if you don't want me around."

"It's okay, Frannie." Finally Aaron had sense enough to close the door and cut off the wind that was zipping through. "I don't mind if Lizzie hears me."

Lizzie rubbed her hands briskly to restore their circulation. Unless Aaron whispered or Frannie had learned to read lips, she'd hear their conversation. She knew she shouldn't be so eager to catch Aaron's words, but this would be too *gut* to miss. He had better have a remarkable reason for bursting in and stirring up Frannie's pain!

She tried to grab inconspicuous glances at Frannie and Aaron, but from the way they were staring at each other, they probably wouldn't have noticed if she skittered across the room and stood right beside them. Would someone please speak?

Frannie blinked. Aaron cleared his throat. At the rate they were going, the rooster would be crowing before Aaron enlightened them on his reason for leaving his bride home and visiting another girl. Lizzie struggled to tamp down her temper. Maybe Aaron had a perfectly innocent, legitimate reason for being here. She wished he'd spit it out.

"Frannie, I'm sorry I left here rather abruptly. I never got to talk to you about it."

Well, he hadn't redeemed himself yet. Lizzie dared not even fidget, or else she might get thrown out of this bizarre situation. She looked at Frannie's face. The poor girl hadn't even moved. She must still be breathing, since she hadn't crumpled in a heap on the floor.

Aaron cleared his throat again. "Frannie, I—"

"You got married! You found a *fraa* almost as soon as you got to Pennsylvania. You let me throw myself at you like a fool over and over again while you knew all along some other girl was waiting for you. You must have enjoyed quite a laugh."

Gut girl, Frannie. Don't let him off easy. Let's see him worm his way out of this.

"Wait, Frannie! Wait a minute." Aaron waved his hands. "I'm not married."

"What?" Lizzie clapped a hand across her mouth. She hadn't meant to speak out loud. Fortunately neither Frannie nor Aaron took notice of her.

Frannie's mouth dropped open. Her eyes grew so large that Lizzie feared they'd pop out and roll across the floor.

"Did you hear me, Frannie?"

Frannie shook her head as if trying to free herself from some sort of trance. "I thought you just said you weren't married, but we received news of your marriage some time ago. Everyone has been talking about it."

"That's the problem. Someone got the wrong information, and the wild rumors spread like fire in a haystack."

"I don't understand."

Me, neither! Lizzie leaned closer so her ears would pick up every word.

"It's all been a big misunderstanding."

"You weren't communicating with a girl in Pennsylvania? You didn't go there to marry her?"

"I did not have any secret admirers in Pennsylvania. I was not communicating with anyone there."

"Then how did such a crazy rumor get started if there wasn't any basis for it?" Lizzie clamped her tongue between her teeth. She was supposed to be a silent observer, a fly on the wall. Now she had reminded them of her presence yet again.

"*Jah.* How exactly did that rumor get started?"

Lizzie sagged in relief. Frannie actually concurred

with her. She didn't yell and tell her to mind her own business.

Aaron swept his black felt hat off his head, ran a hand through his blond hair, and plopped the hat back in place. "My *mudder* often wrote to someone in Pennsylvania—some person she's known since they were scholars. Mamm grew up there, you know. Anyway, this *freind* has a daughter. The two women cooked up the idea for me to visit."

"They wanted to arrange a marriage?"

"Not exactly. They wanted to arrange a meeting. I think they wanted things to work out between Dora— that's the daughter—and me."

"Did they?"

"*Nee.* I came back alone, didn't I?"

"So you said," Lizzie mumbled. This time she knew her whispered words were too low to be heard across the room.

"What happened?" Frannie shifted from one foot to the other as if she couldn't wait to hear Aaron's next words—or else was afraid to hear those words.

"I met Dora. We talked several times. There wasn't any spark like between you and me."

There was a spark between Frannie and Aaron? From what Lizzie had observed, only Frannie's wick was lit. Maybe Aaron's interest had been so subtle Lizzie hadn't picked up on it. Had Frannie?

"But we got the report of your marriage. We heard you were bringing your *fraa* back to Maryland to live."

"I can assure you, dear Frannie, I did not get married. I returned alone."

"Dear Frannie"?

"I still don't understand." Frannie stepped back

and leaned against the rough wall of the shed-turned-workshop.

Aaron reached out a hand but drew it back before making contact with Frannie. "Are you all right?"

"I'm trying to absorb all that you've said and make sense of it in light of the stories we heard."

"'Stories' is exactly the right word. I'm not sure how the marriage rumor got started, but someone made the wrong assumption. I don't even think Dora and I were ever alone together."

A smile broke through the shocked expression Frannie had worn ever since the buggy rolled to a stop in the driveway. "You're free? I mourned in vain."

"Mourned?"

"If you had gotten married, you would have been lost to me forever—not that you and I had any kind of understanding. I figured you didn't share any of my feelings if you could get married so quickly after leaving here." Frannie's voice had dropped and she hung her head.

Lizzie had to strain to hear that last part. She nodded in agreement like she was actually part of the conversation. She did agree with Frannie, though. She, too, had assumed the relationship, such as it was, was one-sided.

"I'm sorry, Frannie." This time Aaron did touch Frannie's arm. "I should have explained. I didn't know this whole mixed-up trip would cause such a commotion. Mamm sent me to visit her *freind*'s family. She wanted me to take a special quilt and some other things she had made. I thought it strange that she didn't want to go herself, but I did as she asked. I never dreamed they had cooked up a plot to try to get me and Dora together. I don't know who started the whole marriage rumor traveling along the grapevine, but the story is completely false. I'm not married—yet." He paused to take a quick breath. "I would like us to get to know each other better, Frannie. I know I should have asked before, but do you think—"

Frannie didn't let the fellow finish. "*Jah,* Aaron. I'd like that." Her smile practically swallowed her face. If dancing had been permissible, she probably would have twirled like a ballerina.

"I know it's late and I have the enclosed buggy, but could we take a short drive now?"

"I suppose a short drive would be all right." Frannie fairly skipped from the workshop beside Aaron with a backward wave at Lizzie.

Just like that? Lizzie opened her mouth to speak, but words did not tumble out. It wouldn't have mattered anyway, because Frannie only had eyes and ears for Aaron. Did her grumpy, morose *schweschder* turn into a perky, animated girl right before her eyes? And all it took was a few pretty words from a fellow she had been ready to hide from mere minutes earlier?

Lizzie shook her head. Maybe that was how love worked. It hit you like a ton of bricks and transformed you instantly. Somehow she wasn't sure that was the way it was supposed to be. Aaron had certainly *seemed* sincere, and she didn't really have a reason to doubt his words, but personally, she would have wanted to check things out a bit more. Frannie certainly had no qualms, though. She'd thrown caution out the window and practically raced out to Aaron's buggy.

I think you let him off too easy, Schweschder, but you got your happily ever after!

Chapter Thirty-Two

Lizzie hopped off the little commuter bus several stops early. The oversized van had been packed, and the heat had been cranked up so high she had expected to see plumes of smoke drift from the vents. Someone had pickled herself in sickeningly sweet perfume that tainted every breath Lizzie tried to drag in. Her stomach flipped over and over. She'd rather walk in the cold the rest of the way to the Zimmermans' house than embarrass herself by getting sick on the bus.

She gulped in frosty air as soon as the bus door closed behind her. Finally a pure breath that held only the faint scent of wood smoke. She wiggled her hands back into the wool gloves she'd shed on the bus and set out at a brisk pace. She sure hoped she got a different bus for her return trip home or that this one got fumigated. Maybe she should have spent the extra money for an *Englisch* driver after all.

If this early December day was any indication, the almanac might have hit the nail on the head. It predicted a colder than average winter this year. Winter had not officially begun yet, but they'd already had a few record cold days.

Lizzie swung her bag as she walked, figuring the increased movement would yield additional warmth. At least the sun shone brightly and the frost had disappeared from the grass. She hummed a little tune as she strode, some silly little nonsense song, not a hymn from the Ausbund. It just seemed to be a whimsical sort of day. Visiting Mary always made Lizzie smile. Catching a glimpse of Stephen or having a word with him had absolutely nothing to do with her cheerful mood. *Right!*

At least Frannie's mood had improved by leaps and bounds. Why, her big *schweschder* had become pleasant to be around—most of the time. She had seen Aaron several times during the past week, and that definitely brought smiles to her face.

Aaron's *mudder* had retracted the rumor *she* had instigated by saying she thought things might work out for Aaron and Dora. She quickly added that she trusted her son's judgment in such matters and would not try her hand at matchmaking again. Hmmm! There seemed to be a lot of those promises going around. At any rate, Frannie definitely exuded more cheerfulness, for which Lizzie offered prayers of gratitude.

A sudden pitiful little sound brought Lizzie to a standstill. She ceased humming and even held her breath to hear the noise if it occurred again. The swirly-headed feeling that lack of oxygen caused almost made her gasp for air when the sound came again. She cocked her head. A plaintive meow came from the little stretch of woods ahead. Lizzie could not ignore an animal in distress.

She picked her way through brambles that had thorns sharp enough to tear into her legs. She jumped over a rotting log and stopped to listen again. The crinkly, crunchy leaves underfoot had obscured any other sounds as she hiked, and she wanted to be sure she was headed in the right direction.

There it was. It sounded like a kitten or a very young cat. The squeaky meow came from somewhere a little deeper in the woods. She needed to hurry. The cry for help tore at her heart and seemed weaker than when she had first heard it. What could have happened, and why had the poor creature run into the woods to begin with?

The trees thinned until only a few old oaks and some scruffy pines dotted a partial clearing around a murky pond. Where was the kitten? Lizzie glanced around. Leaves did not pile up in layers here like they did in the woods, so where could the cat be hiding?

The next meow came from above her. The scraggly pine trees didn't have branches sturdy enough to support the weight of a cat, so she turned her attention to the oaks. There, perched on a branch overhanging the pond, was a little orange and white kitten. Whatever was it doing there? Something must have frightened it into shimmying up the tree, but now it acted afraid to climb down.

"Here, kitty!" Lizzie skirted around the briars and stood beside the old oak. She patted the trunk. "*Kumm*, kitty!" She coaxed and called, but the kitten didn't budge. It continued to stare at her with frightened green eyes and let out another wail.

Lizzie set her bag down and poked her gloves inside. She'd never be able to hang on to tree limbs with gloves making her hands slippery. Besides, the yarn would catch on the rough bark and might make her lose her balance.

She ignored the voice that told her she was crazy to even consider climbing a tree. How many grown women in dresses and bonnets climbed trees? But she couldn't leave the poor kitten stranded where it sat. She'd climbed trees dozens of times during her growing-up years. She could surely do it now.

Lizzie couldn't spend any more time debating with herself. She was growing colder by the minute, and Mary was expecting her. She needed to make this rescue and be on her way. Lizzie glanced around to ensure she didn't have an audience, blew on her hands to warm them, and reached for the lowest sturdy branch.

With a little jump, she grasped the bumpy branch. She swung herself back and forth to gain enough momentum to propel herself up onto it. She reached for the next branch overhead when her feet gained stability on the first one. She paused to catch her breath. Had climbing trees been such hard work when Lizzie was little, or was she simply out of practice?

Carefully she climbed higher. She tested each branch before adding her body weight to it. "Hang on, kitty. I'll only be another minute."

"*Danki*, Stephen, for bringing your *mamm*'s baked treats in to sell today. People like their *kaffi* and cocoa in the cold weather, and nothing goes better with those than a homemade cookie or brownie. Tell Mary I'll settle up with her at the end of the week."

"Sure, Nancy." Stephen only half paid attention to Nancy Stauffer, the owner of the small store, which sold all the essentials, from fabric to food. Something had caught his eye when he glanced out the door.

Not some*thing*, he amended, but some*one*. He mumbled a few niceties and made his escape from the chatty woman. Why would a girl head off into the woods? From this distance, he couldn't discern specific features. He only knew she was Plain by the black cloak and bonnet.

The horse would be fine for a few more minutes. Stephen patted the big animal's head as he strode past. Maybe the girl was meeting a fellow, and the woods were their secret spot. That didn't seem very likely, though. *Buwe* of courting age would be working this time of day.

Stephen picked up his pace. He wanted to keep an eye on the girl and make sure she was all right. The woods here could be a bit tricky to maneuver. It wasn't that the trees were all that dense, but with fallen limbs, uneven ground, swampy areas, and a pond, a person could easily get into trouble. As *kinner*, he and some of the other fellows would romp through these woods, and one of them always wound up getting hurt or wet or both.

He wanted to stay far enough back so he didn't frighten the girl, but he didn't want to lose track of her. She hopped over rotting logs with the agility of a doe. With her last leap, he could see her blue dress beneath the black cloak. Most Mennonite women and girls wore dresses with a small print, but a solid color wouldn't be out of the question.

Then he heard it. A pitiful little meow. That must be what had led the girl through the woods. Her cat had probably run off, and she had tracked it here. Or perhaps she simply liked rescuing animals. Rescuing animals? Who else did Stephen know who would risk life and limb for an animal? He walked faster.

Suddenly he lost sight of the girl. He'd only looked down for a scant minute or two to detangle the thorny vines that had wrapped around his ankle. Where did she go? Frustrated that the thorns held him fast, impeding his progress, he yanked his leg as hard as he could. Mamm would question how he got the rips in his pants.

She couldn't have gone far in those precious minutes he had wasted battling the briars. Could the girl be Lizzie? She was supposed to visit Mamm today. That was the reason he'd delivered Mamm's cookies and brownies. But Lizzie always arrived on the commuter bus or with an *Englisch* driver. She couldn't have walked from her house.

The mournful meow came again. Was it above him? He looked up in time to see the girl crawling along the limb where an orange and white kitten sat. Didn't she notice the limb was a dead one and might not be able to support even her small body? He had to stop her.

Lizzie reached for the branch the cat sat on. It was thinner but seemed sturdy enough. She tapped it and called to the kitten. If it would only trust her enough to walk toward her, she wouldn't have to leave her relative security next to the trunk. But the kitten stared at her without budging. It opened its mouth in a silent meow as if too afraid to even plead for help.

Lizzie sighed. "All right, silly kitty, I'll get you." She began to inch her way along the branch.

"*Nee!*"

A loud, deep voice bellowed below her, but all other sounds were obliterated by the thunderous crack that split the air. Fear shot through Lizzie's body.

Chapter Thirty-Three

Lizzie threw out a hand to grasp the tree trunk but only grabbed a few skinny branches. She'd crawled out too far to reach the trunk. She didn't have time to think of any other means to save herself. She clung to the limb as if it could help her, but another little crack tore it free from the tree.

She sailed through the air, completely powerless to stop her motion. She couldn't even get out a scream. She squeezed her eyes shut and braced for the impact with the cold, hard ground. Maybe she had on enough clothes to cushion her fall a bit and prevent broken bones.

Her eyes flew open with the splash. She had made contact all right, but not with the earth. Lizzie gasped as the cold water sucked her under. Murky water entered her nose and mouth. She sputtered, coughed, and flailed about. Those cushiony clothes became saturated in a matter of seconds, and her athletic shoes turned into concrete blocks. It took all her effort to keep her head above water as the pond fought to suck her down. Why hadn't she realized the very branch she'd been slithering across hung over the middle of the pond? *Would that have stopped you from rescuing the kitten?* Probably not.

The water hadn't yet frozen, so at least Lizzie didn't have to contend with ice. That fact didn't provide a whole lot of comfort, though, since the frigid water threatened to drown her. If she could kick off her shoes, she might be a little more buoyant. But the long dress and cape had wrapped around her body and bound her as tightly as any rope would. The wind that she hadn't paid attention to before now blew its icy breath across the pond.

Lizzie fought against the forces trying to drag her beneath the water's surface. Hadn't someone spoken right before she fell? Did they go for help, or did they leave her here to die? She didn't want to die. Not yet. She kicked harder but couldn't propel herself toward the pond's edge. Who would have thought a little pond in the woods would be so deep that she couldn't stand up and wade out of it?

The cold zapped her strength. Her fingers had grown almost completely stiff. A mighty shiver sent a spasm throughout her body, and she gulped in more nasty water. She gagged and coughed again. She turned her head enough to drag in a shallow breath of air. She was going to die here. Her family would never know what had happened to her. Had the kitten survived? She'd hate for all this suffering to be in vain.

Lizzie tried to blink water from her eyes so she could search for the kitten. All she could see were shapes and colors. Could eyeballs freeze? She tried to call out but could only croak a weak, whispered "Help." How about that? Lizzie Fisher is finally rendered speechless. She almost chuckled. She must be delirious.

"Hang on! I'm almost there!"

There *was* someone else here. Lizzie prayed he would hurry before the pond claimed her as its own property. Her brain would soon be as numb as her body. Her legs had become useless appendages, and her arms weren't much better. She feared her fingers might never bend again if she did make it out of this pond alive. She should close her eyes so she wouldn't see her final descent beneath the water's surface. *Soooo tired.*

"Lizzie!"

Her eyes popped open. Whoever was there knew her name. Or were the angels calling to her? *Dear Gott, I really would like to live a little longer, but if You're calling me home, so be it.* Lizzie's eyelids weighed a ton, as did her arms and legs. They drooped despite her effort to keep them open.

"Lizzie! Open your eyes! Here, grab this branch."

I'm too tired.

"Lizzie!"

She forced her eyes open. She squinted, blinked, and squinted again. A splash beside her made her gasp and gulp in more foul water. Something long and dark landed beside her.

"Grab it, Lizzie! Grab the branch!"

A branch? That's what the thing was? She tried to raise an arm so she could obey the voice, but it wouldn't cooperate. Was her arm caught on something? Why couldn't she make it move?

"Try harder, Lizzie. You can do it."

She knew the voice. It haunted her dreams and sent shivers up her spine. Only right now, her spine and everything else was frozen. How did Stephen find her? She had to make her arms work.

"Can you hear me, Lizzie?"

She tried to nod, but that turned out to be another

impossible feat. "*Jah*." Her voice came out a teensy bit louder than before. With gargantuan effort, Lizzie thrust out her arm. *Please, Lord, let my fingers bend enough to grasp this limb.*

"That's it. You can do this. I'll give you thirty seconds, and then I'm plunging in." He stripped off his jacket and threw it aside. That much she could see. She couldn't let him risk his life for her again. Why was Stephen always around to witness her most mortifying moments? But she'd be embarrassed later. Right now she had to make her frozen body move.

Lizzie's fingers uncurled enough to wrap around the limb. She clung to it as tightly as she could. She heard a grunt before her body sailed across the pond. She gagged and gasped when more water entered her mouth, and she lost her grip on the limb. Gone. Her lifeline was gone. She wanted to wail. Would her arms work well enough for her to doggy paddle to the pond's edge?

She didn't get the chance to kick or attempt a single stroke before more splashes rippled the water around her. Stephen must have plunged in to rescue her. Now he would be as chilled and as at risk for drowning as she was. If only she could touch the bottom with her toes since she was a little closer to the edge. She stretched her leg down as far as it would go, but it did not make contact with land. All she got for her effort was another gulp of water. She coughed again.

"I'm here, Lizzie. I'll get you out as quick as I can."

She didn't know how he planned to do that. His arms and legs would soon grow cold and sluggish, too.

"Sorry. I didn't mean to splash more water on you."

Lizzie tried to smile, but her frozen lips wouldn't budge. "D-doesn't m-matter." Somehow she found the strength to throw an arm around Stephen. She had very little control over her movements and knocked him under the water. Could she fish him out? Was he a *gut* swimmer? Had she caused him to drown?

Stephen's head emerged seconds later. "It's okay. Stop thrashing."

She couldn't even feel that her body thrashed about. She did feel the violent chill that seized her with the next gust of wind. She shivered uncontrollably.

"Let me hold on to you."

Lizzie couldn't answer or nod her assent. She could only flutter her eyes. Would Stephen interpret that as agreement? She would have to let him hold on to her, since she didn't think she would be able to swing her arm out again. Never in a million years would she have believed a person could be rendered useless so quickly in the cold water.

Stephen looped an arm through one of hers. "Your lips are blue. I've got to get you out of here. Try to relax and let me tow you. Don't fight against the water."

Lizzie blinked again. She had to keep her eyelids from slamming closed. She knew she would never open them again. How hard it was to relax a stiff body!

With one strong arm and some powerful kicks, Stephen propelled them through the water. The little pond had looked so innocent, but it was deceptively deep. They had almost reached the pond's edge before Stephen could finally put his feet on the bottom and start sloshing through the water.

"Do you think you can stand?"

Lizzie's feet hit the muck at the bottom of the pond with a thud. She couldn't really feel them, but surely they would hold her up so she could take a few steps to reach dry ground. She tried, but her knees buckled. Apparently her brain's signal had gotten diverted somewhere. She would have slid back down under the water if Stephen hadn't caught her.

He whisked her up into his arms and cradled her close. She tried to absorb whatever body heat she could, but he trembled almost as violently as she did. His sodden work shoes made squishy noises with each step. He didn't release her until he could gently lower her to a sitting position on dry ground. He snatched up his discarded jacket and wrapped it snugly around her.

"Y-you n-need it."

"You need it more. Let me catch my breath, and I'll get you to the buggy."

"K-kitten?"

Despite the seriousness of their situation, Stephen threw back his head and laughed. "Only you, Lizzie. Only you would worry about a cat when you're sitting here shivering like a drowned rat."

"Y-you w-would, too."

To Lizzie's surprise, Stephen wrapped his arms around her and drew her close. He dropped his head on top of hers. If Lizzie didn't know better, she'd have said he just kissed the top of her head—where her bonnet should be. "I thought I'd lost you." His voice was a mere whisper, but she heard it over his wildly thumping heart right beneath her ear.

Stephen rocked her gently in his arms. He hoped they could warm up enough to trek back through the woods to his buggy. He didn't just speak his thoughts aloud, did he? Maybe her ears were too full of water to have heard his murmuring. When had he let his guard down and admitted Lizzie into his heart—the heart that had almost stopped beating when he saw her drop into the pond?

When she reached her hand up to feel her head, he grasped it. Her fingers still had a bluish tint but appeared to be thawing a little. "Your bonnet is now being worn by some creepy pond creature. I'm sure Mamm has one you can borrow."

"*K-kapp?*"

"If you're talking about that grayish brown thing, it is miraculously clinging to a few strands of your hair, but I think it is beyond hope."

Lizzie groaned and shivered against him. He tucked her hand back inside the jacket. He held her a little tighter and pushed long, loose strands of her caramel-colored hair off her face. "I hope I'm not making you colder since I'm drenched, too."

She shook her head against him. "I'm sorry you had to get all wet."

"I couldn't very well stand there and watch you drown. I had hoped the limb idea would work so I could keep my clothes dry to wrap you in." She snuggled a little closer as another shiver shot through her slight body. He had to admit he loved her closeness, even if she was soaked through and through.

When her shivering subsided a bit, Stephen pulled back to look down into her violet eyes. What if he hadn't seen her walk into the woods, if he hadn't followed her? He wouldn't be looking into her violet eyes now or ever again. That very thought pierced his heart and soul. "Lizzie, whatever possessed you to climb that tree?"

"The kitten."

"Cats climb trees all the time. You know that."

Lizzie sniffed and wiped at a rivulet of water that dripped from her hair down her cheek. "I think it was scared to move. It had the most pitiful meow."

"Didn't you notice that limb was half-dead and hanging over the pond? Did you think what would happen if you fell?" Stephen struggled to keep his voice calm. He didn't want to be angry or appear angry. He'd been scared. Make that terrified. Seeing Lizzie dangling from the limb and plummeting into the water had made him physically ill. Even reliving the incident made him want to retch.

"*Nee* and *nee*. I only thought of rescuing the helpless kitten."

"Can you even swim?"

"Kind of."

"How does one 'kind of' swim? Either you can or you can't."

"I can tread water and sort of doggy paddle."

"I should paddle you right now!"

Lizzie gasped. "Don't you dare—"

"Calm down. I think you've had enough punishment for one day. Do you think we can make it to the buggy? We've got to get dry clothes."

"I can make it."

Stephen jumped to his feet. At least he could feel his toes now. He reached down to pull Lizzie to a standing position. "Okay?"

She wobbled. "I-I think so."

He kept hold of her arm as they shuffled through the dried leaves.

"Wait!"

Stephen's heart lurched. Was she hurt? Did she have some injury he hadn't seen, or had frostbite caused severe damage? "What's wrong?"

"The kitten."

"Really? *Kumm* on." He tugged on her arm.

Lizzie dug in her heels and wouldn't budge. He could yank her along or scoop her up in his arms, but she would probably kick and scream the whole way.

"We didn't go through all that to leave the kitten to fend for itself."

"It will go home."

"What if it doesn't have one?"

Stephen clenched his teeth. "Wait right here!" He knew his tone was gruff, but he couldn't help it. He stomped back to where he had last seen the ball of orange fluff, snatched it from beneath a bush, trudged back, and thrust the animal into Lizzie's arms. "Here. Are you always so much trouble?"

"Sometimes more."

Chapter Thirty-Four

"*Ach*, Lizzie! Stephen! What happened to you two?" Mary's hands flew to her cheeks. She stared in horror.

Lizzie hung her head. If she wasn't so cold and miserable, she'd be terribly embarrassed. As it was, she couldn't look Mary in the eye. Once again she had placed her *freind*'s son in danger. She wouldn't blame Mary one little bit if she tossed Lizzie out and forbade her ever to return. She could feel Mary's eyes on her but couldn't formulate a response.

"We had a little accident, Mamm."

Lizzie ventured a quick glance in Mary's direction, but hastily lowered her eyes before they connected with Mary's.

"It's the wrong time of year to go swimming, ain't so?"

Was that a trace of amusement in Mary's voice? Maybe she wouldn't be mad after all. "We weren't exactly swimming," Lizzie said.

"*Jah*. One of us was drowning."

Lizzie's head snapped up. She shot Stephen a dirty look. "I was not drowning." At Stephen's cough, she amended her statement. "Not quite." Finally she gathered enough courage to look Mary in the eye. "I'm so sorry, Mary. It's all my fault that Stephen got soaking wet. I hope he doesn't *kumm* down with pneumonia or something."

"Stephen is a grown man. I trust his decisions. If you were in trouble, I'm glad he happened along to help you. You can tell me all about it after you get dry. Let's get you out of those sopping wet clothes." Mary tugged at Lizzie's arm. "Oh, you've brought a *freind*."

Lizzie looked down at the kitten burrowed in the crook of her arm. "I didn't mean to bring the kitten here. I . . ."

"Was this another risky rescue?" Mary looked from Stephen to Lizzie with the hint of a smile on her lips.

"Something like that." Stephen coughed as if clearing his voice, but Lizzie had a feeling he was trying to cover a laugh.

"You go change!" Mary gave her son a stern look.

"I thought you said I was a grown man and you trusted my decisions."

"True, but right now *I'm* deciding that you need to get out of those clothes and stop dripping all over my floor."

"All right. All right."

"I'm so sorry, Mary. I'll clean the floor."

"You will do nothing of the kind. I'm teasing, dear. I'm so grateful you're safe that I'd crawl around with a rag in my teeth to clean the floor. I was very worried when you didn't show up as planned."

"I didn't mean to cause you concern." Lizzie's *mudder* didn't tease, so she wasn't quite sure what to make of the banter. She was stunned when Mary wrapped her in a warm, loving hug. Would Mamm have done that, or would she have reprimanded her for her foolish behavior?

"Stop apologizing. Let's find you some dry clothes. We can't have you getting sick. My clothes might be a bit big on you, but they'll do for now. Then we'll get something hot into both of you and you can tell me this whole wild story."

Stephen called from the hallway. "You'll have to find her a bonnet, too, Mamm. Some pond creature is wearing hers."

"Shoo, Stephen!" Lizzie smiled as Mary hooked an arm through her free one and led her toward the door. She decided she liked the easygoing, caring relationship Mary and Stephen shared. Dare she say she envied it? Mamm would have made her take the kitten outside and then mop the floor before she even changed clothes. Rules were rules. Animals belonged outside, and floors had to be spotless. When Lizzie had her own home . . .

Fifteen minutes later, Lizzie shuffled into the kitchen in stocking feet carrying her soggy shoes and clothes. The light blue dress with tiny white flowers bunched a bit at the waist from her attempt to gather the extra material beneath the pins. A kerchief covered her damp, re-pinned hair. She stopped in the doorway and smiled at the sight that greeted her.

Mary sat in a high-backed oak chair murmuring to the orange and white kitten purring in her lap. Mamm would never pet a cat, and would never allow one to be in her kitchen. Guilt crept in. Lizzie shouldn't make such comparisons. Mamm was Mamm and Mary was Mary. That was it.

"I'm afraid that dress is about to swallow you up."

Mary looked up from petting the kitten. "'Tis a sweet little girl you rescued."

"I'm not sure who got rescued, me or her. Do you know who might be the kitten's owner?"

"I can't say that I do."

"I was hoping to return her to wherever she belongs."

"We can ask around, but for now, she can join the trio outside."

"I didn't mean to dump another animal on you."

"What's one more? I think Stephen got his love of animals from me." Mary rose and held the kitten out to Lizzie. "Let's trade. I'll spread your clothes out by the stove. Maybe they will dry while we weave."

Lizzie hoped so. How would she explain arriving home in a print dress and a borrowed cloak? She nuzzled the purring kitten.

Mary held up the *kapp*. "I don't think we can salvage this."

Lizzie's free hand flew to her head. The kerchief was fine for right now, but she couldn't show up at home without a head covering.

"I have a bonnet you can wear home, but my *kapps* will be different from yours. You are welcome to have one of my extras, though."

"*Danki*, but if I can borrow a bonnet, that will be fine."

"I doubt your shoes will dry completely. I'm pretty sure my feet are a couple sizes larger than yours, but if you can keep them on your feet, I'll loan you a pair."

Lizzie giggled at the thought of waddling home in oversized shoes and borrowed clothes. That would make a hilarious sight. She probably wouldn't be laughing when Mamm saw her, though. "I'll be okay, Mary. I might squish and squash, but I'll take my shoes off as soon as I get home. *Before I set foot on Mamm's kitchen floor.*

Mary turned back to Lizzie after draping the clothes over a kitchen chair pulled close to the woodstove. "Now, would you like tea or cocoa?"

"Tea will be great." Lizzie glanced toward the doorway.

"I've already sent a thermos of hot tea out to the shop with Stephen. I couldn't get him to stay inside once he got dry clothes."

How embarrassing! Mary had read her thoughts. Did Stephen simply need to get to work or was he reluctant to face her after the words he murmured after rescuing her? Maybe she had caused him so much trouble that he wanted to forget about her altogether.

"Sit down, dear. I'll get the tea. I have freshly baked banana bread, too. Would you like a slice? Or maybe you'd rather have a sandwich or soup first?"

"A slice of the bread will be fine, but I can help you. I'm not an invalid, you know."

"I know, but you've been through quite an ordeal. Your body needs to recover."

Lizzie sank onto a chair and arranged the kitten in her lap. How much had Stephen told his *mudder*? Did he tell her how silly she looked clinging to a tree limb for dear life? She didn't know why, but she wanted Mary to hold her in high regard. If only that limb hadn't broken, she could have easily grabbed the kitten and scrambled back down the tree.

"Are you okay? Are you sure you aren't hurt anywhere?" Mary set a plate with a generous slice of banana bread and a cup of steaming tea on the table in front of Lizzie.

"I'm fine. Only the pride I'm not supposed to have got wounded."

Mary smiled and patted Lizzie's arm before returning to the stove to pour her own tea. "Don't worry, dear. We all have done things that seemed like a *gut* idea at the time but did not turn out as we expected."

"This turned out disastrous!"

"Not at all. 'Disastrous' would have been if you'd gotten hurt or if Stephen hadn't found you. You are both safe and unhurt—and you rescued the kitten."

"True, but I'm still embarrassed to have been caught in a tree, and I'm sorry I caused Stephen trouble. He could have drowned."

"But he didn't. He's a *gut* swimmer. I made sure all my *buwe* learned to swim when they were young, since the county is surrounded by water."

"Smart thinking." Lizzie ventured a sip of steaming tea and savored its warmth. Did any of her siblings know how to swim? They'd gone to the river to fish and play in the water, but she doubted any of them could do more than float or doggy paddle.

"Did you climb the tree because the kitten wouldn't *kumm* down?" Mary broke off a chunk of her own slice of banana bread and popped it into her mouth.

Lizzie gulped. To buy herself a little time, she stuck a sliver of bread in her mouth. If she could keep the day's events to herself or erase them entirely she surely would. She might as well share the details with Mary now since Stephen would most likely do so later—if he hadn't already given her an abbreviated version. Lizzie swallowed and washed the crumbs down with another gulp of tea. "I did. I climbed up when this little rascal acted too scared to move."

After Lizzie had concluded her story, Mary smiled and patted her hand. Surprisingly, Lizzie felt better after sharing the events. Mary didn't judge, condemn, or even criticize. What an incredible person!

"You are an amazing young woman, Lizzie Fisher. You have a warm and tender heart, and you are brave enough to act on your convictions. I am happy to call you a *freind*."

Lizzie's jaw dropped. "I do foolish things. I could have caused your son to drown. I could have caused him to get badly burned in a fire. And yet you call me amazing? Amazingly dumb, I'm thinking."

Mary laughed. "The Lord Gott watched over you both. I truly believe He sent Stephen to help you—both times."

Lizzie still had trouble concentrating a while later as they sat at the loom. Her mind kept replaying Mary's words. Did Gott send Stephen to help her? If so, was it only to help her when she was in trouble or to help rescue kittens, or was it something more? *Don't go there, Lizzie!* She jerked her mind back to the task at hand. "You are doing very nice work, Mary."

"I've had a great teacher."

"*Nee*, I believe you are naturally skilled in weaving, among other things."

Mary laughed. "I'm not sure I have any natural abilities, but weaving sure is fun."

"You have lots of skills. You are a *gut* listener, an exceptional *mudder*, and a terrific *freind*."

"You're a dear to say such things."

"I mean every word."

"I believe you do. I don't think you have a dishonest bone in your body."

Images of hiding art supplies and drawings crept from the shadows of Lizzie's mind. If that wasn't dishonest, it was certainly a close kin.

"And don't think that keeping your art a secret is dishonest. We all have parts of ourselves we don't share with others."

"I'd better add mind reading to your list of talents."

By the time Lizzie was ready to leave, her dress and stockings were only barely damp. However, her cloak, though not wringing wet, was far from dry.

"*Ach*, Lizzie! You can't go out in the cold with that wet thing. Let me loan you a shawl. Or you can take my cloak."

"I'll be fine. The heat will probably be blasting on the commuter bus. That's what got me into a mess in the first place." She set out in damp clothes and a borrowed bonnet and prayed the bus would be on time. Lizzie stopped to pet the kittens and was glad to see the three original kitties had accepted the newcomer. She visited the puppies and gave Sunny an extra pat. Should she stop in to speak to Stephen or leave him alone?

Before she could ponder the subject further, he opened the workshop door and hurried outside. Had he been watching for her?

"Are—?"

"*Danki—*"

They spoke and stopped at the same time. Lizzie gave Stephen her best smile. "You first."

"I was going to ask if you are okay. Any lingering effects from being waterlogged and nearly frozen?"

"Not as far as I can tell. I was going to say *danki* for all you did today. You kept me from drowning. I-I'm indebted to you."

"I'm glad I happened to be at the right place at the right time."

Lizzie shuddered. "Me, too. I'm not sure how much longer I could have survived in that cold water. I thought I was slipping away when you pulled me out." Her cheeks burned at the memory of Stephen's arms wrapped around her. *That was only for warmth, you silly goose!* Wasn't it? Stephen's face must be as warm as her own. It had certainly become a lovely shade of cherry red.

"I'm glad I could help."

"I'm glad you could swim!"

Stephen laughed. "Me, too."

"I'd better walk to the end of the driveway so the bus driver will see me." She turned away before he could read the emotions overwhelming her. Her shoes squeaked and squished, making for a pretty unpleasant experience. But at least they weren't at the bottom of the pond. She would have plenty of explaining to do very soon. *Please, Lord Gott. I know it's a silly thing to ask when there are so many more important things in the world, but could You please let everyone be busy and not notice when I arrive home?*

"Hey, Lizzie!"

She whirled around at the voice that always sent her spirits soaring. She watched Stephen jog to catch up with her. She waited for him to speak, but he stared at her as if in a daze. Should she speak to break his spell or wait for him to collect his thoughts?

Stephen shook his head and cleared his throat.

"I wanted to tell you that the puppies will be leaving in a little more than a week."

Lizzie gasped. Maybe that was why he was acting so strange. He probably feared she would burst into tears at that news. She wanted to, but she wouldn't. "Oh." Now she was the one who couldn't get herself together. Her brain knew perfectly well the dogs weren't going to stay with Stephen permanently, but her heart ached at the thought of their leaving.

"I figured you might want to visit them again before they leave."

"I'd like to do that. I'll be back to work with Mary again next week. Can I spend some time with them then?"

"Absolutely. The new kitten will probably be here, too, if we can't find her owner."

"I'm sorry to have foisted another animal on your *mudder*."

"What's one more? Besides, she loves cats. I've seen her playing with them in the evenings when she thinks we aren't watching."

Lizzie laughed. "That's nice to know. I always find that animals can lighten my troubles."

"That's for sure."

Lizzie stared at her wet shoes. "I'm going to miss little Sunny." *I will not cry.*

"I know you will."

Lizzie jumped at Stephen's light touch on her forearm. That funny tingling sensation traveled up to her shoulder and made her heart flip over.

"I always have trouble letting a litter go, too, especially such a fun one like this one has been. But I raise them to do a special task, and I'm glad I can help people in that way."

Lizzie nodded. It had to take a special person to

love something and let it go so someone else could benefit. Stephen was every bit as incredible as his *mamm*, despite his sometimes gruffness. She thought she understood that better now, after Mary's explanation. "I'd better wait for the bus."

Stephen dropped his hand from her arm. "And I need to finish my cabinet."

Lizzie rubbed her arm as she trudged down the dirt driveway, but she couldn't erase the tingling.

Chapter Thirty-Five

Despite the heat pouring from the vents on the commuter bus, Lizzie shivered the whole way home, making for a long, miserable ride. And the bus must have made a hundred stops, prolonging her discomfort. The only bright side was that the vehicle didn't reek of some sickening perfume this time.

She hopped off the bus at the end of the long driveway leading to the house. What a welcome sight the smoke curling from the chimney made. Warmth. She'd experience it soon. She sped up the lane as quickly as possible. How *wunderbaar* it would be to change into dry clothes. If only she could wrap herself in a fuzzy blanket like a caterpillar in a cocoon.

Please let everyone be busy so I can slip inside to change clothes. Lizzie chanted her little prayer over and over. Five minutes. That's all she needed to race upstairs, pull on a dry dress, pin on a fresh *kapp*, and zoom back down to the kitchen to help Mamm. Was that too much to hope for?

That hope plummeted when she reached the edge of the front yard. Sadie and Nancy abruptly stopped chasing each other when they spotted her.

"Hey, Lizzie's home!" Nancy squealed and ran to meet her. Sadie followed like a shadow.

Great! If Nancy discovers something, the whole world will soon know. She'd somehow have to make the best of this situation. Lizzie forced a smile. "Aren't you two cold?"

"Not a bit. We've been running. Right, Sadie?"

"*Jah.*" Sadie usually agreed with whatever Nancy said. The little girl trotted the remaining steps and threw herself into Lizzie's arms.

"What a nice *wilkom* home." Lizzie hugged the youngest Fisher in a mock bear hug. She held her breath, waiting for Sadie to say something about the damp clothes, but Sadie seemed content to be hugged. If she noticed anything unusual, she kept it to herself. Nancy would be a different story altogether.

"I'm glad you're home." Nancy threw her arms around Lizzie, too. "How are the kittens? Mamm is in a snit because you and Frannie weren't here to help her, and she shooed me and Sadie outside when I offered to help, and . . . Eww! Why are you all wet?"

Even though she talked a mile a minute, Nancy still noticed everything. "Where's Frannie?" Maybe she could head Nancy off the topic of the clothes.

"I don't know. She was gone when we got home from school."

"That's strange."

"What's strange is that your clothes are wet."

"Damp."

"Huh?"

"They're not wet. They're only damp. I'd better get inside and help Mamm." Lizzie detached herself from the tangle of arms surrounding her and strode toward the house.

"Did you fall in a pig's trough or something?" Nancy and Sadie fell into a fit of giggles.

Lizzie whirled around and pressed an index finger to her lips. "Shhh! Our secret, *jah*?"

"You mean you don't want me to tell anyone you came home all wet?"

"Exactly." What were the chances of that happening? Lizzie had better work on a plausible excuse. If Mamm knew she'd fallen in a pond and nearly drowned, she'd never let Lizzie leave the property again.

A quick backward glance assured Lizzie her little *schweschders* had returned to chasing each other and weren't paying one bit of attention to her. She could slip in the front door without Nancy asking why she didn't go in the back door as usual. She tiptoed across the front porch, the squish of her shoes making the only noise. That soft sound would be a warning gong to Mamm, whose ears could pick up a gnat's whisper in the next county.

Lizzie stooped beside the front door and untied the soggy shoestrings. She'd carry the shoes inside and dash up the stairs in stocking feet. If Mamm was in the kitchen as Nancy had said, Lizzie just might have a chance to make herself more presentable before Mamm caught sight of her.

She softly closed the door behind her, zipped across the wood floor, and took the stairs two at a time. She didn't exhale until she had closed her bedroom door behind her. She peeled off the clothes and, with trembling fingers, pinned on a clean dress and *kapp*. Thank goodness she'd saved her old pair of sneakers.

Lizzie heard Mamm mumbling before she even reached the kitchen. The muffled words were punctuated by clanking pot lids, and something heavy slammed on the counter.

"I don't know why I'm doing this alone. Grown girls should be here helping." Thump, clang, clang. "She left early. She should be back by now."

Lizzie couldn't be sure if Mamm was referring to her or to Frannie or to both of them. What she was sure of was that the sooner she got into the kitchen to defuse the situation, the better for the whole family.

"Hi, Mamm. Would you like me to make biscuits, or do you have something else you want me to do?"

"It's about time you got home."

Lizzie's gaze slid up to the little battery-operated clock on the opposite wall. She had actually returned home earlier than usual. She thought better than to mention that.

She pulled out a ceramic mixing bowl and grabbed the canister of flour. Even though Mamm hadn't answered her question, she would go ahead and make biscuits. "Did Frannie take items to Yoder's Store?"

"She didn't do any baking. That girl just took off. She said she had someplace to go and didn't even tell me where or why or when she would be back."

So that was it. Frannie hadn't confided in Mamm, and Mamm was hurt. Frannie had been glued to their *mudder* since birth, like another appendage. Whatever would Mamm do if Frannie decided to have a life of her own? "That's not like Frannie." Maybe Lizzie shouldn't have said that. Mamm might become even more upset. Lizzie rolled dough on the floured board. She should work and keep her mouth shut.

"It isn't like Frannie at all. I don't know what's gotten into her."

"A fellow, perhaps? She'll probably tell you all about it when she gets home."

"Who knows?" Mamm stopped fidgeting with the dish towel and stared at Lizzie as if seeing her for the first time. "What in the world are you doing?"

Lizzie paused with the rolling pin in midair. Wasn't it obvious what she was doing? "I'm getting ready to cut out biscuits."

"Who said anything about biscuits?"

"I asked you when I came into the kitchen. You didn't answer so I assumed you must have set the flour out to make biscuits."

"I was going to make corn muffins. You need flour for them, too."

Lizzie suppressed a sigh and held her tongue in check. If she had started making corn muffins, Mamm would have wanted biscuits. If she had started making blueberry muffins, Mamm would have wanted strawberry ones. That's just the way it was. "I can make corn muffins instead."

"We aren't wasting food. You've already started the biscuits."

"I can make both. You know they won't go to waste. Melvin and Caleb can eat a dozen muffins each."

"Just do the biscuits." Mamm's voice came out in an exasperated sigh.

Lizzie resolved to be cheerful even if it killed her. She cut out perfectly round biscuits and carefully laid each one on the baking sheet. They had to be the prettiest biscuits she had ever cut out.

She wanted to ask all the questions bubbling up inside while she and her *mudder* were alone but didn't want to further alienate the woman. She debated. Everything had become so jumbled up in her head. Her concerns spun until the words spilled out. "Mamm, I just don't understand what you had against the kittens, or any animals, for that matter. Sometimes I feel"— Lizzie hesitated but then blurted—"like I don't do anything to please you." Despicable tears pooled in her eyes, so she stared at the floor. Would Mamm be angry or upset with her outburst? Fear prevented her from lifting her gaze.

"*Ach*, Lizzie. *Kumm*."

To Lizzie's surprise, Mamm's tug on her arm was gentle. She ventured a peek upward and barely stifled a gasp. Mamm's eyes shimmered, too.

"Sit." Mamm pulled out a chair for Lizzie and another one for herself. She sat close and clasped Lizzie's hand in both of hers.

Lizzie sniffed. As hard as it was for her to remain silent, she waited for her *mudder* to speak. She stared at her hand, sandwiched between Mamm's larger ones.

"Look at me, Lizzie."

She didn't want to. She didn't want to see tears in her *mudder*'s eyes. She didn't want Mamm to see the pain, sadness, and confusion that would surely be evident in her own. But obedience won out. She forced her gaze upward.

"You don't have to do anything to please me. You only need to be yourself. I know I don't show it often, but I do love you. I grew up in a house where people did not express their emotions. They didn't hug or say they cared. I'm afraid that attitude became ingrained in me to a large extent. Just because I don't say the words or dole out bear hugs, it doesn't mean I don't care. I love you and Daed and all my *kinner*."

Tears slipped down Lizzie's cheeks. She couldn't remember Mamm ever being so emotional, so expressive. Maybe her gruffness was a way to mask the feelings she wouldn't or couldn't express. Lizzie sniffed again. Harder. "I-I always thought you wanted me to be more like Frannie."

"Why would I want you to be like anyone else? I have one Frannie. I don't need two."

Did she need a Lizzie? Fearing the answer, Lizzie would not permit herself to ask that question. She bit her tongue to keep the words inside.

"I know I must seem mean and grumpy. That's my way, I guess. It doesn't mean I feel that way in here." Mamm removed one hand from Lizzie's and thumped her chest. "I suppose I've been this way so long, it's normal for me—and probably for everyone else, too. Why, you would all faint dead away if I pranced around singing and smiling." She laughed.

Lizzie threw caution to the wind. She might as well ask everything while she had the chance. "What about animals, Mamm? Why do you hate them?" She braced herself. After all, how long could her *mudder*'s calm mood last?

"I don't hate them. I'm afraid of them."

"Of helpless little kittens? What could they possibly do to you?" Lizzie wanted to smack herself for that outburst.

Mamm gazed across the room. Looking into the past, perhaps? She huffed a huge sigh. "I was attacked by a big dog, a German shepherd, I believe, when I was little. I thought he would gnaw me to death. I had to have stitches in my leg. From then on, I did not want to be around any animals, big or small."

"What about Ruff?"

"He was your *grossdaddi*'s dog. Your *daed* inherited him. I didn't have any say in the matter of his living with us after Grossdaddi passed. But I try to stay out of his way."

And she did, too. Lizzie couldn't recall Mamm ever petting the dog, talking to him, or even feeding him. "Kittens wouldn't hurt you."

"All animals can turn on you. I don't trust any of them."

"I'm sure that dog scared you. That must have been an awful experience." Lizzie figured she'd better leave the animal topic behind. She would never change Mamm's mind, so why spoil these few unusual, precious moments of closeness?

A commotion at the back door drew Mamm's attention. She dropped Lizzie's hand and jumped to her feet. She marched toward the door, demanding, "Where were you?"

Lizzie looked up as a breathless Frannie burst into the room. Lizzie shot from her chair and shoved the pan of biscuits into the oven in case Mamm reverted to her extra-critical mode and decided to point out any flaws to Frannie.

"I'm sorry I'm late getting back, Mamm." Frannie patted her chest and gasped for breath.

"I was getting worried. Where have you been?"

Mamm's voice took on a softer, less shrill tone. Lizzie held her breath so she could hear every word of their exchange. Frannie flounced into the room and whipped off her cloak and bonnet. She flung them toward the hook near the door and didn't even mutter when the bonnet missed its mark and landed on the floor. "I've been visiting a *freind*. I'll wash up and help."

"I already made biscuits," Lizzie said.

"Really?"

"I can make biscuits, too, you know." She wanted to crawl under the table when Mamm muttered, "Sort of." The biscuits looked fine to her. Besides, her siblings didn't care what biscuits looked like. They would gobble them up anyway. Wasn't Mamm going to ask Frannie about the *freind*? Lizzie wanted to know who it was. Judging by Frannie's mood, she had a fair idea who this mysterious person was.

"I'm sure your biscuits are fine." Frannie floated across the room and patted Lizzie's arm.

Now she knew some other being had inhabited her *schweschder*'s body. Lizzie offered Frannie a grateful smile.

Frannie smiled in return. "What do you need me to do, Mamm?"

"We're fine now that I've done almost everything all on my own."

"I saw Nancy and Sadie outside. Didn't they help?" Frannie sashayed to the cabinet to pull down a stack of plates.

"They were under my feet, and Nancy's continuous chattering got on my nerves. I was already worried about you, so I sent them outside."

"I didn't mean to worry you, Mamm. I told you when I left, and you knew Lizzie had gone to the Zimmermans'."

"I know. I expected you back sooner, I guess."

Lizzie sailed across the room to take the plates from Frannie. She tried to motion for Frannie to let the topic die. They had tried to placate Mamm. Now they had to let her collect herself and move on.

Thankfully, Frannie correctly interpreted Lizzie's frown and head shake. She grabbed a handful of silverware and followed Lizzie to the table.

"Were you with Aaron?" Lizzie whispered. Frannie's dreamy smile provided the answer. *I guess Frannie made her own match without help from Stephen and me.*

"Tell you later."

Lizzie planned to hold Frannie to that promise. She wanted to hear the details that would explain Frannie's transformation. "*Ach!* My biscuits!" Lizzie tossed the last plate in the general direction of where it belonged and dashed to the oven. She couldn't ruin the biscuits and prove them right. She snatched a hot pad off the counter and yanked open the oven door. Ah! Golden brown. *Danki, Lord Gott.*

"Looks great." Frannie peeped over Lizzie's shoulder at the biscuits.

Two compliments in one day? Was Frannie being facetious? Was she ill? Aaron Kurtz had worked a miracle!

Lizzie could hardly sit still during supper and barely tasted her stew. The biscuits, however, were yummy. When Daed commanded, "Sit still!" she nearly slid off her chair. Relief shot through her when she realized he had been speaking to Nancy and not to her. Nancy looked instantly contrite. Maybe now she wouldn't spill the beans about the condition Lizzie had been in when she had arrived home.

Lizzie offered to play a board game with the little girls after supper to keep their minds occupied and their mouths from tattling. She struggled to concentrate, though, as the events of the day caught up with her. She wanted nothing more than to crawl into her bed, but she had promised to play.

The game dragged on forever. Lizzie couldn't believe only thirty minutes had passed. Had the clock stopped? How could she end this game without hurting the girls' feelings? Sadie's huge yawn provided just the excuse. "Okay. This is the last round. Sadie is about to fall asleep."

"I'm okay." Sadie rubbed her eyes.

"Well, I'm tired, Sadie. I've had a busy day. I'm sure you worked hard in school today and must be tired, too."

"I guess." Sadie glanced at Nancy.

"Oh, all right! I'm tired, too." Nancy started picking up game pieces and dropping them into the box.

Before she fell asleep in the chair, Lizzie hoisted herself out of it and trudged up the stairs. She yawned, rubbed her eyes, and slipped into the room she shared with Frannie. Since the lamplight was so dim, maybe her *schweschder* was already asleep. Lizzie eased the door closed so she wouldn't disturb Frannie.

"Why is your cloak wet?"

Chapter Thirty-Six

Lizzie was instantly wide awake. "Damp. It's damp."

"All right, then. How did your cloak get damp? It wasn't raining where I was today."

"Where were you?"

"Don't try to change the subject, Lizzie Fisher." Frannie stood right on the other side of the door. Her foot tapped the wood floor.

"It doesn't matter how it got damp. I'd much rather hear about your day." They engaged in a staring match, neither willing to back down or even blink. "Something, or someone, has made you awfully happy."

Frannie blinked and giggled. "For sure."

Whew! Now if Lizzie could keep Frannie talking, maybe the subject of the damp cloak could die. "I'm guessing it was some*one*."

Frannie laughed harder.

Lizzie smiled, infected by her *schweschder*'s glee. "Tell me, Frannie!"

Frannie grabbed Lizzie's hand and tugged her across the room to sit on her twin bed. The hand-stitched Log Cabin quilt had already been carefully folded back, so they wouldn't mess it up when they plopped down. "I'm so happy!"

"That's obvious. Let me take a wild guess. Could Aaron Kurtz have been the person you met today?"

Frannie's eyes sparkled in the lamplight. "He could have been."

"Oh you! Was it him or not? Don't keep me in suspense."

"Patience is a virtue."

"I'm not sure I was blessed with that one. Don't make me drag it out of you piece by piece."

Frannie batted her dark eyelashes but kept silent.

"Don't you want to share your joy? You look about ready to burst."

"All right. I did meet Aaron, and we had a *wunderbaar* time."

"So all has been forgiven?"

"There really wasn't anything to forgive. He hadn't gone off to court someone else. You heard everything he said in your shop."

"And you believe him?"

"I don't have any reason not to believe him. He wouldn't need to sugarcoat anything for me, since we weren't a courting couple before he left."

"Are you now?"

"We might be heading in that direction."

"If he's a *gut* fellow and you're happy, then I'm happy for you." *And a teensy bit envious.* Would a fellow ever ask to take her home? Would she ever feel the way Frannie did? None of the *buwe* at the singings had ever made her want to gush like that. But her heart fluttered crazily and her stomach flipped over and over at the memory of strong hands pulling her to safety and gentle arms cradling her. She mentally shook herself. Nothing could *kumm* of that. She'd better focus on

Frannie and be satisfied to rejoice with her. She would banish that envy. Or try to.

"He said he was sorry he didn't speak up and ask me to ride home with him before he went away. He said he won't make that mistake at the next singing."

Lizzie hugged her *schweschder*. "I am truly happy for you. I guess all things do work out for *gut*, if we only wait." *Stephen and I sure wasted our time and efforts trying to arrange a match, though.*

Frannie squeezed Lizzie's arm. "I have cared for Aaron for ever so long. I was afraid he would never notice me."

"I'm sure he noticed you before." *How could he not? She waylaid him after every singing.* "I wish he had told you of his interest before. That would have saved you a lot of heartache."

"For sure, but the important thing is that we understand each other now."

"I'm glad." If he had figured Frannie out in a few short hours, the fellow was a genius. Lizzie had spent twenty years trying to do that. "I hope everything works out for you."

"I believe it will. So you can stop playing matchmaker."

"I've given that up, believe me." Matchmaking was definitely not one of her talents. Maybe Seth would find someone on his own, too. "Can you be so sure already that Aaron is the right one for you?"

"Pretty sure, but we'll take our time. I have known him forever, you know. Now we have to find someone for you."

"Whoa! Don't *you* go playing matchmaker. There is absolutely not a single fellow I'm interested in at the moment." *Are you trying to convince Frannie, or yourself?*

"That could change. Give someone a chance."

"I'm not ready yet." And not likely to take advice from someone who was moping around a week ago, only to be madly in love today. Time to redirect this conversation. "I think Mamm might have been a bit put out that you didn't confide in her."

"Girls don't usually tell their *mudders* about their courting, do they?"

"I wouldn't know, but I always thought such matters were hush-hush. You'll have to tell me all about it in case I ever decide to let someone court me."

"You will."

"I'm not so sure." Blue, forbidden eyes were the only ones that peeked into her dreams.

While Frannie sighed in her sleep, probably dreaming of her beau and a wedding, Lizzie tossed and turned and counted woolly, black-faced sheep. She hoped Aaron was everything Frannie believed him to be. Right now the girl was floating on clouds and actually treating Lizzie like a *freind*. She had become a pleasant person, and if that metamorphosis was due to Aaron Kurtz, well then, Gott bless him.

Lizzie plumped her pillow and turned onto her side. Her own life would be a whole lot simpler if Stephen Zimmerman had never followed her on the trail that day. Then she wouldn't be haunted by those blue eyes. But she wouldn't have met Mary, either. Why couldn't the Zimmermans be Amish?

That probably didn't matter anyway. Despite his tenderness after her near drowning, Stephen probably still thought of her as a bumbling little girl. After all, she seemed to require rescuing at nearly every encounter. And she always seemed to be doing something foolish. If she wasn't running into burning buildings or dropping into murky ponds, she was falling on her backside in the dog pen. Oh well, there wasn't any chance they could have a relationship even if she wasn't a total klutz, was there?

Lizzie flopped back over and stared into the darkness. She was Amish. Stephen was Old Order Mennonite. Similar, but not the same. When she and Stephen were plotting a match between Seth and Frannie, they expected one of them to change their way of life. Could Lizzie expect less of herself or Stephen if they wished to pursue a relationship? And that was a big "if."

She sighed. Would Stephen be willing to leave his church? He had already been baptized. Could she leave, though? Could she turn her back on her upbringing, her faith? Gott was Gott. Her faith in Him would not change. She wouldn't be shunned, but what would Mamm and Daed say?

Go to sleep! His whispered, "I thought I lost you" after the pond rescue had probably stemmed from shock. Those words most likely meant nothing to him—but they meant everything to Lizzie.

One sheep. Two sheep.

Stephen grunted and turned onto his side. He pulled up the sheet and blanket he'd kicked off moments earlier. He was hot and then cold and then hot again. He was miserable. Maybe he had caught a cold or the flu. He didn't feel achy, though. He didn't have a sore throat or a cough. But his heart pounded and flipped, and his agitated brain refused to shut down so he could sleep. What was wrong with him?

A girl with caramel-colored hair and violet eyes appeared every time he squeezed his eyes shut. That's what was wrong with him. Wasn't it bad enough that she popped into his every waking thought? Did she have to invade his dreams, too? Whenever he began to drift off, that little heart-shaped face prodded him awake.

Concern for her safety. That had to be why he'd uttered those words at the pond. After all, she had almost drowned. The fear that had almost paralyzed him when he saw her drop into the pond threatened to overtake him every time he relived the scene. He thought he had lost her.

Anyone would have said what he said, wouldn't they? He'd held her close only to reassure her and provide warmth. Right? Of course. Not. *Admit it, man. You care for her. You care a lot. You almost lost your mind when you thought you wouldn't reach her in time.*

Okay. He cared. Now what? How could anything *kumm* from caring for Lizzie Fisher except heartache? Never in a million years would he believe she would deliberately hurt him, but the fact that he cared for someone not of his faith would cause untold pain if he didn't check those feelings right away. Caring for someone who had been a member of his community had left wounds that had only recently scabbed over. Caring for Lizzie would rip those scars wide open.

How do I stop caring? Stephen kicked the covers off again. Getting over Joanna Brubacher had been a piece of cake compared to what getting over Lizzie Fisher would be like. Joanna had made it easier by dropping him like a hot potato. His only choice had been to move on.

Lizzie was different. She willingly and eagerly gave

up time to help Mamm. She cared about her older *schweschder*'s happiness. She had a super soft spot for animals. She was smart and had a keen sense of humor. It would definitely take a lot of time and effort to get over her.

Did he have to get over her? Stephen bolted upright. His mind spun with possibilities. Could they work things out somehow? Would he be able to give up his family and cleave only to Lizzie? That's what he would have to do if he left his church. But could he ask Lizzie to do something he was hesitant to do?

Lizzie hasn't joined the church yet. Talk to her. A spark of hope burst into flame. Lizzie could join his church and still see her family whenever she wanted. *Whoa, Stephen. Maybe she doesn't feel the same way about you. Maybe your emotions are running away with themselves. Maybe you're setting yourself up for heartache.*

To be honest, he hadn't always shown her his sparkling personality. In fact, there were times he'd acted downright mean. He thought he'd detected some sign of caring in Lizzie's glances and actions anyway. She'd certainly clung to him after the pond incident, but he would probably cling to whoever hauled him out of cold, murky water, too.

Stephen dropped back onto his pillow. He'd have to wait and watch. He'd study Lizzie's expressions and evaluate every word to try to detect her feelings. Asking outright could be risky. That would be his last resort.

Chapter Thirty-Seven

"Doesn't that woman have the hang of weaving yet?"

Lizzie couldn't determine if Mamm was upset that she was planning to visit Mary again or if she'd simply gotten up on the wrong side of the bed. Whichever it was, she would not let Mamm's bad mood spoil her day. She forced a smile. "Mary is doing quite well. She isn't totally confident in herself yet and wants to learn more."

"*Hmpf!* Seems like a waste of time to me."

Lizzie flinched. Did Mamm think her weaving was a waste of time, too? A lump rose in her throat. She tried to cough it out. What she really needed was to get out of the house.

Frannie, who had been a silent observer, offered Lizzie a broad smile. "I think Lizzie's things are beautiful and ever so warm. I love the blanket she made for me."

Wow! Who'd have thought love could so transform a person? Too bad Aaron Kurtz didn't speak up long ago. Lizzie smiled her gratitude at Frannie.

"I didn't mean Lizzie doesn't do nice work," Mamm snapped.

Lizzie would take that as a compliment. From Mamm's tone, she knew a "but" was *kumming*, though.

"But I don't think you need to traipse off to the Mennonite community every chance you get."

"I don't visit that often."

Mamm plunked the mixing bowl onto the counter. Plumes of flour rose from it like a cloud. "Are you planning to join them?"

"I don't have any plans at all, Mamm."

"You certainly haven't rushed to join our church."

"A person shouldn't rush into such a decision, ain't so?"

"*Nee*, but a person shouldn't need a couple of years to make up her mind, either."

Lizzie thought of her art supplies, squirreled away in her workshop. She thought of her pictures of Sunny and the kittens. Was she ready to give all that up? A smiling blue-eyed man appeared in her mind's eye. Was she ready to give up dreams of him? She needed to abandon both. Didn't she? "I need to catch the bus. I won't be late getting home."

"That's what you always say."

Lizzie grabbed her bag and fled. She practically ran all the way down the driveway. *I hope I didn't miss the bus.*

She leaned her head against the bus's cold window. Mamm's words echoed in her brain. "Are you planning to join them?" Not planning. Maybe considering. Would it be so terrible if she did join the Mennonite church? *For Pete's sake, Lizzie, you don't even know how Stephen feels about you. He might only pity you because you get yourself into so many messes.*

It hadn't seemed like pity when he rescued her from the pond. She clearly remembered how tenderly he had cradled her in his arms. His whispered "I thought I'd lost you" was forever stored in her memory.

Lizzie had hardly focused on anything else the past week. She'd prayed for guidance nearly every waking moment. What would she do if he felt the same way she did? What would she do if he didn't? Who could she talk to about her dilemma? Not Mamm. Mary would be understanding, but she was Stephen's *mudder*. Before she had sorted her thoughts, the little bus stopped to let her out.

She took her time shuffling toward the house. Lizzie had to clear her mind and assume a neutral expression. She couldn't appear agitated, or Mary would ask what was wrong. She unclenched her jaw and relaxed the muscles furrowing her forehead.

Black pants and blue shirts danced wildly on the clothesline, the same as on any other wash day. But the flapping laundry created the only sound. It shouldn't be so quiet. On every other visit, the puppies' yapping had greeted her. Lizzie's heart skidded to a stop. The puppies. They must be gone. She didn't get to tell Sunny goodbye. Tears coursed down her wind-chilled face.

Blurred vision made her stop walking. She pulled a hand from her pocket and swiped at her eyes. She didn't have a right to cry over the puppies. They did not belong to her, but her heart crumbled anyway. The more she rubbed her eyes, the faster the tears fell.

"Lizzie! Lizzie! Are you all right?"

When the ache in his arm penetrated his tortured thoughts, Stephen eased up on his sanding. His fingers cramped, and the pain in his wrist ran up to attack his shoulder. He checked to make sure he hadn't sanded a hole through the shelf of the oak cabinet. Thank goodness he hadn't ruined it. He flexed his fingers and rotated his wrist.

The past week had been brutal. He had worked his body so hard that he should have dropped into an exhausted sleep every night. He didn't. He couldn't stop thinking about Lizzie. What was he supposed to do? He'd prayed and prayed but hadn't found any solution to his dilemma.

Mamm had told him Lizzie planned to visit today. He had to do or say something. He couldn't keep going on this way. He would have to express his feelings. He would have to ask her if she thought she could be happy in the Mennonite community, happy with him.

It had become obvious how fond Lizzie had grown of Mamm, and Mamm adored Lizzie. The folks in his community would take to her like flies to honey. Who wouldn't like Lizzie?

The question was would Lizzie want to join them? Could she possibly care enough about him to make such a change in her life? Stephen needed answers, and he needed them today. He *would* talk to her. He yanked open the door and was surprised to see Lizzie standing in the driveway. Was she crying? What had happened to upset her so much? He sprinted in her direction.

Ach! Someone had spotted her, and she hadn't pulled herself together yet. She blinked to see through her tears. Stephen. Of course. Here was another mortifying moment for him to witness. Lizzie rubbed her eyes and sniffed hard.

"Lizzie? What is it? Are you hurt?"

Her heart ached. Did that count? She couldn't get a sound to squeeze past the lump in her throat. She shook her head and then stared at her shoes.

"What happened? Please tell me. I want to help." He gently cupped her chin to tilt her head upward.

"Y-you're always r-rescuing me."

Stephen chuckled. "You make it sound like a crime. I'm glad I've been able to help you. Let's get out of the wind." He grasped her arm and led her toward his shop instead of toward the house. "What happened?"

Lizzie sniffed. "N-nothing happened. I didn't hear any barking and realized the puppies must be gone. I-I didn't get to see Sunny. It's silly, I know." She caught her trembling lower lip between her teeth. She tried to change directions and head for the house.

"I understand. *Kumm* with me."

"Your *mamm* is expecting me."

"I know. This won't take long."

The least she could do was comply with his simple request. She stumbled along beside him, her vision still blurry. "I don't want to keep you from your work. I'll go to the house."

"Not yet, please. I have something to show you." Stephen ushered her through the door and closed it behind them, shutting out the wind.

Lizzie looked at the cabinet. Was this what Stephen wanted to show her? "It's a beautiful cabinet. Maple, ain't so?"

"It is, but that isn't what I wanted to show you."

Lizzie stared at him. What else could be here in the shop for her to see? Had he displayed her drawings somewhere? Her eyes roved the shelves, but she only saw tools of his trade. She sucked in a breath when he stepped closer and placed his hands on her shoulders.

Ever so gently he turned her so she faced a back corner of the shop. "What?"

Stephen kept silent but nodded toward the floor.

Lizzie started to repeat her question but instead looked where he indicated. A golden retriever puppy napped peacefully in a bed in the corner. An ear twitched twice and then was still. One big brown eye popped open at the sound of Lizzie's voice.

"Is it really Sunny?"

Instantly awake, the puppy leaped from the doggy bed and pounced on Lizzie's feet. She dropped to her knees and gathered the puppy to her. When the dog's initial enthusiasm waned a bit, Lizzie looked at Stephen, who had dropped to his knees beside her. His smile lit his entire face.

"I don't understand. I didn't see the other puppies."

"They're gone. They are ready to begin their training."

"I thought Sunny was supposed to go. Didn't they want her?"

"They did, but I wanted her even more. Actually, I wanted her so I could give her to someone else, so the organization and I came to an agreement."

Lizzie's balloon of happiness sprang a leak. Stephen planned to give Sunny to someone. She would have to bid her farewell after all. Tears threatened again, but Lizzie fought them off. "Oh." Maybe Stephen would let her sketch one last picture of the puppy before he gave her away.

"Lizzie?"

"Huh?"

"Look at me."

She didn't want to. Surely he would see the sadness

and pain she didn't have any right to feel. She shook her head and stared at the puppy.

"You, Lizzie."

"What?" He wasn't making any sense, or else her brain wasn't registering his words properly.

"I wanted Sunny so I could give her to you."

"Me?"

"I can't think of anyone who could possibly love her more than you do."

"Mine? Sunny is my dog?"

Chapter Thirty-Eight

"She is."

Lizzie threw her arms around Stephen. "*Danki! Danki!*" She pulled back. Horrified at what she'd just done, she covered her face with her hands. Her cheeks burned. Sunny nudged her to get her attention. "I-I'm so sorry."

"Don't apologize. I, uh, liked that."

"I'm mortified. Grateful for your kindness and generosity, but mortified." To her surprise, Stephen burst out laughing. She ventured a peek in his direction. "What's so funny?"

"You are, you little scamp. You're so adorable when your cheeks are all red and your freckles pop out."

Lizzie couldn't believe it. Stephen found her adorable? With puffy eyes and a splotchy face? He must be making fun of her and she was too naive to realize it. She kept her gaze on Sunny. "It isn't nice to poke fun at people."

"Who's poking fun? I am completely serious. I wouldn't make fun of you, Lizzie. Not ever. I care too much."

"You care? About me?"

"Would I have finagled a way to keep Sunny and

give her to you if I didn't care? I knew you were crazy about the puppy, and I wanted to make you happy."

Lizzie didn't know what to make of Stephen's confession. She couldn't remember anyone ever saying they wanted to make her happy.

"Are you?"

"Am I what?"

"Happy. Did I do the right thing?"

He looked so concerned and so confused that Lizzie had to smile. She touched his arm. "You did a *wunderbaar* thing. I don't think anyone has ever done something so nice for me. I am touched and very happy."

"You had me worried for a minute. I mean, it's not every day I attempt to do something special for someone, and never for a girl, so I didn't know if it was right."

"I'm sure you do nice things for your family all the time."

"That's different. I mean, I care about them, but this is a different kind of caring."

"It is?"

"Don't you feel it, too, or is it all in my head?" This time Stephen's face turned beet red.

"It isn't just you." Lizzie's words came out whisper soft. Maybe he didn't hear her.

Stephen leaned closer. "What did you say?"

"I said, uh . . ."

"Did you say it wasn't just me? Do you mean you feel that same jolt of electricity when we touch? Does your heart pound so hard when we are close that you're afraid it will fly out of your body?"

"Something like that." If she held a piece of paper to her cheeks, Lizzie felt sure it would burst into flame. Thankfully, Sunny chose that moment to leap up and swipe her tongue across Lizzie's nose. Startled, Lizzie shrieked and drew back, nearly toppling over backward. Once again, Stephen came to her rescue.

"Down, Sunny." He grasped Lizzie's shoulders to keep her upright. Obediently, Sunny dropped back onto her haunches.

"She listened to you just fine." Even though Lizzie had regained her balance, Stephen kept his hands on her shoulders. "You're always keeping me from getting hurt."

"I'm glad I'm around to help you."

"You're always around to see me at my least graceful times."

Stephen laughed. "I have seen you poised and proper many times."

"Those have been rare instances, I'm afraid."

Stephen chuckled. "I'd feel exactly the same about you if you crawled around on all fours."

"Somehow I doubt that." Lizzie scratched Sunny's head. "She's a *gut* dog. I hope she isn't upset she didn't get to go with the other puppies."

"I think she feels honored to belong to you."

"Were they going to give her a chance to be a service dog?"

"They usually give all the dogs a chance to prove themselves."

"And you bargained to keep her?"

"I did."

"For me? You did that for me?"

Stephen nodded. "I couldn't bear for you to have to give her up after you lost the kittens. You and Sunny bonded the instant you met. I thought you'd both be happier together."

"I'm sorry I acted like such a *boppli* out there. I hoped I wouldn't be seen. I'm embarrassed over that, too."

"Don't be. You should never be embarrassed because you love someone—person or animal."

"I appreciate your gift, but you know I can't keep Sunny. Mamm won't let me bring her home. She has only endured our old mutt, Ruff, because he is Daed's dog."

"I thought about that, but I still had to get Sunny for you. You can keep her here."

"I've already pawned my kittens off on your *mamm*. I can't ask her to keep my dog, too."

"Mamm loves animals as much as I do. I'll take care of her for you. Besides, Sunny has been here all her life."

"When would I ever get to see her? It's hard to bond with a pet if you aren't together."

"You could visit whenever you wanted. Mamm would love that, anyway."

How about you? Would you like me to visit often, too? "It isn't like our houses are that close that I could just drop by." Lizzie continued stroking the golden fur.

Stephen chuckled. "Look at Sunny's face. I've never seen a more contented dog. I'd say you've already bonded."

Lizzie laughed. "She's smiling."

"It sure looks like it."

"She's a special pup."

"I think you're a special girl."

Lizzie ducked her head. "I'm special at getting you into dangerous situations."

"I'd walk through fire and ice for you any time, Lizzie."

Was he teasing? She raised her eyes to meet his. Her

heart skipped a beat. She saw only honesty—and some other emotion that reached into her soul and made her gasp for breath.

"Do you understand what I'm saying?"

"I-I'm not sure."

Stephen clasped her hand. "I'd really like it if you didn't visit here."

"What?" Lizzie tried to pull her hand away, but his grip tightened.

"Wait. That didn't *kumm* out right, so don't get huffy."

"I don't get huffy."

"Right!"

Lizzie remembered their first meeting and the barbs they had exchanged. She giggled. "Well, maybe a little."

Stephen squeezed her hand. "When I said I'd like you not to visit, that's because I'd like for you to live here."

Lizzie's mouth dropped open. What was he saying? "Live here?"

"*Jah.*"

"Do you want your parents to adopt me?"

Stephen burst out laughing. He threw his arms around Lizzie and hugged her close. "Oh, Lizzie. You are truly one of a kind. Is it any wonder I love you?"

Lizzie pulled back. Her heart stopped. Time stood still. "What did you say?"

"I hadn't planned to blurt out my feelings that way. Are you truly surprised?"

"There have been times when you were sweet one minute and gruff the next, so I wasn't sure how you really felt—oops! I didn't mean to be rude."

Stephen laughed again. "I love your honesty, your

enthusiasm, your generosity. I can't think of anything I don't love about you."

"You really love me?" She never thought she would hear those words from a fellow.

"Is that so hard to believe?"

"I'm surprised."

"Pleasantly?"

"Definitely."

"Could you possibly care about me even though I'm gruff and rude?"

Lizzie laughed. "I think you acted that way to cover up the caring, sensitive man you really are."

"How did you get so smart?"

"I'm a natural genius, I guess."

"Modest as well."

"That, too."

"Are you deliberately evading my question to keep from hurting my feelings?"

"*Nee.*" But she did experience an uncharacteristic shyness at the thought of declaring her feelings. Suddenly she felt hot and then cold. Was she going to be sick? Maybe she needed some air. "I think I need to . . ." Lizzie started to scoot Sunny out of the way so she could scramble to her feet.

Stephen's fingers circling her wrist held her in place. "Please, Lizzie. Can you answer my question? I have to know."

Lizzie's stomach churned. She kept her eyes on Sunny. Stephen deserved an honest answer. She struggled to get one out. "I-I can care. I do care." She raised her gaze to Stephen's glowing face. If pure joy could be captured in a picture, it would look exactly like Stephen's face. She had only a second to look into his eyes before he crushed her to his chest.

"You had me scared. I thought you were going to say I didn't stand a chance at winning your love."

Stephen pressed a kiss to the top of her head that sent chills all down her body. "You don't have to win my love. You already have it."

"You have made me the happiest fellow alive. I knew you were special when I followed you on the trail to the burning house to save those kittens."

"I knew when you left the bag of kitten food at the end of my driveway that you had a soft spot for animals and maybe for silly girls, too. When you kept my drawing and didn't try to discourage my art, I figured you were pretty special. I never dreamed you'd feel the same way about me."

"Did you hope so?"

"*Jah.*"

"Here we tried to arrange a match between our siblings and ended up finding a match for ourselves." Stephen chuckled before pressing another kiss to her head.

Suddenly Lizzie pulled back to look him in the eye. "*Ach*, Stephen! We're forgetting something. Something important."

"What's that, *lieb*?"

"I'm Amish and you're Mennonite."

Stephen's heart sank to his toes. He knew that. He'd thought of the possible problems, but he'd let all those qualms slide to the back corners of his mind in his exuberance over Lizzie's shared feelings. Had they confessed their love for nothing?

"We're not so different." He barely managed to choke out the words.

"That's true as far as our basic beliefs go, but an Amish person doesn't generally wake up one morning and say, 'I think I'll be Mennonite today.' And I don't think a Mennonite person would suddenly turn Amish."

Stephen had struggled with this issue night after night. His mutilated pillow could attest to his angst. His quandary had continued unresolved until right now. Knowing that Lizzie cared for him gave him courage and strength. He loved his family and his community, but he wanted Lizzie by his side for the rest of his life. He looked into her tear-filled violet eyes. "I'll change. I'll join your church."

Lizzie gasped. "You can't, Stephen. You'd have to leave your family, your community. Your parents would be heartbroken. You wouldn't even be able to share meals with them. I won't let you do that to them."

"I want you in my life, and not just to visit Mamm or check on the animals. I would gladly make the sacrifice for you, Lizzie." And he would. It wouldn't be easy, but he would do whatever it took to have Lizzie for his *fraa*.

"*Nee*." Lizzie shook her head.

"Please, Lizzie, don't tell me we have to give up what we've only now found. Can't we compromise on a solution?"

"Only if you'll agree to my idea."

"That's my stubborn, independent Lizzie. What exactly is your solution?"

"It's the only solution, really. I'm sure you must have considered it. I will join your church. I haven't been baptized yet. I would still be *wilkom* in my parents' home and at their table."

"What if I don't want to let you do that? Your parents would be heartbroken with that solution."

"Maybe not." Was that a trace of sadness he detected in her voice?

"Well, your *mudder* would probably chase me off with a broom if I set foot on your property."

Lizzie laughed. "I can just picture Mamm doing that."

"Really? Would your parents throw me out if I came courting? I've never met your family, except for Frannie. They might hate me and forbid you to see me."

"I'm an adult. They wouldn't do that. Don't all parents want their *kinner* to be happy?"

"Are you sure you'll be happy with me, even if you have to change your whole life?"

"I'm sure I would never be happy without you."

Stephen couldn't believe his ears. This remarkable young woman truly cared for him. She would change her entire life for him. He wrapped his arms around her and again drew her close to him—where she belonged.

Chapter Thirty-Nine

"There you are. I was beginning to worry, but then I thought Stephen might have waylaid you." Mary smiled and squeezed Lizzie's arm.

"He did." Lizzie glanced up at Stephen and then returned her gaze to his *mudder*.

"From the light in your eyes, I believe he told you his surprise."

"He told me and showed me." She wanted to squeal and jump up and down like a little girl with a new toy.

"I can also tell that you are happy."

"I think the puppy is the most *wunderbaar* gift anyone ever gave me. But I can't take her home with me. I wish I could. I'm sorry, Mary, but I'm afraid you're stuck with another one of my animals. I finally got Mamm to tell me why she's so against animals. She was attacked by a big dog when she was little, and she never got over her fear. From then on she didn't trust any animal, big or small, so I know I will never be able to have a pet."

"I'm sorry she had to go through such a thing. It's too bad she never got over her fear."

"If leaving Sunny here is too much to ask, Stephen can give her to someone else." Lizzie nearly broke into sobs at the thought.

"Don't be ridiculous. Sunny will be fine here. I'm used to a lot of animals running around the place. Stephen will most likely raise another litter, too. Besides, with Sunny here, that will give you another reason to visit—not that you need a reason, mind you. You're *wilkom* any time."

"*Danki*, Mary." Lizzie shifted her glance to Stephen, who raised his eyebrows in an unspoken question. Lizzie understood and nodded.

He cleared his throat. "Actually, Mamm, Lizzie might have another reason to visit often."

"Oh? What might that be?" Mary looked from one to the other.

"Lizzie is thinking of joining the Mennonite church instead of the Amish one."

"*Planning*. I'm planning to join the Mennonite church." Lizzie spoke with conviction.

"Really?" Mary focused on Lizzie. "Is this something you've wanted to do? Have you thought it through carefully and prayed about it?"

"I have. You know I haven't yet joined my church. Maybe the Lord Gott had other plans for me all along."

"What will your parents say? Won't they be upset?"

"I don't really know for sure and for certain, but it isn't like I'll be lost to them. I won't be under the *bann* or anything." Did Mary think this was a bad idea? If so, she might think a relationship with Stephen was a bad idea, too.

Mary suddenly pulled Lizzie into a hug. "Don't look so worried, dear one. I would be thrilled to have you join our community . . . and perhaps our family?"

Lizzie gasped and glanced at Stephen. His face flushed crimson.

"Mamm! That's, uh . . ."

"Private. I know, Stephen. I'm sorry to put you both on the spot. I only wanted to make it clear that I would be absolutely delighted if that was the case."

Lizzie almost collapsed in relief. She might very well have done that if Mary hadn't still been holding on to her. "*Danki*." Would her own *mudder* be as understanding?

"We can talk to the bishop later, if you like, to see what you'd need to do. Would you want to do that after our little weaving lesson, Lizzie? Or do you need more time to think things through?"

"I don't need to think anymore. I know this is the right path for me to take." She caught Stephen's smile and grinned back at him.

"What do you think your parents will say about your decision?"

Lizzie's smile died on her lips. "They will be surprised, I'm sure."

"Will they accept your decision?"

"It's hard to tell, but I hope so. I'll talk to them this evening."

Lizzie entered her house a few hours later with great trepidation. Stephen had asked to accompany her, but she believed she needed to talk to her parents alone before springing Stephen on them. As it was, Mamm would probably think Lizzie had lied earlier in the day. Hadn't she answered Mamm's inquiry with something about not having any plans to join the Mennonites?

She hadn't really lied, though. Earlier today she wasn't sure of Stephen's feelings. She had known her own heart, but feared she'd misread Stephen's cues.

Now she was sure beyond the shadow of a doubt that she and Stephen were meant to be together. How hard would it be to convince her parents of this? She prayed they would be as accepting and as happy for her as Mary Zimmerman had been. But Mary wasn't losing a *dochder* to another community, another faith.

The visit with Stephen's bishop had gone very well. Mary and Stephen had both accompanied her. The bishop proved to be a very kind, compassionate man. He told Lizzie she could take individual instructions with him to prepare for her baptism rather than wait for the next class in the summer. Lizzie had left the man's house elated and eager to get started. She floated home on a cloud of happiness.

"Is that you finally home, Lizzie?" Mamm hollered from the kitchen.

Lizzie crash-landed the moment she crossed the threshold into the Fisher home. She thought she had made it home in record time. Maybe not. "*Jah*, Mamm. It's me. I'll wash up and be right there." If Mamm was agitated, Lizzie would definitely postpone her revelation until after tonight's Bible reading and prayers. Maybe Mamm would be more receptive then.

Water droplets sparkled like crystals on Lizzie's freshly washed hands when she burst into the kitchen. "What can I do to help?" Her eyes roved the kitchen and stopped on Frannie, who had pulled a huge casserole dish from the oven. She raised her eyebrows in an unspoken question. Frannie barely lifted and dropped her shoulders. That meant Frannie didn't have any idea what was stuck in Mamm's craw this afternoon. Lizzie resolved to be cheerful anyway. "Would you like me to make muffins or biscuits, Mamm?"

"Frannie already made corn muffins."

"Okay." Lizzie headed to the cabinet to retrieve the plates.

"Nancy and Sadie already set the table." Frannie's words were so soft Lizzie strained to decipher them.

"What's wrong?" Lizzie mouthed.

Frannie shrugged again.

If everything had been done, why was Mamm so miffed? Lizzie searched her brain for anything she might have said or done to upset her *mudder* but couldn't think of a single thing. "Is there something I can do for you, Mamm?"

"I suppose not—now."

Did that imply Lizzie could have done something earlier? The evening was definitely not getting off to a favorable start. She certainly hoped Mamm's mood improved by the time they finished supper.

Lizzie wasn't quite sure how, but supper time sped by and dragged all at the same time. She wanted to get the upcoming conversation over with, yet she feared finishing supper and prayers and initiating it. Her stomach became such a tangle of knots she could scarcely force down sips of water. She shuffled casserole and vegetables around on her plate and pretended to eat. She probably didn't fool anyone.

"What's wrong with you?" Frannie whispered while they washed dishes.

"Nothing, why?" Lizzie almost dropped the slippery plate she had pulled from the dish drainer.

"For one thing, you're all thumbs. I expect we'll have

a lot of broken dishes soon. For another thing, you didn't swallow any of the food you chased around your plate."

"You noticed?"

"I did. What's up?"

"I wasn't very hungry."

"Uh-huh. And?"

"And what?"

"Why are you so jittery?"

Should I confide in her? Will Frannie be sympathetic, or will she yelp and spill the beans before I'm ready? "I need to talk to Mamm and Daed later."

"It must be something awfully bad if you're so nervous about it."

"It isn't bad at all."

"I've never known you to be nervous about talking to Mamm and Daed before. Did you sneak another stray animal home?"

Lizzie wished Frannie would drop the subject. Maybe she could get her *schweschder* to talk about something else. "How are things going with Aaron?" Frannie's face reddened. *It's not so pleasant to be put on the spot, is it?*

"You know we don't talk about those things."

"Much."

"Courting is private."

"Aha! You are courting!"

"Shhh!" Frannie clapped a soapy hand across Lizzie's mouth.

"Eww!" Lizzie swiped the back of one hand across her lips. "Now I'm going to taste soap all night."

"You could try eating some of the supper you played with to get rid of the taste."

Lizzie wrinkled her nose. She rolled up the dish towel and swatted Frannie with it.

"Ow!"

"That didn't hurt, and it wasn't as bad as eating soapsuds."

"I guess we're even, then. And I guess you aren't going to tell me your big secret."

"You'll find out soon enough."

"It won't be tonight if you don't hurry up and dry those dishes. I don't have any more room to stack things in the drainer."

Lizzie swirled the towel over the next plate and stacked it with the others.

"What's taking so long in there?" Mamm hollered from the living room. "We'd like to get to bed sometime tonight."

"See what I mean, poky?" Frannie elbowed Lizzie and splattered soapsuds on the counter and on Lizzie's dress. Lizzie dried faster.

"This should be an interesting evening," Frannie said as she pulled the stopper from the sink.

"Interesting" is not the word Lizzie would have chosen.

Chapter Forty

Lizzie and Frannie scampered into the living room and dropped side by side onto the sofa so Daed could begin reading from the big Bible. Lizzie hoped he chose a long passage so she'd have more time to organize her thoughts. But, of course, he chose the shortest one he'd read in a long time, maybe ever. She prayed hard for guidance, for the right words, for her parents' understanding, for a mind that wasn't suddenly blank.

Panic seized her when Daed indicated the silent prayer time was over. She wasn't ready. Was there a way to ease into the subject, or should she simply plunge right in? Melvin and Caleb stood and clomped off toward the stairs. Sadie and Nancy gave a round of hugs and followed their *bruders*. Now if Frannie would leave, Lizzie could dive in and get this whole thing over with.

When Mamm and Daed made motions to head upstairs, Lizzie cleared her throat, which had suddenly gone as dry as the creek bed during a summer drought. Her heart pounded. Apparently Frannie didn't have any intention of leaving. Lizzie nudged her and jerked her head toward the stairs. Surely the girl would get the hint that Lizzie wanted to talk to their parents alone. Lizzie nudged her again.

"I guess I'll go upstairs." Frannie faked a yawn.

As Mamm rose from her chair, Lizzie spoke. "Mamm, can you wait a minute? I need to talk to you and Daed."

Mamm grunted and plopped back onto the rocking chair.

Daed stoked his bushy beard. "What is it, Dochder?"

All the moisture had evaporated from Lizzie's mouth, and her tongue stuck to its roof. Her hands grew so cold and clammy she slid them down the sides of her dress to dry them. *Please help me, Lord Gott. I don't know what to say. Give me the words. Let them understand and not hate me.*

"Well, what is it, Lizzie? We want to go to bed before sunrise." Mamm's fingers drummed on the arms of the wooden rocking chair.

"I know." She cleared her throat. "I'm sorry to keep you, but I need to tell you about a decision I've made."

Mamm clucked her tongue. "I hope it's a decision to join the church with the next baptismal class."

Lizzie's heart plummeted. Her decision was the direct opposite. She wanted to run to her room and pretend she hadn't initiated this conversation. But the memory of Stephen's sweet smile and laughing eyes spurred her on.

"Let her tell us, Anna." Daed reached over to pat Mamm's arm.

"I'm trying to be patient, Emanuel. Please tell us, Lizzie." Mamm sat back in the chair and waited. Although she tried to appear patient, Lizzie could see that Mamm's nerves were coiled as tight as a spring. She really hated to be the one to make them snap.

Her *daed*'s encouraging smile calmed her marginally.

Please don't be disappointed in me. She cleared her throat again. "I-I've decided to join the church, but not our church."

That brought Mamm back to the edge of the chair. She gripped the arms so tightly her knuckles turned as white as cotton. "Which church?"

"The Mennonite church."

"I knew it! Didn't I ask you that this morning? And what was your answer?"

"I wasn't being untruthful this morning. I didn't know for sure then."

"That woman turned you against us. I should never have let you go there. Working on the loom, my foot! She was trying to recruit you."

"Not so, Mamm. Mary had nothing to do with my decision. She was as surprised as you are. She's really a very nice person and would never try to turn me against my family."

"*Hmpf!*" Mamm crossed her arms over her chest.

"And they're Old Order Mennonite, so they aren't too different from us. It's not like I'm joining aliens and leaving the planet."

"I suspect there is more to the story, Dochder." Daed reached across the space separating them to pat Lizzie's tightly clenched hands. "Am I right?"

Lizzie nodded.

"A *bu*?" Mamm's voice rose in pitch and volume.

Lizzie nodded again. "He's ever so nice, Mamm. He wants to meet you both. He wanted to be here with me now, but I told him I wanted to talk to you alone. He makes furniture and raises dogs for a service dog organization."

"We'd like to meet him." At least Daed seemed calm and cordial.

"I can't believe this!" Mamm covered her face with her hands and burst into tears.

"I'm losing my *boppli*!"

Lizzie jumped off the sofa and knelt at her *mudder*'s side. "You aren't losing me, Mamm. We'll still see each other. I haven't been baptized, so I won't be under the *bann*." She pried one of her *mamm*'s hands from her face and grasped it.

"She's right, Anna." Daed scooted his chair closer and took his *fraa*'s other hand. "Lizzie will always be our girl."

Lizzie tried to smile at him, but feared she hadn't been successful. "We'll still have family meals and celebrations together."

"It won't be the same." Anna sniffed.

"It won't be the same when Frannie marries, either, but we'll still be family, Mamm."

"Frannie? Is she getting married and leaving, too?"

"I'm sure she will sometime. That's all I meant." Lizzie certainly didn't want to give away any of Frannie's secrets. Life with her *schweschder* had been much more pleasant lately. Lizzie wanted to keep it that way.

"Our *kinner* are growing up, Fraa. We have to accept that, even if we don't like it." Daed winked at Lizzie. "They will always be our *kinner*, but they have to leave the nest sometime. Your parents probably felt the same way when we married." He leaned over to kiss her cheek. "We have to trust our Lizzie's judgment. We raised a *gut* girl."

Lizzie stepped a bit lighter as she climbed the stairs to her room, relieved the confession and difficult conversation were behind her. Mamm still looked sad, but at least she had stopped crying. Daed hugged her and said he wanted her to be sure and to be happy.

Lizzie was more sure of Stephen than she'd been of anything other than her faith in Gott. She had never believed in love at first sight, but Stephen had been special from day one. How many people would risk their life for a stranger?

She crept down the hallway and slipped into her semi-dark room.

"I knew it!"

Lizzie stifled a scream. "I thought you were asleep."

"Hardly."

"You knew what?"

"That you and Stephen Zimmerman were—"

"Shame on you, Frannie! You were eavesdropping."

"I couldn't help it."

"You could have gone straight to bed."

"Don't get all riled up, Lizzie. I'm happy for you."

"You are?"

"Sure. Didn't I tell you before—when you were trying to fix me up with Seth—that I saw the attraction between you and Stephen? Don't you remember? You denied it, but I was right."

"I remember. And I'm sorry for trying to throw you and Seth together."

"Apology accepted—again. But it worked out, ain't so? It just wasn't the match you intended."

Frannie laughed so hard she snorted, causing Lizzie to giggle. "Shhh! You'll wake everyone up."

"You know very well our siblings could sleep through a tornado ripping the roof off the house."

"Probably."

"For sure."

"Well, Miss Eavesdropper, you probably heard me

tell Mamm and Daed things wouldn't be the same when you married, either. I wasn't trying to hint that you had any plans. I was simply stating a fact. Do you?"

"Do I what?"

"Have plans to get married?"

"Someday."

"Hey, you know my plans."

"But you didn't tell me. I had to hear it on the sly. Are you sure you don't want to stay Amish?"

"It isn't that I want to give up being Amish at all, Frannie. I never wanted to be anything else. I just don't want to give up Stephen."

"He could become Amish."

"He's already been baptized."

Frannie smacked her hand on the bed. "Lizzie Fisher! You wanted me to give up my family and faith for Seth!"

"Actually, I hoped Seth would turn Amish, since he hasn't been baptized, but that's all a moot point now."

"That was a plan that didn't work out, did it?"

"*Nee*, but this plan is a better one."

"I guess you can learn to ride a bike now."

Lizzie laughed. "Maybe. I've never understood why they ride bikes and we ride scooters. What's the difference?"

"Who knows? And your husband won't have to grow a beard like Aaron will."

"Aha! I caught that slip. You and Aaron *are* planning to get married."

"Nothing has been decided yet. Don't you say anything to anyone."

Lizzie pretended to button her lips. "My lips are sealed. You know I'll keep your secret."

"Among the others you harbor."

Lizzie giggled. "You make me sound mysterious. I'm simple Lizzie who likes to weave, likes animals, and—"

"And loves Stephen Zimmerman." Frannie snorted again, sending them both into another bout of laughter.

Lizzie recovered first. "I've been thinking, Frannie."

"I thought I smelled something burning."

"Ha ha! Seriously, I've wondered if the Lord Gott kept me from joining the church because He knew Stephen would *kumm* along and become part of my life. Since I haven't been baptized, I can have the best of both worlds, so to speak."

"Maybe, or maybe your not joining had something to do with another of your secrets."

"What are you talking about?" Lizzie's muscles tensed. What was Frannie getting at?

"Your drawing."

Lizzie gasped. "My drawing? What do you mean?"

"I know you draw and paint. Your pictures are quite lovely."

"You sneak! How did you find my pictures? You've been going through my things!"

"I was looking for yarn one day and came across them."

"You hate needlework. You have to have been rummaging through my things."

Frannie had the decency to look ashamed. "I'm sorry, Lizzie. I was feeling bad about not having any talent, so I looked through your things."

"What exactly were you looking for? You wouldn't have found your own heart's desire under my belongings."

"*Nee*, but I hoped to find some idea or hint of what

makes you so talented. I thought something might give me a sign of what I'm *gut* at."

"*Ach*, Frannie, you only needed to look inside yourself to find your own desires. Don't you see the joy you bring others through your delicious baked treats?"

"You helped me see that, but that was after I had snooped. Forgive me?"

"Sure, but you can't tell."

"I promise. Will you be able to continue your art as a Mennonite?"

"I think so. Stephen and Mary know and they are all right with it, but I will find out for sure."

Suddenly Frannie threw her arms around Lizzie in a tight hug. "I know I haven't been the nicest *schweschder*, but I'm going to miss sharing a room with you."

Lizzie patted Frannie's back. "Me, too."

Epilogue

"Are you too cold? We don't have to walk out here today." Stephen squeezed Lizzie's mittened hand as they hiked through the back fields of the Zimmerman property.

"The air is refreshing."

Stephen laughed. It was a joyful sound that Lizzie would be happy to hear for the rest of her life. "'Refreshing' is putting it mildly. This wind is awfully cold for mid-December. We might be in for a long winter."

"There's nothing we can do about that. We have to accept whatever the Lord Gott gives us."

"That we do." Stephen stopped walking and pulled Lizzie into his arms. "I'm thankful He gave me you." Sunny stopped trotting and waited patiently beside them.

Lizzie laid her head against Stephen's chest. His heart thumped right beneath her ear. Since she didn't even reach his chin, he had to bend down to drop a kiss on top of her head. She could stay in his embrace all day, all week, forever. "I'm thankful for you, too." She knew Stephen had furniture orders to finish before Christmas. She had a few weaving orders to complete, too. With great reluctance she pulled back. "Show me what you are postponing our work to look at."

"All right. I guess we have to move." Stephen took her hand again and led her through a patch of pine and holly trees.

Lizzie picked up on his excitement. He was chattering away like a little *bu*. She smiled. Would she have a *wunderbaar* little *bu* with dark hair and big blue eyes one day? Her cheeks warmed despite the cold wind slapping them.

"How is your instruction going?"

Stephen's question pulled Lizzie out of her daydreams. "Fine. The bishop said I only need to meet with him two more times."

"And then you'll be ready for baptism?"

"*Jah.*"

"Any regrets?"

"Not a single one. We are very similar, you know. But I will have to get used to looking for a black buggy in the grocery store parking lot instead of a gray one. And— don't you dare laugh at me, Stephen Zimmerman—I'm looking forward to wearing that blue print dress your *mamm* helped me make."

Stephen turned his head, and Lizzie knew he tried not to laugh, but a chuckle escaped anyway. She nudged him. "I told you not to laugh."

"I'm sorry."

A moment later they cleared the stand of trees and faced a pretty little open field protected by more stately trees. Stephen wrapped an arm around her and tucked her close to him. "This is it."

"It?"

"Our place."

Lizzie looked up into the eyes she loved. "As in yours and mine?"

"As in yours and mine. Daed is deeding this area to me. We can build our house over there on that little knoll." He pointed across the field a ways. "And over there, we'll have room for our shops."

"Shops?"

"Sure. I'm going to build a bigger shop, since my business has been expanding. And you need space to weave and to draw and to display your items to customers. You've outgrown that shed you work in at your parents' house."

Stephen had finally visited and met her parents, who had admitted he would make a fine husband. He had watched her work in her shop and admired her talent. He wanted her to continue to use her gifts. Lizzie had been blessed indeed.

"What do you think?"

"I think it's a splendid plan. I feel like jumping up and down like Nancy and Sadie would do." With her hand that wasn't tucked into Stephen's, Lizzie reached up to swipe at a tear.

"Why the tears?"

"Happy tears."

"Are you happy, Lizzie?"

"Very."

"You aren't disappointed that our original plan to match Frannie with Seth didn't work out?"

"Not at all. They are on their own." She threw her arms around Stephen's waist and hugged him tight. "This match is ever so much better."

"Our match?"

"Our match."

"Are you sure you don't have any regrets about leaving your church and community?"

"None whatsoever. I'll still see my family and *freinden*, but I belong here with you."

"And I belong with you." Stephen leaned down to kiss the top of her head again.

"A match made in heaven, I'm thinking."

"I couldn't agree more, my *lieb*. And you know what else?"

"What?"

"You can have all the animals you want."

That remark earned Stephen a kiss on the cheek.